# HOME OR AWAY

Kaleigh Allen

Cover art by Emily McDougall.

ISBN: 979-8-9887159-0-0 (Paperback)

Published by Bigger Waves Publishing, LLC
9407 NE Vancouver Mall Dr, Ste 104 #1569
Vancouver, WA 98662

*For Meema;*
*For the wonderful staff at Kansas City Hospice House, who*
*cared for her during her final days on earth;*
*And for the residents of the Garden Village Nursing Home*
*Dementia Unit, who I had the honor of caring for during*
*theirs.*

A Note to the Reader: This story explores themes of
dementia, grief, PTSD, and anxiety attacks.

# 1

GRANGER WAS DETERMINED TO STAY in his hometown absolutely no longer than necessary. He'd be there a few hours, tops, then be back on the road again. The day was bright and sunny with no sign of foul weather brewing on the horizon. His plan was solid.

He didn't want to see any old classmates or go down memory lane, he just wanted to do what he came to do and then get back to his real home in Eugene where his new position at work awaited him.

His phone buzzed at him from the passenger seat just as he parked next to the gas pump. He looked at the screen, rolled his eyes, and sighed before he answered.

"Yeah, Mom?"

"Hi, honey," came her tentative voice from the other end of the line. "I didn't want to bother you while you were driving, but I was… just checking in. Are you getting close to town?"

"I just pulled in," he said flatly.

Her tone lightened when she asked, "to the house?"

The hopefulness in her voice made Granger grit his teeth. He wasn't even at her house yet and already she was getting her hopes up to unrealistic levels.

"To Lester," he corrected. "I'm stopped at Gus's to fill up my tank."

He unbuckled, and froze.

Something down the street caught his eye. It was a head of wavy, red hair. He watched it bob up the sidewalk away from where he sat hidden in his car at the gas station until it disappeared around a corner.

"Granger? Honey, are you still there? Hello?"

He nodded his head automatically. His pulse was going double its normal speed. Finally he pulled his attention back to the conversation.

"What'd you say?"

"I said Jake should be home from school by now, so the door will be unlocked for you. I'll be home in an hour."

"Okay. Hey," he added before she hung up. "Do you know if any of my old high school friends are back in town right now? I mean the ones who moved away."

He kept his eyes glued to the spot up ahead the whole time, watching the place where the red head had disappeared near the old bakery and hardware store.

"Not that I've heard. Why? You don't have a high school reunion this year, do you?"

"I don't keep up with those things. Never mind. I'll see you at the house."

He hung up. He used his right arm to open his car door, but paused. He checked all his mirrors and twisted around in his seat to check that the coast was clear. Finally, keeping his eyes peeled for any familiar faces, he opened the door and stepped out of his car. As far as he could see up and down the street, there was no one he recognized. In fact, he didn't see any other people at all.

His shoulders relaxed but his jaw remained clenched and his eyes continued to sweep the landscape, surveying his hometown while the tank filled.

The "Welcome to Lester" sign was worn down so much it was embarrassing. The hardware store was losing a decent amount of paint. As far as the eye could see, the sidewalks were cracking and grass was growing in all the holes and crevices. Granger had forgotten how worn-out the town was in his six years living in Eugene.

"Afternoon!"

Granger jumped.

But it wasn't Gus. Instead of a short, heavy-set, balding man, the older man leaning against the convenience store doorway was tall, lanky, and stubbled. It was odd to see this stranger wearing the badge with the gas station logo on it instead of Gus himself.

Granger looked around but he didn't see any other employees around. He shoved his curiosity into a corner, though.

The man was smiling at Granger over the top of his car.

"Nice day, isn't it? Mighty nice to see the sun out. First day in two weeks we haven't had any clouds or rain or bad storms. S'posed to storm tonight, though."

Granger looked up at the sky. "When?"

"Few hours from now."

*Crap.*

The lanky man smiled up at the sky. With his eyes half-closed the man had a dreamy sort of look on his face.

"Good to know," Granger said. He turned his back on the man to face the pump, but the unusual quiet of the street was becoming eerie. He reluctantly turned back around.

"Is it always this quiet?" Granger asked.

"This part of town's lots quieter since all the developments went in on the other side."

"Developments?"

The man got comfortable against the doorpost and drew all his words out nice and long, taking his time in telling the tale.

"Yeah. New neighborhoods and businesses and even a new school."

He looked back at Granger, sized him up. The man was starting to seem more familiar to Granger. It was only a matter of time until the opposite would be true.

"You from out of town?" the man asked.

"Yeah."

It wasn't completely a lie.

The man uncrossed his arms and rested his long, calloused, oil-stained fingers in his coverall pockets. He squinted into the distance where Granger guessed the 'developments' were.

"Yeah, 'bout five years ago the city got on this big kick 'bout 'revitalizin'' and whatnot. Made short work of it."

If a police officer could've clocked the speed of the man's conversation, he would've given him a ticket for talking dangerously slow.

"That doesn't sound too bad."

"It's not. 'Less you're a business on this side of town."

The pump clicked. Granger was about to excuse himself, when he hesitated.

"Do you know what high school reunions are happening this year?"

The man shook his head.

"I don't really keep up with that stuff."

The man's smile wilted as Granger got back into his car. Granger saw him look up and down the street while he was pulling away. It was so quiet. So empty. So unlike how Granger remembered it.

Granger shook his head so as to not get distracted by memories of the Lester he used to know.

Granger saw a few minor changes throughout the town as he drove, but nothing big. He figured the guy was probably exaggerating, although he had said there was a new school... that was pretty specific.

*The town isn't that big, though. Why would they need a new school? Unless they were just replacing one of the old ones. Yeah. That's probably what he meant.*

At one point, Granger realized he was sitting forward a little in his seat, his right hand clenching the steering wheel, looking this way and that for that red head of hair and hoping he didn't spot it.

He flexed his driving hand, leaned back in his seat, and kept his eyes straight ahead. He pushed away more memories and forced his mind to focus on the new position at work.

At a stoplight, where he finally started to see more cars and people, he hit the button on the door that rolled his windows down so he could enjoy the spring breeze. He was hit with the familiar scent of freshly mown lawns, the faint yet unmistakable and unwelcome smell of manure from the farms on the outskirts of Lester, and a whiff of something sweet from the nearby icing factory. He closed the windows again at the next stop sign.

With each passing minute, Granger felt a growing urge to turn the car around. When he drove past the playground, he couldn't keep himself from remembering all the times he swung higher and higher on the swing set before launching himself into the air and landing unsteadily on the grass. Feeling the curves and bumps in the road beneath his car reminded him of the season he learned to drive.

He shook his head again, frowning deeply.

*"Hi honey. I, I didn't want to tell you this over voicemail, but I wasn't sure when you'd get the time to talk. I know you're busy.*

*It's your grandma. She's not… doing well. And she's not… Well, I just think you're going to want to come home for this. Call or, or text or something when you get the chance. I'm sorry, honey. Love you."*

When he'd played that voicemail for the first time three days earlier, he first felt annoyed. But when his mother mentioned her mother-in-law, his grandmother, he felt a wave of fear wash over him.

Most times when his mom called or texted she managed to slip in the suggestion that he come visit. In the six years that she'd tried this tactic, it had yet to work.

Until she mentioned that something was wrong with grandma.

Now that it was warming up, residents and tourists in Eugene were going out to dinner more often so they could sit on the patio, eat their Italian food, and watch the cyclists and street musicians. Granger felt bad about taking time off when it was getting so busy at the restaurant, especially since he was just promoted to manager, so he'd waited until his day off to make the five hour drive from Eugene to Lester.

Granger tightened his sweaty grip on the steering wheel again as he turned down the street leading to his mom's house. Even from all the way down the block, his eyes instinctively found the light gray, two-story, split-entry home where he had lived from fifth grade until he graduated from high school six years ago. He recognized one of the two cars in the driveway, a blue sedan that his mother had bought used over fifteen years ago. The other car, a beat-up white Camry, he didn't recognize.

Just before he pulled into the driveway, a petite lady with mousy brown hair hurried down the front steps. She had the appearance of one of those porcelain dolls that broke easily. She wore the biggest smile she could manage, but she still looked slightly worried because of the natural shape of her eyes and eyebrows.

She stood outside his window, bouncing on the balls of her feet a little, while he parked and turned off his engine. Seeing his mother face-to-face for the first time in six years, he felt the slight nudge of a compulsion to jump out of the driver's seat and hug her. But that was a very small part of him, and the rest of him was fixated on the reason why he hadn't seen her in all that time. He took his time getting out, and hugged his mother stiffly with his right arm.

"Hi, baby."

She sounded tearful.

"I thought you weren't getting home 'til later," he said.

"I couldn't wait."

Granger was not a tall man at five-foot-five, but he was taller than his mother. When his shoulder started to feel wet, he pulled away.

A raspy voice yelled out to them from the other side of the screen door, "is he here?"

"Yes, he's here," she yelled back, her voice strained. When she finally let Granger go he noticed there were in fact teardrops on the front of his shirt.

From within the house came the sound of a stampede, followed by a teenaged boy flying through the front door.

"Hey man!" Jake smiled and flung his arms around his older brother. His arms were much longer than Granger expected. And the kid's high, raspy voice was now a low, raspy voice.

Granger couldn't help but crack a smile, and then he couldn't stop it from growing.

"What happened to you, kid?"

"He's grown up," their mother said, still happy crying.

"You're taller than me!"

"He's grown at least a foot since you last saw him."

"You were supposed to be twelve years old forever, Jakey." Granger mussed up Jake's hair and Jake shoved his hand away.

Once they'd wrestled a little bit in the front yard, Granger asked him, "how's senior year? You failing?"

"Yeah right. I'm getting better grades than all of you," Jake said, referring to his three older brothers and older half-sister.

"Except Trevor," Granger said.

"Even him," Jake said with a big grin.

"It's true," their mother interjected. Her eyes shone as she appraised her youngest child. "Jake's GPA is a 4.6 right now because of his college-level classes."

"How? You hate school!"

"Kids change a lot in six years," their mother said, averting her gaze.

Granger's mood changed instantly. Turning away from Jake, Granger quietly asked his mother:

"Is this how it's going to be all weekend? You guilting me for every little thing?"

She didn't respond.

Jake quickly looked from his mother to Granger. "Let's go inside," he said. "I'll grab your stuff from the car."

"I don't have any stuff."

Jake didn't seem to understand.

Their mom looked up again. "Aren't you staying?"

Granger didn't try to conceal his annoyance when he said, "I've gotta get back to work. The owner just promoted me to manager, so I've got training."

He waited in vain for one of them to congratulate him on his news.

"You couldn't get time off to visit a terminal family member?" Jake asked.

Granger opened his mouth to answer the question, but clapped it shut again.

"Terminal? What are you talking about?" He looked at his mom. "You didn't say she was dying when we talked on the phone."

"Well, no, I didn't want to tell you everything over the phone."

His right hand found and gripped the short, iron railing. "Why not?"

She wouldn't look him in the eye and her voice was sheepish again as she explained. "It's been a… a difficult time. I felt like it deserved a conversation in person. I know how much she meant to you."

"'Meant?' She's not gone yet," he said, but then panicked, "is she?"

"No, she's still alive."

He stood dazed for a few more seconds. "She's dying?"

Jake was quiet. Their mother finally responded.

"Yes."

"Is it…" he swallowed. "Cancer?"

"No, not cancer." She glanced around the neighborhood. "Let's go inside. I don't want to talk out here."

She led the way up the stairs and into the house, wrapping her arms around herself as if it was cold outside. Granger searched the sky again for storm clouds in the distance.

*So far so good. I can still beat the rain.*

Inside, Granger pulled his feet up the worn, carpeted stairs and into the living room. It was dark inside, the sun was on the other side of the house. Everything in the room looked the same as it used to.

His mother sat on the edge of the faded navy armchair, hunched forward. He noticed wrinkles around her eyes and mouth that hadn't been there when he'd moved away, and her dull, brown hair had silver strands in it now.

Granger did not sit.

He waited for her to start explaining, but she was evidently in no hurry. Her mouth worked silently in different shapes. With each moment Granger felt another blanket of dread landing softly over him. Even Jake looked grave and pale-faced sitting on the ottoman, watching his mother try to put words together.

"Your grandma has dementia," she finally said. She said it so quietly that he almost didn't hear her over the hum of the fridge in the next room. She teared up again, but these tears weren't accompanied by a smile. She didn't continue.

"So, she's losing her memory?"

When she didn't answer, Jake stepped in, his voice somehow even raspier than before. "Yeah, but it's more than that. She's really not the same as she used to be."

"How so?"

"She needs lots of help with doing regular stuff. And the doctor said it will get worse and she'll need help with even more stuff."

"Like what?"

Jake shrugged. "There are so many possible symptoms, it just depends."

"On what?"

"Where the dementia is, what kind it is."

"The doctors can't tell?"

"Not exactly."

"So, it's a disease. What's the cure?"

"There is no cure," Jake said.

"Not at all?"

Their mom finally joined the conversation. At first when she spoke nothing came out. She cleared her throat and tried again.

"They have some medicine that can help with the symptoms, but that's it."

"So, she has it for the rest of her life, then?"

"It's terminal," she said, nearly whispering. "It *is* the rest of her life."

Granger sat.

The three of them were quiet for a few moments. Brand new leaves rustled outside as a spring breeze blew past the screen door. It had been so warm a few minutes earlier, but now Granger felt a chill, too.

He looked over at his baby brother again, who was hardly recognizable as an eighteen-year-old. Granger could tell just by looking at the kid that he was probably pretty popular with the high school girls. He had thick, chestnut brown hair unlike their mom's thin and dull hair and Granger's own blond hair. And where Granger had lost muscle in the last six years, Jake had gained. But sitting across from him just then with a look that could only be described as sorrowful, Jake looked a lot more like the scrawny little boy Granger remembered.

Granger closed his eyes and rubbed the lids with his good hand. He was the one to break the silence.

"Where is she?"

"*Golden Grove Nursing Home,*" she said.

Granger's brow furrowed, "a nursing home? Since when?"

"This week. We can't take care of her anymore."

More tears slid out of her eyes.

"Take care of her?"

She nodded and dropped her gaze to an old gray stain on the carpet. She pulled at the ends of her cardigan, which were already worn out.

Jake stepped in again. "She needed help with everything. She couldn't go to the bathroom on her own anymore. She needed help eating. She was totally lost."

Granger didn't understand. "Were you living with her?"

"She lived here with us."

"Since when?"

"For the last year," he said. "We had to block off the stairs and move lots of stuff around to keep her safe. But it wasn't enough. She needed more help than we could give."

"What happened to the farm?"

"We've been trying to keep up with the maintenance until your uncle gets back from Africa," their mom said, emphasizing the word 'trying.' "The house is going to him once she passes away."

"Is she going to... pass away... soon?"

Neither his mother nor his brother answered other than offering small shrugs.

"I'm sorry, honey," his mother whispered, looking at him with big, tear-filled, puppy dog eyes.

Anger boiled inside him.

"When can I see her?" he asked, sharply.

"We can go now, if you want," she said.

Through the window Granger saw clouds forming in the distance, moving toward Lester. It had taken him longer than he'd expected to leave his house in Eugene that morning, and it would be a five hour drive back.

Granger didn't like driving in the rain at night with only one working arm. That, combined with this new information about his grandma meant he probably wouldn't get on the road again for awhile.

*So much for a one-day trip.*

# 2

GRANGER STEELED HIMSELF FOR THE reunion with his grandmother. He needed to focus on the problem, to learn more about her dementia, what it was and what could be done. As difficult or emotional as it might be for them to see each other again, he was prepared to keep his head on and his emotions under control. His grandmother had never been a particularly emotive person, so it shouldn't be a problem for him to mirror that.

His mom drove the three of them fifteen minutes out to the edge of town to an area Granger had seldom visited before. Just when Granger was sure she had taken a wrong turn and landed them in the middle of nowhere, she pulled the car off the road onto a long driveway leading up and over a slight hill. A sign appeared along the side of the road saying, *Golden Grove Nursing Home and Hospice.* 'Lo and behold,' as Granger's grandmother would have said, at the end of the driveway was a run-down looking parking lot.

"I didn't even know this place was here," he mumbled.

"It's been here since the seventies," she replied.

Granger could hear her trying to keep her voice free of emotion and keep the conversation light. He didn't play along.

*How could she not tell me all this until now?*

Facing the entrance, the one-story building extended back from either side of the lobby in a 'v' shape. The parking lot was less than half full of cars and the only person Granger saw as they got out of their own was a man in overalls planting some flowers under a window.

When Granger looked behind him he realized why he couldn't see the nursing home from the road. Some woods blocked the view of the main road and the town itself. They hadn't driven that far, but it was so quiet. It was even more of a ghost town outside the city limits than inside them, apparently. Granger shivered.

The three walked through a set of glass doors and stepped into a foyer where three signs were prominently displayed. *Hospice & Palliative Care* was to the left, *Memory Care* was to the right, and the *Lobby* was straight ahead. More signs told him that the non-hospice, non-memory care area of the nursing home was through the lobby. It wasn't a new or fancy building, but it was clean enough and decorated how Granger figured most older folks would like their own homes decorated.

The middle-aged woman at the desk beside the front door gave a sad sort of smile when she saw them. Granger tried to identify the expression on her face.

*Pity?*

Granger already didn't like where the evening was headed.

"Welcome back," the woman said in a soft, feathery voice.

"Thank you," their mother said, signing them in on a clipboard sitting on the desk. "This is one of my other sons, Granger."

The woman nodded politely, but she still looked sad. Granger was relieved she didn't try to make small talk or tell them how sorry she was that their grandma was sick.

Once they were signed in, the three of them headed down the hall marked *Memory Care*. The conversations of residents and their visitors created a low droning sound that followed them as they passed the lobby.

Granger's mother subtly pointed behind them to the woman at the front desk.

"That's Evangeline," she whispered. "She recently moved her mother in here. Her mom died the other day."

Granger peeked behind him to see Evangeline dabbing her eyes with a tissue.

*Oh.*

They walked through a set of heavy double doors, the kind Granger had seen in hospitals. He kept walking until he noticed he was alone. Turning around he saw Jake and their mother still standing by the doors. Granger almost asked what they were doing, but they followed him once the doors closed with a click.

"We have to wait until the doors lock to make sure none of the residents walk out without staff," Jake explained.

The longer he was there, the more Granger felt like he was in a foreign land. He followed his mother and brother down the wide hallway lined with rooms on either side.

Back in the main lobby, the elderly people he saw, who he assumed were residents, were neatly dressed, talking and moving about without the restriction of locked double doors. On the other side of the double doors everything was different.

He passed by an older man who was facing the pea-green wall to their right. He was wearing worn-looking sweatpants, a dress shirt that was unbuttoned in the middle, socks, and no shoes. His white puff of hair was tousled. He stood with his nose six inches from the wall, rubbing the pad of his finger across the wallpaper as if tracing something. The man was calmly but totally absorbed in his activity. Granger fidgeted and walked a little faster.

Then he passed a little lady in a wheelchair. With one of her hands she kept pulling at her nightgown so it came up too high on her thighs, but she didn't seem to care or even notice. She was rubbing two of her fingers together with her other hand, mumbling nonsense and laughing. There was no one else around her.

Granger got a bad taste in his mouth.

He glanced back at the exit, feeling more queasy every time he passed another resident.

One resident further down the hall was talking in a raised voice to a staff member. Despite the staff's attempts to calm him down, he gesticulated more and more wildly and raised his voice even more. The man took a swing at a staff member. A full-on swing. Granger, eyes wide, looked around. The staff member, a woman much shorter than the resident, ducked in time to avoid his fist, but he came at her again. With one little call for assistance, two other staff members were on the spot immediately. By the time Granger, Jake, and their mom passed by, the staff had somehow deftly ushered the man into a room without using any force at all.

The hallway opened up into a miniature lobby with a nurse's

station situated in the middle, and his mother turned into a room on the right side of the hall. Jake followed.

Granger's heart rate was still elevated from the surprise of seeing the man nearly knock out the staff member. It was odd to him that no one else seemed bewildered or a little freaked out by the scene.

*What is this place?*

With one more look down the hall at the three staff members shielding the irate, but quickly fatiguing, resident from other residents, Granger followed his brother inside the room.

The room was small. Somehow the nursing home had managed to pack a set of matching twin beds and a round, wooden table into the space, but it was tight. The walls were a cool and calm green color, possibly to give off the illusion that the temperature inside the room was also cool. It was probably 80 degrees in the room.

Two people sat at the table with their backs to the door: A curvy woman with thick brown hair and a frail woman with short, thin, permed, gray hair. His forehead wrinkled. He quickly stepped back into the hall to double check the nameplate by the door, but the name was correct. Someone must have mislabeled the room.

But Jake rapped on the open door with his knuckles.

"Hey, grandma," he said in his usual pleasant, care-free way.

Granger's functioning arm shot out and reached for Jake. He was about to warn Jake that they had the wrong room. Before he could say anything, though, the younger of the two ladies turned around and smiled at them.

"Julia, your family is here," she said. "We can finish our game later."

A feeble voice came out of the frail, old lady, who still had her back to them.

"What's here?"

On hearing that this little lady had the same first name as his grandmother, Granger reasoned that this was how their nameplates got mixed up. He still stood in the doorway, ready for his mother and brother to figure this out and find the correct room.

"Your family. I'll move so they can come sit by you."

His mother walked further into the room.

"How is she today?"

The woman wore a name tag that said, *Melissa - Activities*.

"Tired. Night shift said she was up wandering around the unit for a few hours in the middle of the night."

Jake, too, walked further into the room.

"Was she looking for something?" he asked.

Granger looked back into the hall, trying to read the other name plates and wondering why it was taking Jake and their mom so long to realize they were in the wrong room.

"She kept mentioning her husband's name, but it was hard to tell what exactly she was looking for. Aimless wandering is pretty common here. A lot of times they don't even know what it is they're looking for." Then she perked up a little and lightly clapped her hands once. "Well! I'll give you the room. Let me know if you need anything."

Jake squeezed between the table and the far wall, then leaned down so the little old stranger could see him.

"Hi, grandma," he said, beaming.

"Hello," the lady said in a soft, floating, unfamiliar voice.

*Did they adopt this lady while I was away? What the heck is going on?*

"It's Jake," Jake explained, taking a seat.

"Jakey is my grandson," she said.

"Right! And guess who else is here to see you."

Jake scooted his chair over and tipped his chin up at Granger. Granger watched all this from his spot in the corner by the door, where he stood completely frozen. An iciness washed over him again, warning him that something was wrong even before his brain fully believed it. He tasted bile in his mouth. The fresh air and the parking lot were just on the other side of the window and they beckoned him.

Jake and mom looked at him expectantly.

He tried to tamp down the feelings bubbling up.

*Hallway. Hallway.*

He wanted to get to the hallway, but at the same time, his morbid curiosity was growing. He couldn't walk away without seeing his grandmother after six years and a five-hour drive.

He walked straight into the danger zone.

His legs were stiff as he moved around the table. He kept his eyes glued to the old lady's profile. The gray hair that had always been long and thick and in a braid down her back was now cut short and styled in the stereotypical old lady perm that she never would have agreed to before. Her once strong and sturdy frame, much like Granger's had been, was now shriveled up. Her bones seemed to be collapsing in on themselves. Her once strong voice now sounded like a mouse's squeak in comparison. Before that moment he never would have thought it was possible for her to get so tiny and frail. That happened to other people's grandmother's, but not to Grandma Julia.

She looked up at Granger, looked right into his eyes. The quick, calculating, I-can-see-through-walls look that could read Granger's soul in a heartbeat had been replaced by a gaze that was more glazed over than a donut.

Granger did not know this woman.

He missed the chair when he tried to sit down, which sent him crashing into the wall. Jake grabbed the chair to steady it while Granger regained his balance and sat.

She turned her gaze back to Jake. Even in his cold sweat, Granger felt like it must have been nearing ninety degrees in the room by that time. He couldn't find his voice to tell his mom to turn down the temperature on the window unit. His mouth was open, but no words were coming out. He looked helplessly at his baby brother for direction.

Jake raised his eyebrows at Granger and nodded. Granger raised his own eyebrows and shrugged.

"It's okay. Go ahead," Jake said quietly.

It was then that Granger remembered his goal: figure out what was going on with grandma and what he could do about it.

Granger cleared his throat and found his voice.

"Hi, grandma."

She pulled her eyes from Jake back to Granger.

"It's Granger, grandma," Jake said.

"Granger," she repeated.

"Yeah," Granger croaked. Sweat trickled down his temple. He pulled at his shirt.

Jake saw this and asked their mother to turn the heat off.

His grandmother repeated the name again.

"Granger."

When she didn't say or do anything else, Granger tried again.

"I-I'm one of your grandkids."

"I have a lot of grandkids, don't I?" she remarked placidly.

Jake chuckled.

Granger looked up at his mother, who was standing quietly behind their grandmother. She was smiling at him, but tears were gathering in her eyes again. He looked back at his grandmother and swallowed down the lump in his throat.

"Remind her of who you are," Jake said.

*Remind her of who you are?*

What weird words.

He tried to ignore the ripping feeling that was happening inside his chest.

"I can't think of anything," Granger told Jake.

"Grandma, you remember? Granger helped out a lot at your house in the summers growing up," Jake filled in for him.

The brothers looked at her. No reaction.

"I, uh, played baseball," Granger volunteered.

Nothing.

"I've got the one arm that doesn't work."

"He's one of my older brothers," Jake supplied.

She looked back at Jake but didn't say anything.

"Sometimes it helps for her to see pictures," Jake said. He leaned back in his chair and looked at a large bulletin board beside the bed. He plucked a picture off and slid it in front of her. It was a picture of the family from ten years prior. The six of them stood in a smiling row in front of the high school with their oldest brother, Levi, in the center wearing a blue cap and gown.

"See, grandma," Jake said, leaning over the picture and pointing. "That's our mom, Allison, your daughter-in-law. Here's Levi, Trevor, Lillian, me, and this one is Granger."

"Those are my grandchildren."

"Yeah! This one is me and that one is Granger, this guy sitting right here."

Their grandmother nodded, smiling at the two of them across the table. But her gaze faded back into that vacant expression. Granger was unused to seeing so little focus behind her sharp, gray eyes. Her expression sort of reminded Granger of how their other brother, Trevor, had looked after getting his wisdom teeth out: distant and loopy.

"Where's Albert?" she asked.

"In the picture?" Granger asked.

"I don't think she's talking about the picture," Jake said.

Grandma jumped a little when her daughter-in-law spoke from behind her.

"Albert went to heaven a few years ago, Julia," she reminded her.

Grandma looked at Granger like it was him who'd said it.

"Is he coming today, too?" she asked Granger.

Granger's eyes widened, unsure how he was supposed to answer that.

"No, no, we won't see him for a while, Julia."

"He said he'll be back in time to mow the lawn before it gets dark."

Their mother cleared her throat and sat down next to their grandmother so they could see each other. "Don't worry, we'll take care of it."

"He said he'd do it. Where is he?" She was looking all over the room and fidgeting in her chair a lot. The Grandma Julia of his youth was not a fidgeter. She looked like she was about to cry or yell at somebody.

Their mother threw a concerned look at Jake. Granger looked from one to the other, waiting for one of them to calm her down.

Jake reached out and touched her hand. She flinched but this brought her attention back to her guests. "Hey grandma, we brought you some cookies."

"Right, the cookies," their mom said. She rummaged around in her purse and pulled out a ziplock containing two chocolate chip cookies. Seeing food right then made Granger want to vomit.

"I can't eat right now, not when Albert is so late coming home!" Her voice didn't even sound like her own anymore.

He had watched his mother turn off the heat but he sure didn't feel a difference yet. His grandmother was now whimpering like a small child who had lost her mother in the grocery store. Granger's queasiness was growing and his emotions were pressing up against the barricade in his head, threatening to burst through the wall.

*Just focus. Think. Don't feel, think.*

His body would not listen to his mind.

Granger stood so abruptly that his chair hit the wall behind him.

"'Scuse me," he said, tripping over the table leg in his effort to get out of the room quickly.

"Where are you going?" his mom asked.

"Outside."

"But Granger, wait—"

He stepped into the hall and sucked in a lung-full of cool air, but with that inhale he also got a host of unwelcome smells.

"Excuse me," he said when he saw Melissa From Activities. "How do I get outside?"

"The way out to the parking lot is just back the way you came. But we also have a lovely, fenced-in patio out back, too, right through those doors."

Granger was already walking briskly back down the hall toward the double doors before she finished her first sentence.

Instead of opening it, when he shoved on the door he collided with it. He recovered and pushed on the door again. Locked.

"Ma'am," he said, "How do I…"

"Punch in this code written right here on the wall. It's to keep our residents from wandering away and potentially endangering themselves."

She typed in the code for him and he burst through to the other side. He tried to breathe but couldn't take in a full, satisfying breath. In the hall he passed a custodian and some old ladies in matching sweaters who were walking and talking. Finally, he opened the glass doors and the fresh, spring air welcomed him, just as the mental retaining wall failed him.

# 3

GRANGER RAKED HIS GOOD HAND through his hair a couple times. He flexed his fingers to try to get rid of the pins and needles in his hand. He was shaking all over.

"Come on," he growled, forcing himself to breathe through gritted teeth. There was a nice, round piece of broken-off asphalt lying nearby. Granger kicked it with all his might. It banged into a hub cap and smashed into pieces. He'd never been good at aiming in soccer. He was relieved to see the car was his mom's and not a strangers'.

He paced the perimeter of the lot, occasionally glancing up at the dark clouds now moving in quickly from the southwest. He was on his second lap when the skies opened. He patted his pockets but found no car keys.

*Oh yeah. We brought her car.*

The rain fell hard and fast. He took a few strides back toward the nursing home, but then paused, turned around, and resumed his trek around the parking lot in the downpour. He tried to focus on the relaxing rhythm of the rain hitting metal and glass and pavement and foliage, but his mind wandered rebelliously.

After ten minutes in the rain, Granger was drenched through to his socks and boxers. Still, he did not go back inside.

Every once in a while a car would pull in or out of the parking lot and someone would run to or from the building with an umbrella or a large handbag or a newspaper over their head. One car pulled in and a young mother and daughter got out and ran toward the building together. Granger wouldn't have given them a second thought or even a second glance except the mother called over to him, startling him out of his thoughts.

"There are umbrellas inside the building if you need one," she yelled over the rain and a low rumble of thunder.

"I'm good, thanks," he shouted back.

He hunched over more and walked on before the conversation could go any further.

Five minutes later, he saw two familiar figures leaving the building. His mother and brother ran out to the car holding umbrellas.

"Have you been out here this whole time? In the rain?" his mother asked.

"Yeah." He was still shivering, but now it was because he was cold.

"Why didn't you come back inside?"

"I didn't want to."

"There are umbrellas in—"

"Can we go?"

She looked down, fiddling with her keychain to find the right key while holding the black umbrella handle awkwardly between her arm and torso.

"I thought you'd come back in," she said, still looking down. "I know it's a lot to take in, honey, but it's not good to avoid it."

"'Avoid it?'"

"I know how you must be feeling. It's so sad—"

"Sad? I'm not sad, I'm mad!"

The keys fell into a shallow puddle at her feet. Jake fished them out for her before she could even bend over.

"I suppose that's to be expected," she said.

"You think? Why the heck didn't you tell me sooner?"

"Come on, man," Jake said in a tone much calmer than Granger's and much more confident than their mother's. "Don't take this out on her."

Granger brushed him off. Granger didn't take his eyes off his mother, who wouldn't lift her eyes to look at him.

"It was so gradual, honey. We barely noticed, ourselves."

"Really? It was 'so gradual' that one day you just woke up and thought 'wow. Grandma sure seems different. Wonder how that happened.'"

Jake took a step forward.

"Are you blaming us?" Jake demanded. Granger looked at his little brother, surprised by the outburst. Jake scoffed. "You could have seen it for yourself if you cared enough to come back every once in a while."

"Jake—" their mom said.

"Lester is not my home anymore. I have a life in Eugene. I can't just leave anytime I want."

"You have a job?" Jake asked.

"Yes!"

"You have vacation time and money for gas?"

"You don't think I have other things to spend my money on, like, I don't know, rent? And other things to do with my time? It's a ten-hour round trip!"

"Why does family always have to compete with your 'life?' I didn't say I think you should move home, I'm just talking about visiting! You'd think because the woman helped raise you that you'd find the time to visit her as she's dyin—"

"Shut up!" Granger shouted.

"Boys—" their mother said.

"I want to know why he hasn't shown his face in six years, mom! I know you do, too."

"Please, get in the car," she said.

"You have no idea what you're talking about," Granger shot at Jake.

"Why wouldn't I? I was there. I lived with grandma, too."

"You don't know half of what we went through. You were too young to remember."

"But who's been here for the last six years?"

"We didn't know how serious it was until a few weeks ago," his mother pleaded, answering a question he'd asked minutes ago. "We thought her memory problems were just because she was getting older. We had no idea it was dementia. We didn't even really know what dementia was!"

"You wouldn't have come back even if we did," Jake said, sounding sullen like the teenaged boy that he was.

The nearby sound of a car door shutting grabbed the attention of all three. A nicely dressed older couple glanced at them and hurried into the building.

"Please," their mom said again. "Get in the car. We can talk about this at home."

At the mention of that last word Granger only thought of Eugene. There was no room in the definition of that word for Lester anymore.

Granger dropped into the front seat and slammed the door.

The sun set, the storm continued. On the drive back to the house, Granger looked out the passenger seat window, seething. Each time he thought of that alter-ego version of his grandma sitting in a nursing home eating mashed vegetables and staring at the four walls in that broom closet of a room, the anger at his mother and brother intensified.

When the car of silent passengers pulled into the driveway, Granger told his mom he wasn't hungry and went straight to the bedroom he used to share with Trevor. Their room looked the same as it had when Granger left home, a year after Trevor left home, except now there were no sweaty clothes heaped on top of the hamper, or empty food wrappers on the night stands.

His plan to return to Eugene that night having been foiled by the weather and the news about his grandma, he was forced to stay one miserable night in Lester.

He looked around his old room, and at his twin bed that was outfitted with a set of his old, dark blue sheets. After such a long day, the bed did look inviting. He blinked to get rid of the dryness in his eyes and realized he had nowhere to put his contacts overnight, since he hadn't packed anything.

Someone knocked lightly on his bedroom door. When he opened it, his mother stood on the other side, holding out a toothbrush, toothpaste, contact solution, and a small container which, he was guessing, was for his contacts.

"Thanks," he mumbled.

He walked to the bathroom. When he walked back to his room with freshly brushed teeth and blurry vision, she was still standing in his doorway, leaning against it and looking into the room.

He slipped past her but didn't shut the door.

"I'm surprised you haven't sold the house, yet," he said while he busied himself with moving the pillows and pulling back the covers on his bed. "After this spring it'll just be you living here."

When she spoke she sounded exhausted. "This isn't a good market to sell in. Better to hold onto it for a little longer."

"You could downsize a lot, though," he said, his back still turned. "I can't imagine you'd lose money."

She said nothing. When he finally turned around he saw her eyes roving across every inch of the room.

"I guess you could turn this into another guest room or rent it out," he said drily.

When she was still quiet, he asked, "why haven't you?"

"Rented out your rooms?"

"Turned it into a guest room. You turned Levi's into a guest room."

Her eyes finally finished sweeping the room and came to rest on him.

"I wanted to keep it the same. Just in case."

"Why didn't you keep Levi's the same, then?" He knew the answer, but he wanted to hear her admit it.

"He only needs it when he and his family come to visit."

"Isn't that the same as what I'm doing now?"

She opened and shut her mouth a few times before she said, "he doesn't need his old room like it used to be. He has a wife and daughter now."

"So, because I don't have those things, I'm not a real adult yet? You have to keep my room looking like a high schooler's room?"

"That's not what I meant."

Granger and his mother looked at one another for a long time.

"I'm not moving back," he finally said. He watched her face as the words landed on her ears. She lowered her gaze again.

*She needed to hear it,* he told himself. *It's no use giving her false hope.*

She shrugged and walked out of the room. "A mother can dream."

When he heard her bedroom door latch he got up and shut his own.

He laid down on the bed with his right hand on the pillow, cradling the back of his head. Even the blurry ceiling had a look distinctive to his old life.

A car turned into a nearby driveway and the glow from its headlights raced across the wall opposite Granger's head, momentarily illuminating a picture on his old desk.

He squinted, but couldn't tell what the picture was. Curiosity pulled him out of bed and over to the desk. Until that moment he'd forgotten that he hadn't been back in that room since he moved away for his freshman year of college, so it surprised him to see a beautiful, smiling, red-headed teenaged girl looking back at him.

He put the picture face down on the dresser and got back in bed.

*Plan. Need to make a plan.*

He wanted to get out of Lester as soon as possible. The town was bringing out the worst in him.

*I guess that makes sense, Lester is the worst of me.*

At the same time, now that he'd seen his grandma, now that he knew how bad things were, he couldn't just leave. At least not without a plan to see her again.

And then there was the question of what he could do about his grandma's situation. Should he try to make her remember him, or would it upset her? Would she immediately forget him again anyway? Was it even possible for her to remember him again? Was dementia really incurable?

Even when he swallowed, the lump in his throat wouldn't go away. He turned onto his right side, facing the wall.

Over the next thirty minutes he formed his plan. He fell asleep around one a.m. with his mother's words ringing in his ears.

*"A mother can dream."*

Dreaming was exactly what Granger did that night. Between dreams he woke up thinking the same thoughts that had plagued him since his head hit the pillow hours earlier.

*They couldn't really have expected me to come home all the time, right? My life isn't here anymore. Home isn't here. Trevor and Levi are gone, too. Jakey will be leaving home this fall. Why all the fuss about me?*

In those half-asleep moments, long-forgotten memories of family ski trips, a Major League Baseball game, and jumping from a tire swing into a large pond floated through his consciousness.

It was an unpleasant night.

# 4

BOTH HIS MOTHER AND BROTHER were gone when Granger awoke, which meant he didn't have to deal with their questions. He relaxed. The stove clock said it was 11:15 in the morning, so he poured himself a bowl of cereal. When he put the milk away, he saw a post-it note with his name on it stuck to the fridge.

"*Granger*

*Not sure what your plans are, but Jake has a game this evening. It would mean a lot to him if you came. We can ride to the school together when I get off work if you want.*"

He rolled his eyes.

*I should've known she'd do anything to keep me here longer.*

After he ate, he brushed his teeth and put his shoes on. He didn't want to put off things at the nursing home any longer, as it only made him clammier.

He grabbed his car keys, along with some other items that he thought may come in handy, and headed out. The temptation to get on the highway and drive southwest instead of northeast out to the nursing home was strong.

At *Golden Grove* he approached the front desk in the lobby where a short, thirty-something man with a receding hairline sat. His name tag said, "Archie."

He smiled at Granger and in a wheezy voice said, "Hello, are you visiting a friend or family member?"

"My grandmother," Granger mumbled.

"Alright, just sign here."

"Thanks," he said mechanically. He had to set down the pile he was carrying so he could pick up the pen connected to the desk by a little silver chain.

"Is this your first time here?"

"Uh, no. I came yesterday."

Archie nodded, "I can always tell which visitors are new."

"Because you've never seen them before?" Granger asked drily.

"Because they all look sorta scared."

"Oh."

Granger picked up his pile again, and then Archie held out a visitor badge to him. Granger set the pile back down on the counter, took the badge, and put the lanyard around his neck with his one good hand. This caught Archie's attention.

"Do you want some help with those?"

Archie had that 'helpful' look on his face. Granger hated that look.

"I'm fine."

The pile was very large and awkward to hold onto, but Granger would manage.

Since he knew where he was heading this time, he looked around a little more. Then he wished he hadn't. A lot of residents sat alone, especially in the memory care unit. Some sat in wheelchairs, looking out the windows or staring off into space. Some mumbled to themselves. Others paced the halls continuously.

One man up ahead strode down the hall with his hands clasped behind his back, looking around with a sharp gaze that reminded Granger of his grandma's, or rather, reminded Granger of what his grandma's used to be. Granger figured the man was a staff member, maybe a doctor or psychiatrist or something. Then a girl wearing scrubs, who was maybe just old enough to vote, approached the man with a little cup of liquid in one hand and a little cup of pills in the other.

"Here you go, Mr. Farley, these are your noon medications," she said in a sing-song voice that seemed out of place in the depressing atmosphere.

Granger couldn't help but stare. The man looked as healthy as he could be at his age. He surely couldn't have been older than 65. He was much taller than Granger, and though he was on the skinnier side, he didn't look frail at all. Granger could even see decent muscles on the guy's arms.

"Medications?" Mr. Farley asked, looking down at the girl with his hands still clasped behind his back.

"Yes, sir," she said.

"I just took medications," Mr. Farley said.

"Yes, you took some around seven this morning, but it's about noon now, so it's time to take some more."

The way the girl didn't miss a beat made Granger wonder if she had conversations like that a lot.

Farley looked at her for a minute, but then accepted the two cups. She watched carefully as he dumped the pills into his mouth and washed them down. He handed her the empty cups, then clasped his hands behind his back and resumed his walk up the hall.

As he got closer, Granger looked closer. The guy looked sort of familiar.

Granger's train of thought derailed when he found himself outside his grandmother's open door.

He could see her sitting in the same place as the day before, alone this time. He had no free hand with which to knock, so he opened his mouth to alert her to his presence. But then he hesitated, worried he wouldn't know what to do or say to interact with her, a stranger.

*I guess I shoulda thought of that before... Maybe I should come back when mom and Jakey...*

Then he thought of dealing with them again, while also trying to deal with his grandma's new reality. While he deliberated, his hands got clammy, which compromised his grip on the stuff he was holding. Before he dropped everything he stepped into the room.

"Knock, knock."

Her head moved slightly at the noise, but she didn't turn around or say anything.

He stepped further inside.

"Hi, Grandma. It's me, again. Granger. Your grandson."

Her head raised.

"Oh, I'm sorry. I didn't know you were asleep."

As he came around the table she lifted her eyes to his, looking groggy.

"It's Granger," he repeated. A tray of food sat in front of her, picked over. "Aren't you going to eat anything?"

"Yes," she said, but didn't reach for her fork.

"Do you remember me? Granger Kyle?"

"Granger Kyle."

"Yeah. I'm one of your grandkids."

She licked her dry lips and shifted in her seat a little. She looked up at the corner of the room where the wall and ceiling met, squinting. He looked, too. There was nothing up there, but when she spoke he realized she was just trying to remember something. It seemed to take a lot out of her when she spoke.

"My grandkids are Steve, Candace, Dave… Rick…" she trailed off.

"Well," Granger began, speaking slowly in case she wasn't finished listing off names. She'd always hated when people interrupted and she had scolded him and his siblings for it repeatedly when they were little. "Steve, Candace, and Dave are your kids. Rick was… well I don't know exactly who he was, he was another family member. Maybe a cousin. I'm Dave's kid."

"Dave's kid… Dave had Lillian, Levi…"

Granger waited again, but she never finished that sentence, either.

"Yep, then there's Trevor, me, and Jakey. Er, Jake."

She didn't respond. Her unfocused gaze drifted lazily away. Granger cleared his throat.

"I brought some pictures, Grandma. Maybe they'll help."

He let go of the frames that were about to fall out of his grip. They clattered onto the tabletop and she jumped.

"Sorry."

He took a seat and scooted up to the table. The wooden chair legs scraped against the wood floor, startling her again. Granger cringed.

He reached across the table and pointed to one of the pictures that was now laying right in front of her.

"This is Levi and Trevor and me with our mom at your farm. I think you took this picture, actually."

He spoke slowly so she could digest every word he said.

"I was about… six, I think, in this picture."

She pointed a crooked and shaky index finger at the picture and said, "that's Allison, Levi, Trevor, Granger."

Granger's heart soared. He smiled broadly.

"Yeah!"

She jumped at his exclamation. He quieted down again.

"And do you recognize the farm?"

"That's our farm."

"Yeah!" he said quieter. But he sat up straighter and scooted to the edge of the chair.

"Why don't those boys have shirts on?"

"Oh, well, we had just gone swimming, or, we were going to go swimming. Something like that. It was summertime."

She was quiet again, but Granger was too excited by how well his plan was progressing to let the conversation end there.

"We used to spend almost every day in the summers at your farm, before we moved there. Do you remember your grandkids at your farm a lot?"

"My grandkids love my farm," she said smiling. "When they come over we make strawberry jam or cookies or rake leaves together."

"Yes!"

She was recalling some of their favorite childhood activities.

Granger looked back at the picture in the frame. If he had been about six years old in the picture then it must have been taken not long before Jake was born. Granger flipped the frame over and twisted the black, fish-shaped tab things that held the back on. With one hand, he popped the picture out of the frame to find the date it had been taken. He was right. It was about eight months before Jakey had been born. Their mom might not even have known that she was pregnant, yet.

"Grandma, this one here," he pointed at the shortest boy in the photo, the one on the far left: blond, barefoot, shirtless, and squinting up at the photographer like his two older brothers. "This one is me."

He pointed from the photo to himself a couple times.

She had trouble following his finger. She looked up at him.

"I'm Granger."

"Where's Granger?"

Granger felt the floor drop out from under him as though he were on an elevator in a fancy building, whooshing down to the lobby from the fiftieth floor.

"Him. Me. It's me. I'm Granger."

"Granger used to love the strawberry jam the most," she said.

"But he hates when his older brothers chase him around the kitchen with their sticky fingers."

The more she talked, the more often she switched from past tense to present tense and back. She laughed, but her laugh now was only an echo of the one Granger remembered. It was like, since her mind wasn't fully there anymore, neither was her body.

"But then as Granger got bigger, he joined in on the fun and he would torment little Jakey with his sticky fingers. But Jakey loved it!"

She searched his face with her eyes, wanting to share the joyful memory, but Granger couldn't muster a very convincing smile. He leaned back in his chair and looked down at the picture again.

That picture had been taken on a great day. It was early summer. He remembered because his mother had been playing outside with them, which meant she hadn't hit the "is it time for school yet so these kids can get out of my house" phase of the summer yet, as she inevitably did every year.

Lillian wasn't in the photograph, which meant she was probably with her mom that day. As a kid, she spent a lot of the summers traveling with her mom, and she never lived with or stayed overnight with her half brothers again once their dad left. Or, as Granger would find out later, after he was kicked out. The date on the picture meant their mom had probably just kicked their father out. Maybe that was why she looked so happy.

His grandma spoke again, saving him from having to think anymore about his dad.

"Where's the priest gone?"

"The... what?"

"The priest. Why's he going?"

"Um... I don't know. What priest?"

"I don't remember his name. They were at a gas station with Phil and Joann."

Granger racked his brain, trying to connect the dots, but she wasn't making sense. Since he'd had some luck with the first picture, he decided to see if they could make any more progress with the others.

"Here, Grandma. Do you remember this picture? I think this was from one of Trevor's birthdays."

She was looking everywhere except at the picture on the table, so he held it up in front of her and shook it a little until she finally focused her attention on it.

"What's that?" she asked.

"Do you recognize anybody in this picture?"

"There's Dave," she said, pointing at 11-year-old Trevor.

"No. Well, he does kind of look like dad. But it's Trevor."

"Trevor."

"Yeah. And look, Lillian is in this one, too. And there's me. That one right there."

She was still looking at the picture, but the interest and focus were gone from her eyes. He swallowed hard, remembering what a good listener she used to be.

When she started to scoot her chair back from the table he quickly held out another picture. He was getting discouraged, but he wasn't giving up just yet.

"This one is more recent. This is from my high school graduation. That's me, Grandma: Granger."

He looked deep into her eyes, hoping to see even the smallest sign of recognition.

"Granger is graduating," she said.

"Yes! That's my high school graduation!"

Her eyes floated from the picture down to the wooden table, and she started rubbing at a spot where the wood grain was darker. He sighed, heavily. He looked again at the graduation photo. He didn't look all that different, although he wasn't as physically fit now as he was then. With a sinking feeling, he reasoned that if she didn't make the connection from this photo, he wasn't sure if she would at all.

He pulled out the last photo he'd brought. One more try.

"Do you know who they are, Grandma? Grandma, look. You see the people in this picture? No... the picture, Grandma. Right here. There we go. Who are they?"

She studied it intently, then looked back at him and asked, "when is Albert coming back?"

The lump in his throat was back. He looked down at his lap, where his left hand laid limp and looking as deflated and defeated as he felt. He opened his mouth to give her the answer he'd heard his mother give her the day before, but when he looked back at her, she was already re-absorbed in rubbing that one spot of dark grain on the table.

Granger was unsure what to do next. His plan had failed, so he threw out his hope of catching up with her. He was a stranger. Just a stranger. With a lifetime's worth of their shared memories and no one with whom to share them.

He looked around her room. Along the top of her dresser were five other framed photos of their family that he hadn't noticed before. The faces of his brothers, half sister, aunts, uncles, grandpa, and even father smiled back at him. On a shelf above the television were her favorite old gardening gloves, formerly a lime green color, but now stained and faded from years of digging in the dirt. There was also a sepia-tone photograph of her and his grandpa on their wedding day, and a small stuffed mule which his Grandpa Albert had given her as a joke one year on her birthday.

Granger knew if she was really herself still, that tiny bedroom would make her feel claustrophobic, which made him feel a tiny bit claustrophobic. Except for the nursing home, and apparently living with mom and Jake for a while, she'd lived in the wide-open country her whole life. The house she and Grandpa Albert lived in for fifty years was a spacious, two-story farmhouse with acres and acres of land. Now, she shared a tiny bedroom with a roommate, and a small, closed-in patio, that wasn't much bigger in size than the bedroom, with twenty other residents.

*Maybe it's good she's not in her right mind. She'd hate it here.*

He looked back at the pictures again. Surely there must be a way to just help her understand who he was. He knew now that it was too much to hope that she would remember anything more than that, but if she could just put two and two together… just one more time, before it was too late. Unless it was already too late…

Granger felt a renewed sense of urgency. But when he felt ready to try again, he saw that she had fallen asleep. He stood up but didn't leave the table yet, partially because he didn't want to wake her a second time, and partially because he didn't want to leave yet. Not with so little progress. He thought about leaving the picture of them at the farm, but he knew his mom would miss it. Throughout his childhood she'd often commented that it was one of her favorites. Maybe he could make a copy.

He carefully re-stacked the frames and awkwardly picked them up again, then tiptoed out of her bedroom.

"Bye, Grandma," he whispered. She didn't stir. Her chin rested on her chest.

He cleared his throat, sniffed, and blinked a few times before turning away.

Outside the room, Melissa From Activities was talking with another resident across the hall in the lobby area. They sat in the kind of armchairs he saw in hospitals and other medical buildings, the kind with the fabric that was made more for being easy to clean than for comfort. Melissa and the resident were talking and even smiling.

It made him feel better, just a little bit, that someone like Melissa From Activities was helping take care of his grandma.

"Excuse me," said a teenage girl in scrubs whose name tag said *Esmerelda*. "Are you still visiting with your grandmother?"

"Uh, no. We're done. Why?"

"I was going to see if she needed to use the bathroom, but I didn't want to interrupt."

"Oh." He squirmed when he was again reminded of the extent of her helplessness.

"She just fell asleep," he said.

"That's okay," she said cheerfully, walking into the room anyway, which Granger found a little irritating.

There were a couple more residents scattered about in the hallways today. And he saw lots of people walking around in navy blue scrubs. Some aides could have been in their sixties or even seventies, while others didn't even look old enough to be out of high school yet. Some aides looked like life had beaten them down. Granger could imagine why, working in a place as sad as *Golden Grove*. But a couple of them smiled at him as they went about their business. One aide walked around with a tray of yogurt and pudding cups, offering them to residents. There were a couple residents to whom she didn't offer anything. These residents sat in wheelchairs silently staring off into space. An older aide sat next to one of these residents and held a spoonful of chocolate pudding right in front of his mouth so that the spoon touched his lips. The resident, who seemed oblivious to the world around him, somehow knew to open his mouth and take a bite. His face lit up.

"There's the smile," said the aide. "You sure love your chocolate pudding, don't you, Smitty?" She gently patted Smitty on the shoulder. Aside from opening his mouth and swallowing the pudding, he didn't do or say anything.

Granger didn't want to see anymore. He headed for the exit, but before he got to the locked double doors of the unit, the frames slipped from his grasp and a few fell to the floor.

"Do you want a bag for those, sir? Or a box?"

Melissa From Activities hurried over to him and took the other frames that were slowly slipping.

He wanted to say 'no,' but his arm was cramping and if any of the frames broke he would have to deal with his mother trying to cover up how upset she was about it.

"Sure. Thanks."

"No problem." She went to the nurse's station and came back with a cardboard box. Granger knew he should have been more specific; a plastic bag with handles would have been easier for him to carry through the building since he had to open doors to get out. He kept his mouth shut, though.

"I should have just taken them out of the frames, but it takes longer with just one hand."

She smiled. "As a mother of three, I understand that when you're in a hurry, you're in a hurry. How was your visit?"

Granger looked over his shoulder at his grandma's door. "I'm not really sure."

He had a lot of questions, and seeing as his mother and Jake weren't there, he figured it was a good time to try and get some answers.

"She got tired really quickly. Is that normal?"

Melissa From Activities nodded. "It doesn't take much for some to get tired. And then there are others." She nodded her head toward the man named Mr. Farley who was still pacing.

Granger remembered the guy from the day before who had tried to hit the staff.

"Why does dementia do different things to different people?"

"It affects the brain and our brains control everything. For some people it messes with their speech, for others it doesn't. Some people get really angry and aggressive and others get more calm."

She looked at him with eyes that looked sad. "It's hard to understand. Mentally and emotionally."

He cleared his throat and tried to smile, "and I was never good at science."

He adjusted the box on his hip as an excuse to look away, feeling that annoying lump in his throat again. He had one more pressing question.

"Is there any way to reverse the disease?"

"Like a cure?"

"Yeah."

"Unfortunately, no."

"But even if you can't totally cure someone, can it get better at all?"

She didn't answer right away. "I've worked here for years, and I'm in nursing school right now, but there's still a lot I don't know. If you want, I could have a nurse come answer your questions."

He glanced over at the nurse's station where a couple people with stethoscopes draped over their necks were busy typing on their computers. They looked like they didn't have time to be disturbed, and although normally, when he felt something was important, he was as persistent and stubborn as his grandma had been, he didn't have the energy this time. Not after the last half hour he'd spent with her.

He shook his head and moved toward the door.

"That's okay. Some other time. Thanks again for the box."

"No problem. What's your name?"

"Granger."

"Hang in there, Granger."

Melissa From Activities went back to the resident still sitting in the armchair, and Granger walked toward the keypad on the wall. Movement out of the corner of his eye caught his attention and he looked up to see Farley pacing toward him. Before the older man turned around to start walking the other way, again, Farley nodded to Granger in greeting. Granger nodded back, still feeling like he should know who the man was. Then Farley looked straight ahead and continued his march to nowhere.

* * *

Granger shut his car door and just sat there until the silence that enveloped him and muffled everything outside became unbearable. He put the key in the ignition and cranked the air conditioning, but still didn't leave the parking lot.

The picture of him and his brothers and his mother at the farm on that hot, sticky summer day looked up at him from the box in the passenger's seat. Granger eyed it.

He'd thought it was a safe memory. It was a photograph of the good old days, before things got complicated… and then totally screwed up. But one memory triggered other memories. Of course, they were all connected.

*Idiot. Why didn't you think of that before?*

Instantaneously, a familiar and profound restlessness came over him. He yanked the gear shift from 'Park' to 'Reverse.' In his haste to leave the parking lot, the farm picture slid off the top of the pile down into the side of the box.

*So much for that plan. She still has no idea who I am.*

The memories he didn't want, nagged him. He turned on the stereo, and turned it up loud.

# 5

"Granger!" Grandma yelled from the wraparound porch. "Get back here and put your shoes on! Lord knows what's hiding in that dirt."

He grudgingly turned around and did not hurry back to the porch.

"No whining. Get back here."

Six-year-old Granger trudged back to the porch steps, stomping his bare feet on the grass. She went back into the house and he heard the smacking sound that the screen door made whenever it closed. He plunked down hard on the bottom step but shot up again right away. He glared down at the pointy piece of gray paint that had chipped off the wood, before brushing it away, sitting more gingerly this time.

His hand-me-down tennis shoes had been worn so much that he could usually slip them on in seconds, which was just how he liked it. But that day someone had tied the laces together. He made a frustrated grunting sound at being delayed further. He held back tears thinking of all he was missing at the creek, which was where his two older brothers had run after getting tired of playing in the sprinkler.

*Not fair!*

His little hands wrestled impatiently with the knot, which only made him more mad. From down at the creek, Granger heard Levi

38

whoop and then a big splash.

He couldn't take it anymore. He stood and headed toward the screen door with the shoes. But before he'd crossed the porch, his mother's voice floated out from the kitchen through the mesh of the door.

"... she said she wouldn't be able to keep me on for next year. I'm not worried about the rest of the summer, but come fall..." she sighed. "I wish Dave was here."

"Dave was dragging you and the kids down to a dangerous place," Granger heard his grandmother say.

"I know, Julia."

His mom's voice sounded different to him than it usually did. He didn't like that, though he couldn't say why. His mom continued talking.

"But even the little money he brought in helped."

"You did the right thing, child. I wish just as much as you do that my son would get his act together, but he can't provide for his family if he can't hold a legitimate job, make sensible decisions, or stay sober."

Little Granger didn't understand much of what he was hearing, but what he did pick up on was this: Dad's not doing something he should or he is doing something he shouldn't, and it's hurting Mom.

While he was frozen in place, trying to make sense of what they were saying, a chair in the kitchen scraped across the floor and he jumped. He looked all around him for a place to hide; he didn't want a spanking for overhearing a grown-up conversation. But then he saw Trevor's other pair of flip flops lying on the porch right next to the screen door. As quietly as he could, he dashed over and snatched them up. He flung his hopeless tennis shoes into the grass and jumped off the porch, landing feet-first in the dirt. On impact, he tipped forward and fell onto his hands and knees, but in no time he was up on his feet again and running, only tripping a few times in the flip flops that he hadn't grown into yet.

He decided to wait until that night to tell Trevor what he had overheard. Since the two younger boys shared a room, Granger wouldn't have to worry about Levi overhearing and making a big fuss. Trevor always kept Granger's secrets. He wasn't a tattle-tale like Levi.

Granger made it to the creek and finally understood why his brothers had been 'hooting and hollering,' as Grandpa Albert would say, more than usual. Grandpa Albert had tied a long, thick rope to the tree hanging over the deepest and widest part of the creek. In his excitement, the conversation about his dad was wiped completely from his mind. In the midst of all the excitement of early summer, the six-year-old wouldn't remember the conversation until weeks later, and by then, it didn't seem so important.

The five of them, Mom, Levi, Trevor, Granger, and little Jakey, lived on Grandma Julia and Grandpa Albert's farm for six years. They were the best years of Granger's childhood. Some of the best of his whole life, in fact. The farmhouse and the creek and all the land between and around it was theirs to explore, and it was Disney World to the boys in comparison to the tiny, two bedroom townhouse with no yard that they had lived in before.

In their townhouse days, when his dad was gone, Granger had one parent. When his dad was there, Granger never knew which version of his dad he was going to get. Some days his dad was the best dad in the world, like an overgrown kid. He played with them and took them on outings. He bought them treats and toys. It was a blast for the boys and their older half-sister. On other days, his dad didn't pay any attention to them except to snap at them for being too loud and rambunctious. This usually happened after long, very loud conversations with Granger's mother.

At the farmhouse, Granger had three parents to get after him, but at least they always acted like parents.

There were uncomfortable times at the farm, of course. There are bound to be when an elderly couple with a farm to run, their perpetually underemployed daughter-in-law, and four little boys all share a house. But they stuck together as a family back then, and his grandma had been the glue.

# 6

THERE WAS NO ONE IN the house to pepper him with questions when he returned to his mom's place, but the deafening silence was unbearable and the four walls were stifling. He needed to move.

He found his shirt with the special running sleeve in a box with other old baseball gear in the bottom of his closet. It was made especially to accommodate monoplegia: it held his paralyzed arm against his body so it didn't flap around while he ran. His mom had been so proud of that purchase for him. He'd only used it once before.

Granger grunted and strained but finally got on the running shirt and slid his arm into the sleeve. Granger caught a glimpse of himself in the mirror and decided to wear his cotton t-shirt over it.

He went outside and started to run.

Movement was white noise. It was soothing. His mind synced up with his body when he moved; things made more sense, problems could be solved. Or avoided. It was why he enjoyed working in the restaurant industry; he was constantly in motion.

The boiling anger inside him fueled the first part of his run. His face got hot and sweaty before the run became taxing, thinking about his mom and brother and all they hadn't shared with him. He took long, powerful strides, running like he used to run in high school, until his body reminded him that he hadn't run in years and begged for him to stop. But when he slowed down, he was gripped by a strong desire to speed up again and find a hole he could jump in or a big rock he could hide behind.

*What's gonna happen? Will she get worse? How much worse? Is this just the beginning?*

He tried to run faster again, but fatigued quickly. He was forced to walk when the stitch in his side made running unbearable. He propped his right hand on his right hip and breathed heavily.

The image of how his grandma used to be came into his mind, and then the image of who she was now. The two versions of her sat side by side in his head, dissonant.

One choked sob escaped him and he covered his mouth to hold in any others that might follow. He couldn't stop the tears from pooling in his eyes, though. He sniffed and blinked them away.

He kicked a rock and glared at it shooting down the street. He punched a trashcan as he passed it. But the tears came stronger and the fight went out of his arms and legs.

He looked around at Lester, and thought of all he hadn't known he was missing. He thought of all his mother and brother hadn't told him, too.

He got back to the house drenched in sweat and already sore. It took twice as long as it used to to restore his breathing to normal. He was so distracted that at first it didn't seem strange to him that the house was still empty. Another note in the kitchen from his mom told him she'd come home to get him for Jake's game, found him gone, couldn't reach him, and so had gone to the game on her own.

He'd forgotten about Jake's game. According to the clock, it had probably just started. He felt a little guilty about the three missed calls and four missed texts from his mom.

*Honest mistake.*

He hopped in the shower and thought about his situation.

*I could leave town right after Jake's game if I wanted. Or I could just go back to Eugene right now...I could say I've left town but stay to visit Grandma.*

It was a hard decision to make. Eugene was beckoning him home. Back to routine and his friends and a life he enjoyed, for the most part. But thinking of his mother's downcast, pitiful, quietly weeping face was unpleasant and uncomfortable. The older she got, the more sensitive and meek she seemed to get.

*Fine. I'll go to the game and then I'll go home. That seems fair enough.*

Granger drove himself to the baseball field, his old stomping ground. His stomach knotted itself over and over again.

He pulled up and took a survey. Two-thirds of the parking lot asphalt was cracked or riddled with potholes, but the other third was perfectly smooth and level, glistening sleek and black in the sunlight.

Granger pulled onto the old asphalt and found shade under a couple of large oaks along the perimeter. Most of the trees in Eugene were still saplings. Eugene was newer, cleaner, and very organized. Most neighborhoods were a grid of cookie-cutter houses with manicured lawns. All the pavement in Eugene was nice and smooth. Meanwhile, in Lester, nature had started to reclaim its territory. Grass and weeds shot up through cracks in the pavement all over the place.

The announcer, Mr. Bernard, who was also a Felton High English teacher, was already commentating on the second inning of the game from the press box. His voice bounced off the bleachers and echoed in the parking lot where it looked like Granger was not the only one coming late to the game.

None of the other stragglers were rushing to the baseball field. Even the few cars that drove past on the road moseyed along. Life happened in slow motion in Lester.

The spring wind blew through the tall trees that stood around the parking lot, sounding like a rushing river. A grasshopper jumped along beside Granger on his journey. Eugene was less than a day's drive from Lester, but they were completely different worlds.

He didn't see anyone he knew well, but he did see a few faces that looked familiar. He pulled his baseball cap down further onto his forehead and discreetly tucked his limp arm into his jeans' pocket with the help of the good arm. He was almost inside the park when he heard:

"Mr. Granger Kyle! It's been awhile!"

Granger knew who owned that quiet, gentle voice. He lifted his head to look at the man standing right next to the gate. Mr. Savoy's smile reached all the way up to his watery blue eyes, and reached all the way into Granger's soul.

Granger was surprised to feel a real smile tug at his face and he readily shook the old maintenance director's hand.

"Mr. Savoy! Good to see you. You still hanging out around the field in case anything needs duct taping?"

Mr. Savoy laughed, "not much needs duct taping these days. A few years ago the school finally got enough money to actually fix the bleachers. And the scoreboard. And the dugout. And the fence."

Granger saw that the rusting, gray chain-link fence around the park was gone now, replaced by a sturdy, shiny, black one.

"But you were the team's good luck charm!"

"Nah, just their number one fan."

Mr. Savoy rested his hands in his overall pockets.

"I see they've upgraded your uniform."

"Absolutely. I think the school worried that the old overalls would unravel one day while I was out mowing the lawn or something."

"That would've been a sight."

"I'd hate to be the one to scar these teenagers for life."

Mr. Savoy removed his own baseball cap to rub his balding head while he gave Granger the once-over.

"You got tall," he said with all the pride of an affectionate grandfather.

Granger laughed, "no, I didn't."

Mr. Savoy shrugged. "Well, I suppose I'm not the best measuring stick." He looked over his shoulder. "I'll let you go now. You'd better head inside if you want to see your brother play. It's one of the last games of the season!"

"Right," Granger said slowly, peering inside the gate. All he could see from where he stood were the backs of the new bleachers. He looked back at Mr. Savoy. "I can spare another couple minutes. It's good to see you're still going strong."

"Not as strong as I used to be. I got cancer four years back. Been in and out of treatment since then."

Granger only then noticed that Mr. Savoy's flushed cheeks did look hollower and his collar bones protruded more than they used to.

Granger reddened and he cleared his throat, "I'm so sorry. Are you doing okay now?"

He shrugged and his gaze drifted away. This time his smile did not reach his eyes when he said, "some days are better than others."

Mr. Savoy was looking toward the row of oaks around the parking lot. No, he was looking past it at the grassy clearing between the parking lot and the road where a decorative concrete bench sat next to a sapling.

*Oh yeah.*

Granger reddened even more and looked at his feet.

"I heard about your daughter. My mom called and told me when it happened. I'm so sorry," he said in a low voice. "What was her name?"

"Linda." Mr. Savoy took a deep breath in, still looking at the memorial. "Loss is a beast unlike any other." He turned his watery, blue eyes back to Granger. "But I don't have to tell *you* that, do I?"

The people brushing past them to go through the entrance talked amongst themselves, oblivious to Mr. Savoy's and Granger's conversation. Mr. Savoy seemed to have forgotten the other people were there, as well. Granger couldn't look Mr. Savoy in the eye anymore. Finally, Mr. Savoy released him from his discomfort.

"Just want you to know I'll be a friend if you ever need one, son."

"Thanks." Granger shifted his weight from one foot to the other.

"Good to see you. You'd better get in there. He's a natural," and patting Granger on his left arm, "just like you."

There was that twinkle in Mr. Savoy's eye again. It was amazing to Granger how quickly the emotions changed behind the old man's eyes. Mr. Savoy went back to greeting the students and parents as they walked in, like their little moment had never happened.

*… used to be,* Granger finished inside his head. *"A natural just like I used to be."*

Granger walked the path between the bleachers and got his first glimpse of the field. He paused.

The baseball field was not fancy or gigantic, but it didn't look like it was falling apart anymore, either. The bleachers were sturdier and the "Home of the Lester Lions" sign was printed clearly and brightly on white vinyl now, instead of being painted on a big, wooden board. But the same spirit lingered in the air. The spirit that was unique to this field, the spirit that was there the last time Granger had stepped foot on the dirt and grass. It was his home field. It was home.

Granger reached out to hold onto the metal cross bracing under one of the bleachers. He blinked rapidly and clenched his jaw. He felt hidden, standing between the two tall bleachers. He could see the field, but the spectators couldn't see him. He just observed for a minute or two. He watched the game without seeing it.

*This was a bad idea.*

Unwelcome emotions swelled inside his chest. His feet developed a mind of their own and turned him around to go back to the parking lot.

"Granger! Up here!"

He looked up and saw his mom leaning over the side of the bleachers he'd been holding onto, waving at him. He hesitated, then very slowly turned back around and went to meet his mom.

He snuck glances at other spectators as he walked up the metal steps. Some of them looked at him as well, but if they recognized him they didn't say anything.

"I thought you might not come," his mom said with a chuckle. She had her eyes glued to the diamond.

"Sorry I'm late," was all he said.

"I'm glad you could come. This will mean a lot to Jake."

For the next five minutes Granger was too paranoid to watch the game. He scanned the whole crowd before he could relax. Finally, he turned his attention to the field. They were in the third inning.

Watching Jake play baseball was like traveling through time, but Granger didn't know if it was like going back into the past or jumping forward into the future. Whatever it was, it was trippy. He knew Jakey wasn't twelve anymore, but he wasn't supposed to be a high school senior playing varsity baseball, either.

"He's so tall," Granger said.

She nodded without looking over at him.

"A lot happens in six years." She sounded disappointed.

*There it is again.*

But she changed her tone, and the topic, before he could defend himself.

"Did you go see grandma again?"

"Yeah."

"How'd it go?"

"I took some pictures with me."

"Did she recognize you?"

"Only in the pictures."

Her voice got higher the more questions she asked him. He knew this technique; he'd grown up hearing it. She was trying to soften him, defuse his anger, avoid conflict. She didn't just dislike conflict, like his older brother Trevor, she feared it. She hated feeling like anyone was upset with her.

She wanted him to relax around her and take down his walls. Knowing what she was trying to do just irritated him more.

"A couple days before you got here, one of the nurses told me that with dementia, people can lose their more recent memories first. They might remember what happened when they were ten years old, but not what happened five years ago or yesterday."

"Mm," he grunted.

"I'm glad she remembers you as a little boy, though."

"You're always looking for the bright side, aren't you?" he said in a toneless voice while focusing on the field.

She went quiet.

"Remembering me as a kid is not the same as her knowing who I am now."

One of Jake's teammates hit a bunt to third base and Jake ran from first to second. His mom was roused out of her thoughts by the noise and clapped along with the other spectators.

"Brings back memories, doesn't it," his mom said, trying to smile.

"Of course it does," he snapped at her.

Her smile drooped and she looked back at the game. She didn't try to make conversation again for ten minutes.

Granger had a hard time fighting the urge to stand, walk back down the steps, and leave.

*Is she clueless? Of course it brings back memories. Why would she bring that up? She's just trying to ease her own conscience with all this chit chat.*

He squirmed, trying not to wish he was down on the field playing again. He sat with his left arm resting in his lap so he could clap his left hand with his right when the Lester Lions scored or when one of the team members made a good hit or had a good run or made an impressive catch. That way, he could cheer along with everyone else while also disguising his monoplegia.

Toward the end of the game, Granger was starting to feel a little guilty for snapping at her. He tried to make amends by starting up the conversation again.

"He's gotten really good," he said, genuinely impressed. "How'd he do when the scouts came?"

Lester was a small, rural town, but they'd gotten lucky fifteen years back when they hired a Lester-born baseball coach who had years of experience coaching really good high school teams from much bigger towns and cities around the country. The coach moved back to care for his aging parents, so the story went, but he still wanted to coach. Since then, Lester High's varsity baseball team consistently competed against the top teams in the state. It was a good team when Granger had played, and it was a good team now.

"He's not going to play in college."

Granger's head snapped toward her.

"What do you mean 'he's not gonna play in college?'"

Granger watched her watching one of Jake's teammates take a few practice swings before stepping up to the plate.

"He doesn't want to keep playing. He said he wants to finish out this year strong, then take a break."

"But..."

Granger squinted at the field as if he might find a reasonable explanation for Jake's decision, there.

"... why?"

"He just doesn't want to keep playing. And I support that decision."

Jake emerged from the dugout and took a few practice swings of his own while he waited for his turn at bat.

"With all his discipline and talent, he could do well. Like, really well. Not to mention get a scholarship. How's he planning to pay for school?"

"A job. He's waiting to hear from one more school to see if he's been accepted, it's the one he wants to go to the most, and once he's decided where he's going, he's going to start applying for jobs around campus right away. He's also been saving a lot from his job at the car wash. He's worked there for four years now, so he's got a decent amount in the bank!"

Even in his shocked confusion, Granger knew one thing for sure: he couldn't leave Lester, yet, not until he could talk some sense into the kid.

*Insane! They're both insane! They have no clue what he's turning down.*

Granger said nothing while Jake stepped up to home plate, hit the ball off the wall in centerfield, sprinted around the bases, and slid into home after the outfielder's throw got past their third baseman. The people in the stands stood up cheering and clapping. Granger's mom stood and joined them. Granger stood, but he was too dumbfounded to cheer or try to clap.

He opened his mouth to ask his mom another question when his mom looked across the bleachers and exclaimed, "oh! There's Devon!"

Granger looked around. "Who's Devon?"

"Jake's girlfriend. Didn't we mention her before?"

His eyes found the girl his mom was waving to. Devon took off her baseball cap so she could fan herself with it, smiled, and waved energetically to his mom with her other hand.

The girl's Felton High baseball cap had been covering a head of dark auburn hair that looked even redder as soon as the sunlight hit it.

# 7

"Go Granger! Yes! Run!"

Jakey's pre-pubescent voice called out even after the other fans' cheering died down. It was the last game of Granger's junior year of high school, the top of the ninth inning. He had just made it to second base and Shawn was now on first. Their team was down by two.

Jesse was up to bat, which was good for their team. Jesse was not as stocky as Granger, he wasn't as big as Shawn, and he looked completely out of control of his body when he hit, pitched, or ran, but he was notorious for hitting the ball hard and getting on base.

The gangling boy stepped up to home plate and adjusted his stance. He was all limbs. His fair-skinned face and black hair peaked out beneath the batter's helmet. Even from second, Granger could see the wild look in his friend's eye.

"Let's go, Jesse!" Granger shouted from second.

"Come on!" Shawn echoed from first.

With his eyes laser-focused on Jesse, Granger got low, his stance wide, ready to bolt.

Jesse got a strike.

Then a ball.

Granger wanted to steal third, but their pitcher was on top of him.

On the third swing, Granger heard a satisfying THWACK!

50

The ball made a beeline for the outfield fence and Granger took off sprinting.

People were yelling… but not cheering. Jesse hadn't pulled off a home run. He'd hit the ball low. Hard, but low. Luckily, the center-fielder didn't nab it from the air. He picked it up off the ground and looked straight at Granger, who was still running at full speed.

The third-base coach wanted him to stay on third, but it was too late, Granger couldn't stop. When he looked ahead and saw the catcher with the ball, he couldn't turn around fast enough. The catcher threw the ball to the third baseman, sealing Granger's fate. He slowed. He wasn't just done hitting for the inning or even the game, he was done for the season if they didn't win. He hung his head on his way to the dugout, counting the months until the start of the next season.

But when Andre hit the ball and brought both Shawn and Jesse home, Granger's spirits lifted.

*We're still in this! We can still win!*

He joined his teammates in the dugout as they clapped and shouted and smacked Shawn and Jesse on the backs. Then they turned their attention back to their boys still on the field.

"You've got it, Marcel!"

Marcel stepped up to home plate. On the first pitch he hit the ball over the second baseman's head, far enough into the outfield that he made it to second and got Andre home.

The dugout went wild, and then quieted down while Hunter walked up to the plate. Hunter racked up two strikes right out of the gate. His teammates leaned forward, quiet, watching the action like hawks. Some of them fidgeted and squirmed. Others were like statues.

If they won the game, they would go on to state for the second year in a row. Six of the players on varsity that year were seniors, including Hunter, which meant Hunter would give it all he had.

*THWACK!*

Hunter hit the ball just above the second baseman's reach and he and Marcel ran for their lives.

Granger and his teammates yelled at the two boys sprinting. Marcel made it home but Hunter got out…their third out of the inning. The Lester High School Varsity Baseball team left the dugout for the last time during the game.

Granger slipped the glove onto his strong left hand, flexing his forearm muscles and pounding his right hand into the glove while he bounced on his toes.

"Go, Granger!" cried the little voice again.

Until all the players were in their places on the field, Granger drank in the sights and sounds. There was a full and lively section of Lester High fans, even though the game was being played at a school an hour away from Lester that day. Jakey and his mom waved at him. Granger smiled. His eyes continued to move across the bleachers. He stood up a little taller when he spotted his brother, Trevor, who was a high school senior. Trevor stood with his hands relaxing in his pockets, talking to two of his friends. Trevor hadn't played any sports in years. He spent all his time outside of school studying, reading, and working. Granger lived for the competition of the game, but Trevor didn't care for it at all. He still came to Granger's games.

The first hitter was just picking up his bat and warming up. Granger's eyes scanned for just a few moments more, until he found the bright red hair. Katie was in a sea of students who were elevating the energy of the whole game. She was all smiles and laughter, standing with several of her cheerleader and football player friends. She never missed his games. She thrived on the energy of them. She followed action and excitement, and people followed her; her passion for life was contagious.

Granger smiled and felt another surge of adrenaline. He straightened up even more, proud of the muscles he'd built up over the year.

The first hitter stepped up to the plate and Jesse, looking like a marionette doll being yanked around, launched a fastball at him. On the second pitch, the hitter smacked the ball into the outfield and sent Granger running after it. He threw the ball in harder than he remembered ever throwing a ball before.

The sun beat down on him and he was covered in sweat and dirt. He'd just taken a drink in the dugout but already his mouth was bone dry. He could feel the skin on his nose burning and several new blisters on his feet, forming. But it was just him, his team, and his favorite game. He didn't have a care in the world for anything else, and any problems he might have could be fixed by playing harder, better, faster.

He smiled.

# 8

HE FROWNED.

"Granger, did you hear me? Granger?"

Granger shook his head, trying to shake away the memory. The taste of it lingered, despite his efforts. In the past six years, he'd gotten really good at blocking out what was behind him, the good and the bad, even though his counselor warned him against doing so. It was a jolt to suddenly be overcome by so many emotions and sensations.

"What?"

"I said you left your car keys on the bleacher."

His mom pointed.

"Oh." He turned back to get them and then rejoined her on the steps.

"Isn't that your wallet, too?"

He went back for the wallet.

"Must've put them in the shallow pocket by accident," he muttered as an explanation. But he was so absentminded at that moment that his words were hardly intelligible.

"What?" his mother asked.

But by that time, Devon had found them. His mom threw him one last concerned look and then greeted Devon. The crowd was moving downstream, giving them no choice but to keep moving. Outside the field, Jake found them and jogged over.

"Great job, sweetheart," their mom said, hugging him.

"Thanks," he said with a smile. He hugged his girlfriend and then turned to Granger.

"You came!"

"Course I did," Granger said, averting his eyes. He decided that giving his little brother the benefit of the doubt wouldn't hurt him. "Great job! You were on fire out there."

"Thanks." Jake's smile widened at the praise. "Have you met Devon? Devon, this is one of my older brothers, Granger."

They each said hello, then his mom started asking Devon about how her family was doing.

Their mother talked to Devon like she was part of the family. Feeling a little awkward, Granger turned to talk to Jake again. Jake looked pleased, but not as excited as their mom was over the team's win. Not as excited as Granger would have been. Granger thought it was as good a time as any to ask Jake about his decision not to play ball in college. But Jake wasn't paying attention to him, nor to the conversation of the two women. Instead, his eyes scanned the parking lot purposefully.

"You looking for something?" Granger asked.

"Shawn," Jake said, still searching. "I guess he's not here."

"Shawn who?"

"Shawn Wills."

Granger's best friend throughout middle and high school. Granger looked around, too.

"Does he still live around here?"

"Yeah."

"Why'd you think you'd see him?"

"He said he would come by the game, if he could get off work in time. He's been helping me lately."

Granger felt a twinge inside.

"With baseball?" Granger asked, trying to keep the jealousy out of his voice.

"No. I've been thinking about majoring in finance when I go to college and, since that's the kind of work he's in, he's been talking to me about it. But he likes to come see the Lions play when he can."

"He's in finance?"

"Yeah. When did you talk to him last?"

"Summer after high school graduation."

"Oh. I always assumed you guys would be close forever. You used to hang out all the time."

"He went to the city for college, I went to Eugene, we lost touch. Don't expect to keep all your high school friends when you go off to college. People move on."

Jake waved to some friends across the parking lot, so he didn't see Granger's eyes flick quickly to and from the red hair as he said this. When he looked back at him, Jake squinted beneath his two bushy brows, probably because of the sunlight, but Granger didn't like the feeling that Jake was trying to read his mind, just like their grandmother used to.

They were at their cars before Granger had a chance to ask Jake about college. He decided to broach the subject once they were out of the heat in the air-conditioned restaurant where their mother wanted them to go for an early dinner. They said goodbye to Devon and put the baseball fields behind them.

The restaurant was on the 'new' side of town, so his mom offered to lead the way in her car. Where there had been only farmland six years earlier there were brand new, cookie-cutter house neighborhoods. They passed a new strip mall housing a fancy tech store, a frozen yogurt shop, and a specialty shoe store. Granger couldn't ignore the night and day difference between the old part of town and the new. He didn't know which of the two was more of a surprise. Bridges had been rebuilt. The roads were smooth and black with bright paint. There were chain coffee stores on street corners everywhere. The restaurant they pulled up to, a pizza place in yet another strip mall, was also new.

"It's nice, isn't it?" his mom asked when they got out of their cars.

"It's different," he acknowledged. He followed the other two inside. "All this happened in six years?"

"It was crazy fast," Jake said.

They slid into a booth and a server brought them menus.

"It doesn't even look like Lester anymore."

"You sound disappointed," his mother said.

"I just expected the old Lester."

"Nothing stays the same forever," Jake said distractedly, focusing on his menu.

Granger picked up his own menu instead of responding.

After they ordered, their mom started asking more questions about the game, which Jake answered readily but without the amount of enthusiasm Granger expected.

"Jordan's been upset all season," Jake explained, "because he's been on the bench so much. But he's not taking the game seriously anymore. Coach even said so. He's not in it like he was last year."

Jake sat back and propped his elbow on the top of the booth.

"I thought he was hoping to play in college," said their mom, who was sitting next to Granger.

"So did we. But the way this season is going, it doesn't look good for him."

"Maybe he's got too much on his plate to focus on baseball. Senior year can be hard," she said.

"He's smart. School's always been pretty easy for him."

"Well, maybe something's going on at home?"

Granger tried not to roll his eyes. His mother was incapable of thinking negatively about anyone.

"Or maybe he's just slacking," Granger posited.

"Baseball's always come naturally to him," Jake said as if he didn't hear Granger. "He'd do really well in college."

Granger had found his in.

"Like you," Granger said.

"Yeah, but I don't want to play in college."

"Why not? You're good, too."

Jake shrugged one shoulder, "I just don't want to. The last couple years some of the guys from the team who've graduated have come to our practices when they're home from college on break. They're tired of playing in college. They said it's basically a full-time job. And I'm already getting kind of burnt out from it. You played baseball for, what, ten years? I'm sure there were times you got tired of it."

Granger picked up his red plastic cup of ice water and stared at the condensation on the side while he lifted it to his lips.

"Nope."

"You never even thought about taking a break?" Jake challenged playfully.

Granger sipped and then set the cup down. "No. I would've kept playing if I could have. No question."

Jake shrugged, "well, that's fine. That's what you would've done. I'm not you, so…"

"And I support his decision," their mother said, again.

Granger almost let it go. Almost. He was so close to letting it go. But instead he leaned forward and rested his good elbow and forearm on the table.

"But the scholarship," he entreated. "Even if you don't love it anymore, it's money for school. You would throw away the chance to get half your tuition paid for. Or even more than half?"

"I'm getting a job," Jake said.

"You'll have to work a lot more at a job to make up for a lost baseball scholarship, especially with your skill level."

"I haven't 'lost' anything. College baseball isn't on the table at all. I made that decision months ago."

Granger pressed. "What is this really about? Come on, you can tell me."

"I told you. I just don't want to keep playing. It's exhausting and I'm just tired of it."

"Tired of practicing? Of traveling for games? What?"

"All of it. I'm just tired of so much baseball."

Granger scoffed, "I don't get it."

"Are you mad at me?"

"I don't think you've thought this through."

"Granger—" their mom said.

"Yes. I have. Like I said, I've thought about it for months now, maybe even a year. I've made my decision. I have a plan. Mom is fine with it. It might not be the decision you would have made, but I'm not you."

"Boys," their mom said in a weak whisper, glancing at other tables where customers were starting to notice their argument as their voices got louder.

"It's not about me—" Granger said.

"You sure about that?" Jake interrupted.

"— you're throwing away a great opportunity—"

"I've made up my mind, so just drop it."

"Seriously—"

Jake smacked his open palm on the tabletop, causing the

silverware to rattle. "Drop it!"

Granger was stunned into silence.

It was in that moment that it really hit Granger: Jake was not a kid anymore. He didn't look like one, he didn't talk like one, and he didn't act like one. Granger didn't know what to do with the adult version of his baby brother, who spoke with such willpower, confidence, and authority. It was unsettling, but not unimpressive. Of course at that moment, Granger was more annoyed than proud.

The people at the tables nearby got quiet at Jake's outburst. They were definitely looking now.

Their mother let out a shaky exhale. "Can we not do this here? Please?"

Granger looked away from his brother, his temper still flaring. His good hand was shaking a little under the table.

"I just wanted a nice family reunion this week," their mom said. "Please, don't argue."

Granger looked over at her. Her body and her voice were both shivering. "I can't take it, not with everything else that's going on…"

Jake's demeanor and tone changed instantly. "Sorry, mom."

Granger bit his tongue to keep his first response from escaping.

"Sorry," he finally echoed.

"Promise me you won't do this with Trevor and Levi, too."

"What are you talking about?" Granger asked.

"They're coming to visit for a few days. To see your grandma."

"When?"

"Tomorrow."

He sighed heavily, closed his eyes, and rubbed his face from his forehead down to the blond stubble on his chin.

"Mom," he said, wearily.

He knew what was coming next: more tearful requests that he stay, this time to see his brothers. He'd have to go without his razor yet another day.

"Can you at least tell me these things ahead of time?" he asked.

"Sorry," came the weak reply.

"It's one surprise after another," he muttered.

# 9

"Tell me about one of the happiest moments in your life."

"The happiest?"

"Yes."

...

...

"I guess whenever I played baseball. Especially in high school."

Dr. Jenkins watched him as he spoke, leaning back slightly in his chair, his right ankle resting on his left knee and a legal pad in his lap.

"What about those times made you the happiest?" he asked. His tone was not rushed. It was never rushed.

"I don't know. I liked playing baseball."

Dr. Jenkins nodded, but didn't say anything. He just kept looking at Granger, waiting for him to continue. Granger exhaled and felt the familiar headache coming on. He always got headaches from his counseling sessions. He'd had no idea when he started his sessions that it could be so exhausting. And it hadn't gotten much easier, even after seeing his counselor twice a month for the last year.

"Playing baseball, I felt like I really knew what I was doing. It felt good. I felt sure. I felt like *me*."

"What in your life makes you feel that way now?"

Granger shrugged. "Nothing."

More silence.

"Do you want to play baseball again?"

Granger was angry with himself when he couldn't stop his eyes from stinging. He leaned forward in the plush armchair and rested his right forearm across his knees. His left arm lay limply in his lap.

"Yes." He tried not to sound impatient, but he wasn't very successful.

"It's just a question," the doctor reminded him gently. "Notice the anger but don't let it take over."

Granger took a deep breath.

"I want to play all the time," he said, moving his gaze to a distant spot on the dark red, Persian rug.

"Why don't you?"

Granger's voice was hard as he asked, "'why don't I' what?"

"Why don't you play?"

Granger felt the lump in his throat growing. He glared at the rug and sniffed loudly. He didn't want to cry again. He dropped his head and shook it. "I know what you want me to say but I can't."

Two months earlier, Dr. Jenkins had asked him the same question. Only then, Granger had responded by yelling, *"because my left arm doesn't work anymore!"* And he might've called Dr. Jenkins a name or two.

"You don't have to say anything. It's just a question. I just want you to think about it. Sure, you might never play the same again, but that doesn't mean you can never play again."

Granger sat up and looked at Dr. Jenkins. "But that's why. I know there's adaptive technology, and I've been working with my occupational therapist for over a year now, and I know the stories of the people who've lost limbs but still find a way to do what they love, like surfing or running or whatever…"

His counselor waited.

"But… to get out there again… to try to play, knowing that I'll never be able to get back what I lost. The ability. The scholarship…"

Granger looked back at the carpet. "It wasn't just the game."

The counselor didn't say anything for a minute. Granger wiped away angry tears. He'd broken down in front of his counselor for the first time after six months of counseling. He still didn't like to do it, but he trusted Dr. Jenkins a little more now.

"You're right," Dr. Jenkins finally said. "Life changes. Things happen. Life would've changed anyway, whether you had the accident or not."

Granger looked out the window. He could only see blue sky because they were on the third story of the building.

"Like your relationships with your dad, and with Katie."

"Those things with my dad and Katie wouldn't have happened if I hadn't had the accident."

"But your relationships with them still would've changed. In some way. Over time."

"So I'm just supposed to suck it up, huh?"

Dr. Jenkins shifted in his chair. "When I think of that phrase, 'sucking it up,' I imagine a person pushing down their feelings and running through the brick wall head-on because they feel like it's either that, or give up. Neither of those options are healthy."

"So what then?"

Dr. Jenkins lowered his voice a little. "You are allowed to feel hurt. You are allowed to be sad and angry. Things, painful things, have happened to you that you have not asked for…"

Granger swallowed.

"…but not everything in life is stuff that happens *to* you. There is so much of life that *you* choose, that *you* do. We can't always prevent the things that happen to us. But we still have choices that we can make. Lots of them. You can make one of them right now. And in the next moment. And the next…"

# 10

*HOW DID I LET THEM talk me into staying even longer?*

Granger hung up his phone and rubbed his eyelids. After a ten-minute long discussion, Granger had convinced his boss not to penalize him. His boss didn't think Granger's situation qualified as a family "emergency," because no one was in the hospital or actively dying. Granger tried to explain.

"She's got dementia, and she's losing her memory really fast, so she'll probably never remember me again. And I just found out about it…"

"Well why didn't you call me two days ago, when you left Eugene? You're telling me this *now*? Now I've gotta push back your training *and you've* gotta find someone to cover tonight's shift last minute. You'd better hope someone's available."

Granger had forgotten all about the shift he was scheduled to work that evening. He couldn't keep track of the days of the week; they were all running together.

When he hung up the phone after the conversation with his boss, he called seven of his coworkers, until he found someone who could fill in for him at the last minute.

"Only if you agree to take my shift for tomorrow," Brandon negotiated in his squeaky voice.

"Yeah, fine, that works. Thanks."

In a tiny sitting area on the side of the nursing home furthest from the memory care unit, Granger poured himself some coffee to try to get rid of his headache. He stepped one foot into the hall to head back to his grandmother's room, but then paused and looked around at the little room. The little, *empty* room. Residents, those not in the hospice or memory care units, of course, passed by on their way to dinner, completely absorbed in their own conversations. He pulled his foot back in and sank down into a chair at the table closest to the coffee pot. He relaxed his shoulder. He stretched out his neck.

The sounds of pleasant mealtime chatter, silverware scraping against plates, and quiet, canned jazz music drifted from down the hall. He tried to shut his brain off for a while, but the diners' light laughter captured his attention. He wondered again what his grandmother would think of the place, if she were really there. She'd always liked the quiet solitude of the country.

He thought that getting some quiet solitude of his own would do him good. He wanted to get his mind off of things for a while.

It did the opposite.

Sitting in that little room, alone, his thoughts drifted straight to the dementia. He felt the unwelcome sorrow tug at his mind and heart even stronger than before.

He shook his head as if his mind could be cleared like an Etch A Sketch, and pulled out his phone.

He had a new text from his roommate, James, and another from their friend, Marcus.

To his relief, some of the sharper edges of Granger's mind dulled as he pulled his attention away from life in Lester, back to life in Eugene. He really liked living in Eugene. Things were simple for him there. He had a townhouse, a roommate, a job, and friends who'd known him since college and not a moment before. He relaxed even more when he counted less than twenty-four hours until he would be back in Eugene. In that moment, for the first time since he'd driven back into the Lester city limits, he didn't feel like anyone or anything was spying on him, trying to peer into the depths of his soul.

After about two minutes of this reprieve, his phone notified him that his battery was at 5%.

He shoved the useless thing back into his pocket, slumped down in his chair, and stared at the wall while he drank the tepid coffee.

His headache was not going away without a fight. He closed his eyes to block out some of the light, but his contacts were drying out, which added to his discomfort. He wasn't sleeping well in his old bedroom, and he was feeling it in his neck muscles.

There was a small couch, the kind made specifically for small children, in one corner of the room. Granger eyed it with a heavy head and even heavier eyelids. It looked so plush. He was trying to envision how he would fit onto it when he heard approaching footsteps and voices. He jolted awake, but when he didn't recognize their voices, his guard eased back down again.

"But I wanna play with Sammy," the disembodied voice of a little girl said firmly. "Why do I have to be here?"

Granger silently commiserated with her.

"I never get to do anything fun," she whined.

"Mm, you're right," said a young woman's pleasant voice. "You never ever get to play. You never get to have sleepovers with the Traegers, or go to the pool with the Carlson girls, or ride bikes with Tina."

"That's not the same," the girl whined.

In mock innocence, the woman's voice asked, "it isn't? How so?"

"Because that was just for one day."

"So it doesn't count."

"Yeah."

"I see. So what does count?"

"What?"

"If that doesn't count as playing with friends, what does count?"

Silence for a beat. "Playing with Sammy."

If he'd been feeling more like himself, the unexpected sound of the woman's snort would have made him smile.

They came into the room. Granger saw them a split second before they saw him. "They," were a little girl and a young woman holding a baby carrier.

The little girl had wild, brown curly hair, an expressive face, and a pep in her step. The young woman had the same big, brown eyes and small mouth as the girl, but her brown hair was straight and shoulder-length, and she did not have the same energy.

When the woman finally saw Granger, she nodded politely, and changed her course.

"Izzy," she said to the little girl, who was already walking deeper into the room, having spotted the bookshelf and toy bin in the corner. "Izzy," she said once more, more firmly. When she had the little girl's attention, she made a small jerking motion with her head toward the hallway.

"Oh, I don't mind if you stay," Granger said quickly. "I'm just taking a coffee break. Come on in."

Izzy didn't wait for a second invitation. She darted over to the books and toys before the woman could respond. The girl's feet, which she'd been dragging on the carpet a few seconds before, were suddenly as light as a paper airplane. The woman set down the baby carrier next to another table and thanked him.

"I would put up more of a fight," she said, "but to be honest I don't have it in me today."

She collapsed into a chair.

"I know the feeling," Granger said, feeling more fatigued saying the words aloud.

"Rough day?"

He nodded and took another sip of his coffee. While she peeked inside the baby carrier at her feet, his grandmother's voice floated through his head: *"always be polite to strangers, especially young parents; you don't know what sort of hell they've walked through."*

Somehow, until that moment, he hadn't realized who she'd been thinking of whenever she said that.

So, despite his fatigue:

"How old?" Granger asked, nodding his head at the baby carrier.

She looked inside. "I'm not sure. Maybe three months? Four?"

At the look on his face, her small mouth broke into a pleasant smile and she laughed.

"He's not mine. I'm just watching him while his parents are in one of the rooms."

"Oh." He gave a half-hearted chuckle, but if she'd asked, he couldn't have told her what they'd just been talking about. "Sorry," he said distractedly.

"Don't worry about it," she said, pulling her eyes to where the little girl played in the corner.

Granger's thoughts were not in the room with them.

… *"always be polite to strangers, especially young parents"*… Over the years their grandmother gave lots of lessons and advice to the four unruly boys and their half sister. She could find a lesson in just about anything, which annoyed them to no end as elementary and middle schoolers. But she ignored their whining complaints and made them listen to her anyway. *"Someday you're gonna need to know these things, and so I'm gonna make sure you do."* He recalled other words of wisdom from her:

*"No, chores aren't fun. But the fun won't last long if you don't take care of the hard stuff first."*

*"No, Granger, go back and look again. There are still tomatoes on that plant, I can see them from here. If you don't pick them, they'll go bad, and then we'll be out of tomatoes. If you're doing a job, even if you don't particularly like the job, don't do it halfway. It'll make you lazy."*

*"Go play, boys. Go explore. Your work's all done for the day and you need to stretch your legs and your imaginations. Go on, I don't wanna see you again until it's dark."*

*"It's time for bed, boys. No more yammering. You need your sleep."*

*"Tomorrow we are gonna rest. We've gone too long without a good rest day and it's wearing on all of us. This goes on any longer and none of us will be much use anymore. So, tomorrow we are only gonna do what we absolutely have to, and then the rest of the day we are gonna rest."*

She dispensed wisdom left and right, and her grandchildren rarely appreciated it at the time. Granger wondered how people would react if they found one of her little proverbs hidden inside a fortune cookie. The thought made him smile. But he could imagine those people forgetting all about the words of wisdom as soon as they threw the little slip of paper in the trash on the way out of the Chinese restaurant.

*"Life's probably gonna be hard for you, Granger. It's hard for most people. Trying to deal with your problems on your own will just make it harder. Remember that. But be careful who you let help you. Some people will only drag you farther down."*

*"Drag my father down?"* Granger had asked. She paused, she thought for a minute. She looked at her grandson, who was growing up, but who wasn't grown up enough, yet.

*"I said 'drag you farther down,' as in, they'll only make your life harder."*

"Are you okay?"

Granger's green eyes flicked up to the big, pretty, brown ones watching him with a concerned, or maybe just confused, look. He noticed then that he was sitting forward in his chair, leaning his right forearm against the table, and he'd been glaring at his brown paper cup. He forced his muscles to relax.

"This place is difficult to be in," she said in a matter-of-fact way. Her words weren't sickly sweet. They didn't drip with 'well-meaning' sympathy. She didn't have a soothing smile ready for him when she said it. She wasn't even looking at him when she said it. His guard eased down a little more.

He exhaled and looked back at his cup. "Yeah. It is." He cleared his throat. "Are you visiting family here, too?"

She shook her head, "Izzy and I volunteer."

"Why?" he asked, too tired to conceal the stupefied tone.

"Long story," she said with a yawn. "It's our way of saying thank you to some people."

Granger studied her profile. She may not have been gorgeous, but she was attractive. He couldn't deny that he was a little glad not to see a ring on her left hand. Up close, she looked shorter and younger than he'd first thought. She probably wasn't much older than him. He was starting to think she looked familiar when he stopped himself: everyone and everything was starting to look familiar, not because it was, but because he was too worried it might.

While he was still studying her, trying to figure out if he knew her or not, she looked back at him. He smiled politely and looked back at his coffee cup so she didn't think he was a creep.

He didn't expect what she said next.

"I don't want to make you uncomfortable. But... I can offer a listening ear. If you want to talk. I'm not a counselor or anything, but some people find it helpful just to say things out loud to somebody. That's why I come. Well, it's one reason."

She nodded down to where the little baby slept.

Granger's answer was quick, automatic. "No. Thank you, though."

"No problem."

She went back to watching the girl sift through the toys in the bin. The sound of the little plastic toy pieces being mixed around and dug into was a nostalgic one to Granger.

Maybe it was because they were totally unconnected to each other, maybe it was because she didn't seem the type to get under his skin, or maybe it was because she was just a disarming sort of person and his exhaustion was disabling his filter, but even though he'd immediately declined her offer, something in his brain leapt down to the tip of his tongue, and it wouldn't go away even when he told it to.

*"There are some moments in life when you just know you gotta do something,"* his grandmother's words suddenly reminded him. *"Something good for your soul or good for somebody else's soul. This is God trying to help you out. It's a good idea to listen."*

When he spoke, the words came out slow and choppy, but they came.

"My grandma. She has dementia."

The young woman didn't say anything, didn't even move. The only indication that she was listening was a slight flick of her eyes at the sound of his voice.

"She... " he exhaled loudly and rubbed his right hand over his face. He didn't know why now, of all times and places, he was most on the brink of breaking down. He was now also keenly aware that at any moment his mother or brother could walk through the door. He glanced at it. It was empty, so he went on.

He kept the tears at bay but his voice sounded strangled as he continued, "my family didn't tell me about the dementia until a few days ago." He looked back down at his cup. "She practically raised me."

He didn't say anything more for the next few minutes. In the silence, Granger didn't hear traffic, or his family trying to politely pressure him into staying longer, or old people slowly losing their minds. Besides the clinking of glasses, etc. from down the hall, there was only the quiet noise that the baby carrier made as the woman rocked it gently with the toe of her tennis shoe, a bird out the window making a non-musical sound, and the sound of Izzy turning the pages of a book.

Izzy gasped, "Look, they have Junie B. Jones now!"

The young woman cringed and went over to the girl.

"Sorry," she mumbled to him.

"Don't be," Granger said. He offered a weary smile. "That was all I was gonna say, anyway."

He glanced back at the doorway. Still empty, to his relief.

On her way back to the table, the woman said, "I'm still teaching her how to read social cues." She rolled her eyes. "Apparently I still have some work to do."

She leaned back in her chair and brushed her silky, brown hair away from her face unceremoniously.

"She yours?" he asked.

She nodded.

He was curious about the little family, but he didn't feel the need to feign any more interest than he actually felt. The stranger seemed genuine enough and chill enough to not appear offended by the flat affect that he was left with since he was so emotionally drained.

"I can see the resemblance. You don't look old enough to have a kid that age, though," he observed.

*Wait... did that sound rude?*

"Sorry," he said. "I didn't mean... That was supposed to be a compliment..."

"Then I'll take it," she said with a side smile. "Because today I feel twice my age. I had her when I was in high school."

She didn't offer any more information than that, and Granger didn't want to put his foot in his mouth again. He hoped he hadn't been rude. She was either a very chill person, or she hid her feelings well. Or he was as bad at reading people as Izzy apparently was.

She walked back over to her daughter, who wanted to show her something on the bookshelf, and Granger went back to his coffee. He found he didn't mind having other people in the room, at least not these people. Izzy's little voice was actually a welcome distraction. The only kids he was ever around were the customers at the restaurant, and he only interacted with them long enough to bring them crayons and take their macaroni and cheese orders. He rarely saw his half sister's kids, and he'd only met Levi's baby girl once.

"Ooh," Izzy said, hopping up onto her feet and grabbing another book from the shelf. "There's another one!"

The little girl sat cross-legged on the floor and started reading aloud with an impressive amount of gusto, using a different voice for each character and including lots of sound effects.

"A little quieter, Izzy," said Izzy's mom.

At every sound from out in the hall, Granger tensed, but no one came in the room looking for him. Izzy's mom got up to get herself a cup of coffee then returned to the table, the baby carrier ever at her side.

"I forgot how heavy these things are," she said, setting it down carefully. "Do you have kids?"

A laugh that sounded almost like a bark escaped his lips. His hand flew up to cover his mouth. "Sorry," he said, much quieter.

She bent down to peek in the carrier, then gave him the all clear; the baby slept on.

"No, I don't," he continued. "Sometimes I can barely take care of myself. To be someone's dad? At this point in my life? I feel like that'd just be irresponsible. I don't know how some people do it."

As his mouth was moving, his brain started to wonder if maybe he should shut up.

"Not you," he added hurriedly. "I meant me. You seem responsible. And, y'know, like, er, a good mom."

One side of her small mouth curved up and one eyebrow lifted.

He sighed, "wow, I'm on a roll today. Can you pretend you haven't heard a word I've said?"

Her expression had a slight mischievousness about it.

"No."

"Bummer."

She smiled easily, but not excessively. Not annoyingly. And whenever the tone of the conversation had turned serious, she didn't try to conceal the shadows that lay just beyond her quick wit and dry humor.

"I'm Granger. I don't think I said that before."

"Nina. Nice to meet you. Are you from out of town?"

His phone buzzed in his pocket and on instinct he pulled it out.

"Sort of," he said.

His battery was almost dead, but it had enough juice still to get a text message from one of his older brothers.

Nina said something, but he didn't hear her. He reread the text, and then reread it again, squinting at it more and more. Nina said something else. He held up his hand and shook his head.

"Hang on."

His phone died just as a river of coffee ran off the table and onto his pants.

He said some words that, later, he would regret saying in front of the elementary schooler listening from the corner.

Nina, who'd apparently been trying to warn him about the spill, was already offering him some paper towels from across the table.

He took them, feeling his face get red. He was awake now.

"I gotta go," he said, and stormed out of the room without another word or glance behind him. He threw the remainder of his room-temperature coffee into the trash can on the way out and felt more than a few drops splash on him. Then he had to backtrack and reach his hand into the garbage to retrieve his dead phone. He would rather have just left it there.

# 11

*"CANT GET AHOLD OF MOM, u with her? Need to ask her about the will."*

That was all Levi's text said.

When Granger plugged his phone in with Jake's spare charger that night, he texted his oldest brother:

*"Don't try to get ahold of mom tonight. She had a hard day."*

He didn't mention the text to Jake or their mom; he was going to deal with it himself.

Granger ruminated over it half the night and then he was up with the dawn the next morning, not long before he heard a car door closing somewhere just beneath his window. He heard someone walking across the driveway toward the house, and could tell by the gait, and the early morning hour, that it was Trevor, not Levi, who'd just arrived.

Granger slipped out of his room and opened the front door just as Trevor reached it.

Trevor was the second oldest and the second tallest of the brothers, after Levi on both accounts. He was fit, well-dressed, and clean-shaven. His brown hair was gelled only enough to manage fly-aways. His checked, long sleeve, button-down was neatly tucked into dark jeans and his brown loafers looked freshly polished. Well, they would've looked that way to someone who knew anything about loafers and leather and polish, but Granger didn't, to him they just looked shiny.

They did their usual handshake, and Granger stepped aside to let his older brother in. Trevor was the only one in the family that Granger had seen in the last six years. They tried to hang out every four months or so. The two middle brothers were closer to each other than they were to any of their other siblings, so, although Trevor's return complicated Granger's plans, Granger was nevertheless glad to see him.

Trevor kept his voice low as they talked.

"How long have you been here?"

"'Bout a day and a half. What time did you leave this morning to come down here?" Granger looked at the time. "It's barely six thirty."

"Five fifteen. I woke up at four and couldn't go back to sleep. How is everybody?"

Granger shrugged. They walked to the kitchen for some coffee. While Trevor slid out of his squeaky clean loafers so he wouldn't wake the others, Granger stretched his working arm above his head, and learned that his green t-shirt and black basketball shorts were past the point of needing a wash.

They brewed some coffee and settled in.

"Things have been a little tense," Granger finally admitted.

Trevor nodded. "How's Grandma?"

"Forgetful."

"How's life in Eugene?"

"Great, actually," Granger was able to honestly say.

"Nice."

The two sipped in silence for the next forty minutes. Trevor was even less of a talker than Granger, which Granger didn't mind in the least. But more than once, Granger felt the urge to tell Trevor about Levi's text. He could've used Trevor's skilled listening ear. But he kept the information to himself. He would deal with it.

"How were you gonna get in?" Granger asked, instead.

"What?"

"You didn't know I was awake. How were you going to get in the house if no one was awake?"

"Oh. Mom gave me a key."

"She did? Why?"

"In case I stop by when they're not here, or awake."

"Do you come down here a lot?"

"About every other weekend."

Granger finished his coffee and went to the sink to rinse out his mug.

"I didn't know you came that often."

"I didn't used to. I started coming more often about a year ago."

"So, you saw grandma start to…"

"Yeah, but I didn't know what I was seeing for a long time. She was acting strange but that's all I knew."

"When did you know for sure? That it was dementia."

"Couple weeks ago. Why? When did you find out?"

"When I got here."

"Oh." Trevor looked at his mug with his thick brows knit together. "Mom said she was updating you. Well, at least that's how I understood it." He looked up at Granger. "I should've told you anyway. I'm sorry."

It was the first genuine apology Granger had gotten since being in Lester. It wasn't too much of a surprise that it had come from Trevor.

"Thanks."

"She really didn't tell you anything?"

"She'd make comments about how Grandma was doing, sometimes. But they were really vague," he said, trying to remember the few conversations they'd had over the last year. "It didn't sound like anything was wrong, until the other day when suddenly Grandma was dying."

Jake appeared in the kitchen then, looking groggy and surprised to see them.

"Did we wake you up?" Trevor asked him.

Jake shook his head. His voice was raspier than usual when he said, "just getting some water." He, too, checked the time. "You're here early."

"Yeah."

"Levi here yet?"

"No."

Granger excused himself to shower and find something clean to wear, and to formulate his plan for confronting Levi right when he arrived, before he could get to their mom. She didn't need any more stress at the moment.

\* \* \*

But Levi was already leaning against the kitchen counter talking to Trevor and Jake when Granger got out of the shower. Granger silently cursed his poor planning, but luckily their mom was still asleep.

The biggest change in Levi's appearance since Granger had last seen him was the man-bun. Granger nearly gagged. As if the soul patch wasn't bad enough on its own, now it had a friend. Levi wore faded jeans that were ripped and stringy at the hem, an obscure 70s rock band t-shirt which he wore unironically, and flip flops. He was telling a story, gesticulating emphatically, when he noticed Granger was in the room. His face lit up and with two long strides he had Granger in an embrace, holding his mug of tea out to the side in one hand.

This greeting was enough to throw Granger off. He responded to Levi's questions of "how ya doing? How's work?" with monosyllabic answers.

Granger seized the earliest opportunity to enact his plan of getting Levi alone so he could confront him.

"Need help getting your stuff from your car?" Granger asked.

"Nah, I already brought it in. Thanks!"

"Oh." Thinking quickly, "Trevor? Do you have stuff to bring in?"

"Just one bag. I can get it later."

"Don't worry about it, I'll get it. Levi, wanna give me a hand?"

"Come on, Granger," Levi said. "Let's catch up, first! I just got here."

Granger was out of ideas, and he was out of patience. He was pushed past his limit when Levi grasped one of Granger's shoulders affectionately and told him how happy he was to see him.

"How long's it been?" Levi asked.

The dam burst. Granger threw Levi's hand off his shoulder.

"What were you thinking?" Granger hissed. "She's not even dead yet!"

Levi looked taken aback. His smile vanished. Jake and Trevor looked from Granger to Levi and back again.

"What are you talking about?" Levi asked.

"Your text last night."

"What text?" Jake asked.

"About the will?" Levi asked.

"You say you're 'reformed' or whatever and then you do something totally selfish and insensitive—"

"Whoa, whoa, whoa, hang on a second—" Levi said, setting down his tea and putting his hands up in defense.

"She's not even dead yet!" Granger repeated.

"I just wanna have a look."

"At her will?" Jake asked.

"Yes." Granger said, hoping Jake was about to side with him.

Levi turned to Jake, "it's pretty standard to look over these things when someone's on their way out."

"'On their way out?'" Granger repeated. He felt his rage bubbling to a point that was making it hard to whisper instead of yell. "Since when have you been interested in money?"

"It's not about the money. I want to know what we'll be dealing with when the time comes."

While Levi was keeping his cool, Granger was letting the smoke come out of his ears unhindered. Seeing Levi's serene affect, which was so unlike the angst and aggression he used to hold onto so tightly, triggered some dark compulsion inside Granger to spit a few words at Levi which would have made their mother gasp. Jake checked to make sure she wasn't standing in the doorway, and Trevor uttered a low warning to Granger. But Granger felt a morbid satisfaction in seeing the muscles in Levi's jaw contract.

"We're losing her fast enough without you wanting to speed things along."

"I'm not trying to speed things along," Levi said firmly. "I don't want her to die, of course I don't. She's my grandmother, too. And after all she did for me…? But if before she got dementia she didn't fill out everything she should've, the legal process could get dicey."

"She didn't know she was going to get dementia!"

"Didn't she suspect it at all?" Trevor asked their youngest brother.

Jake shrugged, "if she did, she didn't let on."

Levi looked back at Granger, "I'm a lawyer—"

"We know."

"You don't know how often families go to blows over muddy instructions once the person dies."

"So you're an expert and I don't know anything?"

"We haven't even looked at the will yet and you're already losing it!" Levi was finally losing his cool, acting much more like his old self. "I'm trying to save us from a major headache."

"'A headache?!' You're calling her 'a headache?'"

Trevor and Jake both shushed them, and checked the doorway again.

"No, I am not! If you're putting up this much of a fight *now*, when it's completely uncalled for, just imagine how it's going to be when there's something *really* wrong."

"Don't act like you know everything. We know you have the fancy job—"

"You know I'm a public defender."

"—and it's bad enough she can't remember us anymore and she's dying—"

Levi's expression changed.

He looked at Jake. "She's doesn't remember you anymore?"

"Not very often," Jake said. His eyes fell.

"What?" Granger spat. "You haven't been to see her?"

"He's been here more often than you think," Jake said to Granger, flatly. Granger could tell by the way he said it that what he really meant was 'he's been here more often than *you* have.'

Before Granger could form his next argument, Levi addressed him again.

"Hey man, I'm sorry."

With a response like that, most of the fire drained out of Granger against his will, and left him even more exhausted than he'd been before. He wasn't ready to be done being angry. Levi still needed some sense knocked into his skull. But Granger could hear their mom stirring down the hall. He needed to cool off and come up with a new plan.

"Whatever." Granger turned away. "Don't mention the will to her. We haven't finished this."

Out of the corner of his eye he saw Levi extend a hand. Granger pretended he didn't see it.

# 12

Twelve-year-old Granger and thirteen-year-old Trevor lay in their beds wide awake, trying to lay perfectly still and quiet. It was dark except for a little bit of gold light from the street lights sneaking in between the slats of the blinds. It was so late at night, or early in the morning, that thirty or forty minutes passed between the cars driving by.

The two boys had already speculated aloud to one another about what sort of trouble Levi had gotten into, but the longer they waited to hear the sound of their mom's car pulling in the driveway, the quieter they got. They each lay still, excitedly worrying that it was even worse than they'd previously thought, and wondering silently for the last hour about the horrible things that could be happening, or would be happening, to Levi.

Hours before, just after the boys climbed into bed, their mother poked her head in the room. All she said was that she had to go pick up their brother, she would be back soon, and they should call Grandma or the neighbors, Mrs. and Mr. Marsh, if there was an emergency.

"Don't wake Jakey up, I didn't tell him I'm leaving. Just let him sleep."

And with that she was whisked away into the night, taking with her any chance of her twelve and thirteen-year-olds falling asleep before she got back.

The two boys listened hard for the sound of their mom's car. They heard seven-year-old Jakey cough a couple times from down the hall, but otherwise he didn't stir. Sometime after one in the morning, the boys finally heard the car pull into the driveway. Granger held his breath, wishing his heart would stop beating so loudly in his ears; he didn't want to miss a thing. The front door opened and closed quietly, and then:

"You're going to work this summer. End of story."

"Fine. I don't care."

"And you're going to pay back the bail money."

"What? How?"

"Shh, keep your voice down."

"I can't make that much in one summer!"

"You messed up, Levi. Big time. And your grandparents took the hit for us since I didn't factor *bail* money into our budget this month. So you're going to pay it back."

"I'm going to have to work, like, twenty-four/seven this summer!"

"So be it."

"When am I going to have a summer vacation? And hang out with my friends?"

"Keep your voice down, Levi. It's obvious that hanging out with your friends isn't doing you any favors. You've made some pretty stupid choices with your 'friends.' No. I don't want to hear it. You're not entitled to complain. You brought this upon yourself."

Granger, and he assumed Trevor, also, heard Levi huff dramatically, "there's no way I can make that much money. And this is my last summer of high school! I deserve a summer!"

"Vacation is not a right."

"I'm not doing it."

"Yes. You are. Your grandmother and I worked it out. In fact, it was her idea. You're going to go live with Grandma and Grandpa for awhile."

"You're kidding me. You have to be joking. There is no way I am doing that. Are you kidding?"

There was no way little Jakey was still asleep. Even their mom wasn't trying to whisper anymore.

"Not at all," she said.

"Because of one night?"

"Because of the past *year*! Your actions affect those around you — listen to me, young man — your actions affect other people. You need to learn that before it's too late. You have three little brothers, Levi. Like it or not, you're a role model for them. That's why your grandma and I agree that it's not good for them to have you around right now. Until you can work through whatever you need to work through, you cannot be in this household."

"Is this what you did to Dad, too? Kicked him out just like this? Lot of good that did us."

Granger lay paralyzed in his bed, stunned that Levi would say such a thing but also straining his ears to make sure he didn't miss their mother's reply. The whole house was frozen in silence.

"Yes." Her voice sounded quieter, but no less intense.

And then, after a moment, they heard Levi say just as quietly, "I wish you'd left instead of him."

Neither Granger nor Trevor dared to breathe.

They waited, and waited, and waited.

"Go to bed," she finally said. "Your grandfather will be here to pick you up tomorrow at eight. And if you sneak out before then, I will call the cops. If you end up in jail, I will not bail you out again."

Levi stormed down the hall and slammed his bedroom door. Almost at the same time, Granger and Trevor exhaled.

A few moments later they heard the slow squeaking of another door's hinges, and the sound of little feet padding down the hall.

"Mommy? Is Levi going away?"

"Jakey," their mom's voice said, sounding distant and hollow. "Let's go back to bed. We'll talk about it in the morning."

None of them slept much that night.

# 13

THE OTHERS KEPT UP THE conversation on the way to the nursing home. Granger sat quietly in the backseat. He let his anger at Levi be the fuel to forming a new plan. He was coming up empty, though.

Levi was not one to be easily swayed. He might have changed a lot in the last decade, but he was just as stubborn and headstrong as ever. Granger knew going into it that Levi would put up a fight, he'd been prepared for that. The problem was that Granger didn't know what to do next. Granger could picture Levi standing in court week after week, weaving his stories, arguing so eloquently and changing people's minds. Granger could only keep trying to put a stop to this will nonsense. For their mother's sake.

Their grandma was putting together a puzzle, the kind with only a few, big pieces, when they arrived.

"These pieces are harder to lose and harder to swallow than regular sized puzzle pieces," Melissa From Activities explained.

Inviting two more people into their grandmother's room maxed out the space. Granger let Levi and Trevor go in with their mom and Jake to visit her first. After Granger had been waiting forty minutes, he realized he should've expected they'd be awhile; Levi was as talkative as Jake.

Still tired and wondering if it was his now-permanent state of being, Granger was sitting so far down in the armchair that if someone had come along behind it and tipped it forward just a few degrees he would've slid onto the floor. He had his legs spread out in front of him. He stared straight ahead and rested his head in his right hand, his elbow propped up on the armrest.

*Come on, think. What do I do about Levi?*

He couldn't remember the last time he felt so tired. His limbs felt heavier in Lester, like he was wearing weights on his wrists and ankles.

*I just want to go home.*

Granger opened his eyes and looked up when the unit doors opened and a small group walked in. A middle-aged man and middle-aged woman led the way, but they kept turning around to talk to the people following behind them: Nina and Izzy.

Granger sat up a little.

The four visitors walked right up to the resident named Mr. Farley, who was out pacing, per the usual.

"How you doing, dad?" the middle-aged man asked.

"Doing just fine, son. How are you?"

"Doing good. Do you want to go in your room so we can visit?"

"My room?"

"I can lead the way."

Neither Nina nor Izzy noticed Granger sitting further down the hall. For the first time, Granger thought back to his conversation with Nina the evening prior. He'd actually been feeling relaxed until the end. He remembered how he'd left them, and he cringed.

*Jerk.*

He was so tired and distracted, he'd completely brushed her off. Then he'd blown up at Levi.

*Levi was being insensitive.*

*But Nina wasn't.*

*I need to get out of this town. I need sleep.*

He was convinced it was the exhaustion turning him into a guy he didn't even recognize.

*I'll apologize to her when I see her next.*

If he saw her again.

"Granger?"

Levi had poked his head out of the room.

"You want a turn?"

Granger stood up like he was lifting an elephant on top of his shoulders.

"Hey, man," Levi said. "I really am sorry about earlier. And the text."

"But you still want to see the will?"

Levi hesitated, "let's talk later. Go see her now."

Granger walked past his brother into the room.

He needed a new plan, quickly. He was supposed to leave Lester in just a few hours, but if he did, Levi was sure to broach the subject of the will with their mother, and Granger couldn't let that happen. He could just imagine how she would break down, sitting by while Levi calmly perused over the paperwork that would soon divide up his grandma's possessions like it was a card game.

Their mom went to talk to the nurse. So, all the brothers congregated in the room again. Jake was sitting next to her watching her put the puzzle together and talking about nothing in particular.

"She's getting tired," Jake commented when Granger sat down in Levi's empty chair. "She's had a big day. Lots of faces."

Trevor watched silently from over by the bed, an expression of quiet pain on his face. Levi looked in the room but stood in the hall so he could hear the nurse's report. He nodded slowly and looked from the nurse to their mom to their grandma with his hands in his pockets and a solid frown in place.

Their grandma set one of the pieces down in the wrong spot and looked up, looking at her family as if she hadn't realized they were still there.

"I should come more often," Trevor said after a few minutes of silence.

"I wish I could," Levi said. "But work has been so hectic lately, I haven't been able to get away."

Granger noticed Trevor fidget and share a look with Jake.

"Does she look thinner to you guys? More tired?" Trevor asked.

The other three looked at their grandma. She was in her own world again, not paying any attention to them or their conversation.

"Not Grandma. Mom."

They all turned to look at where she stood in the hall.

"Now that you mention it…" Levi said.

"She didn't look like that last time I was here," Trevor said.

"She cries a lot," Jake said. "And I don't think she's sleeping much. And sometimes she forgets to eat. I have to remind her."

Granger wondered if he looked as guilty as he felt, or as guilty as his two older brothers looked. They were all still processing Jake's words when their mom joined them in the cramped room again wearing a forced smile. "You boys ready to eat?"

Jake led the way.

Jake seemed to know more about what was going on than all the rest of the brothers combined, and maybe even more than their mom. Jake was clearly the best option for an ally. Granger knew he had to let him in on his plan.

When they all left the room, Mr. Farley was out pacing the halls again. He was wearing a sweater vest over his button down, slacks, and loafers. If it wasn't for the untucked shirt and untidy hair, Granger still didn't think he would be able to tell that Mr. Farley was a resident. At that point, Granger was sure he knew Mr. Farley from somewhere, but it wasn't from anywhere he'd been recently. He had been someone in authority over him… when he was a kid…

He watched Mr. Farley pace, his hands clasped behind his back, as one of the aides approached him.

"It's your walking day, Mr. Farley. And you're in luck, it's stopped raining! Are you ready sir?"

Mr. Farley sighed and looked at his wrist. "Now where did my watch go?"

"Here, you can check mine," the aide offered. "It's 10:30 in the morning."

"What time will the kids be here?"

"The kids? Your kids?"

"Well, them too. But what about the students?"

The aide hesitated, but then answered, "we'll be back by then. We won't be gone very long."

Mr. Farley seemed satisfied enough with this answer. And Granger finally remembered who Mr. Farley was.

# 14

The phone rang.

"Lester Elementary School," said the secretary.

Granger sat against the whitewashed, cinder block wall on a bench just inside the school office, his feet dangling eight inches off the floor. He watched his classmates leave for the day through the big office windows. Some of them happened to glance in and see the "troublemaker" on the infamous bench. Many of them turned to their friends to point him out, indiscreetly. Granger looked down at his toes when his face got hot, causing his straight, sandy-brown hair to fall into his eyes. He busied himself with pushing and pulling his dark green, dollar store backpack across the bench.

*Swish. Swish. Swish.*

But in no time the halls cleared and it was only Granger and the grown-ups left in the school. Granger had to tilt his head way back to see the faces of the people walking by. When his neck started to hurt from doing that, he went back to watching his feet dangle or watching his backpack go *swish, swish, swish,* or admiring the things in the 'lost and found' bin that sat under the secretary's desk. The 'lost and found' was a clear plastic tote, big enough for Granger to fit into, empty, if he'd tried. It was mostly full of jackets, glasses, and shoes, with one or two lunchboxes in the mix. Not very interesting. Except for the pair of shoes pressed up against the side of the bin closest to Granger. Not only were they brightly colored, they had wheels under the heels. *Wheels.* Granger's little eyes grew wide, seeing the coveted shoes up close and unattached to anyone else's feet. He couldn't believe someone would lose them and not come looking for them... until he remembered that the Principal banned them two months earlier.

He dropped his gaze back down to his wheel-less shoes, giving them a scathing look before tucking them as far beneath the bench as he could reach.

*Swish. Swish. Swish.*

"Ahem."

The secretary was giving him the eye. He stopped his backpack mid-*swish* across the bench.

The door to the front office finally opened, and when he looked up, his grandmother was looking straight at him. Usually, he wasn't fooled by her most common facial expression. He'd lived with her long enough to tell when her frown actually meant she was unhappy. Today, she really was unhappy.

She didn't say anything and she didn't take her eyes off Granger as she passed him. Her posture was perfect, or was it stiffer than normal? He was a little relieved to see her in her long, floral dress instead of her work overalls. The dress was old and faded and saw just as much dirt and elbow grease as the overalls, but at least she didn't look quite so out of place among the office workers in their professional clothes.

The office door closed after another figure walked in. Trevor trailed behind their grandmother wearing the same backpack as Granger except in dark blue. She pointed to the bench and Trevor sat down obediently, keeping his wide eyes glued to the long, gray hair in a braid down her back. His feet could almost reach the floor.

"What'd you do?" he whispered to Granger.

Granger's insides twisted.

The secretary hung up the phone.

"I'm Granger Kyle's grandmother."

"Are you his guardian?"

The secretary was new.

"I'm one of his primary caretakers. Granger and his mother and brothers live with me and their grandfather."

"Oh," the secretary said. She adjusted her glasses and moved some papers and file folders around on her desk with her fingertips like she was worried about messing up her nails. She finally picked one up.

"You're Julia Kyle?"

"I am."

"I see your name now," she mumbled. "Sorry, I was expecting Mrs. Benson."

"It's 'Ms. Benson.' And Allison couldn't leave work early to come down here, so I came."

The secretary paged the Vice Principal without looking up again, and tapped her pencil rapidly on one of the file folders while they waited. Granger wondered if his grandma made her nervous, too.

"Mrs. Hartman, Granger Kyle's grandmother is here."

Mrs. Hartman's electronic voice over the speakerphone said, "I'll be with them in a minute. I'm just finishing up a call."

Their grandmother did not try to squeeze onto the bench next to the two of them. She didn't even lean against the wall. She remained standing, almost unmoving, next to the secretary's desk, facing the Vice Principal's door.

Trevor nudged Granger in the rib cage and mouthed, "what'd you do?" again, his eyebrows raised higher this time. Granger's tongue suddenly felt enormous and dry in his mouth. He was, ironically, saved when Mrs. Hartman's door opened and she stepped out to greet their grandmother.

The two ladies were the same height, but their grandmother was older and leaner. Mrs. Hartman in her jacket and pencil skirt looked like a president compared to their grandmother. Granger always wished Mrs. Hartman would wear sweatpants or fuzzy slippers or do a crazy hairdo whenever he had to go see her.

The women shook hands and introduced themselves. Mrs. Hartman had on what Granger referred to as her 'serious smile,' which was not really a smile at all in his opinion.

Their grandmother followed Mrs. Hartman inside and made a jerking motion with her head, which told the boys to follow.

"Come on in," said Mrs. Hartman.

*No, thanks*, Granger thought.

Mrs. Hartman got right to it once the three visitors were sitting in a row across the desk from her.

"I called you in today, Mrs. Kyle, well, actually I called his mother in today, because Granger was fighting on the playground during recess."

Mrs. Hartman looked right at him and he really wished Trevor wasn't there to witness his humiliation.

Mrs. Hartman continued, "this is the third time this year. What happened today?"

He tried to speak but nothing came out until he cleared his throat a couple times.

"Nothing. Aaron and I were just playing. We weren't real-fighting."

"Mrs. Lake said you punched him in the stomach."

"He punched me, too."

"He didn't seem to think it was very funny. He reported it to Mr. Havencroft after recess, and he didn't say you were just playing."

Granger decided he wasn't going to be playing with Aaron at recess anymore.

"We were! Maybe he got mad but we started out just playing. He was showing me stuff he learned from watching boxing on TV with his dad and uncle and he said he was gonna do some of it to me and I said okay so then he punched me and then I punched him back and then he acted like I actually hurt him and then he ran—"

"Were you 'play-fighting' the other two times?" the Vice Principal asked.

He looked at his lap. "I don't know," he mumbled.

"What do you mean, 'you don't know?' I think you do know."

"I don't remember."

"Try," his grandmother said.

"The last time," Mrs. Hartman said looking at another paper on her desk, "you were in the hallway walking in line with your class when you shoved another boy in the back."

"He was walking funny and he said that's how I walked and he was laughing at me and he wouldn't stop."

"And the first time, you were in the boys' bathroom and you knocked the trash can over and started kicking the stall doors. What was your reason for doing that?"

Granger was quiet.

Mrs. Hartman waited.

"When Mrs. Lake asked the other boys what all the noise was about, they said you weren't just 'playing' around. They said you just got mad all of the sudden and started kicking things. Your teacher said you'd been in a bad mood most of the day and the rest of that week."

Granger looked past his lap to where his worn, hunter green backpack lay on the floor beneath his feet.

"Granger."

He didn't say anything.

"Granger," Mrs. Hartman said more forcefully. He met her eyes, his head still tilted slightly down.

"Do you remember that?"

He did.

He'd kicked so much and so hard that he'd actually broken a toe. When his family asked him how he did it, he said he tripped.

"Were you mad that day?"

"Yes."

"Why?"

He didn't say anything.

"Grange—"

"When did that first incident happen?" his grandmother asked.

More papers were shuffled.

"October 6th."

He waited for his grandmother to say something, but when she didn't, he chanced a look up at her and saw that she was looking back down at him. At first he thought she was waiting for him to explain himself, like Mrs. Hartman was, but her expression was... different.

She turned back to face the Vice Principal.

"Do we need to pay for the trashcan?"

"No. Fortunately, it was getting replaced that month anyway."

His grandmother nodded. "Okay then. I'll talk to his mother when she gets home this evening and then we will talk to Granger. Let me know if things don't get better."

She stood up, a surprised Granger and Trevor following suit before she could change her mind.

"Wait," Mrs. Hartman said, also looking surprised. "I would like to make some sort of a plan so this doesn't happen—"

"I understand, but I think his mother needs to be part of this discussion, don't you?"

"Well, yes. I guess you're right."

"Like I said, call us again if things don't get better. Don't forget your book bags, boys."

The outer office was a little emptier when they walked out. The school nurse was gone for the day, and the new secretary was just hurrying out the office door as they came out, probably so she didn't have to face Granger's grandmother again. But a tall figure was approaching Mrs. Hartman's door when they opened it. He had his hands clasped behind his back. Whenever Granger saw him, whether at assemblies, Field Day, or just walking in the halls, he was always standing or walking just like that.

He introduced himself to Granger's grandmother with a smile as they passed. "Farley Wilcox. Principal."

"Julia Kyle. Grandmother to these two boys. Nice to meet you."

"Nice to meet you, as well. Have a good day, boys. See you on Monday!"

None of them said a word until they got into the car.

Granger's grandmother looked at him in the rearview mirror.

"October 6th?" she asked.

Granger shrugged.

"Do you remember that that was the day after my birthday party?"

Granger didn't answer right away, but then he admitted, "yes, ma'am."

"When your father dropped in, unannounced."

It wasn't a question.

Granger just looked back at her in the mirror.

"We will talk about handling anger appropriately when your mom gets home."

Then she fixed her eyes on the road.

But he felt a small weight lift off his tiny shoulders.

"And you both need haircuts tonight."

# 15

GRANGER WAS FINE WITH HIS mother's suggestion that they get an early lunch. It meant he could talk to Jake and then get out of town even sooner. He was not prepared for her next suggestion, though.

"A picnic with who?" he asked.

"My church small group."

"No."

"Granger…" she pleaded.

"We don't know any of them," Trevor added. "Won't that be awkward?"

"I've gotta get back on the road ASAP," Levi said.

"Me too," Granger said, grudgingly agreeing with Levi.

"It won't last long," she said. "Please? You don't even have to stay the whole time. It's just… I told them I'd come by."

It wasn't her words, but Jake's look at them from over her shoulder that had the biggest effect.

"Fine," Levi said. "I can stay for a little while. It might be fun!"

Granger, on the other hand, could not think of anything less fun, and almost wished he had a root canal appointment to go to. He silently cursed his healthy teeth.

He'd been to church before. When the boys and their mom lived on the farm, they went with their grandparents to church most Sundays. For a hyper, grade-school-aged boy, sitting still on a stiff wooden pew wearing stiff, itchy clothes for a whole hour and then being forced to stand and politely listen to old people talk about you and smile over you and ask you stupid questions about yourself was somehow even worse than it sounded.

*Talk talk talk talk talk.*

Young Granger hated the small talk. He didn't remember anything of what the preacher said, but his ears rang with the incessant chatter of the church people before and after the services. All he wanted to do was go home, change into his regular clothes, and play down by the creek for the rest of the afternoon.

But there he was, all grown up and going to a church picnic.

Their mom couldn't stop beaming as she introduced her three oldest sons to all twenty-five people gathered around the park picnic tables.

"I thought you said this was a 'small' group," he whispered to her.

"I guess some extra people came," she said, smiling.

"How come you get a pass?" Granger asked Jake, who for some reason didn't have to be introduced to each person.

"I've already met most of these people at church."

"I didn't even know you and Mom went to church."

"Yeah, for the last couple of years."

Jake was polite and responsive to each person who started up a conversation with him. He seemed completely at ease, though most of the people there were at least their mom's age. Levi, in a similar manner, didn't know a stranger. The first person he shook hands with just happened to have been in the Peace Corps, just like him. Once he heard that, they couldn't have pulled Levi away if they'd tried.

There was a free moment between introductions when Granger seized his opportunity. He pulled Jake aside and explained the situation of the will from his own perspective.

"I already know about the will," Jake said. "Levi said something about it last week."

Granger hadn't expected that. "And?"

"I don't see a problem with it."

"You don't?"

"No."

"How do you not see a problem with it?"

"It makes sense that he'd want to know what to expect."

"No, it doesn't."

"Why not?"

"Because a will is something you read *later… after*. Not now. Not when she's still alive."

"Things won't change much between now and then," Jake said.

"Of course they will! Now, she's alive. Then, she… won't be."

"But everything else will be the same. I mean, she's alive now… but she's not really here anymore, is she?"

Jake didn't even flinch as the words left his mouth.

Granger stared at his little brother as if he didn't know him. First Levi, and now Jake. Anger ignited inside his chest again.

"How can you say that?"

Jake's bushy brows came together. "You think she's still in there?" he asked, slowly.

Granger, scowling, looked away and didn't say anything. What could he say?

"She's not going to get better," Jake said.

"I know that," he snapped.

Jake looked around them. "Let's talk after. It's getting more crowded."

"Forget it. I'll talk to Trevor."

Granger turned and went to find Trevor, leaving Jake in the dust. He would convince Trevor to help him keep the will discussion off the table, and then he was getting the heck out of Lester. He wasn't about to sit through a picnic.

But then suddenly his mother was in front of him saying, "Granger, Trevor, I want you to meet some more people," and before he knew what was happening, he found himself face-to-face with a young woman and a frizzy-haired little girl.

Suddenly the need to talk to Trevor didn't seem as urgent anymore.

Nina stuck out her hand and smiled. "Hello again."

"Hi!" he said, maybe a little too enthusiastically. He shook her hand, cleared his throat, and tried to take it down a notch.

"You're part of my mom's small group, too?" he asked, nonchalantly.

She looked around, "I'm part of any group that offers free food. I just wander around town looking for clubs to join."

He smiled. His attitude toward the picnic was changing quickly. Maybe he wouldn't prefer a root canal after all…

"Actually, no," she said. "I'm part of the other small group that's here for the picnic."

"That explains why this 'small group' isn't that small."

She looked over at his mom and then back at him. "I didn't realize you were one of Allison's sons."

"I am. For most of my life now, actually. I think she even gave birth to me."

"Is that so? Interesting. Do I get to meet your other brothers?"

"At your own risk."

"Duly noted."

"This is Trevor, a year older than me, and that hippie over there with the leather bracelets is the oldest, Levi."

"Oh yeah," she said with a look of realization on her face. "I think I was in school with Levi."

His mom had been watching their interaction with fascination, and when Granger looked at her he knew exactly what she was thinking. Luckily, she didn't share with the group, but only asked, "do you two know each other from school?"

"No," Granger said. "We met at the nursing home the other day."

He gave Izzy, who'd been standing quietly at her mom's side, a small salute. She smiled briefly, but her attention was mostly on the playground where a dozen kids were already playing. She kept tugging at Nina's arm.

"Alright, go on, but—" Nina began.

Izzy darted away. She was already halfway to the jungle gym before Nina finished her sentence, "no pushing!"

"Oh, that's right," Granger's mom said to Nina. "I forgot you two volunteer up there sometimes."

Granger still felt the need to apologize to Nina for the day before, but his entire family was standing around them.

Just then, a young guy walked up to their little group and put his arm casually around Nina's shoulders, to Granger's disappointment.

"This is my brother, Luke," Nina explained to the Kyle family.

Granger didn't feel disappointed anymore.

Just as he shook the guy's hand, Granger recognized him.

"Luke," Granger said, filled with surprise. "Luke Lanzo! You're siblings?"

"Granger Kyle!" Luke said.

"We were in the same grade," Granger explained to his mom. "And we were in the same cabin at summer camp a few years in a row."

"I remember," she said, looking pleased at Granger's unexpected warmth toward someone from Lester. Granger was surprised at his own reaction.

"How's it going?" Luke asked. "You still live around here?"

"No, I live in Eugene now."

"Nice! You still playing baseball?"

Granger froze.

There it was... the question.

It took more strength than he expected to finally say:

"No."

Granger didn't know what compelled him to do it, but he looked down at his left arm and tried to lift it. Using all the strength in his left shoulder he could only shrug, his arm remaining lifeless. He watched Luke's face change from curiosity to understanding to embarrassment. Nina watched with an unreadable expression on her face.

Luke cleared his throat.

"That's right. I forgot. I'm sorry."

"Don't be," Granger said, forcing a smile onto his reddening face. "It was a long time ago. So, what do you do?"

Luke launched into a fascinating explanation of his job as a plane mechanic. Jake had found his way over to them by that time and was unabashedly enthralled by the subject, asking Luke one question after another.

"I've been living in Texas for the last few years, I just came up to visit. I'm staying with Nina and Izabelle for the next couple days."

"Oh, did your parents move away?" Granger asked.

It was Luke's turn to hesitate. "Um, no, they still live around here."

The Lanzo siblings shared a look.

Nina piped up, "our parents and I aren't exactly on speaking terms. So Luke splits his time between us when he comes to visit."

The second awkward silence of their conversation was interrupted by a balding, heavy-set, middle-aged man in a polo and khakis standing on a picnic bench and announcing that everyone should find a seat.

A second's pause was all it took for Jake to start up the conversation about aircraft maintenance with Luke again, and he continued to pepper Luke with questions even after they were all seated. Trevor excused himself to take a phone call, Levi was still standing in the same spot on the grass, talking to his new friend from the Peace Corps, and their mom had wandered off to talk to someone else. Of the only other people he knew at the picnic, one was sitting directly across from him needing to be apologized to, and the other was cutting in line for the monkey bars.

Now that he knew Nina was Luke's sister, something gnawed at him. There was something he should remember about the Lanzo's, but he didn't know what. Something that happened a long time ago... Granger glanced across the table at Nina, and she looked right back at him. She looked nervous, even a little shy, unlike before. The look on her face made Granger wonder if she knew he was trying to remember something about them. She looked like she was just waiting for him to figure it out.

He knew the feeling.

He put his curiosity aside and smiled at her.

"I think I saw you at the nursing home earlier today."

The shyness and nervousness disappeared. "Oh? I didn't see you."

"Probably for the best, I might've been rude to you again. Sorry about yesterday. I had just gotten this text—"

"Say no more. You're forgiven."

"Just like that?"

She accepted the paper plate her brother handed her and shrugged, "why not?"

"Thanks."

She smiled, "don't mention it."

"So do you fly the planes or just fix them?" Jake was asking Luke.

"Both. The maintenance is how I make a living. The flying is for fun."

"When did you start flying?"

"Junior high."

"That young? Where'd you learn?" Jake asked.

"There's an airfield about thirty minutes from here. I went twice a week until I graduated and moved away."

"Oh yeah! I've seen some small planes flying around. Cool! Did you ever fly in the Air Force?"

"No, never wanted to. The military isn't for me. I prefer to fly for fun. If you're ever interested I could take you up some time. I like to take friends and family when I get the chance."

"There's nothing scarier than letting your little brother take you up in a plane that *he's* flying," Nina said.

Until he looked back at Nina, Granger hadn't noticed the wind picking up, but across the table she was battling against it, her brown hair whipping into her eyes over and over again. He looked up at the sky. No clouds... yet.

"He's taked me flying a bunch of times, too," Izzy added, squeezing herself between her mom and her uncle.

"Izabelle's my best customer," Luke said proudly.

She beamed. "We go up a hundred thousand miles off the ground!"

"Not quite. More like 2,000."

"I'd love to learn to fly," Levi said. He rested his arms on the wooden picnic table and leaned forward. "What do you have to do to get certified?"

Out of the corner of his eye, Granger saw Izzy wiggling in her seat. She was staring straight at him.

"What happened to your arm, mister?" she asked, suddenly.

"Izzy!" Nina said, mortified.

Granger's brothers glanced over at the noise, but went right back to listening to Luke's tales of flying.

"What?" Izzy asked innocently.

"That's not polite." She looked at Granger. "Now *I'm* the one that's sorry."

"It's okay." He almost left it at that. "Actually, to tell you the truth, I don't mind it so much when kids ask. I don't know why."

"I think I do," Nina said. "Curiosity is one thing, pity is another. So is judgment."

"Huh. Yeah, I think you might be right."

He wished he could remember what had happened to the Lanzo's all those years ago...

He turned back to Izzy, who's brown eyes were wide in anticipation. "I was in a car accident a few years ago. I got hurt, and now my arm doesn't work."

Another gust of wind blew some napkins down the table and they all reached out to save them.

"Does it hurt?" Izzy asked.

Nina still looked a little uncomfortable about her daughter's invasive questioning, but also maybe looked a little curious, herself.

"It's mostly just numb. I can't really feel anything there."

"So, you can't move it?"

He tried to lift his arm again. "That's all I got. And even this is an improvement."

"Can I feel it?"

"Izzy..."

"You can, but it doesn't feel any different than this arm. Except it doesn't have as much muscle anymore."

All the muscle he'd worked to build in high school, that he'd been so proud of, was gone. And not just the muscle in his bad arm.

She poked his left arm gingerly and watched his face to see if he would feel it. He couldn't pass up the opportunity to gasp and hold his arm like she'd hurt him, which made her jump.

"Just kidding," he said.

She exhaled and laughed.

"That's such an old man joke," Nina laughed.

"It is," Granger said. "Like that old substitute teacher in elementary school who would pretend to take his thumb off to freak us out."

Nina laughed again, "I remember him. He was crazy."

But Izzy wasn't done with her investigation. She looked across the table with innocent eyes.

"Is it gonna get better?"

He felt his smile falter.

"No. Not all the way."

"Oh."

Oh. That was how he often felt, even years later. It wouldn't get all the way better?... oh.

"But it's okay," he lied. "I can still do lots of stuff. Like drive and work and get dressed and mow the lawn."

"But not baseball?"

She must've overheard some of the conversation earlier.

"Not baseball," he confirmed.

Granger didn't want to hurt the kid's feelings, but he was ready to be done talking. The dark cloud that had hovered constantly above Granger for nearly four years, that he was finally keeping at bay, threatened to drift overhead again.

"Alright, that's enough questions about Mister Kyle's arm," Nina said.

He made a face. "Gross, no. Please, call me Granger."

"Thanks for letting me touch your arm, Granger," Izzy said.

The guy in the polo and khakis hoisted himself onto the picnic bench again and called for everyone's attention. He announced that he was going to pray for their meal and then they could all go through the line.

Everyone bowed their heads and closed their eyes, even Granger's brothers. He followed along, but felt all his muscles tense up. He opened his eyes and looked around once during the prayer, and saw Izzy looking at him and his arm. When he caught her, she closed her eyes quickly.

"Alright," the host said after a collective *Amen*, "better eat quick because it looks like a storm's coming in."

Granger looked at the sky and his pulse immediately quickened. A few people laughed, but the thunderheads gathering in the distance were no joke. Granger didn't want to be finishing off his watermelon when the incoming storm finally blew in, he wanted to be on the interstate, well past it. It wouldn't be a mild one, by the looks of it.

They ate quickly, especially Granger.

He tossed his plate into the trash can, took another peek at the sky, and went to find Trevor ASAP. But when Granger tried to make him see his perspective of the will business, Trevor shocked him by saying almost the same thing as Jake had.

"It isn't speeding her death along," Trevor said. "It's getting us ready for what happens next. It's gonna be harder for us than for her."

Granger gritted his teeth and walked away, waving Trevor's words away with the wind.

He didn't have any more time to find an ally within the Kyle family. Part of the sky was clear and bright blue and sunny, but the other part, the bigger part, the part that was moving toward them, was full of dark, dark gray clouds.

# 16

THE FIRST RAINDROPS FELL WHEN they pulled into their mom's driveway. The wind had picked up even more by the end of the picnic, sending everyone scrambling to pack up and leave as quickly as they could. The clouds were low in the sky, moving quickly, and the wind was pulling the trees taut, stripping off the weaker of the brand new green leaves and flower buds and sending them north by northeast with no sense of meandering in their path. The thunder was getting louder and more frequent, too. It all gave the impression that they should be grabbing Toto and calling out for Auntie Em.

He'd lost precious time.

"I knew I should've left this morning," he said, slamming his car door and running after his mother and brothers into the house.

"You'll just have to wait it out," his mom said once he was inside.

"I can't. If I don't leave now I'll be late for work and I'll be in huge trouble."

"Won't he understand if it's a weather delay?"

"I'm already in hot water with my boss."

"But honey, you can't drive in this!"

"I'll be fine," he said as he started to sweat. "It's moving quickly. By the time I get to the edge of town it'll be halfway over."

She gave him a look that told him she clearly believed this was nonsense.

He went straight to his old bedroom and grabbed the few items he'd brought or borrowed.

"And if I leave soon enough, I can miss it," he yelled over his shoulder, with no proof to back up his theory.

"Who are you trying to convince?" Levi shouted from down the hall.

He yanked the borrowed phone charger out of the wall.

The lights flickered.

Not a little, momentary flicker. An earnest, struggle-to-come-back-on flicker. They were without electricity long enough for the appliances to make that noise that sounds exactly like how dread feels.

Granger closed his eyes, breathing heavier than a moment before.

*Control. It's all about confidence and control. You can do this.*

He imagined a long stretch of highway, and how the wind would pummel the side of his car. Even in his imagination he was on high alert, gripping the wheel with a one-handed, white-knuckled grip.

He opened his eyes, looking up at the ceiling light and then at the houses across the street, until the power surged back on.

Granger glanced over his shoulder when there was a knock at his open door. A rumble of thunder rattled the whole house. He finished rolling up the phone charging cord with a shaking, clammy hand.

"What's up, Jakey?"

"Do you know when you'll be back in town?"

"Uh, no. I don't know. I'll just have to check my work schedule. My boss might not let me leave for a while, after the way this week has gone."

"You should've told him what was going on before you left."

"No kidding."

Jake invited himself in, walking over to Granger's bed with his hands in his pockets. He waited.

"I'll let you know, okay kid? I'll check my work schedule as soon as I get home. I just got promoted, you know, so my vacation time will be kinda tight for a while."

"Oh yeah. Congrats, by the way."

Jake seemed a little lackluster.

"Look," Granger sighed, "I'm sorry I kinda jumped down your throat about the baseball thing. And... stuff..."

Did he still think Jake was making a mistake? Absolutely. Would he still try to convince him to change his mind? Most likely. But he couldn't stand to see the kid so broken up about... well, about anything.

"Don't worry about it," Jake said. It almost seemed to Granger like that wasn't what had been bothering him. "Are you coming back for my graduation?"

*Dang it. Graduation.*

"Um.... Yeah... yeah I'm planning to. I might have to do some begging at work but I'll try."

"You promise?"

Granger paused before he stood up. He looked at his little brother. "I'll really try."

"I guess that's better than promising and not following through," Jake said with a shrug.

Granger knew who Jake was referring to when he said it. With a hard edge to his voice he agreed. "You're right. It is."

He tossed the charger back to Jake.

"What about this fall?" Jake asked.

"What about it?"

"I was just thinking... I'll be leaving for college, and then she'll be all alone."

"Trevor and Levi can visit, too. And they live a lot closer, so it should be easier for them."

"I just know how much it means to her when *you* come to visit."

There it was again. Frustrated, he asked, "why me, specifically?"

"You know why," Jake said.

Granger didn't contradict him.

"She'd feel better if she knew you'd be around a little more."

Granger looked around him on the floor for his jacket. He looked in the closet, looked in the corner. "I get that, but I also have a full time job."

"So do Trevor and Levi."

"I told you I'd check my schedule."

"Here," Jake said, tossing him the jacket from across the room. Granger caught it and pulled it on effortlessly using the one-arm technique his occupational therapist taught him years ago.

He stalked out of the room before Jake had a chance to go another round. Another explosion of thunder jarred the picture frames on the hallway walls as Granger walked by. In the living room, he crossed between his mom and the TV.

"Wait—" his mom began.

"I'm coming right back inside I just need to make sure my—"

"No, Granger, listen," she said, turning up the TV volume from her perch on the edge of the couch. He sighed and turned to face it. The weatherman he'd grown up seeing on the screen was again greeting him with fantastic news.

"… of the storm moving across the western part of the state. In Franklin, Guston, and Karney we're getting reports of 65 to 75 mile-per-hour winds and quarter-sized hail. Contrary to prior predictions this system is moving more north than northeast. It's on course to hit Trayfield and Lester within the half hour, possibly sooner, with Kenison and Fairfax getting less damaging winds and hail to the south…"

"Looks like it will be a fun drive," Granger said.

Dang it, Monty Lewis, he thought. Why couldn't you deliver some good news for once.

His brothers walked in the room during the report. Levi was just hanging up the phone after telling his wife that he'd head out once the storm passed.

"You're still leaving?" Levi asked. "You can't be serious."

"I have to get back by 5:30."

"You're an idiot if you try to drive in this."

"There haven't been any sirens yet, it's just a tornado watch."

"Look at it out there!"

"I can't be late for work!" Granger said.

"You work at a restaurant, not the White House."

Granger dropped his things on the ground and in two strides was face-to-face with Levi. His voice was measured and quiet at first, but it quickly changed.

"I am so sick of you acting like you're better than me because of your stupid job."

"And I'm sick of you holding a grudge against everybody. I'm not making you feel insecure about your life, Granger, you are."

"Boys, please," their mother pleaded.

Granger shoved Levi with his right hand.

To his surprise, Levi shoved right back.

So, Granger shoved harder, causing Levi to run into an end-table and knock a lamp to the floor.

Trevor and Jake moved when they saw the first shove and as soon as the lamp hit the floor they were between the other two.

"Cut it out, guys," Trevor said in the authoritative voice he rarely used. He had one forearm on Granger's chest and one on Levi's.

"I thought you were supposed to be some peace-loving hippie," Granger jeered.

Levi's expression was anything but peace-loving hippie at the moment. Angry Levi was back.

"You don't fool me," Granger went on, yelling to be heard over the thunderous cacophony in the sky above their house. "You act so selfless and caring but then you wanna know what you'll get from her as soon as she's dead."

He was out of options. He could not protect his mom from Levi's scheme, he knew it. He turned to look at her. She was watching the scene in horror with tears in her eyes.

"Did you know about that, Mom?" Granger asked, not caring to try to be sensitive. "Grandma's not even in the ground yet and Levi's trying to extort her."

Levi growled and lunged forward, "I am not!"

Trevor and Jake held him back but he had the advantage of size over them and he pushed them away.

"I'm not gonna hurt him," he bellowed at the two scrambling to try to get between them again.

"Coulda fooled me," Jake said. But Jake and Trevor didn't get between them again.

Granger could still clearly see Levi's anger, but Levi's approach changed instantly. He towered over Granger as he neared. Granger stood up as tall as he could to face him.

"Listen here," Levi ordered over the sound of thick branches hitting the front window. "Janessa's grandpa got dementia four years ago and two years later he died. It was hard on the family, but they were doing okay, considering. Then his will was read. After the man got dementia but before he died, one of his grandkids and one of his kids both went through nasty divorces. But of course, he hadn't included that change in his will. No one thought of that until after the will was read. It was a bloodbath. Their family used to get along pretty well, they even liked each other, until the will reading. Since then, most of them don't talk to each other anymore. Now, do you see why I wanted to be prepared? We have a hard enough time dealing with our own crap. And Dad's crap. Just look at us. We haven't been together like this in six years. You haven't even come home since then. I don't know the last time I talked to Lillian. Jake and Mom have been carrying all this Grandma stuff on their shoulders all by themselves. We don't need anything else making it harder!"

Every person in the room was quiet, but nature made up for it with plenty of noise.

"I have to go," Granger finally said. His jaw set.

"It's not safe to drive in this," his mom pleaded again. "Especially not with one arm. I'm sorry, but you know I'm right." She pointed at the muted screen with the TV remote. "They've already reported about a dozen cars off the road. And half of those are on the highway to Eugene. At least stay until it clears. I'm sure your boss will understand."

Granger didn't hear anything after *"especially not with one arm."*

A gust of wind wider than the door itself slammed into the front of the house just then, throwing the door open so hard that the doorstop at the bottom couldn't prevent it from making a handle-shaped dent in the wall.

"I can't lose my promotion. And if I don't leave now, the storm will be even worse. It's mostly wind and thunder right now. And I'll be moving away from the storm, not with it. I'll call you when I get through it if that makes you feel better."

He gave this speech quickly, amid the protestations of everybody. He had enough sense to hurry over and give his mom a quick hug. Then he bounded down the steps and slammed the front door behind him to make sure it latched all the way.

The wind shoved him backwards more than once on his journey to the car. He surveyed the skies again, swallowed, and looked back down at the ground.

*What are you doing? Are you insane?*
*I can do this.*
*Who are you kidding?*
*I have to make it back in time for work.*
*Idiot.*
His mother and brothers were on the front steps still trying to

convince him to come back inside when he whipped out of the driveway. He turned on his car radio, leaned forward, and held tight to the steering wheel. Wherever he looked, Lester residents were hurrying to find shelter, their hair standing on end like cartoon characters. But he wasn't the only car on the road, which gave him some comfort. He followed someone until they turned off into a grocery store parking lot. Another car pulled into the bank across the street.

He made himself inhale and exhale, forcing himself to relax the muscles in his back and right arm.

And then, as he drove, the wind died down.

Granger chuckled, thinking of his mother's worries.

"See? It's fine. I beat it," he said to himself. He mentally patted himself on the back for his successful immersion therapy: he was scared to drive in the storm, but he'd done it anyway.

*Dr. Jenkins would be proud.*

Even the big, fat, sporadic rain drops had stopped. All would be well. He was driving out of the city limits, finally starting to ease into his seat.

Then Granger felt the hair on the back of his neck stand up.

The sky started to turn a little green, and so did his face.

The truth that he'd been trying to deny, was settling in. In confirmation of his fears, the music on the radio was interrupted by three familiar dial-up-internet-esque beeps followed by a high, sustained tone.

Granger could feel the picnic lunch trying to come back up his throat.

A staticky, robotic, man's voice gave Granger the news: "The National Weather Service has issued a Tornado Warning for the following counties... at 11:52 a.m., Doppler Radar reported a tornado touchdown five miles outside of Lester county..."

His eyes widened just in time to see that he was approaching something large and wide and dark. It wasn't the funnel, but it wasn't much help to him, anyway. It was a massive wall of rain. It hit his car like a shower of bullets. He was pretty sure there was some hail mixed in. He could no longer see the road. At all. He veered off to the right slightly, hoping he was on the shoulder, and slowed. A check in his rear-view mirror informed him that at least if he was driving in the same direction as the rain, there was some visibility of the yellow and white paint.

He didn't have time to regret his decision. He spun his '99 Nissan around like a Nascar racer taking a high-speed victory lap and headed back to Lester just as the town's tornado sirens started to wail.

He gritted his teeth and growled at the robot-man still listing off counties, "Why do we live here?"

He didn't care about the speed limit anymore. He sped down Main Street debating how much time he had before he needed to pull off the road and dive into a ditch or a gas station. He didn't see a funnel yet, but he couldn't see much of anything anymore. He pressed down harder on the gas pedal.

By some miracle, he pulled into his mom's driveway in one piece. He pried his cramping hand off the steering wheel, jumped out of the car, and sprinted up the steps. The front door swung open just before he reached it.

"Oh thank you, Jesus," his mom cried, throwing her arms around him.

"What's going on? Why aren't you guys in the basement, yet? Where's Levi?" Granger yelled. The noise of the storm was starting to sound like a freight train.

"He followed you," Trevor yelled back.

"What? Why?"

"Because you were stupid enough to try to outrun a tornado," Trevor said.

Trevor looked outside and then whipped open the door again. Levi stumbled into the house, his hair dripping wet.

"Didn't you see me as you passed? Coming back into town?" Levi asked. They were both still breathless.

Granger shook his head. "I couldn't really see anything."

Levi shook his head, but he didn't blow a fuse. Instead, he laughed and clapped Granger on the shoulder.

Down in the basement they collapsed on the couch and bean bag chairs. Levi found a towel for his soaked locks.

"Did you forget to close your sunroof?" Trevor asked.

Levi shook his head. "I couldn't see anything through my windshield so I thought sticking my head out the window might help. It didn't. I was lucky I saw him drive by. Or shoot by, I should say."

Granger's heart was still pounding and his breathing hadn't calmed down yet. Part of him wanted to laugh off the excess adrenaline like Levi, but suddenly he felt like he might pass out. He fell down on a beanbag hard.

When he closed his eyes he could see the storm coming down the two-lane road right at him, but in his mind the scene was darker. It was nighttime. And he wasn't the only one in the car.

# 17

GRANGER SHUT HIMSELF INSIDE THE basement bathroom. Shaky and clammy, he managed to find the toilet in time to be sick, but it didn't leave him feeling much better. He sat on the cold floor in the dark with his eyes closed and breathed through his nose, willing himself not to puke again.

Someone knocked on the door after a while.

"Honey, are you okay in there?"

"Fine, mom," he said, his voice raspy from throwing up.

But she slid inside and closed the door behind her.

"Mom!" His protest was weak.

She flicked the light on and he shielded his eyes.

There was a night light resting on the counter. She plugged it in and turned off the big light again.

"I just wasn't feeling well," Granger said with his arm still covering his eyes.

"I know. You've been in here forty-five minutes."

That was news to him.

"Did you have an attack?" she asked quietly.

He didn't respond.

"How long has it been since you had one?"

He swallowed down the horrible taste in his mouth.

"Over a year."

She sat next to him and held his wrist to check his pulse.

"Is it better yet?" she asked.

"Not quite."

They sat in silence while Granger tried to regulate his breathing.

He was still angry with her about a lot of things, namely not being forthright about his grandma's condition a lot sooner, but the attack had rattled him. He didn't pull his wrist away from her.

"I hate these," he whispered.

"Me too," she said.

The storm quieted down over the next fifteen minutes.

"How are you now?" she asked him.

"Better. Tired."

He knew there was no way he would have the energy to drive back to Eugene that afternoon.

"So much for making it to work on time."

"Well, it wasn't for a lack of trying," she said. "Will your boss be really mad?"

"Yeah. Not much I can do about it now, though."

They sat for a few more minutes like that.

"I knew about the will, honey."

Granger turned. "You did?"

"Levi first mentioned it a few months ago."

Granger huffed, "of all the—"

"I'm not upset, Granger."

"You're not?"

"No. I admit at first I was a little shaken. I didn't want to admit she was as bad off as she was. But now she's even worse. I've made my peace with it. He's just trying to help. That's all."

Granger certainly didn't agree with her, but he didn't have the energy to fight her on it at that moment.

His brothers did him the favor of pretending not to notice when his mom helped him out of the bathroom and up the stairs into his old bed again. He felt like an oversized toddler getting tucked in for an afternoon nap, but his legs were so fatigued that he needed the assistance. He collapsed onto the mattress and his shaking hand couldn't even get his shoes off. She slid them off for him. He mumbled his thanks and turned to face the wall.

The tornado had just barely missed Lester; the house was still standing. The afternoon thunderstorm that was left seemed like a drizzle in comparison. Down the hall he could hear his brothers talking and laughing, and he was laying in bed because he could barely stand.

It was still raining when he awoke later that evening. His thoughts immediately went to his job, wondering if he'd jeopardized his promotion. He couldn't afford to lose it. The landlord had jacked up his rent not too long ago, and his old wages wouldn't cut it anymore. Of course, he would try to explain to his boss that he'd been delayed by the storm, but what if that wasn't a good enough excuse? What would he do then?

He sat up and took a deep breath before pressing the button to call his boss. He braced himself.

"Hey Tony. I know I missed my shift. I'm really sorry. There was this storm—"

"I saw."

"Oh, right. Well I'm really sorry about not making it—"

"How far away are you right now?"

"Um, about five hours."

"And when did you try to leave?"

"Around noon."

"And it's almost seven now."

"Yeah."

"So why are you just now calling in?"

Granger didn't answer. Once he'd made it back to the house, making a phone call had been the last thing on his mind.

"Look, Granger, you're a good employee. That's why I promoted you. I don't know what's been going on the last few days but this isn't like you. So, I'm gonna give you another chance. But if you drop the ball again, I'm gonna give your promotion to somebody else."

"It won't happen again."

"This pushes back your training even more. Now you won't be done until mid-May."

Mid-May. Jake's graduation. Granger weighed his options.

"Not a problem," he said.

"I'll see you on Monday, then."

The smell of ground beef and tomato sauce welcomed Granger into the kitchen where his mother and brothers were making dinner. As he walked in, a hacky sack almost beamed him in the face. He caught it less than a foot in front of his nose with his good hand.

"He's still got it," Jake shouted, throwing his hands up.

"But how's his throwing?" Levi teased. "Catching is one thing… it doesn't look like he gets to the gym as much as he used to. Come on, show us what you got."

Granger didn't enjoy being patronized. He set the hacky sack down on the counter and nudged it over to Jake.

"Oh, come on," Levi said.

"I don't feel like playing."

Granger let his brothers provide the entertainment and conversation during dinner while he focused on his three and a half servings of spaghetti and salad.

"Did you call your boss already?" his mom asked while they cleared the table.

"Yeah."

"Did you lose your promotion?"

"No, amazingly."

"Oh good. I was worried."

*Evidently not too worried, or you wouldn't keep trying to get me to stay longer.*

"What'd he say?"

"That I can't miss any more work, obviously," he said. "My training's been pushed back. I won't finish until mid-May now."

"Mid-may?" Jake asked.

"Looks like I probably won't make it down for your graduation. Can't take time off during manager training, company policy. Sorry, kid."

The kitchen got quiet.

Granger didn't want to disappoint Jake, he really didn't. But he needed the promotion and he needed time away from Lester again. He hated who he was, in Lester.

"But, you could come just for the weekend, couldn't you?" their mom asked.

"No guarantees. Some of the training happens on the weekends."

"Don't worry about it," Jake said. "At least you tried." He tossed the hacky sack once, caught it, set it down on the table, and stood. "I've gotta finish my homework. G'night."

When they heard his bedroom door shut, Levi turned to him. "Did you really try?"

"Of course I did."

"It's a high school graduation. It's a big deal."

"You think I don't know that? I tried, okay?"

Levi scoffed and excused himself from the table.

Trevor sat silently for a beat until he, too, excused himself. He kissed their mom on the head and went to their room.

Granger sat at one end of the kitchen table, his mother sat at the other.

"You're disappointed," he said.

"I'm just sad."

He nodded, took one last drink of his water, and got up.

"Night, Mom."

# 18

LEVI AND TREVOR WERE WAITING for him in his room.

"Shut the door," Levi said quietly.

Granger shut it because that's what he was going to do anyway, not because Levi told him to do it.

"You're being a real jerk, you know that?" Levi said.

Granger ignored him. He yawned and walked toward his bed.

"It's not just that you aren't trying to make an effort, it's like you're going out of your way to hurt them."

"Is that so?"

"He's right, Granger," Trevor said.

Granger faced Trevor, feeling like he'd been bitten by his beloved childhood dog. "You, too?"

"It's his graduation," Trevor said. "It's important."

"Yeah, I know that, but if I miss my training again I'll lose my promotion. I can't afford that."

"Have you tried to get the time off? Really?" Levi asked.

"Why is everyone interrogating *me*? I have a job just like you two. And I live way further away than you guys do."

"We've been making an effort to come visit," Levi said.

Granger rolled his eyes. "Please, Levi, enough with the 'good guy' crap."

"Look, I don't know what happened between you and Mom and —" Levi started.

"You're right. You don't. So just accept that my relationship with them is not the same as yours is. It's… complicated."

"I would've thought that, if anything, your senior year would've made your relationship stronger," Levi said.

"Well, it didn't."

"Don't you think it's time to change that? It's been, what, six years? Seven? You're not doing yourself any favors."

Granger threw his arm up, "alright then, what do you suggest, Lifestyle Guru?"

Levi ignored the dig. "Act like you care. I know you do. Really try to come for graduation. Stay for church in the morning."

Granger snickered. "I'm not staying for church in the morning."

"Why not? We are."

"Since when?"

"A few hours ago. Trev and I have to get back to our lives, too, but we agreed to stay for church tomorrow."

"Why?"

"Because it means so much to Mom and Jake," Trevor said. "And we both feel guilty for not being around as much as we should."

Granger turned his back on Levi to face Trevor. If anyone would understand him, it would be Trevor. He tried to read his brother's expression.

"I have to get back to Eugene," he said, watching Trevor's face.

"I know," Trevor said.

"I have responsibilities there."

"Yeah."

"There's nothing for me here."

Trevor thought for a second. "You have 'great opportunities that you can't miss out on?' You 'promise you'll be back when you can?' I don't know, Grange, you're starting to sound like someone else we know."

Though his tone was calm and unprovoking, his words cut all the way through.

Granger gritted his teeth. "*I* don't make promises I can't keep."

"Because you don't want to let people down?"

Granger pictured the disappointment on Jake's face, on his mother's face, when he didn't show up to graduation.

Granger turned away from Trevor and walked back to his bed.

"Get out," he said to Levi.

The bedroom door opened and closed.

As he slid into bed and faced the wall he said to Trevor, "wake me up in time for church."

"Is that Trevor's shirt?" his mom asked first thing the next morning.

"It is," Granger said.

"It looks nice on you."

"It's a little tight."

"You should've told me you were out of clean clothes, I could've thrown them in the wash."

"I washed my clothes last night."

"Then why are you wearing Trevor's?"

"I needed something nicer to wear to church than my T-shirt and basketball shorts."

He purposefully kept busy pouring his coffee so he wouldn't see her reaction. But she must've put in extra effort to tone down her excitement, for his sake.

"You look nice," was all she said, though he could clearly hear a smile in her voice.

She was equally surprised to hear that her two oldest sons were joining them for the service.

"Wow! Alright then," she said, trying to maintain her composure. "Let's go!"

Jake seemed surprised but not disappointed. Whatever tension or disappointment he may have been feeling he was hiding behind his usual golden retriever disposition.

The church was a sanctuary with a hallway of classrooms flanking either side. The sanctuary had windows up near the tall ceiling that let in streams of sunshine. It smelled like new paint. The wood panel walls were glossy white, making the whole room bright.

"Do you remember it?"

Granger looked at Jake.

"Remember what?"

"The church."

"Should I?"

"It's the one we came to with Grandma and Grandpa."

"It looks a little different, though," his mom said. She pointed out many of the church's features and introduced the guys to even more people. All she needed was a vest and a little flag to lead them on their tour.

"Dude," Levi said to Granger under his breath, "you look like you're out for blood."

"I can't help it that I don't want to be here."

"Yes, you can."

"I'm here. Leave me alone."

Levi left his side, shaking his head.

Regardless of his standoffish behavior, a half a dozen smiling old ladies approached Granger one or two at a time to greet him and ask him about himself before the service started. His eyes lingered on the exit.

When Levi recognized a short, white-haired couple a few rows from the back he hurried over to them.

"How does he always know someone?" Trevor asked. "No matter where we go."

"Didn't he used to come every week with Grandma and Grandpa when he lived with them?" Jake asked.

"Oh, yeah."

Jake's posture was relaxed. He didn't seem to mind wearing a button-down or even the thin tie he was sporting.

"You've been coming for a while?" Granger asked, his eyes narrowed.

"Yeah. We like it."

Granger wanted to know why they'd started going to church again all the sudden. It didn't seem like the right time or place to ask, though.

While they waited for their mom to finish a seemingly endless conversation and lead them to their seats, Granger let his gaze float around the big room, which was how he spotted Nina, Luke, and Izzy across the sanctuary, beneath one of the high windows. They were in conversation with yet another elderly couple, and didn't see him. Aside from the Kyle brothers, Nina, Luke, and Izzy were some of the only younger people in the sanctuary, but it didn't look like it bothered them that much.

"Do you know Nina and Izzy Lanzo well?" Granger asked Jake.

"No, but I know who they are."

Levi was back from his visit and asked what they were talking about.

"I didn't recognize her at first, at the picnic," Levi said.

"You know her?"

"Yeah, she was maybe a year or two behind me, but we were in high school together. I know she dropped out before she finished. I'm surprised."

"Surprised at what?"

"Her. Her life. The fact that she goes to church. All of it."

Granger was about to ask why Levi found that surprising when it hit him.

"Whoa. No way," he muttered.

"What?" Trevor asked.

"I remember you telling us about her," he said, his eyes wide. "I *knew* she looked familiar."

"What do you mean?" Trevor asked.

"Is that the girl, then?" Granger asked Levi. "The one involved in that whole… scandal?"

"Yeah, that was her."

"What are you talking about?" Trevor asked.

Under his breath, Levi reminded them of the story. "The word on the street was that her boyfriend got her pregnant and then ran away, and might've gotten locked up for murder. The girl's parents were pastors somewhere in town and they kicked her out of their house when she got pregnant. She never came back to school."

"How do you remember that?" Trevor asked.

"How do you not?" Granger asked. "I remember everyone in school talking about it for weeks. People were saying all sorts of things about her: her boyfriend murdered someone, she helped her boyfriend murder someone, her boyfriend killed her parents…"

"Her boyfriend threatened to kill her, she killed her baby, she was in witness protection…" Levi added.

Trevor raised his eyebrows.

"Maybe you were sick that week," Levi speculated.

"I remember Luke missing a lot of school around that time. Everybody was talking about him, too," Granger said.

The three brothers glanced over at the Lanzo's without thinking. When they did, Nina was looking directly at them. The look on her face was the same nervous, uncertain one she'd given him at the picnic table the day before.

They averted their eyes.

"I think she knows we know," Granger mumbled.

"How? She can't hear us all the way over there," Trevor said.

"I think she's been waiting for us to figure it out," Granger said.

"What makes you say that?"

"I don't know," he lied.

"Poor girl," Trevor said.

"Don't say that," Granger said.

"Why not?"

"She wouldn't want pity."

"How do you know?" Levi asked.

Granger shrugged.

Finally, their mother finished talking and led them down the aisle to an empty pew.

"It's so weird, though," Granger said to Trevor. "I met her at the nursing home the other day. She's not at all what I imagined she'd be like."

"How so?"

"Don't you think someone with that kind of past would be more of an outcast? I mean, in this town at least?"

"I don't know, maybe."

"She seems so... I don't know... healthy. Normal."

Their conversation was interrupted by their mom, who leaned around Jake and asked Granger how he was feeling.

"Fine," he said, not understanding why she was asking.

"I know it's been a while since you were here. Just..."

Granger waited.

"No pressure, okay?"

"No pressure to do what?"

Her eyes darted around the room a little before she looked back at him, "I just don't want you to think I expect anything."

Granger still had no idea what she was referring to, but at that moment there was movement up front. A group of people, some with instruments and some without, took their places at the back of the platform while another man stood up at the front of it and addressed everybody.

Granger hadn't been in that church in about a decade, but as soon as he sat back and felt the stiff wooden pew pressing uncomfortably into every vertebrae, it felt more familiar. The hubbub died down and the people on the platform started playing their instruments and singing. He recognized the tunes of some of the songs, but none of the words. He wasn't much of a singer, anyway, so he busied himself with reading the words from the hymnal Jake was holding. Jake sang along whether he knew the song or not. During the music part of the service, Granger tried to figure out what it was about church that Jake and their mom were so drawn to. But that led to similar questions about Nina.

He couldn't figure her out. It was true, they'd only met a couple of days ago, but the picture of her that he had in his head, the one he'd formed from reports of her back in high school, did not seem to match the woman currently sitting across the sanctuary.

The pastor got up to speak and everybody sat down. It wasn't long before something about the sanctuary started making Granger drowsy, just like it had when he was a kid. He shifted in the pew. He yawned. He shifted again. It didn't matter that the pew was highly uncomfortable, he could've fallen asleep in five seconds if he let himself. He tried to pay attention to the sermon so he wouldn't nod off, but the preacher's voice was too calming. He had to let his mind wander to more interesting things or he would wind up slumped over, snoring.

He thought about Eugene and what the weather might be like for his trip back that afternoon. He thought about work and his promotion that hung in the balance. Finally, he thought about being back in Lester. Katie and her red hair briefly floated across his mind and he realized he hadn't been keeping his eyes peeled for her. A discreet look over the portion of the sanctuary he could see told him there were no red-headed females of the right age present. He only hoped the same was true for the pews behind him.

*She wouldn't be here. Although I never thought I'd be here...*

During his visual sweep of the sanctuary he saw Nina, Luke, and the top of Izzy's frizzy brown curls. Izzy wiggled every once in a while, and leaned over to her mom and her uncle, between whom she was seated, more than once to whisper something in their ears. He couldn't see Luke's face, but saw his shoulders shake slightly after one such Izzy-whisper. Aside from whenever Izzy needed to share something with her, Nina was attentive to the pastor's sermon. She seemed genuinely interested in what he was saying.

He didn't know her, he acknowledged that, but he could not figure her out. He was finding himself more and more intrigued by her, especially now that he knew who she was.

*Maybe Levi was wrong, maybe that was some other girl.*

But Granger now clearly remembered the pregnant girl being Luke Lanzo's sister. The two people were, in fact, one in the same.

Granger pulled his gaze back to the front of the room when he realized he'd been looking across the sanctuary for too long, just in time for the pastor to finish his sermon.

"That's it?" Granger asked Jake when they all stood.

"What'd you expect?"

"It felt a lot longer when we were kids."

# 19

"Granger, stand up," Grandma hissed.

He groaned, "Trevor was doing it, too."

"Trevor. Up. And stop fussing with your dress shirt. You can take it off as soon as we get home. It's just for a couple of hours."

Levi was standing on the other side of their grandma, uncharacteristically a perfect angel that morning in all of his ten-year-old glory. But Granger knew his secret: Before they left for church that morning, Granger overheard his mother promise Levi extra cookies for dessert if he 'set a good example for his younger brothers.'

"Granger, stop wiggling so much. You might run into somebody," Grandma said.

He squirmed more. "It's so itchy."

"It's not that itchy, you're just used to those real soft, cotton shirts. You'll itch more if you keep wiggling around like that. Try not to think about it."

They walked into the sanctuary and found themselves right at the back of a long line of people making their way steadily down the aisles to find seats. Levi looked down at the wiggly Granger out of the corners of his eyes, but kept his head straight ahead like a soldier.

Granger was going crazy; he couldn't stop scratching. Trying not to think about the itchiness only made him think about it more. He was only six, after all. Before his grandma could stop it, he lost his balance and stepped on Levi's toes.

"Ow! Hey!" Levi shoved Granger. Granger stumbled back and landed on his butt in the middle of the aisle.

"Ow!"

"Boys!"

"He stepped on my foot!"

"It was an accident!" Granger whined.

She pulled him to his feet. His sore rear end took his mind off the itchiness momentarily.

"Why couldn't I stay home with Mom and Jakey?" Granger asked.

"They're only staying home because Jakey is sick. You're not sick."

Granger faked a sneeze and a cough. She didn't even turn around.

They took their seats in a pew about halfway up the aisle. Granger didn't like how dark the sanctuary was. The wood panel walls made him sleepy, but his mom and grandma would never let him nap.

"But why not? At least I wouldn't get in trouble," he'd reasoned after church a few weeks earlier.

His grandmother had rolled her eyes, "do they let you nap in school?"

"Yeah. In preschool."

"You're not in preschool anymore."

Then she'd given him a chore to do before he could think of a good argument.

That day was the same as all the other Sundays. The sun streamed through the high, stained glass windows. The choir wearing dark green robes settled into the choir 'loft,' as his grandmother called it. Everywhere, old ladies in their 'Sunday best' slid into the pews. And just like every week, there were at least three gigantic hats blocking Granger's view when he sat down.

"I can't wait 'til I'm older," he mumbled. "I hate being short!"

"Oh, hush now," his grandma chided him.

He looked up at her and didn't know how she wasn't squirming from itchiness. She was wearing one of her two nice outfits, the outfits she only wore to church and weddings. The one at home was a light pink one with matching jacket and hat. This one was a light blue one with matching jacket and hat. Granger liked them only because they reminded him of cotton candy.

He slid back into the pew and winced when he remembered his injured rear.

Finally, the service started. And thus began the hour-long exercise in restraint, in which he was never successful. At least when everyone stood to sing he didn't have to be quite as still and he could whisper to Trevor without being overheard. But then the singing ended and the worst part began: the sermon. Suddenly, the itchiness was back with a vengeance. He wanted to rip off the dreadful crisp, long-sleeved, button-down shirt. After squirming in the pew and talking to Trevor got him in trouble another handful of times, Granger was made to sit right next to his grandmother: the seat of shame. That didn't solve the itching problem, though. He found a few creative ways to scratch without causing as much of a scene, but apparently it was still too much.

"Granger," his grandma whispered, lightly gripping his arm. "Just sit still."

"Itchy," he said through gritted teeth.

She studied him, then she sighed, checked her wristwatch, and looked back at Granger.

"Come with me," she whispered. "Levi, Trevor, stay here and behave."

Granger jumped up. He didn't know why they were leaving the sanctuary, but he was ecstatic. He followed her into the empty women's restroom where she set her handbag on the counter and opened it.

"Unbutton your shirt."

He unbuttoned faster than he'd ever done anything in his short life. He whipped his undershirt off next. After scrounging around in her purse, she pulled out a bottle of hand lotion and turned to face him.

She froze and her eyes widened.

"What?" he asked, instantly freaked out by her reaction.

He looked down at the red spots covering his torso.

"What is it?" he asked her, even more panicked. "Why are there spots?"

"Well, crap," was all she said.

He wasn't allowed to say that word. The situation must be really, really bad.

He started to cry.

*I'm going to die!*

She knelt down in front of him and helped him put his shirts back on, gingerly. "Shhh, it's gonna be okay. It's just chicken pox."

"The chicken pots?" Granger blubbered.

"Pox. Lots of kids get it."

"Am I gonna get better?"

She laughed softly, "yes, you will. But this lotion won't help much. We need to get you home."

Once he was re-dressed and calm he looked up at her.

"I'm sorry for getting after you, baby," she said.

This apology surprised him. "It's okay."

"Didn't your mom see the spots when she helped you get dressed this morning?"

He shook his head, "she only helped me button. She said to get dressed by myself today."

"I guess she was with the baby most of the morning, wasn't she?"

He felt better that she didn't seem shocked anymore.

"You said a bad word," he finally pointed out.

She laughed and picked up her handbag.

"I'm sorry. I wasn't expecting to see chicken pox. I was worried about it spreading."

But then her smile fell. "I wonder…"

"What?" Granger asked.

She led Granger back out to the foyer where she instructed him to stay put. About a minute later she emerged from the sanctuary with Levi and Trevor. She paused only long enough to check their chests and then she ushered them all out to the car. Trevor and Granger exchanged a glance once they were safely in the back seat, and Trevor offered Granger a sly grin. Granger grinned back, proud that he had single-handedly saved himself and his brothers from dying of boredom that day. But then he remembered how itchy he was and he was miserable again.

Later that afternoon, while Granger was getting bathed in oatmeal and covered in pink dots by his mother, his grandmother started on Levi, who was also covered in them. Levi confessed that he found them the day before but, scared of what they might be, said nothing. Even though Trevor got chicken pox the next day, it turned out to be a pretty great week for the boys. They got to miss school, get out of chores, and eat a few extra cookies.

It was one of Granger's best, and most miserable, memories of that church.

# 20

"YOU OKAY, HONEY?"

Granger looked up. He blinked away the memory until he remembered where and when he was.

His grandmother's face, with all the strength, solidity, and kindness that emanated from a bronze bust of Mother Teresa, vanished. His mother was looking at him with her tender, open-hearted hopefulness.

"Fine. We should get going."

"Oh. You looked like there was maybe something bothering you."

"I'm fine. Let's go. I gotta get out of town."

The five of them left the church behind and drove to the outskirts of town once more.

The nursing home felt the same as any other day of the week, except some of the older folks were in their Sunday best. As soon as they walked in the front doors, they were greeted by the sound of singing from down the hall.

"I wish your grandma could at least go to the services here," their mom sighed.

"Why can't she?" Levi asked.

"They tried a couple times but she got upset," Jake answered.

"I think it was too noisy and busy for her," their mom said.

"That's sad," Trevor said.

"Jake and I sometimes come and have a little service in her room with her on Sundays," their mom said. "But she doesn't seem to realize what's going on."

Granger couldn't remember his grandma ever missing church when he was a kid. To most people, his grandma and her dedication to her faith were synonymous. The ache in his chest came back.

She was sitting up at her table when they got there, with her back to the door. Someone had turned on a radio for her, and from it came the sounds of a man with a slow, baritone voice introducing the next hymn while an organ started up in the background. She was looking out the window at a hummingbird, bobbing her head and tapping her foot slightly. And then all of a sudden she opened her mouth and started singing along, matching the pitch and lyrics perfectly.

*When peace like a river, attendeth my way,*
   *When sorrows like sea billows roll;*
   *Whatever my lot, Thou hast taught me to say*
   *It is well, it is well, with my soul*

Granger, Levi, and Trevor looked at their mom and little brother, bewildered.

"How can she remember that?" Levi asked.

*But not remember us…*

"The nurse said," Jake began as they filtered into the room, "there are some things people with dementia can remember for a long, long time, even when they've forgotten most other things. Songs are one of those things."

Their conversation upon walking into the room had startled her a little.

"We shoulda knocked," Jake said. "I forgot."

"Good morning, Julia," their mom said in a chipper tone. "It's Allison and your grandsons."

His grandma's face lit up when she saw them.

"You!" she said, looking at each of them.

She recognized them, at least a little bit.

Granger blinked away the moisture in his eyes.

"Hi Grandma," they each said.

She didn't call anyone by name, which Granger knew he shouldn't hope for but did anyway, but reached out and grasped each of their hands one by one. Despite the dementia's fading and softening of her persona, her grip was still firm. After she'd greeted each of them, she turned back to the window. The hummingbird was gone now.

The room was uncomfortably crowded, but none of them offered to step out or suggested they take turns this time. They settled in as best they could, and another song came on the radio. Like with the last, she sang the opening verses.

"She seems so much more... peaceful..." Trevor said softly. "When we were growing up, I felt like she never sat still."

"She did," their mom said. "But you rarely saw it. It was usually early in the mornings or late at night. I'd find her sitting on the porch or at the kitchen table, very still."

"I saw it when I lived with them again senior year," Levi said. "I'd come in after midnight sometimes, thinking she and Grandpa were asleep, but she'd be up at the kitchen table still. I thought she was waiting up for me," he laughed, "to bust me for being out past curfew."

The room got very still. They sat and listened to the radio with their grandmother. But after awhile, Granger started to squirm in his seat. The ache grew the longer he sat there. His car was out in the parking lot, waiting for him. He could leave whenever he wanted. But he couldn't. It was like someone had cast a spell on the room, and everything hung suspended in midair, even time. They sat there, and an invisible force seeped in that was so thick it made it hard for Granger to breathe. Gravity pulled on him with a greater strength, from the inside out. He felt an aching in everything: in the inches between him and his family, in the room's furnishings, in the organ music that swelled over the radio waves, in the glass of the window, in the flowers and sunshine outside.

The force of it all had snuck up on him. He'd thought he was prepared when he arrived in Lester, thought he could handle it without being overcome by it. Because he *had* to be able to handle it without being overcome by it. But now...

Granger felt a flutter of panic deep down, even while the ache remained.

He stood.

His family, even his grandma, looked up at him. Levi's, Trevor's, and their mom's eyes were red and watery.

Granger cleared his throat.

"I need to get on the road."

No one responded. He was thankful no one protested.

The room felt off-balance to Granger as he waded through the thick emotion toward the door, toward the thinner air on the other side of it.

Seeing him move, the others finally stood, too.

Levi and Trevor said goodbye to him, but stayed in the middle of the room.

"Aren't you guys heading back now, too?" Granger asked, trying to keep the emotion out of his voice.

Levi looked back at their grandma. He put his hands in his pockets. "In a bit."

Granger didn't feel like prolonging the goodbye. He put an arm around his mother and gave her a quick hug. It wasn't quick enough for him, and it wasn't long enough for her. She looked down and wiped her eyes with the pads of her fingers as soon as he stepped away.

Granger caught Jake's eye. There was still disappointment in his little brother's face. They said goodbye with a handshake, and Granger moved on. He was almost done, almost free.

Granger hurried around the table and bent down to hug his grandma.

"Bye, grandma," he said. But his strained voice in that moment gave him away. "See you soon."

The song on the radio ended and the room got eerily silent as he stood up, waved once more, and stepped out of the room. He didn't stop walking.

*Faster.*

He moved through the halls feeling like he was in a dark tunnel, and all the people he passed were mere holograms hovering near the walls of it.

*Faster.*

This time, when he broke free of the building, he did not feel any freer.

# 21

HE WAS BACK IN EUGENE, right where he should be. Things could finally get back to normal.

And yet, a few weeks passed and he still didn't feel the relief he expected. So, he dove into his manager training, throwing himself into his work. When he woke up early with the remembrance of the grandma he'd left behind in Lester, he went to work and helped the scheduled employees bus tables, fill napkin holders, do the dishes, anything. He thought of his mom and Jake more in those few weeks than he had in the six years prior. Their looks of disappointment were seared into his brain.

*I shouldn't have gone back*, he thought to himself one early spring morning. *Things were going so well until I went back.*

Going home had made life messier, and he'd been a bus boy and a server and a dishwasher long enough to want to scrub all the messy things clean.

*I'll just have to pick up where I left off. I didn't backslide too much. I've got my promotion now, things are looking up already.*

He went straight home that night despite invitations from his coworkers to go out after work. He then declined his roommate's invite to join him and some friends for a late night movie. He felt too heavy, again, too weighed down by something that wasn't physically there.

"Hey, man," James said from the doorway of Granger's room. "Are you sure you're okay?"

Granger waved his roommate off, "I'm fine. Just tired. Have fun at the movie."

James ignored his answer. "Do you think maybe you should go back home again? You've been a little… off… since you got back."

"I'll go back when I can swing it with work," Granger said, stretching and yawning.

James thought for a moment, then slipped into the room and shut the door behind him.

Granger forced a laugh, "don't worry about me, man! Really! You should be worried about Deja waiting for you downstairs."

James didn't laugh. "You don't talk about your home or your family much, at least not since I've known you…"

"For good reason," Granger said, still trying to keep the conversation light.

James didn't crack a smile.

"I know it's your decision, and I don't know the whole story, but it looks a lot like you're avoiding things instead of confronting them. And it's not doing you any favors."

Granger felt a prick of annoyance toward his well-intentioned friend. James seemed to be able to read the annoyance on Granger's face because he backed toward the door with his hands up in defense.

"I just had to say it. I'd want someone to say it to me. Well, probably not, but I'd need someone to say it to me."

"Don't worry about it, man," Granger said again, trying to sound carefree, but sounding stern instead. "Thanks for checking in," he added, to be polite.

James nodded and left the room, clearly feeling the tension, too.

*Dang social workers.*

Granger laid in bed ready for sleep. Three hours later he was still staring up at the ceiling.

*It's a mental thing. I just need to get Lester out of my system and focus on the good things going on.*

He chewed on the idea of scheduling an appointment with his therapist. It would be his first one in a few years.

*I don't need to see Dr. Jenkins. Not for this. After all those years of monthly therapy appointments, I can handle this on my own.*

He spent all night trying to recall everything he could from his past therapy sessions that might help him. He was decided on one thing at least: going back to Lester wouldn't do him any good. He needed to stay in Eugene, where he'd been doing well for so many years. Next, he needed to fill his life with more good things to get past the bad. Yeah, that sounded like something Dr. Jenkins would say, although he couldn't remember a specific time when he'd actually heard the therapist say those exact words.

The next few days felt like breaking in a new pair of shoes: a little odd, a little uncomfortable, but getting better all the time. And then one night, after staring up at the ceiling for hours, worrying about his grandma and wondering how long she'd have left, Trevor's words floated through his mind:

*"I don't know, Grange, you're starting to sound like someone else we know."*

That was all it took to screw everything up.

Granger fought against the comparison. He refused to accept that he was anything like that low-life. He could think of a whole host of reasons why they were different.

But one by one, the similarities revealed themselves.

They both wanted to be free from Lester, and everything connected to it.

They both had made promises to come back, only to wait years to do so.

They both stayed away when the others wanted them to be there.

They both ran when things got hard.

*Unlike him, though, I haven't been exploiting them for my own selfish gain.*

As he laid in bed, even though he was exhausted and perpetually on the edge of sleep, thinking about that man made his heart pound loud and fast in his chest, his whole body tense, and his face get red and hot with anger.

In his mind (because if he'd let himself say them out loud, he would have yelled them, and James was trying to sleep in the adjacent room) he rattled off a list of his favorite choice words to describe his dad. He wished doing so would make him feel better, but it didn't. It never did.

*I am not him.*

*You sure about that? There's not a whole lot of proof to the contrary.*

*Just because I don't live there anymore doesn't mean I've hurt and abandoned my whole family.*

*Just think of the look on Jake's and Mom's faces. What other proof do you need?*

*No! He was the dad! He had more responsibilities! He had five children and a wife to think of and he didn't! But me? People leave their hometowns after high school all the time, that doesn't make them heartless ba—*

*Excuses, excuses.*

Therapy had done him some good, but he wished it hadn't made him so dang self-aware. The warring in his mind fatigued him and kept him awake all night long, again.

In the morning, he pulled himself up by his metaphorical bootstraps and trudged into work.

"You look horrible," his boss said, gruffly. "You hungover?"

"No, just not sleeping much lately."

"I didn't know you were an insomniac."

"Me neither."

"Well, since you're here early, we might as well get started on your training for the day."

"Fine by me."

And because his mental and physical fatigue had sapped all his remaining strength, he added, "and could we talk about my training schedule? I've got my little brother's graduation coming up…"

# 22

REMARKABLY, GRANGER FOUND HIMSELF DRIVING down Lester's Main Street once again. It was a bright and beautiful day. The sun passed behind the occasional cloud and the resulting contrast in light and temperature seemed to further animate the town. Summer was almost upon them and the town was seizing the opportunities that the warm weather afforded them, before the sweltering heat of July came and made them all lethargic.

At a stop light next to a tire store, where a sign reading "ConGRADulations Wyatt" hung in the front window, Granger wiped his right palm on his shorts. His heartbeat accelerated again.

*You've driven too far to turn around now. Come on, you did it once already. You can do it again.*

His family knew he was coming. Right after he'd gotten the 'OK' from his boss he'd texted his mom and shaken off the last of the guilt. The relief was as tangible as it was unexpected. The guilt was gone, but the discomfort at the idea of returning wasn't.

Granger kept driving.

*It's just a few days. I can do a few more days.*

He remembered his boss's words before he left:

*"It's a high school graduation? We coulda had this discussion months ago. Why didn't you say something sooner? A few days is all I can give you, then you'd better be back here or we are gonna have a problem."*

There wouldn't be a problem, because Granger wouldn't get delayed this time.

137

Jake was out front mowing the lawn when Granger pulled in. Jake saw him immediately, but took his time turning off the lawn mower, stretching out his back, and walking over to the driveway. He was stoic, but he was the first to extend a hand.

Granger shook it.

"I packed more clothes," Granger said, stuffing his right hand in his pocket.

Jake nodded.

"So I don't have to rush back so soon," Granger went on, as if that was the reason why he'd been in such a hurry to leave the first time.

Jake played along. "Nice. You wanna come in? I need some water."

"Sure. You want some help mowing?"

Jake looked around the yard with his hands on his hips. "You could finish mowing while I start in with the trimmer, if you want."

"Sure."

Granger didn't even take his things into the house before taking over the mowing. He was halfway across the yard before Jake came back out with two glasses of water. Granger wasn't thirsty, but he accepted it with a thank you and the two sipped and surveyed what was left to be done. Granger noticed new mulch, new planted bushes, and a spinny little lawn ornament.

"Looks nice," Granger said, not knowing anything about landscaping or whether the yard actually looked nice.

"Mom wanted it to look better than usual."

"Because of your grad party?"

"Because Janessa's coming."

Granger smiled. The two finished their water.

"I'm glad you got to come," Jake said.

"Me too," Granger said. He looked at the new grass stains on his tennis shoes. "Sorry about... y'know... the whole..." he couldn't find the words he was looking for.

"Don't worry about it," Jake said. And he seemed like he meant it.

Granger wiped some sweat off his brow and looked down at his empty glass, his throat dry.

"I'm sorry, too," Jake said.

"For what?"

Jake shrugged, "pushing you. Pressuring you."

"Don't worry about it."

In the awkward, quiet moment that followed, Granger busied himself with taking an extensive visual survey of the new mulch.

"We'd better finish the lawn before Janessa shows up," Granger said.

Jake nodded and grabbed the Weedwacker. The deafening silence was finally broken by the purr of yard tools.

Trevor, Levi, Janessa, and Elizabeth arrived all at once after dinner. The noise in the house tripled in an instant. Everyone was excited to see Levi's wife and baby girl, even Granger.

"She slept through the whole last half of the car ride, which was a miracle," Levi said, setting down the baby carrier as Elizabeth's uncles and Grandma Allison circled around. "So she's in a better mood now than you'll probably see all weekend. Enjoy it while it lasts."

Their mom and Jake laughed. Levi did not.

It was only once Levi knelt down to unfasten Elizabeth's seatbelt that they saw Janessa standing behind him.

"It's less than two hours from home but it feels like eight when she's screaming. I wish she was like those babies that find car rides soothing," Janessa said.

She dropped all the bags she was carrying, some of which landed with a loud thud, and then opened her arms wide and turned to Jake.

"You did it, Jake! End of senior year! How does it feel?"

"Like I have to go back in the fall."

"Soak up all your freedom!"

"I will! I'm glad you guys could come!"

"We wouldn't miss it!"

She turned to hug Trevor next.

"Trevor, how's work? Have they found a replacement for your coworker yet?"

"No, not yet."

"So you're still doing all her work, too?"

"I am."

"Hang in there, buddy."

"Thanks. I'll take all the encouragement I can get."

Granger looked over at Trevor. Were those dark circles under his eyes and not just a trick of the late evening light?

"I didn't know one of your coworkers left," Granger said.

"Yeah, in February."

"Is that Granger? The one and only?" Janessa squeezed through the small crowd. "How the heck are you, man?" She wrapped him in a hug.

"I'm good, how are you?"

"Tired, what else? It's been awhile! When were we last all together?"

"A few years ago, I think."

"At least. Good to see you."

He smiled. She turned away to hug the last person.

"Allison? Where'd she go? There you are. How are you, Mom?"

As Janessa moved from person to person, asking about their life and work and such, she yawned about every thirty seconds. Both new parents looked seconds away from sleep when they all finally settled in the living room.

"I like what you've done with the mulch out front," Janessa said to their mom. "That's pretty new, isn't it?"

"I told you she'd notice," their mom said to Jake.

The floral tattoos covering both of Janessa's arms from shoulder to wrist spoke of her enduring passion for all things gardening and landscaping, even though she'd sold off both of her businesses in the last few years.

When it got late enough, their mom left to go rock her granddaughter to sleep, and Janessa could hardly keep her eyes open, so she turned in not long after. Granger looked around the room at Jake and Trevor sprawled out on the couch, and Levi who was lying flat on his back on the floor. He was tempted to go to bed when the silence set in, afraid of any sort of awkwardness that might follow. But then the image of Nina Lanzo and her own brother, talking and laughing together, still close after the things they'd gone through, flashed across his mind.

Granger glanced at all three of his brothers, all together again.

He picked a topic at random.

"You got lucky," Granger said.

Levi opened one eye to see that Granger was addressing him.

"What makes you say that?" he asked groggily from the floor.

"Janessa. I've always thought she was way cooler than you."

Levi chucked his dirty sock at Granger's smirking face.

"But seriously," Granger said, "your life seems so stable now compared to ten years ago. You guys are good together. You got lucky."

Levi closed both eyes again. "I disagree. Luck had very little to do with it."

"You don't think you got lucky meeting Janessa?"

"Meeting her? Maybe. But everything after that was a lot of hard work."

"You make it sound so romantic."

"It is. But not all the time. You know she almost called off our wedding?"

The three of them looked at Levi in surprise.

"True story. About a month before we got married."

"What happened?" Granger asked.

"I was nervous about the wedding, because... y'know... marriage... and I started to run."

"You were going to leave her at the altar?" Jake asked.

"No, not like that. I mean the closer we got to the wedding, the more often I would disappear and kind of go off the deep end. Like, one day I just decided to go skydiving. I found this company who would take me up that same day. It was a shoddy company, and they probably should've been closed down. They almost forgot to give me a helmet, and I almost landed in a tree."

Trevor opened his eyes at that, "you what?"

"And one weekend, me and an old high school buddy took a spontaneous road trip to Las Vegas and I only told Janessa I was going when we were crossing the state line from Kansas into Colorado. I missed two wedding planning appointments and one of our pre-marital counseling sessions."

"Yikes," said Jake.

"Before that, I went bungee jumping with a harness that didn't fit right. I put a lease on a motorcycle. I bet a couple thousand on a horse race. I signed up for this super intense obstacle course race. I did anything and everything."

"How did you afford all that?" Jake asked.

"I didn't. I put it all on a credit card. I was about to get married and saddle my wife with a butt-load of shiny new debt."

"Nice wedding present," Trevor said from his end of the sectional sofa.

"And that's why she almost called off the wedding?" Granger asked. "Because of the debt?"

"No. She almost called it off because she saw me react like Mentos in a Coke bottle as soon as I got a little uncomfortable and scared."

"She was afraid you'd do that kind of stuff whenever you got too stressed?" Trevor asked.

"Yeah. She didn't know what to do with me. I think it really freaked her out. And she doesn't get freaked out easily. A month before our wedding she called me when I was on my way back from Las Vegas, and said we needed to talk as soon as I got back to town. She gave it to me straight."

"What changed her mind?" Trevor asked.

"Honestly? I don't know. It doesn't make any sense, even now. She's a smart woman. We were this close to splitting and she had every reason to do it. But at the end of that conversation, something changed. Obviously, I promised I'd get some help, and I have, but that promise alone shouldn't have been enough. She had no reason to believe I wouldn't do it again, but she did."

"She knew about all that stuff from the beginning of your relationship, though, didn't she?" Granger asked. "Your old anger problems and your recklessness and stuff?"

"Yeah, she did."

"And... she was okay with that? Even when she saw that you weren't, like, cured?"

"She's never expected me to have all my crap together. And don't get me wrong, she's wonderful. I love her. But she's got her own problems, too. She's not perfect, either. We've learned to work together. I think that's why our problems don't get worse."

Granger couldn't help his mind from wandering to Katie, and their last few fights as a couple.

"I don't think I've ever heard you talk about your marriage before," Granger said.

Trevor and Jake echoed his statement.

"You've never asked," Levi said lightly.

Later that night as Granger lay in his old bed again, he thought about Levi and Janessa. He hadn't meant to open up that particular conversation, but it was interesting food for thought. To a stranger, the couple would seem like a match made in fair-trade-coffee-drinking, vegan-eating, yoga-loving, peace-advocating, long-hair-and-tattoo-having heaven. But the strangers wouldn't know about Levi's jail time, or both of their unstable childhoods, or Levi's anger management problems, or their mountain of debt. Granger had underestimated both of them. The first time Levi brought Janessa home, Granger was convinced their relationship would last about as long as Levi's ability to manage his anger. But he'd been surprised on both fronts.

The most surprising thing was, despite everything, their relationship wasn't just surviving, it was strong. Granger didn't get it.

The three older brothers were finishing lunch the next day when from down the hall their mom exclaimed:

"Oh no!"

"What?" Levi yelled back through a big chunk of his sandwich.

"Lillian can't make it."

"I didn't know she was gonna come," Granger said.

"Of course she was," their mom said. "It's her brother's graduation."

None of the brothers were close with their half-sister. She was ten years older than Granger, and she'd spent most of her childhood, especially after the boys' mom kicked their dad out, with her own mom in Chicago.

"She really wanted to come but the kids came down with the stomach flu."

"Did she come to all of our graduations?" Granger asked.

"I don't think she came to mine," Trevor said.

"That's because she was in labor," their mom said.

Jake appeared in the doorway in a navy blue cap and gown. "Did you say Lillian can't come?"

"I told you to iron your gown, it looks like you just took it out of the plastic bag! There are big square creases all over it."

"Jake's clearly the favorite son, he doesn't have to wear the hand-me-down one," Levi said.

"This is the hand-me-down one," Jake said.

"It looks brand new," Levi said.

"All three of you wore that exact cap and gown," their mom confirmed. "And now it's Jake's turn!"

"Why did you fold it back up after Granger's graduation? Why not just hang it in a closet?" Jake asked.

"Go iron it," she replied. "Hurry, please."

Jake groaned, "I'm going to be late!"

Janessa came out of the guest room trying to hold onto a squirmy Elizabeth.

"Let's get this show on the road," she said. Her face was flushed and her previously relaxed but tidy hair-do now looked disheveled. She handed Elizabeth off to Levi, who had just enough time to shove a baby carrot into his mouth before his hands were full of his eighteen-month-old.

Janessa shed her vegan leather jacket and fanned herself. "I should've waited to get ready until after I got her ready," she said. She lifted her thick blonde braid off her tanned shoulder and leaned over the sink to open the window and soak up the breeze.

Elizabeth shrieked and started writhing around. Her dad's arms strained to keep a hold of her but she had the intensity of both her parents combined, which made his attempt futile. He set her down on the floor where she kicked and screamed.

"What'd you do?" Granger asked.

"I wouldn't let her eat the plastic bag on the counter!" he said, barely audible above her screaming.

"We'll wait outside," Granger shouted to the rest of the family, and he and Trevor hurried to the front door.

They could still hear the noise inside the house from outside, but Granger smiled and laughed as he shook his head.

Granger tensed up at the football field. He kept his head down while the family walked up the ramp to the metal bleachers. He wished he'd brought his baseball cap. Eventually, the temptation to look grew until he gave in and peeked at the growing crowd. He was surprised to see so many unfamiliar faces, and so many faces in general. It was hard to find enough space for the six of them to sit together.

As it got closer and closer to the start of the ceremony, Granger watched hundreds of people flood in. He got less and less nervous about bumping into someone he knew.

"How big was his class?" he asked his mom.

She looked down at the ceremony program in her hand, "five hundred and fifteen."

He raised his eyebrows.

"How big was mine?"

"Um, I think about two fifty. It was just a little bigger than Trevors."

"Why is his class so huge?"

"They're all this big now, or bigger. Lester's grown a lot since you left."

"How? Why?"

"It's a nice town to raise a family in," she said. "What's Eugene like these days?"

He shrugged, "pretty much the same as when I first moved there."

"Do you still like it there?"

"Yeah, that's why I still live there."

He regretted how cold that sounded.

"I like how alive it feels. It's not a whole lot bigger than Lester but it's all so new and young and there's lots to do."

This was evidently more information than his mom had been expecting to get out of him, and she looked pleased about it.

Granger turned to talk to Trevor so he wouldn't have to keep making small talk with her. He was already getting irritable from the heat, and he was afraid he'd say something rude again.

Janessa leaned around Levi. "So, Granger," she said, "what's the story? What's been keeping you in Eugene so long? Why haven't we seen you much?"

Granger swallowed and fidgeted on the bleachers ever so slightly. "Work. I've been really busy."

"For six years?"

"Well, you know how life gets."

"Uh, huh," she narrowed her eyes. "You work at a restaurant?"

"Yeah."

"Do you own it?"

"No, but I did just get promoted to manager."

"I heard! Congrats!"

She wasn't done scrutinizing him.

"How's life going for ya?" she asked.

"Not bad. Can't complain."

"Tell me about it," she urged.

"Yeah, I'd like to hear, too," Levi said.

Trevor leaned forward to listen, too.

Granger felt restless. "You know, it's just life. I work at the restaurant. I work a lot."

"And... friends?" Janessa asked.

"Yeah, I have friends."

"And... do you do anything fun?"

"Yeah, my friends and I hang out when we can."

"... And anything else?"

"That's pretty much it."

"Well I can see why you wouldn't want to leave all that excitement," Janessa said.

Elizabeth started squirming again and her parents discovered she needed another diaper change, so Granger was spared further interrogation by his sister-in-law. He relaxed again. Until he felt Trevor looking at him.

"What?" Granger asked.

"Everything all good?" Trevor asked.

"Yeah, it's fine," he said, nonchalantly.

Trevor was quiet for a minute and then, in his unobtrusive way, asked, "is life pretty stressful these days?"

Granger could answer that easily and honestly.

"Not really. Life in Eugene is pretty chill."

Another minute passed, then Trevor asked, "do you still go to therapy?"

Granger felt his teeth clench together. "No."

Trevor didn't press.

Granger could feel himself getting sunburnt as the afternoon progressed, and the aching in his back and butt from slouching on the bleachers intensified. He wasn't the only one leaning this way and that, slouching and straightening, stretching his legs out and crossing them again, as the day wore on.

"I think she's getting too hot," Granger heard Janessa whisper to her husband. They were taking turns holding a sleeping Elizabeth and wiping beads of sweat from their foreheads.

"I'm gonna take her to the car," she said. "Where are the keys?"

Levi handed them to her and started to stand.

"You stay. They'll be calling his name soon. Hopefully."

When a bead of sweat dripped off of his own eyebrow, Granger wished he had volunteered to take his niece out to the shaded parking lot and air conditioned car. Now, he was stuck frying like an egg on the metal bleachers.

The ceremony lasted hours. Hours. But eventually every name was called and every navy-clad student was holding a diploma. After an agonizing, ten-minute long descent of the bleachers behind hundreds of other families, they met Janessa and Elizabeth who were busy napping in the cool car.

They heard Jake's raspy voice calling to them from across the parking lot. He came over to them beaming, even though he had huge sweat stains under his arms and down his back.

"Thank goodness it's over!" he said.

"And thank goodness you're the last person who has to wear that gown," Granger said.

Jake was in heaven, getting to introduce everyone he knew to everyone else he knew. Granger met so many of Jake's friends and classmates that he lost count after fourteen. Their mother took pictures constantly.

"My last one," she said tearfully when he showed her his diploma.

"Aw, come on, mom," he said, hugging her.

"Alright, family picture," Janessa announced. "Everyone get together."

"Aren't you gonna be in it?" Jake asked.

"First, you five," she said, setting Elizabeth's baby carrier down at her feet.

It felt weird to line up alongside them all, huddling together and smiling for the camera after all that time had passed. It felt unnatural, though they'd done the very same thing many times before.

Jake snagged a passing friend to take a picture of them all. Janessa grabbed Elizabeth and they slid into place next to Levi, who reached for his daughter. Granger watched his brother with his family.

Granger hadn't spent this much time around him since Levi's days of street racing on the outskirts of town during math class, getting suspended for his outbursts at school, and disappearing for twenty hours at a time, only to return home in the middle of the night unable to walk straight and covered in strange injuries. If nothing else could convince Granger that Levi might have really changed since then, seeing him with his stable, happy little family might.

*Click.*

Everyone stepped apart.

"I should head back to the house," their mom said as if she was just talking to herself. "I still have a lot to do to get ready for the cookout tonight. I need to run to the store for a few more things first, though."

Granger felt that nudge inside again.

"I can go to the store for you," he offered.

"You don't have to do that," she said, waving away his request. "I don't mind."

"I'll go. What do you need?"

As he expected, she didn't argue further. She pulled out her folded up list and handed it to him.

"I'll go with Granger," Trevor said.

"Thank you, both," she said. "For the napkins and plates... Jake, what color did you say you wanted? Blue?"

But Jake wasn't paying any attention to them. He was looking at something in the distance just past Granger's right ear. It was the look on Jake's face that made Granger turn around.

There was a man watching them from a few yards away.

Granger's blood turned ice cold.

# 23

THE WORLD AROUND THEM SLOWED to an agonizing pace, and then tilted on its axis a few degrees too many. For a few seconds, Granger couldn't make sense of what he was seeing.

The muscles in his right arm tensed up, and then he felt pain. But not in his right arm… in his left arm. He looked down at it. It was still hanging by his side, completely limp. He touched his left forearm; he couldn't feel his fingertips on his skin. But still, he felt pain.

He looked back up at the man, who was still looking at all of them. The man took one step forward.

Granger took a step backward without thinking, and swore.

"What are you doing here?" Granger demanded.

His mom didn't chastise him for his language. The whole family stood just as still as him, looking at the man with wide eyes and pale faces.

The man staring back at them with an almost sheepish look on his unrefined, stubbled face was no taller than Granger, but he had Trevor's dark hair, Jake's thick eyebrows, and a gaze as intense as Levi's. He was under a tree with his hands in his pockets, walking forward very slowly.

"Just thought I'd come see my boy graduate," he said.

He looked from pale face to pale face, and offered them something resembling a half smile. Granger snapped like the first crack in a glow stick. His legs shot him forward.

"Get out of here. Now," he said.

"You shouldn't be here," Levi added, still holding his daughter.

"You saw the ceremony?" Jake asked. His voice was quieter than the others, and raspier than normal.

Dave appeared to relax a little at Jake's question.

"Whole thing," he said. The man turned and nodded toward the football field fence. "From right there."

The top of Dave's forehead did indeed look freshly sunburnt.

He took another couple steps toward them.

"You need to leave right now," Granger shouted, throwing his right hand out in front of him as if he could arrest Dave's momentum without physical contact.

Dave froze. They never broke eye contact.

"You weren't invited. Leave," Granger said. He didn't expect his voice and hand to shake like they did.

"Actually, I kind of was." Dave said it in such a congenial way, Granger felt the glow stick crack a couple more times.

The hair on the back of Granger's neck stood on end. He lost his voice. Completely dissociated from his body, he watched the man approach them. His feet remained frozen until Dave stepped off the curb.

"I'm warning you!" Granger yelled, advancing several purposeful steps. He felt a hand on his right arm. It was his mother's.

She was holding him back.

Granger stared at her, fully realizing what Dave had just said.

He looked from his mom to his dad and back.

"Did you... invite him?" he choked out.

"Not exactly," she said. "Not to the ceremony."

Dave said something, maybe an apology for showing up so unexpectedly, Granger didn't hear it. His head started to pound. He withdrew his arm from her grasp and backed away from her.

"You invited him?" he asked again, feeling the knife dig into the place between his shoulder blades.

"Granger, just listen, please," she said.

He did not.

He ran to his car, jumped in, and peeled out of the parking lot.

As soon as he got behind the wheel, the headache got worse. He knew he shouldn't be driving; he could barely see. He winced and gasped with the pain that started behind his eyes, ran down his chest, and shot into his paralyzed arm. Once out of sight of the football field, on one of the lesser-traveled country roads nearby, he slammed on his brakes and threw the car in park. Unable to see anything, he grasped desperately for the door handle, found it, and shoved the door so hard that he fell onto the gravel.

He gasped and wheezed on his hands and knees.

It felt like his heart was coming out of his chest, or being squeezed into a thousand pieces. He clutched at his chest. He wasn't sure what would kill him first, the pain or the fear.

He collapsed with his back against the front tire of his car, and waited for the heart attack to end him. But when it didn't, he realized what was going on. Against the pain and fear, he forced himself to breathe very, very, very slowly.

Eleven minutes later, the pain started to ease and some clarity returned.

*Panic attack.*

His heart rate started to slow.

He focused on the quiet of the flat, treeless farmland around him, on the metal hubcap behind him and the hard gravel under him, on the smell of grass and dirt, on the heat from the sun. And he sent up a silent prayer of thanks to God for Dr. Jenkins, who'd taught him to do all that.

His eyesight still hadn't returned, though.

*Oh wait.*

He opened his eyes.

*Oh good.*

He was okay. He was covered in dust and pock marks from the gravel, but he was okay.

Just as he acknowledged this, he heard another car coming down the road. When it pulled up beside him, Levi and Trevor got out of it.

"He's gone," Levi announced to Granger.

"Are you okay?" Trevor asked.

Granger took another deep breath. His older brothers approached him, towering above. His face reddened and he looked down at the ground.

They were close enough now to see the situation; him on the

ground all dirty, his car in the middle of the road still running with the door wide open.

"Are you okay now?" Levi repeated, squatting right in front of Granger.

Granger nodded.

"That wasn't cool of him. At all," Levi said. "He shouldn't have come. And she shouldn't have invited him."

"No," Trevor agreed. "But he's gone now."

Granger nodded. He looked down at his shoes.

Trevor and Levi surveyed their surroundings, letting the silence envelope them, too. Then they sat down in the gravel.

"You'll get your clothes dirty," Granger pointed out to Trevor.

"I can wash them."

Granger's face got even redder, sitting with the two of them like that. He couldn't look either of them in the eye.

"I almost hit him," Levi muttered after a bit. "If I hadn't been holding Elizabeth, I probably would've."

Granger looked up at Levi, who was looking out in the distance with a hardened expression on his face. Some of Granger's mortification faded at the realization that his brothers were as shaken up by, and engrossed in their own thoughts of, the situation as he was.

"You should've," Granger said.

Levi just shrugged.

It was quiet again, but then Granger sighed and amended his statement, "no, it's good you didn't."

"Probably," Levi grumbled.

"What happened after I left?" Granger asked.

"Not much. He left a minute after you did. He finally seemed to get that we didn't want him there."

Granger shook his head. It was unbelievable.

After a little while, Levi stood.

"You feeling okay now?" he asked.

His legs shook, but Granger was able to stand on his own.

"Should we head back?" Levi asked.

Granger nodded.

"I can drive your car," Trevor said with a look at Granger's trembling hand.

Granger didn't protest.

"Someone still needs to go to the store for mom," Levi said.

"We can still go," Granger said. He wouldn't mind some more time before facing his mother.

It was a quiet ride to the grocery store. But when Trevor rejoined Granger near the entrance with a shopping cart, Granger voiced his thoughts.

"He's gotta be here for money. He only ever wants money."

Trevor thought about this. "What about the last time he came around?"

"He was just easing his own conscience, trying to feel less guilty. And I'm still not convinced he wasn't also after some money."

"Maybe."

They wandered down the first aisle.

"Jake's too old for something custody-related," Trevor mused. "But I guess they're not even technically divorced…" He leaned his forearms on the grocery cart as they moved along, his eyes looking glassy.

"It's gotta be money, then…" Granger swiveled around and looked at Trevor with wide eyes. "What if he's trying to get Grandma's house?"

"Her house," Trevor repeated, trying the idea on for size.

"Yeah. It's got to be worth something. The house plus the land."

"She would've already decided who the house and land are going to. In her will."

Suddenly, Granger was a little keener for Levi to get his hands on that will and decipher all the legal jargon for them. Surely she wouldn't have left Dave anything too big or valuable.

"I doubt he's thought of that. He doesn't have the brains."

"I think he does," Trevor said. "He managed to hide a lot. For years."

They found the hamburger buns and Granger started piling packages into the cart. His hand had finally stopped shaking.

"Well, even if he does know that, he can't possibly make any changes to her will now. Can he?"

"I don't think so." Trevor's brow furrowed like he was thinking hard, then he exhaled. "I wish I knew more about that kind of stuff."

"We'll ask Levi when we get home."

Trevor looked down at the cart. "That's probably enough."

Granger looked down. "How many do we need?"

"40 buns."

"How many is that?"

Trevor did the math quickly. "96."

"Oh."

They returned most of them to the shelf and then moved onto the next thing on the list, each getting lost in their own thoughts as they walked the aisles. Granger wandered back into dangerous territory. The longer Granger thought about what had happened after the ceremony, the more rapid his breathing became again. He got more and more tense, but this time, he felt another emotion. An emotion he was more used to: anger. He was mumbling a long string of strong synonyms for 'jerk' when he made eye contact with a lady reaching for some two liters on a high shelf just as he was.

She froze.

"Not you!" he said. "Sorry."

She pulled the two liters down quickly and walked away with a huff.

"He really wasn't talking about you, ma'am," Trevor called after her. But she was already in the next aisle over.

They headed to the frozen food section for lemonade.

"I thought he was still in prison," Trevor said under his breath.

"So did I. He should be. I always thought he got off too easy."

They walked in silence for a few more minutes, only talking when trying to remember which chips their mom wanted.

"What was she talking about?" Granger asked. "She knew he was coming?"

"Sure sounded like it."

Granger felt his chest start to tighten again.

"What was she thinking?" he growled. "That woman—"

"Watch it," Trevor warned.

"She shouldn't have—"

"I know."

"How could she?"

"I don't know."

"Why aren't you as angry about this as the rest of us?"

"Who says I'm not?" Trevor put a couple packages of ground beef in the cart.

Granger considered Trevor. Trevor had always been an even-keeled kind of guy, but had he been acting more subdued than usual lately?

Granger didn't dwell on the thought too long, there were other things that needed to be dealt with. It didn't matter how deeply he breathed, his body remained tense, and he felt that dark cloud stretching over him again.

*I gotta get out of town. ASAP.*

"It is interesting…" Trevor said.

"What is?"

"That he showed up for graduation. It's a big milestone for Jake, and he was actually there for it."

Granger didn't like Trevor's tone. It sounded almost optimistic.

"He showed up on their fifteenth wedding anniversary, too. Remember? And then the next day he left for Bermuda and we didn't see him for three months. And he showed up for your sixteenth birthday. High. He stayed for a week and then we didn't see him for eight months."

"I know, but… what if he's really changed?"

Granger laughed.

"I'm serious."

"Oh, he's definitely changed. Didn't you see him? You used to be the spitting image of him. Prison really did a number on him."

"You think prison could affect the outside that much without affecting the inside?"

Granger's smile faded and his eyes narrowed. "What are you saying?"

Trevor hesitated. "I'm just curious…"

"Are you kidding me right now?" Granger asked.

Trevor looked away and moved further down the aisle.

"You would give him another chance to let you down just to see if he's really changed?"

"Why shouldn't I?" Trevor challenged. "Do any of us really deserve second chances?"

"He's way past second chances."

The two brothers eyed each other. Since the moment Granger had seen his dad standing across the parking lot, his sights were set on one thing and one thing only: Eugene. His home, sunny and happy and drama-free, beckoned him.

But if Trevor and their mom still couldn't see Dave for who he was... If they were willing to let him back in again... If they still hadn't learned their lesson...

*Haven't I had to deal with enough, without this? If I leave Lester, at least Jake and Levi will be here to talk some sense into the other two.*

But what about when Levi left in a day? Would Jake be as steadfast as he needed to be to keep Dave away from them? Granger never thought Trevor would be having second thoughts about Dave, but if he was, could Jake be having them, too?

*This isn't my responsibility. They're all adults. They can fend for themselves. If they want to let Dave wreak more havoc, so be it.*

That settled it. He would leave right after the party that evening.

"Is that everything?" Granger asked.

"Almost. We need plates and napkins. I don't know what aisle they're in. Why don't you look over here and I'll look over there."

Granger found them quickly, but couldn't remember what color he was supposed to get. He waited for Trevor to find him, but after five minutes he was still standing alone in the paper products aisle. People were starting to give him weird looks as they passed by. He'd just resolved to go find Trevor when Trevor rounded the corner. As he turned, Granger saw something fall to the floor right next to him.

Maybe the thing had slid off the slippery hamburger bun packages in the cart, or maybe Trevor had knocked something off one of the end-cap displays. Or maybe something had worked its way up and out of his pocket. Trevor picked the thing up and shoved it into his pocket so smoothly and quickly that Granger could've convinced himself he'd imagined the whole thing.

But the object looked familiar.

So familiar that Granger immediately pretended he hadn't seen it.

And suddenly a new door opened, behind which was a room full of new things to wonder and worry about.

Granger cleared his throat and tried to sound normal. "What color plates did Jake say?"

Trevor thought about it. "He never said."

They loaded up with blue plates and napkins and went to the

check-out. The whole time, Granger wondered if Trevor knew that Granger knew what was in his pocket. He probably did. A bright orange prescription pill bottle was hard to miss.

Granger didn't have enough mental space to deal with more than one big problem at a time. So, he decided:

*If Trevor hasn't mentioned it, I won't ask about it and I won't worry about it. It's probably just… prescription allergy medicine. Yeah. It is the season for it.*

And with that, Granger shoved one problem out the car window as they drove and let the other problem take up all the space.

It was the most eery party-preparation atmosphere Granger had ever experienced, not that he'd thrown a lot of parties in his life. The brothers were clearly all thinking about Dave, as evidenced by their very purposeful evasion of the topic and the extended periods of silence. Their mother did not broach the subject, but scurried from room to room under the guise of 'needing to finish getting everything ready before the guests came.'

In the few minutes the family had alone together between the party prep and the arrival of their guests, their mother answered Levi's direct question, assuring them Dave would not be at the cookout. That didn't stop any of them from looking up every time the front door opened, though. It wouldn't have been the first time Dave showed up without an invitation.

It felt strange to be at a party after the day they'd had. That morning Granger had actually been doing okay, and then he was facing his father, and then he was on his hands and knees in some gravel trying to remember how to breathe, and then he was seeing Trevor come back from the pharmacy section of a grocery store carrying a bottle of pills. Now, he was serving hamburgers to people he'd never met. He was tired, to say the least.

Jake managed to maintain his trademark, smiling sociability throughout the duration of the party, but when the front door shut behind the last guest, a shadow fell over his face.

Levi and Janessa were washing dishes and talking quietly when the others entered the kitchen. Levi pulled his hands out of the soapy water and leaned against the counter while he dried them. Trevor finished covering a tray of cookies with plastic cling wrap. Jake pulled out a chair from the kitchen table and plunked down in it. Granger, yawning, remained where he was by the fridge, knowing if he sat down he'd spend the whole night there. Janessa peeked over her shoulder and set down the bowl she'd been drying.

"You don't have to leave, Janessa," their mom said wearily.

"It's okay," Janessa said. She gave their mom a smile and a tender squeeze on the shoulder, then headed back to the guest room where Elizabeth was already sleeping.

The brothers hardly breathed as they waited. The sound of the frogs in the nearby creek came in through the open window above the sink. Their mom studied her hands. With her head tilted down, the dark circles under her eyes were more prominent. From that angle, Granger could also see how thin her face was getting. He looked down at the floor, too.

"Your dad contacted me a few weeks ago," she said. "At first I was suspicious, but he wasn't asking for anything. He just kept reaching out to ask how we were and to tell me what he'd been up to recently."

"Which is..." Levi prompted. He had his arms crossed over his broad chest, and his expression was hardened again.

"He got out of prison in December. He's been working in a bottle factory in the city, and making good money. And he's been clean the whole time, too."

"He would have to be," Levi said. He set the hand towel, now folded, on the counter instead of looking at her. "As part of his parole."

"Maybe so," she said. "But that counts for something, doesn't it? He's doing what he's supposed to. He's working on himself."

She got quiet again. Granger looked at her. She was chewing the inside of her lip and staring at the linoleum floor. There was no fight left in her. She was like a broken slap bracelet: curled up inside herself indefinitely. Granger didn't know how her frame could hold her up any more. He was on the verge of pulling up a chair for her to sit in, until he remembered what had made her this way. And now, yet again, she wanted to let the culprit back in.

"So then what?" Granger asked.

She took a deep breath. "I was careful." Her eyes flicked to Granger's. "I really was. After a few weeks it seemed like he was really in a better place than he used to be. That's when he asked if he could come visit. He didn't know you three didn't live in Lester anymore, so I told him. But I knew you'd be here for graduation. Or, at least, I hoped you would be."

She rubbed one hand over the other, making her knuckles red, in stark contrast to her fair, nearly translucent complexion.

She shook her head. "He wasn't supposed to come to the ceremony."

The brothers remained silent, and Granger wondered if they were biting their tongues as hard as he was. The frogs soloed again, and Granger was about to mount his soap box when Levi spoke.

"When were you going to tell us?"

"Tonight. I wanted everyone to enjoy the ceremony and the party, first."

"He's never showed up at the right time before. Why start now?" Granger said.

"I think he's really changed," she said.

He glared at her. "Forgive me if I don't believe you."

She looked like she'd touched a hot burner on the stove.

"How long will he be here?" Trevor asked.

"I'm not sure. I think a few days."

"What do you want us to do?" Levi asked.

"The plan was for him to just come by once or twice while you're all here. Starting tomorrow. We didn't make any specific plans. But if you're not comfortable with it…"

Granger let out a low, humorless laugh.

"Doesn't seem like we have much of a choice," Levi said, speaking for all of them.

"You do! And you don't have to… I mean… I know you'll never have a perfect relationship. I'm not expecting… I just think this could be good. You're all adults now. We've all had some time to… recuperate."

Granger caught both Trevor and Jake sneaking a peek at him.

"If he's really changed—" Levi said.

"He hasn't," Granger said.

"—I guess we'll find out," Levi said.

Granger looked up at Levi, who was giving a pointed look to Granger. Granger wished he could read the expression, but he couldn't. Now Levi was buying into all this, too? Levi?

"So, you'll give him another chance?" she asked.

Levi shrugged.

"You've got to be kidding me," Granger said to Levi.

*What the heck is happening to these people?*

But then Levi turned his back to them all and dunked the potato salad serving spoon in the soapy water. Trevor slowly straightened. He gave their mom a limp hug before walking down the hall. Jake stood, gave her a quick kiss on her cheek, thanked her for the party, and went to bed.

She looked across the kitchen at Granger, her grayish eyes barely meeting his.

"You're making a mistake," he said.

"What if I'm not?"

"Mom—"

"When someone throws you a lifeline, you take it," she said.

"What do you mean?"

"We need something. Some sort of closure, or healing."

"We're doing fine."

"No, you're not."

The fire in his stomach didn't need much kindling, but he couldn't risk burning her even more. By the looks of her, she was right about one thing: she needed a lifeline. He couldn't just rip it right out of her hands.

*But maybe…*

The wheels started turning in a different direction.

*Maybe I can toss her a different lifeline.*

He pushed himself off from the wall where he'd been leaning with a giant exhale, feeling suddenly thrice his age. As he passed her, he reached out with his good hand and patted her arm once.

"I'm only doing this for you," he said, mustering as much compassion into his tone as he could. "Go to bed, mom."

"There's more to clean up, first."

"I'll do it. You need some rest."

She looked over at Levi. He nodded. "We'll take care of it. Get some sleep."

Granger and Levi were up an extra hour, cleaning. Granger finally fell into bed, glad he didn't decide to drive the five hours back to

Eugene after the party. Of course, as so often happens, there was a disconnect between his mind and body that night: his body wanted to sleep, his mind was wide awake.

He wasn't going to leave in the morning, he'd decided that. There was a lot to be done in Lester before he could head back home. But he also wasn't ready to face Dave again, even with a warning. That dark cloud over Granger was growing bigger and darker by the minute. He was fully aware he was about to do something he'd sworn he'd never, ever do, and for good reason. Eventually sleep overtook him, but only because the anxiety and physical tension in his body wore him out after several hours.

# 24

GRANGER AWOKE THE NEXT MORNING with the feeling that he'd dreamt everything that happened after the graduation ceremony. Unlike a dream, though, the memory became clearer the more he woke up. He laid in bed staring up at the ceiling for a long time. The decision he'd made late the night before didn't sound like a good one anymore. A better decision would be to get out of bed, gather his things, climb into his car, and drive home. It sounded like such a good idea, that Granger got out of bed and started gathering his things. Trevor was already out of the room, which meant he couldn't ask questions. Granger felt more and more relieved the quicker he packed. The dark cloud over his mind even started to dissipate.

His mother's voice drifted down the hall from the kitchen, though he couldn't make out what she said. One of his brothers responded, and she said something else.

Granger paused.

*She'll only let him in again. She said herself that she thinks this is her only lifeline.*

He looked at the pair of shorts in his hand, then he set them down, sat down on the bed, and sighed. He rubbed his forehead roughly with his palm.

He thought of his other plan, the not-as-good one, again. He looked at his duffle bag. He looked at Trevor's bed.

*One day. I'll give it one day. That's all.*

He tossed his bag back into the corner and exited his room. The dark cloud followed him out.

When they took their seats on vinyl chairs around the greasy diner table later that morning, they were all sporting dark circles under their eyes. Little Elizabeth was the only perky one of the bunch. She wiggled and giggled and squirmed and wanted more than anything to take off running through the restaurant with a metal fork in her hand.

Half of them took turns trying to keep Elizabeth entertained while the other half watched the kitchen door for signs that their coffee was on its way.

They looked over the menu while they waited for Dave to show up. Granger was thankful they'd chosen one of the less popular breakfast/brunch restaurants in town. Other than the Kyles, the only patrons were a few older people reading newspapers or talking quietly with one another over cups of coffee.

At one end of the table, Janessa and Levi were collecting and hiding all the forks, while at the other end Elizabeth, who was sitting in Jake's lap, grabbed a green crayon and stuck it in her mouth. Jake made a panicked noise and grabbed it, causing Elizabeth to laugh and put it in her mouth again.

Granger couldn't keep his leg still, it bounced constantly under the table. He checked his watch. When he looked up again his mom was looking at him.

"He'll be here," she said. She was fidgeting, too.

He wondered how she could misread his nervous energy so completely.

Granger just raised an eyebrow. He sat back in his chair with one ankle propped up on the opposite knee and held his menu in front of him. The foot on the floor kept bouncing. More than once he sat forward in his chair, ready to walk out the door to his car in the parking lot, but he made his butt stay in the chair and acted like he'd only leaned forward to take another sip of water.

His eyes instinctively found the door when he heard a noise, but it was their server bringing a fresh pot of coffee from the kitchen.

She surveyed the quiet bunch.

"Ya'll definitely need this, don't ya?" she asked with a big smile.

"I'll get another pot ready for ya."

They passed the coffee pot around, and then around again just to get it away from Elizabeth's reach. Granger took a sip and then picked up his menu again. He bored a hole into the plastic with his eyes, but he had no idea what the menu said.

Levi checked his phone. A couple minutes later, Trevor checked his phone. Their mom glanced at the door over and over.

"I don't know how much longer—" Levi said.

The diner door opened and Dave came in. Granger's heart rate sped up immediately and his right hand gripped the edge of his chair. All his nervousness vanished, replaced by deep loathing. Granger glanced over to Levi, who still looked like he wanted to punch Dave, but he was obviously trying to rein in his own anger. Granger made himself sit back in his chair again. Dave spotted their table and hurried over to them. When he sat down in the empty chair he was out of breath.

"I'm so sorry I'm late. I was... I'm sorry."

"Something tie you up?" Levi asked, in a way that suggested he knew what kind of answer was coming.

But Dave shook his head, "no, no, no. No excuses from me. It's something I'm working on. No excuses, I shoulda been here sooner."

The brothers shared a quick look while their mom offered Dave the pot of coffee.

"We're glad you made it," she said.

Dave had bags under his eyes and his face was still unshaven. Granger was amazed how much older his dad looked after only six years. His hair was thinner and graying at the temples, and the skin on his face had deeper creases. He appeared to be taking better care of his clothes than himself, at least. His jeans and rain-splattered navy windbreaker were classic "Dave," so down-to-earth and earnest looking, such an unassuming appearance.

"How long were you waiting?" Dave asked their mom.

"Not long," she lied with a shake of her head.

She sat up straight at the edge of her chair and started directing the conversation like she was sorting mail at a post office during Christmastime, shooting messages down and across the table, trying to bridge the gap between Dave and Levi, Dave and Trevor, Dave and Granger, Dave and Jake, Dave and Janessa, and Dave and

Elizabeth, all at once. She talked more in five minutes than she had the entire day before.

Dave acknowledged all the unsolicited information she provided with the appearance of interest and gratitude. Granger watched his every move. It occurred to Granger that he couldn't remember the last time he'd seen his dad sober. Dave was definitely sober now. His big brown eyes were focused, and while his bushy brows were expressive, he wasn't frenetic. He moved at the pace of... well, of a middle-aged man who's been off drugs and in prison for the last half decade.

When Dave looked at Granger, Granger looked down and picked up his menu again.

*Remember the plan.*

"Have you ordered yet?" Dave asked.

"No, not yet," Trevor said.

Dave accepted a menu from Trevor and with one last tentative look around the table, turned his attention to the food.

*The plan.*

Their server came back and took their orders. Again, Granger watched Dave.

"I'll take some oatmeal and half a grapefruit," Dave said politely and succinctly. And that was it. He made no attempts to flirt with the server and charm her into giving him some sort of discount.

*It's because he knows the sort of pressure he's under right now. Plus mom's right here.*

"What? No triple stack of pancakes and a double side of bacon?" their mom asked in a voice higher pitched than usual, like she was trying with all her might to keep the conversation light and easy.

Dave shook his head, "I can hardly eat anything good anymore. A couple years ago I had to go on this heart-healthy diet. It was rough but I've gotten used to it."

Granger's brothers were about as talkative as Granger throughout the brunch, which seemed to contradict their earlier willingness to meet up with Dave, to his relief. Even Jake, ever the diplomat, only smiled politely.

"How was the drive down yesterday?" their mom asked.

"Fine," Dave said after swallowing some grapefruit. "But I'd forgotten that highway's always under construction. I'm pretty sure they've had lanes closed since 1980." He laughed. "I should've expected it, but it's been awhile since I've been on that highway."

His smile vanished when he looked at Granger.

There was another uncomfortable lull in the conversation. Between bites, Dave peeked at his sons and seemed to decide he had the best chance at civil conversation with Trevor; Dave wasn't stupid. He sat up a little straighter and addressed his second oldest son.

"So, Trev, your mom tells me you're an accountant."

"That's right," Trevor said. He didn't avoid eye contact but he didn't smile, either.

"Do you like it?"

"It's a good job."

"I'll bet you're a natural at it. You always were good at math."

Trevor didn't say anything else, so Dave went on.

"I remember when you were just a little guy," he said, "you were maybe five years old. We got you a set of building blocks for Christmas, but instead of building something out of them, we looked over and you'd lined them up all around the living room in this pattern and you said 'there's a hundred and seven!' You were so proud! That was the only time I ever saw you do anything with those blocks." He chuckled to himself. Their mom had a tight-lipped smile.

Granger saw an opening. When he set down his coffee mug it made a nice, sharp, solid sound on the table. He looked across the table at Trevor and in a full voice asked, "those were the blocks we used for the entrance to our clubhouse, weren't they?"

"They were," Trevor said, quieter than Granger.

"And we used them to have tower-building contests, right?"

"Yeah."

"And they were the boundary for our race tracks when we'd race those cars?"

"Yeah."

"Hmm, we sure did use those a lot, didn't we?"

Granger looked at Dave.

"Ah," Dave said, looking down. "Well I'm glad they ended up being fun after all."

"So am I," their mom said with a big smile at all of them. "Does anyone want more coffee? I've got the pot over here if anyone wants anymore."

Elizabeth squealed in reply.

Chipping away at Dave's facade was going to take a lot of work if Granger's openings were going to be as small as that one. He was waiting for Dave to trap himself so Granger only had to point out his inconsistencies to the others, but Dave wasn't making it easy for him. Dave may have been an idiot for how he treated them, but he was crafty and cunning, too.

"How old is she now?" Dave asked.

"Eighteen months," Janessa answered, since Levi was digging through the diaper bag.

"I can't find it," came Levi's muffled voice from under the table.

"Hold on one sec," she told him. She handed Elizabeth back to Jake for a moment and ducked down to help Levi.

Dave watched the handoff and smiled. His smile looked sad.

*She's his granddaughter, and he's never met her before,* Granger realized. He worried that Dave would ask to hold Elizabeth, but he didn't.

It was then that Granger remembered the second part of his plan. Jake was having trouble keeping Elizabeth away from his forkful of eggs, so Granger stepped up to the plate.

"I can hold her," he said. "Hand her over."

Jake raised his eyebrows but handed her to Uncle Granger. With one arm Granger situated her on his lap like he knew what to do with an eighteen-month-old, and looked up to see his mom looking at him again. She, too, looked surprised. He forced a big smile onto his face that said *"see? Everything is fine."*

"Eighteen months, wow," Dave said. "Time really flies."

"You mean when you're in prison?" Granger asked, sounding innocent.

Their mom tipped over her glass of orange juice just then. The table scrambled to mop it up before it spread too far. When it was cleaned up as well as could be with a couple paper napkins, Granger spoke up again. He had to keep trying.

"Sorry, I just wanted to be clear about what you were referring to. Time hasn't flown by so fast for us, is all. You know, since we had to pick up the pieces you left behind."

He didn't look in his mother's direction, but kept his eyes fixed on Dave's.

"Granger," Trevor said. Granger ignored him. The dark cloud was getting bigger and darker, but defensiveness was giving way to offensiveness. He was committed to his plan.

"That's why I came down here," Dave said, holding his stare. "I know I've missed a lot, and left a lot of pieces behind, like you said. I wanna make up for lost time, and try to pick up what's left of my mess."

"We cleaned it all up already," Granger said. "Six years is a long time to be cleaning. And we were already pretty good at it."

"Well, that may be. I have to at least try."

"By all means, why not kick an injured horse while it's already down? Makes sense to me."

Granger knew he was sending mixed messages, (were they fine? Were they not fine?) but he didn't have time to think about any of it, he had to keep up with Dave if he was going to expose him.

"I know I've said it before," Dave said quietly, "but this time I'm telling the truth."

Granger scoffed.

"You don't believe me."

"Never do."

*At least, not for the last six years.*

Dave thought a moment before he tried again. "I want to make up for lost time."

"How much of it?" It was Jake that asked the question. His tone was not accusatory.

"As much as I can."

*What if we don't want to make up for lost time?* Granger stopped himself short of voicing the question. He knew his brothers were on the fence about Dave's return just enough to maybe push back against his question, and he needed Dave to be the common enemy, not himself.

The next five minutes were quiet at their table. Granger worried about what might be going through his brothers' minds, but especially Jake's. Jake who was still so young and impressionable. And trusting. Granger tried to figure out his next steps while half his food stared up at him from his plate.

Everything Dave said and every movement he made grated on Granger's nerves. He wondered how much longer he could stand to be at the same table as him. His mom looked discouraged again. She poked at her uneaten toast. Granger's heart sank a little. He couldn't afford for either part of his plan to fail. If it did, there would only be more problems. If he couldn't convince his mom he was okay and their family was okay, she'd only unravel further. And if he couldn't keep Dave away from the more trusting and gullible members of the family, their wallets would wind up empty and their family more broken than before.

The whole meal passed and Granger's heart rate still hadn't returned to normal. His hairline was dotted with perspiration from being on high alert. He felt different emotions come in waves, each as unexpected and powerful as the last. He couldn't relax, no matter how much he breathed. He looked at the diner door more and more; his car was just on the other side.

*Soon.*

He tried to ignore the black cloud hovering on the edges of his mind and focus on his plan. He waited for more opportunities to chip away at Dave's act, but the man was perfectly behaved the rest of the morning.

"We should probably get going if we're gonna see Grandma one more time before we leave," Levi announced.

"Leaving so soon?" Dave asked.

"I have work to do this weekend," Levi said.

"But it's Memorial Day."

"The life of a lawyer," Janessa explained.

"Oh. When are you boys leaving?" Dave asked, looking from Trevor to Granger.

"Tomorrow," Trevor answered.

Dave nodded.

"Why? How long are you staying?" Granger asked.

Dave shrugged, "a couple weeks."

Alarm bells went off in Granger's head. He shared a look with his brothers.

"A couple weeks?" their mom repeated. "I thought you were just in town for the weekend."

"I got some time off for vacation, and to come visit Mom."

"You did?" she asked. Her voice sounded squeaky.

"You're gonna visit Grandma?" Granger asked.

"Of course." A shadow passed over Dave's face. Granger looked away. He held his tongue for his mother's sake.

*A couple weeks?*

Granger could not stay there 'a couple weeks.' He *needed* to get back to work soon. His plan was developing some holes.

Their smiley server brought the check. His mom, still looking dazed, pulled out her wallet.

"I've got it, Mom," Granger said quickly, pulling out his card.

"I can get it," Dave said, waving Granger's card away.

"No. I've got it," Granger said, putting his own card directly into the server's hand.

"Granger—" his mom said, shaking her head.

"My treat," he said. He forced another smile.

It certainly was a treat; he'd gotten a glimpse of the total and almost let Dave pay after all.

Granger signed the receipt like it was no biggie, but he could hear his bank account yelling at him, *"WHAT ARE YOU THINKING, MAN?"*

They left the diner in a long line. Levi and Janessa headed to their own car with Elizabeth, who was upset they were leaving. Granger watched with narrowed eyes as Dave walked and talked with Jake up ahead. He was about to catch up to them when he felt a hand placed gently on his good arm.

"I'll pay you back," his mom whispered.

"Don't worry about it, really. I told you, I got a promotion."

*If only it was as much of a pay raise as it sounded like it was.*

"Well, thank you," she said.

An idea popped into his head. "Did I tell you I'm gonna try to come visit again next month?"

"No! Why?"

"'Why?' To see you guys. I thought you wanted me to visit."

"I do, I do!"

"Well there you go."

He expected her to be happy about this news, but she still had creases between her eyebrows.

He forced a smile again and put his arm around her shoulders.

"You don't have to worry about me."

She looked up ahead to where Jake and Dave were talking.

"Of course I do," she said.

His plan wasn't going so well.

# 25

THE DAY WAS ALREADY HALF over. Granger decided he didn't have the time to prove to his mother that he was doing fine or that Dave was untrustworthy, at least not by any means other than directly. And he had to convince her before he left town the next day.

Dave, luckily, didn't invite himself along for their visit to Golden Grove after brunch.

If their grandma's room had felt cramped before, it was claustrophobia-inducing with the seven of them. Levi and Janessa were allowed the first and the longest slot of the day, since they were leaving town straight from the nursing home. Mom gladly took Elizabeth for a little while.

She, Granger, and Jake found a quiet alcove in the building to wait in while Trevor went to find the restroom and some coffee. They sat next to a wall of windows and listened to the rain pitter-patter on the roof. Their mom walked around the alcove slowly, and gently bounced the eighteen-month-old, talking to her quietly. As Elizabeth's eyelids got heavier and heavier, the lines on his mom's face softened.

He needed to talk to her about Dave, but he couldn't remember the last time he saw her looking so at-peace. Did he really want to ruin the moment for her?

"I loved having boys," she said just then, a pleasant smile on her face. She looked at Jake and Granger, who were sitting in some armchairs. "But I always wanted at least one girl, too."

She and her step-daughter, Lillian, hadn't been close when Lillian was a child. Their relationship now, from what Granger gathered, was the best it had ever been.

"You didn't have your hands full enough with all of us?" Granger asked.

She smiled down at Elizabeth, who was seriously threatening to fall asleep now.

"Not at all."

"That's not how I remember it," Granger said mildly, reclining a little in his chair.

"It was hard at times, I'll give you that, but you four were God's greatest gift to me."

"Even though half our DNA is from *him*?" Granger asked.

"Yes," she said without hesitation. "Believe it or not, many of the qualities I love most about you boys, you got from his side of the family."

He couldn't deny that his Dad's genes were strong in him and his brothers.

He shook his head, "I like to think we got those from Grandma and Grandpa, not him."

She only chuckled.

"I can't imagine living paycheck to paycheck with four little boys was a walk in the park for you," he said, trying to keep them on topic. He kept his voice low so he wouldn't wake his niece.

"We made it through, though, didn't we?" she asked.

Her eyes betrayed the toll that the years of trial had taken on her. But still, she was not hardened. He didn't understand it.

Granger saw his opportunity and opened his mouth with the word "Dave" on his tongue, but she spoke first.

"I let the stress get to me lots of times, I admit. If it weren't for your grandma…"

She blinked back her tears since she didn't have a free hand with which to wipe them away. "She did more for us than you'll ever know. Did more for me than I deserved."

He felt the stupid lump in his throat again and tried to swallow it away.

"I shudder to think of where we might be without her and your grandpa," she said. "I just hope she knows what she's done for us."

Granger looked out the window and blinked a couple times. On the other side of the glass, fat raindrops dripped off the leaves in the garden, making the plants look like they were crying.

The conversation was veering further and further away from where he needed it to go, but the lump in his throat was preventing him from course correcting. He needed a minute to collect his thoughts.

He stood up and cleared his throat. "I'm gonna go find some more coffee, too. You need some?"

She smiled back down at her granddaughter and shook her head. He left the two of them and Jake, who'd been listening quietly, in the alcove and headed toward the front of the building, his usual path when he needed to get away for a while. He passed Trevor coming back from the bathroom and pointed him to the alcove where the others were waiting. The clock on the wall told him they'd been there thirty minutes already. He found it interesting that he wasn't itching to get out of the building after five minutes like he had the first few times. He wouldn't say he felt at home there, but he was more comfortable in that memory care unit than he was sitting down the table from his father.

He walked all the way to the other side of the building but found all the sitting rooms occupied, so he poured himself a cup of coffee and snagged a chair at the little café table by the front doors. The lobby was mostly empty. On the side opposite from Granger, Archie was reading something while he manned the check-in desk, looking up occasionally to greet the people who walked past. Granger leaned on the table with his good arm and hung his head. As soon as he did, old questions started floating through his mind and new questions formed. He wished he could turn his brain off like he could in Eugene. In Lester, his brain just wouldn't leave him alone. The situations with his grandmother, his mother, Jake, and Dave circled in his mind like a carousel.

He exhaled and rubbed his face with his right hand again. He wanted a nap.

"Granger?"

He lifted his head to see Nina and Izzy standing on the other side of the little café table.

"Hi! Sorry, I didn't see you there," he said, perking up. "How you guys doing?"

Izzy had her arms crossed and a pout on her little face.

"Not very good, I'm afraid," Nina said with a sigh, putting a hand on Izzy's curly head. "We're having a little disagreement about whether or not ice cream qualifies as a meal."

"I see," he said. "You know, I had a gigantic ice cream sundae for lunch once," Granger confided in Izzy.

That got the little girl's attention. She whirled around to face her mom. "See mom! *He* got to do it!"

Before Nina could defend herself, Granger finished his story.

"It was awesome... until I threw it all up."

"Oh," Izzy said. "Why'd you throw up?"

"Too much of the sweet stuff. My mom said it was a bad idea but I did it anyway."

She didn't seem to like that. Or maybe she just didn't like him. It was hard to tell.

Izzy pouted and glared up at her mother simultaneously.

"It's not fair," she said.

Nina raised one eyebrow at Izzy, who's angry expression wilted and who, in a nicer tone, asked, "can I have it for dessert?"

"Not three scoops, but maybe one, after dinner, if you fix your attitude, missy."

Izzy must've decided she was getting an offer for a good deal, and she very politely asked her mother if she could go play with the toys in the corner of the lobby for a while.

"For a little bit."

Izzy left the two adults in the dust again.

With his shoe, Granger lightly scooted the other chair out from the table and motioned to it. "You wanna sit?"

"Sure, thanks."

Granger nodded over to where Izzy was playing. "Wouldn't it be nice to be a kid again? Or even better, to be a kid forever!"

She shook her head, "I think I'd hate to be a kid forever."

"Why?"

"I don't know, I was always so excited to be an adult!"

"But now that you're actually grown up... still think it's worth it?"

She tilted her head back and forth like she was thinking it over.

"Remember how much easier it was to be a kid? Less

responsibility, less stress… No taxes," he said, giving her a pointed look.

She smiled. "Good point."

He relaxed in his chair, starting to feel more like himself again.

"My brothers and I had acres of farmland to run around in when we lived with my grandparents. We had a creek and a tire swing and trees to climb and a field to play baseball in. It was the life."

"You lived with your grandparents?"

"Yeah, we moved in with them after my mom kicked my dad out. I was about five."

"So, she's your mom's mom?"

"My dad's."

"That's cool."

"What is?"

"That you guys still have a good relationship with your dad's parents even though your parents aren't together anymore."

"We loved living on the farm with them. Best five years of our childhoods."

Thinking of the farm brought back to mind all his questions and problems. He took a slow sip of his coffee and lost himself in his thoughts. But after a few seconds, or maybe a few minutes, a noise brought him back to the present.

"Hello?" someone was saying to him.

He looked up at Nina. "Sorry, what'd you say?"

"I just asked what it was like living on a farm. Everything okay? You kinda spaced out there for minute."

"Sorry." He sat up and tried to focus on the conversation again. "I've been doing that a lot lately. I'm just trying to figure out what to do about some… well, it's nothing. Just family stuff."

"Gotcha. Do you wanna be alone?"

On the one hand, talking to Nina had been the most enjoyable part of his return trip to Lester so far. But on the other hand, getting some time alone so he could think about his next steps might be exactly what he needed.

"Actually, yeah." He quickly added, "It's nothing personal."

She was already standing up.

"Don't worry about it," she said. "I understand. I wouldn't have asked, otherwise! Good luck."

She started to walk away, and suddenly there were words coming out of Granger's mouth.

"My dad's back in town."

She turned around and saw that he was talking to her.

He went on. "We don't have a good relationship. And *I* didn't want to be back here, but I especially don't want *him* to be back here. I'm afraid he's going to scam my mom or my little brother or something."

Still standing in the middle of the lobby, one of her feet was pointed toward him, the other was pointed toward Izzy. She remained where she was, but asked, "scam them… like… out of their money?"

"That's my guess. He doesn't have the greatest track record with money. But even on the off-chance he's not here for money, he's still a risk. Every time he comes around he just lets people down. And my mom can't handle… I keep trying to warn them, but they won't listen. It's like they've completely forgotten all the other stuff he screwed up." He sighed. "Does it really make me a jerk for wanting to protect them from getting hurt again?"

She shook her head. "No."

He looked down at his coffee cup. "I think my family would disagree with you."

"Probably."

When he looked up at her again, she was still standing perpendicular, like she was waiting to see if he'd continue. After a moment's thought, he used the toe of his shoe to nudge the other chair again, as a silent invitation to her. She couldn't completely suppress her smile as she turned back to the table and accepted the seat a second time.

"I just don't understand *why* they think the way that they do," Granger said, leaning into the conversation fully. "It all seems pretty black and white to me."

Granger went over his many questions in his mind again, looking for answers. When he came up empty, he exhaled heavily and asked, "so, do you have any sage wisdom to give me?"

"No."

He threw up a hand in mock outrage, "then why did I just spill my guts to you?"

"How should I know!" she laughed.

"Come on, you don't have any advice? I thought this was the reason you came here," he teased.

She smiled, "I know next to nothing about the whole situation with your dad. You want my advice based on zero prior knowledge?"

"Yes. I want you to say, 'yes, Granger. You're absolutely right, Granger. Stick to your plan and everything will be just fine.'"

"So you don't want advice, you want affirmation?"

"A hundred percent, yes."

She laughed, and he couldn't help but laugh along with her.

"Well, thanks for listening anyway," he said in a more serious tone.

"No problem. I hope you can figure out what to do."

"Thanks. But I go back home tomorrow so I think I'm just gonna have to stick with the plan I've got."

"Which is?"

He took a deep breath. "Convince my mom that he can't be trusted, and convince her that she doesn't need the two of us to make up for me to be 'okay.' She's always worried about me. At least that's what she says, but then she ignores me when I say 'hey, mom, you know the thing that would really suck for me more than anything? Spending time with Dave.'"

"You told her that?"

"Not in so many words."

Nina thought for a moment. "Do you two talk much?"

"Who? Me and my mom? We talk enough."

She nodded and looked out the window, "I like your mom. She's nice."

He chuckled, "yeah, 'nice.' Sometimes a little too 'nice.' When you're as nice as she is, you're just asking to get stepped on."

It was then that Granger remembered what Nina said at the picnic, about being estranged from her own parents. And now knowing that it might've had something to do with the scandal surrounding Nina, he asked, as delicately as possible, "was this kinda how it went down with your parents?"

"No, actually. I had the opposite problem."

"Oh."

"The week my parents found out I was pregnant, they kicked me out of the house."

"You don't have to talk about it if you don't want to," he said, trying to backtrack.

She gave him a look, "oh come on. That was totally a leading question. You wanna know the details, I don't blame you."

*Apparently I am completely transparent. Great.*

"Okay fine," he said. "But there's a reason I asked *you* for advice and not someone else. *You* know what it's like to have a difficult relationship with your parents. I wasn't trying to be like those people who just wanna be entertained by other people's drama, I promise."

"I know, which is why I'll tell you what happened."

He was tempted to protest more, to show her that he really was a decent person, but he really did need advice.

"How old were you?" he asked.

"Seventeen. It was my senior year."

"Did you have someone to live with?"

"No."

Granger shook his head, disgusted with her parents.

"How'd you make it?" he asked.

"I worked several jobs at once while I was pregnant. I had the time, since I'd dropped out of school. I hit my lowest point a little bit after Izzy was born. Right before she was born, I landed a more decent job, they hired me even without a high school diploma, and they let me go on maternity leave. And then a week after I went back to work, postpartum, I was laid off. Along with nine other people. I was out of work for three months."

"Three months?"

"Yeah. The economy really tanked here."

"I remember."

"I still don't understand why it tanked, all I know is that, suddenly, there was hardly any work in town, and any work I did find was just impossible to do while also being a single parent. I couldn't make ends meet. I was glad to have WIC, and Luke snuck me money to buy groceries when he could, but at the tail end of those three months I got an eviction notice."

"What happened?"

"I met the Wilcox's."

"Wilcox. As in, Farley Wilcox? The one who lives here? Used to be the elementary school principal?"

"His daughter-in-law, actually. Annette Wilcox. Her husband is a pastor at Good Shepherd Church. I met her one day when I was out grocery shopping. I hadn't had a shower in a few days because they'd shut our water off, and I'd just been crying about the eviction notice on the walk to the store with Izzy. She walked past me in the aisle and stopped me. She asked if we were alright and I broke down again right there next to the baby formula. I don't know why, but I just spilled my guts about everything. We stood there for like thirty minutes while I bawled and she listened. Then she held Izzy while we walked around the store together, shopping. She paid for all my groceries and gave me an extra $50. And then she invited me to the free thanksgiving dinner the church was hosting for the community. That's when everything started to turn around for us.

"Jack and Annette invited us over for meals all the time. We got to know them pretty well. And then it got a little strange..."

"Strange?"

"Yeah. We started receiving a bunch of gifts and food on our doorstep and checks in our mailbox. I got diapers and formula and baby clothes and gift cards and toys and all sorts of stuff."

"From the Wilcox's?"

"No. That was why it was weird. I didn't recognize a single name from any of the notes or checks that were left."

"That is weird."

"It went on like that for over a year. Every week we would get something. There was not one week when we didn't. After knowing the Wilcox's for all that time, I agreed to go with them to their church service for Christmas Eve. I'd been really reluctant to go back because... well, did you ever meet my parents?"

"I saw them at school events, I think, because of Luke. But I don't think I ever met them."

"They're very religious. Very traditional. They went to the same church every week in Trayfield for over twenty years. They probably still go every week. I didn't want anything to do with church after Izzy was born. So I was surprised when I went to the Wilcox's church and found out that all the gifts Izzy and I had been getting were from people at that church. The only thing they knew about me for over a year was the thing that my parents kicked me out and cut me off for, but they just kept giving and giving and giving. And when I started coming to their church every week, they were genuinely welcoming. They didn't treat me badly or make me feel like I was worse than any of them."

Granger looked down at his almost empty cup.

"Wow," was all he could think to say.

"And your grandma was one of them."

He looked up at her.

Part of his heart softened at those words.

"She's always had a heart for the struggling moms," he said.

"And for struggling teens whose parents have let them down."

He nodded in agreement.

He was very proud of his grandma.

"You know," he said, "she's the one who really encouraged my mom to kick my dad out when I was little. If she hadn't... who knows what else might've happened. I think she got a lot of flack for that, but I'm really glad she did it. I don't want to deal with my dad now, but I'd rather deal with him as an adult than as a kid who didn't know any better."

"But I thought you wanted to stay a kid forever," she teased.

"I'm starting to see your side of things," he said with a smile. "So, you really haven't talked to your parents since they kicked you out?"

"They send a letter around Izzy's birthday some years. It usually says something like 'we wish your daughter a happy birthday. Best wishes, Dan and Marie.' So, at least they acknowledge her existence now. It's progress."

Granger scoffed, "'Dan and Marie?' Not even 'Mom and Dad?' Even Dave still wants me to call him 'Dad.'"

"In some ways, I'm glad we have the distance. They could be suffocating at times. Very strict, lots of rules, not much in the way of affection. Everything Luke and I ever did was merit-based. They weren't afraid to show their disappointment or disapproval. My dad didn't speak to me for a whole week once when I got a D on a math test. And if I hadn't been kicked out, I might never have really met Jesus. But of course I wish we were still a family. A better family. Izzy deserves to be loved by her grandparents, you know?"

"Yeah, she does."

Granger thought for a minute. "If they opened up to you again, would you try to patch things up? So Izzy could get to know them?"

"I think I would, but not just for Izzy. I'd want a second chance with them for my own sake, too."

Granger shook his head. "You're a better person than I am. No matter how many times my dad tries to patch things up, I'll never trust him."

"I can understand that. It's different for you. At least a little bit."

"I wish my mom could see that. All she sees is her husband trying to be a good dad. It's like she's blind to all his mistakes and his whole past."

"Or maybe she's just forgiven him?"

"Yeah, well, that doesn't make sense to me, either."

Across the lobby, they saw Trevor walk by. Granger guessed that his mom had changed her mind about wanting coffee.

"Does your brother Trevor look a lot like your dad?" Nina asked.

"Yeah. Trevor's taller and takes better care of himself, but they do look a lot alike."

"Does he have a scruffy beard?"

"Yeah, why?"

"I've seen him in here a couple times. After seeing him, I can see the family resemblance between all of you."

"He's been here?"

"Yeah."

"Was he alone?"

"I think so."

Granger thought about this, but then shrugged. "She *is* his mother, I guess even the most messed-up people can still care about the person who raised them."

"Yeah, look at me," Nina said with a grin.

Granger smiled, "you don't seem that messed up."

Nina tilted her head sideways and was quiet for a second. "You know," she finally said. "I remember you."

His palm got sweaty.

*Oh no, what does she remember about me?*

But she didn't seem angry or judgmental, so, very carefully, he responded. "I remember you, too. Or at least, I remember hearing about you."

Nina snorted. "Of course you do. The whole town heard about me." She shook her head with a wry smile, leaned back in her chair, and crossed her legs. "I always knew I would be a celebrity, but coming into fame so young really jump-started my career."

Granger smiled at her sarcasm.

"At least you got Izzy," he said. "That's way better than what I got."

She looked over at the little girl playing and her tone softened. "Getting Izzy was the purest form of grace I've ever encountered."

"She's a good kid," he said. "Funny, too."

"I'm glad she's got a good sense of humor. The first few years of her life weren't easy."

They listened for a few seconds as Izzy very animatedly narrated an outlandish story starring a plastic giraffe, a toy car, and a Ken doll.

Granger laughed.

"She keeps me on my toes," Nina said. "Izzy's dad had the same witty sense of humor and striking personality."

Granger shook his head, "I remember Pete. And I don't know you guys that well, but it's pretty obvious Izzy got her personality from *you*."

"You knew Pete?" Her expression was unreadable.

"We weren't even close to being friends, but I knew who he was. I heard about him a lot. Everybody did."

She looked out the window, "yeah. He always left his mark."

"He was pretty famous around school for his big mouth."

"You're not wrong. He was always wrapped up in a cause, and not in a good way."

"He's how I first heard about... let's see... the 2010 earthquake in Haiti, Bin Laden's death, uhhh what else... every detail of the Obama administration, the housing market crash..."

"That sounds like him."

"I've never felt so informed or accosted in my life. He made one of our teachers cry once. He argued with her and humiliated her until she broke down in front of the whole class."

She nodded with a cringe.

Maybe he'd gone too far. Her openness, like the other times they'd talked, had given Granger his own dose of curiosity and bravery.

*Take it down a notch*, he told himself.

Granger had no idea what she'd seen in the guy that was so attractive to her, but it was ancient history and she'd been so young, so he decided not to ask about it. He circled back around to the beginning of the conversation.

"I heard a lot about you when all that stuff went down, when you dropped out of school" he said. "You're not what I expected."

"Well, to be fair, you still don't know me that well."

"That's true, but still."

"So," she said, "what *did* you expect?"

*Oh.*

He cleared his throat and shrugged to avoid answering.

"I'm curious!" she said with a little smile. "You said I'm not what you expected, so what'd you expect?"

*Nice going. You really backed yourself into a corner there, didn't you?*

He shook his head, "you know, just… different. I don't know."

She eyed him.

*How am I supposed to be honest and also not come across like a jerk?*

"I'd rather not say, okay?"

She smiled. "Your mom and grandparents didn't raise a fool, did they?"

"I may not be a genius, but I try not to be a complete idiot."

She chuckled. "Okay. I'm gonna guess."

"Guess?"

"My guess is that you expected me to be completely irresponsible and unfit for motherhood. Oh, and 'trashy,' which I think is a horrible way to describe anybody, for the record."

It was a good guess. He thought very carefully before he spoke. "I heard a lot of rumors," was all he said.

"I bet you did. I guess that's the problem with town gossip, even the true parts turn out to be not that truthful."

He looked away, wondering how many rumors he'd spread about her… about anyone.

"You're right," he said. "What'd you hear about me, then?"

"I'd rather not say," she said with a smile.

He chuckled.

"But rest assured," she said, "you're not what I expected, either."

"In a good way?"

"In a good way."

They said goodbye to Levi and his family in the parking lot and little Elizabeth cried when her parents took her from Granger's hip, which made him feel good about himself as an uncle, then the others went back to their mom's house for the afternoon. As soon as they pulled in, Trevor excused himself. No one knew where he was going, all he said was that he was 'going out for a while.' Jake went to his room to play video games. So, it was just Granger and his mom in the kitchen.

"I should probably start dinner now," she mused.

Granger looked at the clock on the stove. "It's two o'clock."

"I need to marinate the steak so we can cook it tonight."

"Steak? You don't have to go all out for us, Mom."

"It's no problem."

Granger might have been able to believe her if she didn't already look frazzled and exhausted.

"Are you sure you don't just wanna do macaroni and hotdogs for dinner?"

"I already bought the steak, I don't want it to go bad."

She was already pulling spices out of the cabinet for the seasoning.

"I'll help you, then."

He wasn't sure if she heard him or not; she was mumbling to herself while looking over a recipe. While he washed up, he looked through the window above the sink at the rain falling in the backyard. A wave of nostalgia hit him. For a second there, he could almost convince himself he was a teenager again, still living at home, with his whole future ahead of him. If he tried hard enough, he could feel what it felt like to be the high-school version of himself: angsty, excited, hopeful, frustrated, impatient.

He leaned into the feeling. It wasn't something he'd ever experienced before, but the more he leaned in, the easier it got, until finally, he felt like he was stepping back into the body of his younger self. He was a teenager again. Jake wasn't in high school, yet. Trevor was still living at home, too, he was just out with friends at the moment… But Granger couldn't hold onto that feeling for long, couldn't remain in the shoes of his younger self. It just wasn't possible; the shoes didn't fit anymore.

There were three things that grounded him back in the present: the absence of feeling in his left arm, the lack of anticipation he felt for life, and the image of his mom, who could not be mistaken for the same woman that she was six or ten years ago.

*Maybe I should let it go, just forget my plan. She's got enough to deal with already.*

*But if I don't…*

He tried to keep his tone measured and free of anger. "I really don't think you should trust him, Mom."

She paused only briefly, her knife hovering just a millisecond longer over the carrots she was chopping.

"I know you don't."

He thought of his conversation with Nina.

"I know you're trying to give him a second chance, and it's very… noble… of you, but I don't think it's a good idea."

"I know. You think he'll only take advantage of us."

"Yeah, I do." He finished drying his hand and approached the counter where she was.

She set the knife down and wiped her hands on a towel. "Here's the recipe for the marinade. Do you want to measure the… actually, you know what, I can work on the marinade. You can… let's see…"

"I can do the marinade. It's no problem."

"No, there's something else I need prepared for dinner, I just can't remember…"

She wouldn't look him in the eye.

"Mom," he said emphatically. "I can do it."

There was a moment of awkward silence that followed.

She looked at him. "It's just… it might be hard to hold the plastic bag open when you're ready to add the seasoning."

With his thumb and forefinger he plucked the bag from her hand. "Well then, I'll just figure out how to do it a different way, or," he dropped his voice to a sarcastic whisper, "I'll ask for help."

He turned toward the spices and away from her. To prove his point, he immediately pulled a bowl out of an upper cabinet and finessed the zippered plastic bag onto it so that it remained, at least partially, open.

He guessed that she saw it, because he didn't hear her go back to chopping until after he'd gotten the bag situated.

Chop.

Chop.

Chop.

"I'm sorry," she finally said. "I forget that you've had six, almost seven, years to figure these things out."

*'If only you came around more often, I'd know these things, honey,'* he finished for her.

"I'm so glad you came home this weekend," she said. "Thank you. It means the world to Jake. And thank you for coming to brunch this morning. It was good to see you and your dad talking—"

"I went to brunch for you, not for him."

"I understand that."

She chopped some more.

"Granger, I don't expect him to completely rejoin the family or be the husband and dad he should've been, but from talking with him over the last few weeks, he seems ready to have a — a very small — part in the family again."

Granger shook his head as he poured a tablespoon of garlic powder into the bag. "I'm telling you, this is exactly how I expect him to act. He gets buddy-buddy with us again and has all this 'proof' that he's changed and then it turns out he's full of… that he's completely fooled us."

"He's made mistakes," she granted. "But we all have."

He wrestled with the lid of the Worcestershire sauce. "Not mistakes that bad."

"I don't think we can judge one person's sins as worse than another's."

"Maybe not, but you can judge the size of someone's mistake by the consequences of their actions, by how many people got hurt."

His face and neck were starting to feel flushed the more they talked.

Her voice was shaky and almost shrill as she said, very slowly, "I know that I could be wrong about him, and I know I could suffer the consequences for letting him back into my life, but that is a risk I am willing to take."

Granger turned to face her. "But are you willing to let him hurt Jakey? Or other people? You realize by letting him back into *your* life, you're letting him back into *Jakey's*, too?"

"It's Jake, not Jakey," she said.

"Whatever. Have you thought about what trouble Dave could cause for Jake? Have you even talked to Jake about this? Maybe he doesn't want a relationship with Dave, either."

She stuttered a little when she said, "that's between me and Jake."

"In other words, you haven't talked to him, have you? Mom, you're so careful, too careful, about everything. Except for Dave. Why is he your weakness?"

"Don't forget that I was the one who kicked him out when you were little," she said. Her hands were shaking so much she had to put her knife down.

"And that was the best decision you ever made."

"No, it wasn't."

"Are you saying you regret doing it?"

"No, I'm saying I've made better decisions in my life. Granger," she signed deeply, "I've learned from my mistakes. I know what to watch out for. I've known him almost my whole life. I know him."

"Sometimes I don't think you do. I think you have this idea in your head of what he could be, but when has he ever measured up to that standard?"

"It's not fair to hold him to a certain standard if it's unrealistic for him."

"Are you hearing yourself?"

Jake came into the kitchen just then. "What's going on?"

Granger got to the point. "Has he asked you for money?"

"No," she said.

"Has he mentioned being short on cash or anything like that? Did he bring up how he's getting by at all? He might not ask for money outright, you know."

"He only mentioned that he has another factory job and he's living in the city."

"He'll sneak it in at some point, I know he will."

"Granger, will you never forgive him?"

Granger laughed loudly, humorlessly. "Forgive him? You people are so determined to ignore the horrible things other people have done. You're fooling yourselves. I'm not going to let myself be blinded like you are. I'm not stupid."

Jake stepped toward their mother, who was shaking all over, and said in a firm voice to his brother, "that's enough. Talk about something else."

"He will only take advantage of you again if you let him!" Granger said. "You did the right thing kicking him out, so why would you let him back in? Both of my arms might work right now if you hadn't!"

"That's enough!" Jake said in a voice that shook the kitchen.

She had tears streaming down her face now. "I know, I know, and I think about that all the time—"

"Do you?" Granger challenged. "Because it seems like you're blocking it out and just pretending it didn't happen."

"Granger," Jake said.

"I've wished so many times I could change what happened," she cried.

"You could keep it from happening to Jakey! Or someone else!"

"I can make my own decisions," Jake said, his voice still booming. "And you need to take a walk."

"You're siding with her on this?" Granger yelled, aghast.

"Get out!" Jake yelled. "Look at her! Look what you're doing!"

Their mother was crumpled over the counter, sobbing, still holding a carrot in her hand.

"I said get out!" Jake said, shoving Granger out of the kitchen.

"Don't touch me!" Granger said, shoving back.

"What's going on?" Trevor asked, coming through the front door.

"I cannot believe you people," Granger shouted from the hallway. "I've had it. You're all on your own. I'm out of here."

He stalked to his bedroom and shoved the door open so hard it slammed against the inside wall.

"Granger, wait!" he heard his mother say as she ran after him, with Jake on her heels. "Don't leave. I'll never forgive myself for what happened to you, but it was a mistake what he did. Don't forget about all the good he did for us."

"I can't forget if there's nothing to remember."

Granger was only in his old bedroom long enough to shove his dirty clothes and toothbrush into his duffle bag and grab his phone charger. "All my memories of him are of his 'mistakes.'" He marched out of his room and toward the front door.

"You're leaving?" Trevor asked. "What's going on?"

"You're a real jerk, you know that?" Jake said to Granger.

"*I'm* a jerk? *I* am?"

"Yeah. You are."

"Well you're a blind, hard-headed child trying to pretend you're an adult. And you," he said, turning to Trevor. "I saw the pills. I know you're hiding something. You coward. When things go sideways you just sit in the background sucking your thumb. Stand up for once! And you!" He rounded on their mom. "I've had it with you. It's because you were too weak to say 'no' that we got in that mess six years ago, and it's why we're in it now. It's weak and it's selfish—"

From out of the corner of his eye Granger saw Jake coming for him, but at the last second, Jake was shoved off his path, and it was Trevor's fist that connected with Granger's face.

Their mother yelped.

Granger saw stars. The last time he'd been punched was middle school. It had been one of his brothers that time, too.

"*Now* you take a stand?" Granger yelled at Trevor. "*Now?*"

"That's right, I *am* on meds. For 'generalized anxiety' and 'major depressive disorder.' You might know that if you cared about anyone other than yourself. But I don't air my dirty laundry for all the world to see like you do," Trevor said, getting right up in Granger's face and looking down on him. "Somebody's got to be the drama-free one in this family and it sure isn't gonna be you. If you weren't so conceited and always looking to cause trouble maybe you'd notice the other people in this family. Ever think you might not be the only one struggling?" He scoffed. "You hate him, but you're more like him than you realize."

Granger punched Trevor right back.

"Don't you ever say that to me again," he bellowed.

"Get out," Jake yelled, coming for him again.

"I don't want to hear from any of you again," Granger yelled at the three of them before opening the front door. "And that includes Levi. You hear me? I'm done with you all."

He slammed the door behind him and didn't look back.

# 26

"Granger, come help me pick these tomatoes," Grandma called from the garden.

It was ninety degrees already and so humid that after they finished breakfast their mom said she wished she could take a second shower.

Granger stood inside the kitchen, looking out at his grandma from the other side of the screen door. He ran his fingers over the mesh screen, making the "zipping" sound he liked so much.

"Do I have to?" he whined.

"Yes. It's one of your chores."

"But what about Trevor and Levi?"

"They woke up early and did their chores already. Come on."

"But it's so hot!"

"Which is why we need to do them now. And quickly. Come out here now, and no more whining."

She gave him the eye, and he didn't want to get in trouble first thing after breakfast, so he groaned but pushed the door open. The screen door squeaked on its hinges and slapped against the doorframe when it closed. His dirty, bare feet padded across the wooden porch, down the steps, and into the garden after his grandma.

"Put the tomatoes in here," she said, placing the bucket down beside him. Before she turned back to the green beans, where she was working at double her usual speed, she plopped her own wide-brim work hat on his little head. It helped keep the heat away, a little.

To Granger's young eyes, she was an old lady. But she worked and worked and worked and never seemed to get tired. He could see beads of sweat on her neck and forehead already, though. Her long, gray hair was in a braid down her back, as it always was, so Granger could see part of her face from where he stood by the tomato plants. The face she was making as she focused reminded Granger of his dad's, whom he hadn't seen in two months.

"Come on, Granger, get started or we'll be stuck out here during the hottest part of the day."

Granger slowly got to work, but he was distracted.

He often wanted to ask about his father, but he was scared that either he wouldn't like what he heard, or that the adults would get mad at him for asking. No one ever told him why they'd moved to the farm, or why his dad never came back, or why no one talked about his dad when he or his brothers were around. But the curiosity was more than the young Granger could bear.

"Did my dad pick tomatoes when he was little?" Granger asked.

"Oh yes. It's an important job."

"Did he like it?"

"Not all the time. I do remember one time, when he was about your age, your father said he wanted to own this farm someday."

"Did he?"

"No, he traded in that dream a long time ago."

"Why?"

"Lots of people change their minds as they get older."

"What did he change his mind to?"

She didn't respond right away, just kept picking green beans. Granger thought maybe she hadn't heard him.

"He wanted to be rich and have fun," she said finally.

Granger thought about it.

"That sounds good," he reasoned. "'Cause then you could buy stuff you need. And not have to be on food stamps like us."

She looked over at him, and he was surprised to see that she looked sad. He must've said something wrong.

"Right?" he asked.

"You have a point, there, but I think it's better to have just enough money than to be too rich."

"Why?"

"There's nothing wrong with being rich, but having too much money can destroy some people." Under her breath she added, "although not having any money at all can do the same."

*Destroy?*

His mind went to a movie he saw at a friend's house the week before, a movie his mom and grandparents didn't know he'd seen, where an alien came to earth and started destroying everything. He felt the blood drain from his face.

"Is that what happened to Dad?" he asked very quietly.

"Pretty close," she said.

He felt braver since she was answering some of his questions. So, he set down his empty bucket and turned his whole body to face her.

"What happened?"

She looked at him and then at his bucket. He was afraid she'd snap at him to get back to work, but instead she put down a couple green beans and sighed.

"A lot happened. It's hard to pinpoint everything that led to where we are today. All I can say is your father got stuck at some point along the way."

"Stuck?"

"Stuck. A lot of people get stuck here and there in life. It's normal to get stuck sometimes. But he just never got un-stuck. At least, he hasn't yet."

Granger thought hard before he asked, "do you know where he is?"

"I have a rough idea."

"Where is he? What's he doing?" Once the floodgates had been opened, Granger let all his questions pour out.

"Don't you worry about that, you hear? All you need to know is he's not here. This is where he's supposed to be."

She turned back to the green beans. Granger turned back to the tomatoes and started picking them in silence. The heat of the day covered his head and neck in dots of sweat.

"I'm gonna play baseball when I grow up. That's a good job, right?"

"It can be. Whatever you decide to do, follow the example of your grandpa, and your mom, and your aunt and uncle, not your dad. Whatever you do, do your job honestly, work hard, and don't abandon the people who need you the most."

# 27

"Do you want to talk about Katie?"

"What about her?"

"Whatever you want to tell me."

…

…

"We met in high school. We dated a few years and then broke up a few months into college."

"What happened?"

Granger shrugged, "we wanted different things. It just didn't work out."

"What did she want?" his therapist asked.

"She wanted to move to New York and be on Broadway. She went to the fine arts college here in Eugene. She loved musical theater."

"Does she still attend the fine arts school?"

"No. She dropped out before she finished her first year."

Granger shook his head and, despite himself, snickered.

"Is that funny?"

"It was a mistake."

"Why do you say that?"

"She was only nineteen. She'd barely started her musical theater major and she decided she was ready for New York City."

"You don't think she was ready?"

195

"She had no experience, no education, and no money."

"There are plenty of people who move to New York in that very situation," Dr. Jenkins pointed out.

"But she could've gotten four years of practice and learning the business before she tried to make it out there. She was too impatient. I told her that."

"How'd that go over?"

Granger leaned back in his chair. "She got mad and we yelled at each other and then she left my dorm. That was the last time we talked."

"So, she went to New York?"

"Yeah."

"What happened?"

Granger looked out the window.

"I don't know," he mumbled.

"Oh?"

Granger kept his eyes on the window. "Well, I might've heard something, but I don't know how accurate it is."

The doctor waited.

Granger sighed, "I heard she's doing okay for herself. She's not on Broadway, but she's doing lots of small, paid acting gigs."

"Do you two keep in touch?"

Granger looked at the doctor. "No. The last time we talked was our last fight. I just said that."

"That's right, sorry. Do you *wish* you still talked?"

"Of course. I wish we hadn't broken up."

"If she came back to town today and wanted to get back together, would you consider it?"

Granger opened his mouth, but something stopped him from answering. He'd thought through that scenario a lot over the last year. He'd been on a date, some double dates, and a couple group dates, but none of those girls were Katie. He thought he knew the answer to Dr. Jenkins' question, until the doctor asked it.

"I don't know."

The counselor let the silence hang between them again. "What did *you* want?" he finally asked Granger.

"What?"

"You said you wanted different things. She wanted New York,

what did you want?"

"Well, to finish my degree."

"So, you broke up?"

"It wasn't just that we wanted to go down different paths. We started to fight a lot more. Right after the accident, she was really supportive and seemed to understand what I needed. But over time, it's like she got impatient waiting for me to get over it."

"'Get over it?'"

Granger listened to the small water feature on the bookshelf while he thought about his answer.

"Get over… being stuck. That's what she told me one time, that I was 'stuck.'"

"What do you think she meant by that?"

Granger leaned forward in his seat and exhaled. "That I couldn't move on. But how can I? After the accident… I felt like someone hit 'pause' on my life. Everything just froze."

"And when did that change for you?"

"It hasn't. I still feel frozen."

"And you haven't hit the 'play' button again because… ?"

"I don't know how."

Present Day

*Stuck.*

    *Stuck.*

Granger pulled out his phone and dialed.

*"Dr. Jenkins' office."*

"Hello, I'd like to schedule an appointment."

# 28

"Run, Granger! He's almost got it!"

Granger pumped his little legs harder at his grandma's words.

She had stepped out onto the wraparound porch to look down on the makeshift baseball diamond, situated between her farmhouse and the creek, just as an eight-year-old Granger was running the bases. Trevor and his friend, Ty, shouted similar encouragement as Granger, the youngest player in the game, sprinted with everything he had in him. Levi and Trevor's other friend, Colby, scrambled to field the ball and get Granger out.

Levi, being four years older, had much longer legs than Granger, and once Colby threw the baseball to him, he overtook Granger in just a few long strides.

"Out!" Levi yelled.

"Agh!" said Granger.

Levi and Colby celebrated. Trevor and Ty sulked. Granger tried not to cry as he stomped back to his assigned position in midfield. He knew he was lucky his older brothers were letting him play at all since it was Trevor's turn to have friends over, so he didn't want to get kicked out of the game by being a cry-baby.

"It's okay, Granger," Grandma yelled, "better luck next time."

But he didn't have better luck next time. He struck out during his next two turns at bat. While he marched back to his position to the

198

sounds of the other team's hoots and hollers, Granger decided he'd had enough. Instead of stopping in midfield, Granger picked up speed and ran to the house.

"Hey, wait!" someone called.

"Grange, come back!"

"He's upset," one of the boys snickered.

"That's okay, guys. Now we have even teams," said another.

Granger couldn't stop the angry tears once he turned toward the house. He bounded up the porch steps and flung the screen door open. His grandma, standing at the kitchen counter, looked up when she heard the racket.

"They didn't kick you out of the game, did they?" she asked in a threatening tone.

He wiped away angry tears. "No."

"Then what's wrong?" she demanded to know.

"I don't wanna play anymore."

"Why not?"

"I just don't."

"Did something happen?"

"No." He plopped down on one of the old, wooden kitchen chairs with a pout on his face.

She gave him the eye.

"They're older and better than me. I don't want to play with them anymore."

His grandma dumped the chopped carrots into a large pot on the stove and then started rinsing a head of lettuce in the sink. She didn't say a word until she'd finished adjusting the water temperature.

"What if you were playing with Trevor and some of *your* friends? Or with little Jakey?"

"Jakey's only two!"

"And he wants to play baseball with you already! So, what if you were playing with him and Trevor instead of all those older boys? Would you play better?"

"Yeah! 'Cause Trevor's only a little bit bigger than me and Jakey's a baby!"

"It sounds like you feel intimidated by the older boys."

"What's 'intimidated?'"

"You feel like you don't play well because you see how good the older boys are. You're comparing yourself to them."

"But they're better than me."

"So what?"

"So... I don't want to play with them."

"I thought you liked baseball."

"I do."

"Don't you want to get better?"

"Yeah."

"Playing with people who are better than you is how you get better."

"But I'm not getting better, I'm getting worse."

She shook her head, "it only feels that way right now. As long as you play baseball, you're going to have games where you don't do well. If you want to be a good baseball player, you have to keep working at it. Don't you want to keep playing baseball?"

"Yeah," he pouted.

"Well, just because something's hard doesn't mean you give up on it. That kind of attitude can lead to all sorts of trouble."

When he didn't respond, she glanced over at him and asked, "you hear me, young man?"

"Yes, ma'am."

"Then get your butt back out there, Granger Scott Kyle."

Her voice had that tone that told him the conversation was over; the matter was closed. Granger slid off the chair and, with his head bent low, obediently walked back out the door and rejoined the game.

# 29

"YOUR THREE O'CLOCK APPOINTMENT IS here," the receptionist said when the doctor opened his office door and looked out at the small sitting room. "He's a new client: Kyle Granger."

The doctor adjusted his glasses and pushed up his shirtsleeves to fight off the increasing heat of the summer afternoon. Though the air conditioning blasted cold air through the vents, the heat had somehow discovered a way to seep indoors through the tiniest of crevices.

"It's 'Granger Kyle,' actually," the doctor said kindly to the receptionist. Still standing in his doorway, Dr. Jenkins turned his attention from the receptionist to the young man slumped down in the chair across from the front desk. The man, whose leg was bouncing incessantly, half-smiled and half-grimaced, and raised a hand in greeting to the doctor.

Dr. Jenkins stepped aside to let Granger into the office, and turned again to the receptionist. "And Mr. Kyle is not a new client."

With a confused look, the receptionist looked back at the client notes on the computer.

Dr. Jenkins shut his office door.

The only noise in the room came from the air conditioning unit. Dr. Jenkins waited to see if Granger would move or break the silence, but the man clearly wasn't in a rush to get started.

"I apologize for the confusion in the waiting area. New receptionist," the doctor explained to Granger.

Granger nodded. He was still standing in the middle of the room. His right hand drummed a quick, staccato rhythm against his leg. His eyes were roving over everything, but were expertly avoiding the doctor.

"Something looks different in here," Granger said.

Dr. Jenkins remained standing, mirroring Granger, and put his hands in his pockets. He looked around his office.

"Yes, I switched some things out. That picture is new, and I think this lamp came after your last session, too."

Granger nodded again and continued looking around.

"Would you like to sit?"

Granger took a seat. He cleared his throat. "Thanks for seeing me."

"I'm glad I could fit you in. It's been awhile."

"Yeah. I was doing pretty well, so…"

In the pause that ensued, the doctor adjusted his round glasses and did a quick, subtle, visual assessment of the young man sitting at a ninety degree angle from him in a matching armchair. It had been a few years since Granger's last session. The young man looked paler than before, made more evident by the dark circles beneath his eyes. His sandy blond hair was longer and shaggier than the doctor had ever seen it before.

Dr. Jenkins settled into his armchair.

"What brings you in today, Granger?"

"I need something to help me sleep," Granger said. His leg resumed bouncing now that he was sitting again.

"You've been having trouble sleeping?"

"Yeah."

The doctor reached for his notepad and pen and began to take notes.

"Trouble falling asleep, or trouble staying asleep?"

Granger thought about it. "Trouble falling asleep. I want to sleep, but I can't."

Dr. Jenkins asked a question he could guess the answer to: "Are you tired when you lay down to go to sleep?"

"I'm exhausted." Granger dragged his good hand down his face from his hairline to the stubble covering his jawline.

"When did it start?"

Granger shrugged. "Not sure. Maybe a few weeks ago."

"You said on the phone that you'd been in Lester for a while, right? You've been back in Eugene for how long now?"

"Almost a month, I think."

As always, Dr. Jenkins waited between questions, in case Granger had more to say.

"How was your trip?" the doctor asked when Granger didn't expound.

"Fine."

"Was it difficult at all?"

"No, not really. I didn't have much of an issue sleeping until I got back to Eugene."

"Were there any other 'issues' while you were there?"

Granger yawned. "Oh, you know, just the normal family drama."

"'Drama?'"

"Yeah."

Dr. Jenkins noticed when Granger's leg started bouncing just the tiniest bit faster.

"And that wasn't stressful?"

"No, I'm used to it."

"You know," the doctor said gently, "'family drama' may be 'normal' for a family, but that doesn't mean it's healthy."

"You're telling me," Granger laughed. The doctor noted that the young man still wasn't looking him in the eye. At least, not for more than a couple seconds at a time.

The second hand on the wall clock ticked several times before the conversation continued.

"Do you want to talk about what happened in Lester?"

"No. Thanks. I really just need a prescription for a stronger sleeping pill."

"A 'stronger' one? So, you've tried over-the-counter sleeping aids already?"

"Yeah. Like three or four."

"Did any of them do anything?"

"I felt more tired, but I still couldn't fall asleep. But I heard about this one sleeping pill on TV a couple nights ago. I wondered if I could try that. It was called... what was it called? Hang on a second... "

Granger rifled around in his pockets, and then his wallet.

"I wrote it down in case I couldn't remember it," he said as he searched. He shook his head. "Sleep deprivation has been really screwing with my memory. And, get this, the other night when I went out to my car after work, I couldn't find my car keys. Then I realized that they were already in the ignition; I'd left my car running and unlocked the whole time I was at work."

Dr. Jenkins couldn't help but lift his eyebrows in surprise.

"How long had you been at work?"

"Well, only about forty minutes," Granger said. At that moment, his expression changed. Again, Dr. Jenkins noticed.

"That's a pretty short shift," said the doctor.

"Well, it was supposed to be six hours, but there was a little... problem."

"A problem?"

"Yeah, it was no big deal. I kinda got into an argument with my boss and he sent me home."

"And that wasn't a 'big deal?'"

"Nah, things will work themselves out. Anyway, I don't want to take up too much of your time, I really just came in for a prescription."

Dr. Jenkins honed in on the presenting symptoms: Granger was jittery, he was avoiding eye contact, his voice was too high and too loud, and his smile never reached his eyes. He was pale, unkempt, and his face was breaking out. Dr. Jenkins assessed and could think of a few different possible explanations. Some were better than others.

Dr. Jenkins deliberated, letting the clock tick for five seconds before he set down his notepad, pen, and glasses on the side table. He mentally buckled down and looked straight at Granger.

"Insomnia, absent-mindedness, argumentative... Do I have it right so far?"

"I wouldn't say 'argumentative,' we just had a disagreement."

"Have you had disagreements with anyone else in the last two or three weeks?"

"I mean, just little ones. Disagreements are normal. But it's easy to get irritated with people when you haven't slept in weeks."

"Oh, absolutely."

"So you believe me?"

Dr. Jenkins' brow crinkled. "Why wouldn't I believe you?"

Granger didn't have an answer.

"Have you been taking any stimulants? Legal or illegal?"

"You mean am I on drugs? No way."

"It's just a question. I have to ask, because of your symptoms."

"I swear I'm not on drugs. I don't touch any of that stuff."

"My question included coffee and energy drinks… caffeine can have a strong effect on people."

"Oh, well, I only drink coffee before work, to stay awake. But it's only one or two cups a day."

Dr. Jenkins made a note of that on his pad and then turned back to his client.

"I definitely think you have insomnia."

"Great. What medication do you think is best?"

"Well, as you know, I always explore the non-pharmacological options first."

Dr. Jenkins saw from Granger's expression that this was not the response he wanted to hear.

"Look, Doctor, you're excellent at what you do. I know from experience. And normally, I would totally be up for trying the non-medication route first, but I'm desperate here." Granger's voice cracked. "I need sleep."

"I know you do. I'm guessing these last few weeks have been very difficult without it."

Granger nodded. Dr. Jenkins was not surprised to see the sleep-deprived man's eyes grow moist.

"But I think we need to talk about the events preceding the insomnia. We've talked before about how one thing can affect many other things."

Granger shot out of his chair just then, making purposeful strides toward the door. "Look. I appreciate all this, Doctor, I really do, but I really don't have time for all this, okay? I just needed something strong to help me sleep, something besides booze, and I have to be at work in an hour and a half so I really can't do any digging into my personal life today because I need to be able to hold it together at work so I can try to fix this mess with my boss —" Granger reached for the door handle. Dr. Jenkins was standing by this time. "— so, I'll come back and see you some other time, okay?"

To Dr. Jenkins' surprise, Granger paused after he opened the door. The moisture in his eyes was pooling, threatening to spill over at any second. He looked at the doctor like he was waiting for him to say something.

"I understand," the doctor said. "Take care, in the meantime. But remember, it might be a few more weeks before you can get another appointment."

Granger didn't move. His right hand held the door handle in a white-knuckle grip, like it was the only thing keeping him upright. He tapped his foot and chewed on his lip.

"Can you make it that long?" Dr. Jenkins asked.

Granger tried to laugh, but it came out as a choked sob, and the next time he blinked, a tear ran down each of his cheeks. He looked down at the door handle and, without moving his feet, pushed the door lightly shut, leaving the inquisitive-looking receptionist staring on the other side.

And then came the inevitable emotional breakdown brought on by a lack of sleep: still standing by the door, several more tears escaped his eyes.

"How come... I'm not better?" Granger whispered.

Dr. Jenkins, who was still standing in the middle of the room, felt his heart break a little. As if it were his own son standing in front of him.

"It's a process, Granger. No one's reached the finish line."

Tears streamed down the man's care-worn face.

Dr. Jenkins offered him some tissues, which Granger accepted, and they returned to their armchairs.

"I'm so tired," Granger whispered again.

"What's been keeping you awake?"

Granger took a shaky breath and mopped the tears still rolling down his cheeks. "I keep reliving moments with my grandma."

"Your grandma," the doctor repeated.

Granger nodded. "She's got dementia. I don't think I mentioned that before. That's why I went back to Lester a couple times this spring. She's in a memory care unit at a nursing home there."

Dr. Jenkins' heart broke in a couple more places, remembering when his own mother got dementia.

"This is your dad's mom? The one who helped raise you?"

"Yeah."

"Well, it's no wonder you're having trouble sleeping."

Granger sniffed and helped himself to a few more tissues.

"You hadn't been back home in quite a while, had you?"

"About six years."

"Was it difficult to be back?"

Granger hesitated, but then nodded.

"Were other family members visiting your grandma?"

Granger nodded. "My mom and Jakey, er, Jake, live there still. But Trevor came back, and Levi and his wife and daughter… and my dad."

It hadn't taken a very lengthy review of the notes from Granger's past sessions for the doctor to remember the details of the father-son relationship. As one well-practiced in the art and science of therapy, Dr. Jenkins forced a completely neutral expression onto his face and asked, "and how did that go?"

Granger only shook his head.

"I see."

The clock ticked for a while, and Granger emptied the tissue box.

Dr. Jenkins very delicately began again, "I'm sorry you were in such a painful situation, but I think you can be proud of yourself for taking such a brave step."

Granger sniffed. "I had to go back. It was my grandma…"

"Yes, I understand. She's one of your most powerful positive relationships from Lester. I'm glad you went back."

"Part of me wishes I hadn't. Things were going so well until I went back."

Dr. Jenkins crossed his ankle over his knee again. "Tell me about how things were going up until then. We haven't talked in a while."

"I was doing good. I was moving up in my job. I was getting along with my friends. I had a social life."

"How'd you feel about all that?"

"Good. Stable."

*Stable. Now we're getting somewhere.*

"Did you feel at peace? Did you have joy in your life?"

Granger looked caught off guard. "Um… I don't know. Maybe. I hadn't thought about it."

"But you liked feeling 'stable.'"

"Yeah."

"Did you feel 'unstable' in Lester?"

"Yes. I felt like I wasn't myself."

"Do you want to talk about Lester?"

"No," but then he added, "not yet."

"Alright, what would you like to talk about?"

"My sleep."

"Alright. You said you've been arguing with people in the last few weeks," Dr. Jenkins said. "Now, I know I've seen you mostly at your lowest in life, rarely at your healthiest, but as long as I've known you, you've had an argumentative side." Granger cringed. "How is this different?"

"I was doing better with that," Granger said. "I really was. I was biting my tongue more. Trying to think first. But now that I'm not sleeping... People at work have been arguing with me a lot lately. And I got in this big fight with my roommate a few nights ago. We never fight."

"What was the fight about?"

"Honestly, I don't really know. I was a little tipsy."

No sooner were the words out of his mouth than Granger looked like he wished he could take them back.

"Were you out drinking with some friends?"

"No. I was alone."

"Have you been going to bars a lot lately?"

"What's 'a lot?'"

*I think that answers the question.*

"How many days a week? On average."

"Maybe three. Or four."

Granger looked at the floor.

"That's surprising," said Dr. Jenkins. Granger said nothing. "I remember you telling me that you tended to avoid that scene... on account of—."

"I did. I do."

Dr. Jenkins looked at the bouncing leg, the untied shoes, the scraggly blond beard, the untidy blond hair, the pale face, and the watery, shadow-rimmed eyes. The clock told him their session had come to an end. He knew his next client would be arriving any minute.

From the pocket on the side of the armchair, Dr. Jenkins pulled out a smaller pad of paper and clicked his pen.

"I think you should come back, Granger."

Granger didn't respond, but watched the doctor write. The young man looked absolutely defeated, even when the doctor ripped the slip of paper off the pad and handed it to him.

"This will help you sleep, but it won't solve your problems. I'm prescribing continued talk therapy for that, and maybe some group therapy… we'll see."

Granger nodded.

Dr. Jenkins pointed his pen at the prescription. "As a reminder, do not take that with alcohol."

"Thanks, Doc."

"And remember to call if there's an emergency."

"I will. I'll see you next time."

# 30

AT THAT POINT, THE SLEEPING pills were Granger's life preserver. As long as he had them, he could manage without alcohol. As soon as he got home from work each day, no matter what time it was, he popped a pill into his mouth, drank a glass of water, and hit the pillow. He was a little groggy when he woke up each morning, but he'd gladly take groggy over sleep-deprived. In the hours before his next shift he did what he could to maintain normal life: he filled his car up with gas, he bought some food at the grocery store just in case his appetite came back, he did only enough laundry so that he'd have clothes to wear for his next shift, and he brushed his teeth. Everything else fell by the wayside, but he was sleeping again. At least he was sleeping again.

This was how life went every day until his next session with Dr. Jenkins. And then every day until the next session. The sleeping pills and Dr. Jenkins were the only things keeping him upright. At least, that's how it felt to Granger.

"I feel like a mess inside," Granger said to the doctor during their third session.

"What do you mean by that?"

"I thought I had everything finally figured out. And then, just like that, I was flat on my back again. No matter where I go lately, things fall apart, and it feels like everyone around me thinks it's my fault."

He looked at the doctor. "Is it my fault?"

"I think the situation is probably too complicated to place all the blame on one person."

"Hm… I hope so."

"Do you trust yourself, Granger? To make good decisions?"

"I don't know…" He rested his elbow on the armrest of his chair and leaned his head on his hand. "I've never thought about it."

"I'd like you to think about it this week."

"Okay," he said without argument.

"In the meantime, I'd like to give you a glimpse of yourself through my perspective. Is that alright?"

"Sure."

"You've said a couple times now," Dr. Jenkins read from his large notepad, "that you 'feel like life is falling apart.' But over the last four weeks you have been diligent about avoiding alcohol. You have not missed any work or been sent home because of fights with coworkers or your boss. You have kept up with your hygiene, even if it's less than you would do normally. And you have come to every one of our sessions so far, ready to talk."

Granger kept listening.

The doctor continued, taking another look at his notes, "you said in our first session that you, 'wish you hadn't gone back to Lester' because things got so 'out of control' when you did. And yet, here you are, getting things back under control."

"I'm not, though."

"I think you are. It's slow-going, I know. But I can see what a difference even three weeks has made. I expected your first visit back to Lester to be bumpy. But you're figuring it out. Not only that, you went back twice!"

Granger tapped his foot slowly on the carpet as he thought.

"I think you need to give yourself more credit," the doctor said. "You said in our second session that you don't want anything to do with your family anymore." Dr. Jenkins set down his pad of paper and took off his glasses. "I understand why you'd think that, given all that's happened. You crave stability in your life that you haven't felt from your family in years. But I have trouble believing you don't want anything to do with them."

"Why?" Granger asked, feeling defensive.

"Because you've been bringing them up more and more, and in ways that make your concern for them evident."

Granger shook his head, "I'm bringing them up because I need to process everything. I'm angry at them."

"You can be angry with them and care deeply for them at the same time."

Granger shook his head again.

"Last week, you talked for almost ten minutes about what a mistake you think Jake is making by not playing baseball in college. And today, when I mentioned Trevor in passing, you told me about the pills and the depression and anxiety and you wondered how long he'd been silently dealing with his own problems. And your mom--"

"My mom," Granger said with venom in his tone, "makes me madder than all of my brothers combined."

Dr. Jenkins eased up.

"Because she could have prevented so many painful things, but didn't," Dr. Jenkins said, repeating what Granger had told him before.

"Yes. And because she pretends none of it happened. She thinks she can make up for it by worrying about me and babying me."

"Do you think she's responsible for the things that happened to you?"

"Yes."

But Granger closed his eyes and pinched the bridge of his nose to fend off the headache. He took a deep breath. "No. Not responsible. But she could have done something to stop it. What's the phrase? A 'sin of omission?'"

"So, you *don't* hold her responsible?"

"No. But I want to. And I hate the way she tries to put a bandaid on the problem instead of actually fixing it."

Dr. Jenkins didn't say anything for a while. When he did speak again, he said something unexpected.

"Have I ever told you about my older brother, Charlie?"

Granger looked over at him, puzzled. "I don't think so."

Dr. Jenkins rarely shared personal anecdotes during their sessions. The doctor fiddled with his glasses.

"Charlie lived his entire adult life without part of his right leg."

Granger was shocked this was the first time he was hearing about Charlie. He would've thought a story like his was the kind of thing a counselor would share with a monoplegic during their first or second session.

"I was always impressed by the creative ways he figured out how to do things."

Granger braced himself for the pep talk: *"How to thrive when you only have three working limbs!"* He was already annoyed with Dr. Jenkins for delivering such a pep talk, and was surprised that the doctor would share such trite advice, as it was out of character for him.

"I miss him very much. He died five years ago this month."

"Oh, I'm so sorry."

"Me too. He killed himself."

The pathway of Granger's expectations took a sharp left turn. It was no longer a mystery why Dr. Jenkins hadn't shared that story during their first or second session. Granger, thoroughly humbled by his incorrect assumption, kept his mouth shut.

"Charlie was in the military. When I was nineteen, he went MIA during an assignment overseas. When he was found three months later, he had a fresh, severe injury to his leg. He was shipped home and got part of his leg amputated."

"He was missing for three months?" Granger asked, aghast.

"Yes." The doctor shook his head, or maybe he shuddered from reliving a nightmare that had been someone else's reality.

"He never talked about what happened during those three months. All I know is that the injury happened toward the end of it, and that he came home with severe PTSD. It lasted the rest of his life. He did amazingly well with the prosthesis, but the PTSD was debilitating. He could never maintain a romantic relationship, even though he tried. He couldn't keep a job for more than a few weeks. He wasn't safe to drive because of the flashbacks —"

Granger's gaze flicked from Dr. Jenkins' haunted expression to a loose thread on the rug.

"Right when he came home, I took him everywhere I could think of that would be peaceful. We went to a lot of parks. We ate a lot of hot dogs, which were his favorite. We avoided anywhere with large crowds or lots of noise. Until he moved out, I stayed up late almost every night, talking with him and trying to take his mind off things. I would sit in his room with him after he woke up screaming. I went with him to his physical therapy and occupational therapy appointments. I asked him questions about what happened, thinking maybe if he could talk about it…"

He cleared his throat. When Granger looked up again, Dr. Jenkins was looking down, his brows knit tightly together and his eyes misty.

"He moved out of our parents' house eventually, but a few years later moved in with me. At first he seemed to be doing better, but he wasn't."

Dr. Jenkins shook his head again. "I did all I could think of, trying to help him all those years. I sacrificed nights and weekends with my wife and kids to spend time with him. But he just kept on suffering. It was… gut-wrenching… to watch. I wanted to help him so badly, but no matter how much I did, it wasn't enough. How do you help someone who's living in a never-ending nightmare right before your eyes? And how do you live with yourself when you can't?"

When he looked at Granger, Granger realized these weren't rhetorical questions.

Granger swallowed the lump in his throat.

"At least you tried," Granger croaked.

"Do you think that's enough?"

"I guess… I guess it was all you *could* do. It has to be enough."

Dr. Jenkins watched Granger, and nodded.

"So how do you think your mom *really* feels that she couldn't protect her child? How do you think she *really* feels that she hasn't been able to fix it?"

Granger looked down at the carpet again. The recent moments with his mother flickered in his memory.

"I get it," Granger finally said, so softly that he almost didn't hear himself say it.

# 31

GRANGER HAD THE NEXT TWO days off from work, and with it being summer break, the high school and college students were picking up shifts left and right, leaving no openings that he could fill. His plan B was to sleep for forty-eight hours. Unfortunately, the sleeping pills and therapy were helping so much already that he was wide awake by 9:30 the next morning.

He called work again.

*"Sorry, everyone showed up for their shift, and no one's called in yet."*

He hung up and tossed his phone away.

The longer he laid there staring at the ceiling, the more he worried.

*What am I going to do to keep myself busy for the next two days?*

He'd been avoiding the bars successfully. He hadn't blacked out or gotten into another drunken fight with his roommate. But it helped that all he was really doing was working and sleeping. Now that he couldn't do either... and his next counseling session wasn't for another week.

He felt sweat forming on his forehead.

He sat upright in bed and fumbled around for his cell phone again. After a couple tries, he dialed the correct number.

He sat back against the pillows while it rang, feeling untethered.

*"Dr. Jenkins' office,"* said the receptionist.

"Hi," Granger said immediately. "This is Granger Kyle. Is the doc available? I really need to talk to him."

*"He's with a client at the moment. Is this an emergency?"*

"Uh, define emergency."

*"Are you or someone around you at risk of harming self or others?"*

"Uh, no, I guess not..."

*"Then would you like me to have him call you back when he's free?"*

"Yes, please. Do you know when that might be?"

*"No, I don't. He's got a pretty full day."*

"Oh. Okay."

*"But if an emergency develops, please go directly to the emergency room and call us from there."*

"Okay."

He hung up.

*Well, now what?*

*"Give yourself more credit,"* the doctor had said. Maybe Dr. Jenkins was right. Maybe he'd made more progress in the last six years than he thought he had.

*"Do you trust yourself?"*

Did he? Could he?

*Not really,* he had to answer honestly.

He tilted his head back, resting it on the wall behind him. *'Trusting myself' hasn't been going too well.*

Then, from out of nowhere, Granger heard another voice inside his head.

No, not a voice, it wasn't audible... but it was *like* a voice. It was whispering something to him.

He tilted his head to the side and squinted, trying to figure out what he was 'hearing.' He wondered if he was 'hearing' his conscience talking to him, or maybe it was God, or maybe he was delusional.

The 'voice' wasn't going away. It was such an odd, but not uncomfortable, experience, that he started to lean in a little bit.

He was doubting his own inner voice lately, but the other 'voice' seemed more trustworthy. He wasn't sure how he knew that, but he did. It was a faint voice, but it was there. And the more he paid attention to it, the more he recognized it.

It wasn't his own voice, he knew that. He'd heard the 'voice' before, and it often sounded like his grandma's, but it wasn't. Sometimes it had sounded like Dr. Jenkins, but it wasn't his either.

The 'voice' sometimes told him things he didn't want to hear, compelled him to do things he really didn't feel like doing, but the 'voice' hadn't steered him wrong, yet.

He hadn't heard it in so long, he'd forgotten about it.

He still didn't know what it was saying, since there were no words, but he ignored his own stream of consciousness for the moment and listened to the other 'voice.' And the message started to become clearer.

His breathing slowed. His forehead dried. His stomach settled. He swung his legs over the side of the bed and stood up. As soon as he did, the soundless voice urged his feet forward; he suddenly felt like going for a run. He didn't question it or argue, though he felt more than a little strange about the whole thing.

*It's better than the alternative,* he reminded himself. He pulled on his tennis shoes and left the house.

He took it very, very slowly. Almost immediately, his mind wandered again to his counseling session from the day before.

Progress. Had he really made progress?

He thought about the kind of guy he'd been six years ago. His temper wasn't gone now, he was still holding grudges, and his patience with his family was thin, but six years ago he wouldn't have even thought of setting foot in Lester again. Even one year ago. And sure, it had disrupted the good life he'd so carefully created in Eugene—

*Was your life really that great before going back home?*

He didn't know if he'd asked the question or if the other 'voice' had.

He thought of the loneliness and anonymity he'd gotten so used to over the last six years. He had friends, but not close friends. James was his closest friend now, and they still felt like strangers sometimes. He liked Eugene because it wasn't Lester, but was Eugene really home? He kept telling himself that he didn't feel like himself in Lester, but really, he felt more like himself in Lester than he had in all the time he'd lived in Eugene. He just didn't *like* who he was in Lester.

*Maybe that could be different.*

*What are you saying? You're not really considering moving back to Lester, are you?*

*No, no, of course not.*

He pictured his mother's sappy, pitiful face as she asked him to move back to Lester, and the resulting fire in his legs propelled him forward with more ferocity. But the surge of adrenaline subsided and he had to slow to a walk. Likewise, the anger subsided when he remembered Dr. Jenkins' story.

For the first time, he allowed himself to think of his mom from another perspective: that of a mother who was not infallible, who had not been tough enough, nor omniscient enough, to protect her child from the reckless selfishness of someone she still trusted more than herself. A mother who knew she could never fully make amends for her lapse in judgment.

He wiped his eyes and his nose and picked up the pace to a slow jog again.

He wished Dr. Jenkins hadn't told him about Charlie so he could stay angry at his mother forever. The anger made sense to him. She deserved it, after all. It was just and it was justified.

He turned his attention to Jake for a reprieve.

Surprisingly, with his newfound perspective, he saw in himself pride for his little brother that he hadn't thought much of before. Despite their disagreements and despite changing a lot in the last six years, Granger had to admit he was relieved by how well his brother had turned out. And impressed. Granger felt a pang of jealousy, another feeling he'd been repressing, and put thoughts of Jake aside.

Trevor came next, accompanied by a wave of pure guilt. He needed to fix things with Trevor if with no one else.

*But I was the victim, not Trevor. He should feel bad for me.*

Granger's exhausted mind searched for something completely different to think about for the rest of his jog.

*Red hair.*

He slowed to a walk again.

He hadn't thought of Katie in weeks. More than weeks, even. Over a month! Even his final days in Lester had been free from worries about seeing her or thinking about her. It was a nice change.

He dragged his sore body up the steps to his townhouse and stumbled, breathless, into the kitchen for some water.

"Oh, there you are."

Granger jumped, not expecting his roommate to be home.

"You okay?"

"Tired," Granger wheezed.

"What happened to you?"

"I went for a run."

James raised his eyebrows. "Are you okay?"

"Thirsty." Granger chugged some water and then coughed out half of it into the sink. He drank slower after that.

"I thought maybe you went out or something."

*Out.* That was code for 'drinking the day away,' lately.

"Nope. Went for a long run."

"Good. That's good."

"What are you doing home?"

"Forgot my lunch." James reached into the fridge and pulled out a sandwich. "What are you doing the rest of the day?"

"I don't know yet. I hadn't planned that far ahead."

James scrutinized Granger. "Maybe we could hang out tonight."

"I thought you and Deja were going to a movie tonight."

James shrugged, "we can watch something here. She doesn't like movie theaters anyway. Too many kids. She says it makes it hard to relax and enjoy the movie."

"That's okay, you guys do your thing. I'll watch something here—"

"No, no, it'll be fun. We can get pizza. Let's do it. I'll text Deja and tell her. She'll be thrilled."

Granger thought about protesting more, but in the end he just shrugged. He wouldn't mind having some company in the evening. It would make it easier to avoid going 'out.'

James was halfway out the door when he poked his head back inside and yelled to the kitchen, "oh, and you got some mail. Real mail, not just ads. It's here by the front door."

Granger thanked him and heard the door shut. Once his heart rate was back to normal and he'd guzzled enough water to fill a large fish tank, he wandered to the living room. He was about to plop down on the couch and see what games were on when he remembered that James' girlfriend was coming over that night, so maybe he shouldn't cover the couch in fresh sweat.

He sighed and turned toward the stairs for a shower when something purple and shiny caught his attention.

He took his foot off the bottom step and walked over to the front door. It was a purple envelope half-covered by shiny stickers. On closer inspection, Granger saw that they were all baseball-themed stickers.

*Must be one of James' nieces or nephews,* he thought.

He sorted through the other mail since he was already there, but didn't find anything with his name on it. He picked up the purple envelope and flipped it over. There in the center was his own name, and in the left-hand corner...

"Izzy?"

Confused and curious, he opened the envelope and pulled out a folded piece of purple construction paper containing even more stickers. In purple crayon, written almost illegibly, were written these words:

*Dear Mr. Kyle,*

*I hope you are feeling good. In Sunday school we prayed and writed letters for people who are sad right now and I prayed for you. I am sorry you are sad. How is your grandma? I hope she is okay.*

*From, Izzy.*

He didn't know what to think about the letter. He was not used to getting mail from children, especially not from children he barely knew.

He set the letter down on the table by the door and went upstairs for his shower.

When he came back down, clean, he started rummaging around the living room and kitchen. After a nice, long search he found what he was looking for. Standing at the kitchen counter, he wrote his response on a piece of printer paper. He was out of practice. He hadn't written a personal letter since his pen pal assignment in fourth grade, and he couldn't remember the last time someone had sent him one, either. But Izzy had, and she didn't even really know him.

It was a short reply, only long enough for him to thank her for the letter and assure her that he was doing 'fine.' In the last line he said hello to Nina.

He stepped back and looked at his work. Why had he felt compelled to write her back? He had a feeling it had something to do with her and her own dad. He stood in the kitchen staring at the letter for a while. Then he reached for his phone and, with only a slight hesitation, dialed his mom's number. It rang several times before there was an answer.

*"Granger?"* It was not his mom's voice.

"Jake? Is that you?"

*"Yeah it's me,"* Jake yelled into the phone.

Granger furrowed his brow. Jake's voice sounded odd, and there was a lot of noise in the background.

"Is everything okay there?" Granger asked.

*"What?"* Jake yelled.

"Is everything okay?" Granger yelled back.

There was a commotion on the other end of the line that made the hair on the back of Granger's neck stand up.

"Hello? Jake?" Granger yelled.

*"Hang on one sec."*

Granger heard muffled voices and more commotion. Jake was talking to someone, but the other voice didn't sound like their mother's, either.

*"Granger, you still there?"*

"What's going on? What's all that noise?"

*"We're in an ambulance."*

Granger gripped the phone tighter and shouted into it so Jake could hear him. "Who are? Why? What happened? Is someone hurt?"

*"Yeah it's... hang on one second..."*

"No, Jake, wait."

Too late. Granger waited, seeing as he had no other choice.

When Jake finally addressed him again, he said, *"Sorry, the EMT's need information. We're on our way to the hospital. Something's wrong with Grandma."*

"What? What's wrong?"

*"... has been acting... but she won't let any of the..."*

"Jake," Granger yelled. "Jake, I can't hear you."

*"...driving through a thunderstorm... sorry I'll try to... we've got... raining and hailing..."*

"It's Grandma? Did you say she's acting strange?"

*"... call you at the hospital..."* was all he heard next.

"No, Jake, just talk fast. Tell me what's going on. How is she acting 'strange?'"

*"She's been yelling and throw..."*

His voice was covered up by a clap of thunder that sounded like a skyscraper hitting the ocean.

*"... nursing home thinks... but she won't let anybody..."*

"So, you're in the ambulance with her?" Granger asked, trying to make sense of it all.

*"No. I'm in the ambulance..."*

"What? Jake, what'd you say?"

*"... ambulance with mom."*

"Grandma's not there?"

*"...ma's in another..."*

"She's in another ambulance?"

*"Yes."*

"Why are you and mom in an ambulance?"

*"... through a lamp..."*

Granger pulled the phone away from his ear for just one moment while he grunted in frustration. "What? 'Through a lamp?' What does that mean? Jake I can't—"

*"Grandma threw a lamp and hit... so..."*

"She threw a lamp? Wait, she hit somebody?"

*"Yes. Mom."*

Granger froze.

*"Hang on, Granger... need to answer more..."*

Granger sat down in the closest chair. Dazed, he listened to the muffled chatter on the other end of the line as he started to put the pieces together.

*Jake and Mom were in an ambulance? Grandma was in another ambulance? Grandma was acting weird... throwing things... and she... she'd hurt Mom? Jake was answering the EMT's questions...*

"Jake! Jake," Granger yelled into the phone. It took a couple tries until Jake finally responded. "Why are *you* answering the EMT's questions?"

*"Because mom..."*

"What? I didn't hear you."

*"... knocked..."*

"Jake, say it again."

*"... got knocked out..."*

Granger stared at the fridge.

Then he shot up, ran to the front door for his car keys, and left the house, locking it behind him.

Jake was still trying to convey information to him through all the noise and static caused by the storm, but Granger interrupted him.

"Jake, I can't hear anything. I'm coming to Lester. Text me when you can. Do you hear me? I'm on my way."

# 32

IT WAS ALREADY DARK WHEN he pulled into the hospital parking lot, made darker by the black storm clouds moving in. Granger parked and ran toward the fluorescent lights of the Emergency Room's covered entrance with his shoulders scrunched up to his ears. His basketball shorts and T-shirt, which hadn't kept him cool enough earlier in the day, were now insufficient in light of the quickly-dropping temperature. The sprinkles of rain that came sideways on the wind were cold pin-pricks on his bare arms, legs, and neck.

*You're here for them. Be there for them. Be a man and be there for your family.*

He ran under the overhang, jumping out of the way of another ambulance just pulling in. He blinked a few times as he entered the building, letting his eyes adjust to the bright lights.

The Emergency Room was full of people. Granger immediately felt the unpleasant, turbulent energy that's always found in a packed ER late at night. He swallowed to try to get rid of the metallic taste in his mouth.

*You're here for them.*

He scanned the rows of parents, children, old people, young people, bleeding people, vomiting people, and crying people. Granger spotted his family across the room at the same moment Jake spotted him. Granger didn't expect the relief he felt in seeing their faces. Trevor, Levi, and Jake all stood to meet him, and Levi immediately pulled Granger into a bear hug.

"Good to see you, man," Levi said.

"You, too." Granger cleared his throat.

"I was surprised you called," Jake said. "Good timing, though."

Neither Jake nor Trevor offered a hug or handshake. Granger shoved his right hand into his pocket. He didn't know what to say, so all he did was nod his head.

"I'm glad you did," Levi said, giving Granger an affectionate, but not gentle, swat on the arm.

Granger cleared his throat again. "Me, too. I, um…" He looked at Trevor and Jake, "I'm sorry about the way we left things. I shouldn't have… well… I'm sorry."

Every word made him want to shrivel up inside, but he had to say them, he'd decided that on his five-hour drive.

"We're good," Jake finally said. "Don't worry about it."

Granger could see the shadow of Jake's boyish grin underneath the somberness. Granger gave him a light shove.

Granger turned to Trevor, next. His older brother stood at a little bit of a distance, still with his hands in his pockets.

*What happened to us?*

They nodded to each other. It would take longer to patch things up with Trevor, Granger could see that.

"They're both still in there?" Granger asked.

Levi nodded. "We haven't gotten many updates."

"What happened at *Golden Grove*?" Granger asked Jake. "I tried to call and text you after we got disconnected but I couldn't get a hold of you."

"I ran my phone battery down," Jake explained. "Didn't you hear what I told you on the phone?"

"I got maybe half of what you said. The storm kept cutting you off."

"Oh. Well, the nursing home called a few times this week," Jake said, "to tell us that Grandma's been acting strange. She's been rejecting food and medication and help, and then earlier today they called again and told us she was getting really aggressive. She was hitting and kicking staff, and screaming. They're pretty sure she's got a UTI. When they called, I was at work. Mom went up to the nursing home to try to calm her down. They said grandma grabbed a lamp and threw it. It hit mom on the head and gave her a concussion."

The brothers were quiet. The rest of the ER continued its soundtrack of disquietude and suffering around them.

Over an hour passed, and the ER didn't get any less full. They stood most of that time, since there weren't many chairs available. Finally, someone came out to the ER lobby and called their mother's name. Levi shook Jake, who'd been there for almost seven hours and who was dozing where he sat on the tile floor leaned up against the wall.

"You can come in and see Allison Benson, now," the nurse said. "She's awake but a little groggy. We're trying to keep her awake because of the concussion. She'll be a little sore, and she has several stitches on the back of her head."

"Thanks," Jake said, "and Julia Kyle? How's she?"

The nurse wrinkled her brow and looked down at the chart she was holding. "Oh, you're not here to see Allison Benson?"

"No, no, we are," Jake said, quickly. "She's our mom. But we're also here to see Julia Kyle. That's our grandma."

The nurse shook her head, "I'm sorry, this area of the hospital is only for ER patients, if you want to—"

"They're both in the ER," Levi cut in.

The nurse looked at her chart again. "They're both in the ER? Was this the car wreck?"

"No," Levi said, "our mom and grandma were brought to the ER at the same time in two different ambulances. From *Golden Grove Nursing Home.*"

"Oh, they were both nursing home residents," the nurse said. "I understand now."

"No. No," Levi said, shaking his head. Granger could tell from his voice that he was trying to remain calm.

"It doesn't matter," Granger said. "Can we see Julia Kyle? She's our grandma."

"We're on her list of visitors with the nursing home," Jake said.

"I'll go check," said the nurse. "Wait here."

They all took a step forward.

"Can we wait in our mom's room?" Jake asked.

"Oh," said the nurse. "Right. Sure." And she walked away looking slightly confused.

"Where is her room?" Levi called after her.

"Right. Sorry," she said, turning around. "I'll show you the way."

Levi shook his head as they all followed the nurse through the door. The noise from the lobby subsided, but the beeping of machines and the crying from down the hall replaced it.

"Here's her room," the nurse said. "I'll be back in a little while to check on her."

"And to tell us which room Julia Kyle is in," Levi reminded her.

"Oh, right. Yes."

"I guarantee she'll forget," Granger muttered when she was gone.

"No doubt," Jake said.

"She's probably over-worked," Levi granted, "but if it takes her more than ten minutes, I'm going to find another nurse. Or I'll just start looking in rooms."

The brothers turned to face the room. It was not a room, in fact, but rather a small area with hospital curtains for walls. Jake slowly reached for the curtain that served as a door and pulled it back. They all shuffled inside.

The hospital bed took up eighty percent of the space, and the machines next to it took up another ten percent. Their mother was lying in the bed in a hospital gown. Her translucent skin looked even paler under the hospital lights, and her graying brown hair was messy and frizzy against the pillow.

"Is she asleep?" Trevor asked.

"She's not supposed to be," Jake said. He raised his voice. "Hi, Mom."

She stirred, but barely.

"Mom," Jake said, raising his voice and getting closer to her ear. "Hi, Mom. You need to wake up. You can't fall asleep, okay?"

"If she can't fall asleep," Levi said, "why'd they lay her bed down like that?"

He reached for the bed remote and pushed a button. Something started to beep, but the bed didn't budge.

"That's not the remote for the bed," Trevor said. "I think it's that one over there."

"Where?" Levi asked.

"That one, by Jake."

"Jake, is there a remote by you?"

Jake picked up a remote. "This is a TV remote."

Granger looked around. "There's not even a TV in here."

"Maybe you adjust the bed manually," Levi said. He and Trevor bent down to look under the bed.

"There's a lever there by your foot," Trevor said.

Levi pressed it and the bed jerked and started to sink to the floor. That woke their mom up.

"That just lowered it," Jake said, who'd almost fallen off the edge. "Raise it back up."

"I'm trying," Levi said.

"Hi, Mom," Jake said again.

"Hi, Jake," she said, fighting to keep her eyes open. She looked the way Granger had often felt in his high school English class.

It took the brothers a full five minutes to figure out how to raise the bed again.

"What are you all doing here?" their mom asked once she saw and heard them all.

"You're in the hospital," Jake said. "You think they wouldn't come as soon as they heard?"

She smiled weakly at each of them. When she saw Granger, her eyes filled with tears and she reached out for his hand.

"Hi, Mom," he said, his voice catching. He edged around the bed so she could grasp his hand. "You weren't supposed to wind up in the hospital when I left."

She smiled. "I know."

His brothers were busy trying to figure out what the other remote could possibly be for, so Granger lowered his voice and leaned in. "I'm sorry for how I left."

She nodded. "I forgive you. And I'm sorry, too."

"I've, uh, still got some work to do, I guess."

"Don't worry. We all do."

He cleared his throat and turned to Trevor. "Trev, go ahead. You need a turn."

The brothers swapped places.

Levi looked at the time. "I'm going to find out where Grandma is."

"I'll come with," Granger said.

Granger followed the massive shoulders and towering frame of his oldest brother out of their mom's 'room' and into the hall. It was late, but the ER was as lively as a mall in the middle of a Saturday afternoon in the 1990s. After questioning numerous hospital employees, the brothers were finally directed to the correct room.

Their grandmother was sleeping, hooked up to an IV.

"Well, at least she's calm again," Granger said.

"Yeah." Levi approached her and patted her hand.

Granger approached her other side and reached for her other hand, but then pulled back.

He looked at the unfamiliar face, and tried to find traces of her former self there. Any that were still there were nearly impossible to spot. And yet, the past six weeks had still been full of worry that before he made it back to see her again, this new version of her would be gone, too.

He steeled himself, reached out, and covered her hand with his own.

Without warning, he was crying. Tears ran down his face and dropped onto the thin, scratchy white hospital sheets. His grandma's chest moved up and down with her breathing. It was not a peaceful expression on her face, just a still one.

He and Levi were lost in their own thoughts when a staff member's voice interrupted them.

"… the last room on the left," the voice said from the hall.

"Thank you."

At the sound of the other voice, Granger and Levi snapped to attention. They looked at each other. They each wiped their eyes just before Dave pulled back the curtain.

"Oh," he said, looking pleasantly surprised. "I wasn't sure if anyone would still be here, it being so late and all."

Levi stood up and shook Dave's hand. "We just got to her room, actually."

Dave nodded at Granger with a tentative expression on his face, then, turning back to Levi, he asked, "how's your mom?"

"Stable, but she has a concussion. Did the nursing home call you?"

"Yeah. And Jake."

Before there was even time for a lull in the conversation, Dave poked his head out into the hall again. "Lillian, over here."

"Lillian's here?" Granger asked.

Dave nodded. "We drove down together."

Their older half-sister swept into the room wearing a rain-spattered trench coat over her pink sweatpants and sweatshirt. Her blonde hair, which was usually styled so carefully whenever Granger saw her, was now pulled back into a messy ponytail. She dropped her expensive-looking handbag next to her pink flip flops when she saw her brothers.

"Levi! Granger!" She hugged each of them. "How are you both?"

Granger wasn't sure how to answer that question. "Fine."

"Good," Levi said, sounding exhausted. "Good to see you."

"How's she doing?" Lillian asked, looking at their grandmother.

"Looks like they're pumping her full of fluids," Levi explained. "She's calm now, which is good."

Lillian scooted past them and reached for her grandmother's hand.

"Has she been asleep long?"

"We have no idea," Levi admitted.

There was movement on the other side of the room. Granger looked over to see Dave gingerly sidling around the other side of the bed toward his mother. Granger wordlessly moved out of the way to allow passage. He couldn't help watching Dave. The man reached out a hand, too, but it fell short. He stroked the sheets with his fingertips, instead. He started to pull the sheets up a little, like he was going to cover her up more, but he stopped.

Lillian saw and, after dabbing under her eyes with manicured fingers, pulled the sheets up to cover their grandma's shoulders. She sat on the edge of the bed right next to their grandma. Dave remained standing.

Granger felt the anger bubbling just under the surface, as it always did when he was around Dave, but he was surprised not to feel any satisfaction in Dave's shame.

"If you want to stay with her for a few minutes," Levi said to them, "Granger and I can go check on the others and let them know you're here."

"Sure, that's fine," Lillian said, wiping away more tears as she looked at their grandma. Dave stood awkwardly off to the side, not saying anything.

The nurse was in their mom's room again, so Trevor remained

inside while the other three waited in the cramped hall.

"Is she still having trouble staying awake?" Granger asked.

Jake yawned, "yeah. They said they don't want to release her for a while, to keep an eye on her."

He yawned again.

"You doing okay?" Levi asked Jake.

"Just tired." His eyes were barely open.

"How long have you been awake?"

"Uh, I don't know," Jake mumbled. "Since, like… four thirty?"

Granger looked at the time. "It's three in the morning. You've been up almost twenty-four hours?"

Jake shrugged.

"I'll drive you home," Levi said.

"No, I'm gonna stay here."

"And do what? We can take turns being up here."

Jake shook his head, "no, no I want to stay." At that moment, he took a step backward and ran right into a vitals machine on wheels, sending the machine careening into the wall and himself onto the floor.

Granger and Levi helped him up and the three nurses who came running at the sound of the commotion made sure both Jake and the vitals machine were okay.

"Let's go," Levi said to him, pointing to the exit.

Jake sighed.

Dave came out of their grandma's room just then. When he saw them he walked right for them.

"I'll take Jake home," Granger blurted out. "You stay, I can go. I'm sure you've been awake longer than I have, anyway, so I'll be a more alert driver."

Levi looked from Granger to Dave, who had almost reached them, and then nodded.

"You wanna tell Trev? When I get back, you two can go home for some sleep." Granger said. He pulled his car keys out of his pocket. "Come on, Jake."

Jake yawned again and followed. They walked away right before Dave reached Levi.

The two brothers left the cacophony of the ER and walked out into the night. Granger had forgotten all about the storm while they were inside. Even after all the time that had passed, it didn't seem to be abating, but growing. The wind whipped around them, and big, fat drops fell fast.

"Good luck sleeping through this," Granger yelled behind him. He turned around when he didn't hear a response. "Jake?"

After redirecting Jake toward the correct car, Granger put his key in the door. At first, he didn't hear the voice over the storm.

"Hey! Wait up!"

Granger looked up and saw Dave running toward them with the uneven gait of someone who wasn't used to running.

"What is it?" Granger yelled back.

"Can I get a ride?"

"What?"

"A ride! Can I get a ride?"

Lightning lit up the sky and thunder clapped directly over their heads. Before Granger could protest, Jake had gotten into the backseat and Dave had climbed into the passenger seat. Granger got into the driver's seat and shut his door so he could hear. They were all dripping wet from the storm and when the lightning lit up their faces, Granger could see how out-of-breath Dave was.

"Where do you need a ride to in the middle of the night?" Granger asked.

"To your mom's house. She just told me she left something for me there. Paperwork for your grandma that I need to sign."

"What paperwork?"

Thunder clapped again.

"For the funeral home. I'm still your grandma's primary medical power of attorney, so I have to sign off before… you know… before she's gone."

More thunder. Granger looked in the backseat to see his younger brother laying sprawled out, fast asleep.

*I am not about to be in a car with this guy.*

But he pictured his mother lying unconscious in a hospital bed and tried to tamp down his anger.

He growled and jammed his key into the ignition. "Fine."

He pulled onto the road just as more lightning filled the sky, despite every fiber of his being warning him this was a bad idea.

# 33

GRANGER TURNED THE WINDSHIELD WIPERS on to their full speed and squinted through the glass. He could just barely see the lines on the road. In order to get to Lester, they first had to drive through a few miles of open country on a two-lane highway, with no lights nearby to help illuminate the way.

"Stormy night, huh?" Dave said from the passenger's seat.

Granger didn't respond.

*Just get home, drop Jake off, get the papers, and come back. It won't take more than an hour. You can manage forty-five minutes in a car with him.*

"I didn't realize we were expecting a big thunderstorm tonight," Dave said.

Granger didn't respond.

"How's work been go—"

"Shut up," Granger said.

"Sorry?"

"Stop talking. I'm not going to do this with you."

"I was just ask—"

"I said shut up."

Granger pressed down on the gas pedal, hoping he could shave a couple minutes off their trip. He kicked himself for agreeing to give Dave a lift.

A couple minutes later, Dave spoke up again. "I know you don't wanna talk… but can't we find any common ground?"

"Was I not clear?" Granger spat. "I don't want to talk to you."

"Now you listen here, son," Dave said, firmly. "I know you don't like me. I know you haven't forgiven me. But I am still your father and your elder and you will at least hear me out."

Granger gritted his teeth, full of hatred, but he didn't protest.

"I know what you think of me," Dave said. "I know you think I'm only here to milk whatever little money your mom and grandma have left. But when I say I've been rehabilitated, and am still making progress every day, I'm dead serious."

"Forgive me if I don't believe you."

"It's still the truth, whether you believe it or not."

"Maybe in your deluded mind, but as far as I'm concerned you'll always be a weak, good-for-nothing, gambling, drug addict."

Was that relief he felt? He'd wanted to say those words to his father for so long. He'd fantasized for years about confronting his dad and giving him a piece of his mind. And maybe decking him, too.

At a slight bend in the road, the car hydroplaned. It was a long three seconds before Granger regained control of the car, and it only heightened the amount of adrenaline coursing through his body.

"Slow down, Granger," Dave said.

*Slow down? SLOW DOWN??*

Granger let out a hysterical laugh.

"What's so funny?" Dave asked.

"You wouldn't listen to me!"

"I am listening to you."

"That night. I told you to slow down and you didn't! You couldn't have slowed down even if you tried."

Granger's pulse quickened even more, and his breathing got more shallow and rapid. It was getting harder to see the road. His father was talking to him, but something was wrong with Granger's hearing. Everything around him sounded muffled and distorted, even as the noise outside the car was getting louder. When a swirling gust of wind tried to shove the car off the road, Granger felt himself being pulled back in time to a night very similar to the present one.

# 34

FALL 2012

Granger stood up for the seventh-inning stretch and smiled down at the field as the two teams swapped places. It was shaping up to be a good game and a great night. The pitcher took the mound and readied himself.

Just before the pitch, Granger glanced at the empty stadium seat next to him and then up the concourse steps once more. His dad had gone to the bathroom fifteen minutes earlier, and it was hard for Granger to believe he would willingly miss this much of an MLB game. He was starting to get a strange feeling. But then the batter down below struck out and all thoughts of his father's whereabouts fled from Granger's mind.

Five minutes later, Dave Kyle came barreling down the concrete stadium steps and plopped into the aisle seat next to his son.

"How's the game going?" He asked Granger, energetically.

"We're ahead by three—"

"Nice! We sure picked a good game to see in person, didn't we!"

The game got wilder and the score got closer and the crowd got louder. But right before the end of the eighth inning, his Dad turned to him.

"Hey, kid, we should probably get going."

Granger looked at his dad, stunned. "What? Now? Why?"

"Well it is a school night, after all."

"But Mom said it was okay. We both heard her."

"I know, I know. I just couldn't live with myself if you missed school tomorrow."

Granger looked from Dave to the field and back again, thoroughly confused and fighting off some major disappointment.

"But—"

"Come on, son," Dave said in his 'dad' voice, which Granger hadn't heard in years. "It's time to go."

His dad stood and headed up the steps to the concourse. Granger sat for a moment watching him with his mouth open.

"Come on, son," Dave yelled over the noise.

Granger stood and trailed behind him, still holding his bag of popcorn and looking over his shoulder every now and then to catch just one more glimpse of the game below. He couldn't remember ever feeling as sad as he did when he turned around in the massive parking lot to see the gargantuan stadium silhouetted by the bright lights within, and to hear the echos of the music and cheering.

Granger had to jog to keep up with his dad as they walked a quarter of a mile through rows of vehicles. Although he'd been hesitant to spend time with his dad, he had to admit he'd been having a good time. He might even say he was having a *great* time. He just couldn't understand why they'd left early. His dad loved baseball just as much as he did, and it was a perfect night: their team was winning, Granger would get to go to school late the next day, his dad bought food from the concession stand for them, and even the weather was great. The thunder and lightning in the distance were still miles from the stadium.

Granger took one last look at the stadium. A couple up ahead of them got into their own car, and when they turned their headlights on, Dave yelped and covered his eyes. Granger looked over at him. Once he recovered, Dave laughed. And laughed and laughed.

"Man, what a game, huh?" he asked Granger.

"Yeah. It was a good one."

Dave put a hand on Granger's shoulder, which was now the same height as his own. "I'm sorry, son. I wish we could've stayed, too."

Thunder rumbled very quietly in the distance.

With his finger in his key ring, Dave spun his car keys around. Faster and faster they went until they shot off his finger and he had to lurch forward to catch them, which prompted another round of raucous laughter.

"I'm glad we did this, son," he said. "I've really missed you kids."

"Really?"

"Yeah, yeah, yeah! I'm glad your mom let me come visit. I've missed so much already. I shouldn't even call you a kid anymore, you're so tall!"

"I'm 5'5"."

"And heading off to college next fall! Man, you've got so much potential, kid. I swear I'm gonna see you playing in a stadium just like this one day. Just remember your old man when you're famous, okay?"

When they made it to the car, a gust of wind shoved Granger's door open with so much force that he had to catch it with both hands to keep it from hitting the car next to them.

"Hey," Dave said, "whadya' say we head to my place in the city for the night?"

"I thought you wanted to take me home so I could go to school tomorrow."

"Oh, come on," Dave said. He had the look and energy of a little kid about to enter a candy store.

Granger was suddenly glad they'd left early. He didn't know what was going on with his dad, but he wanted to be back home in Lester as soon as possible.

"I haven't asked my mom about staying the night. I don't think she'd be very happy about it."

"Fine, fine. We can head back. It won't be as fun, though! You won't get to try out my new Xbox!"

His dad sped out of the parking lot and onto the highway. Granger cast a worried glance at him.

Ten minutes into their hourlong drive from the city to Lester, the wind picked up even more. Granger could feel it shoving the car from the side, trying to push it off the road. The lightning got brighter and the thunder got louder. Dave turned on an old rock radio station, and the broadcast got interrupted a couple times for emergency weather notifications, which made Dave, who was singing along loudly, to pound on the steering wheel in frustration.

"Oh, come on!" he said, along with a few other words. "They

interrupted the best part!"

Thirty minutes into the drive, the lightning and thunder were in unison. The heavens opened up and it started pouring. The sound was deafening. The rain came at their car sideways, helping the wind to push the vehicle off its course.

"Maybe staying in the city for the night is a good idea..." Granger mused.

Dave didn't seem to hear him. He was singing his heart out to a song Granger didn't know.

A few minutes later, Granger tried again.

"Maybe we should slow down a little," he suggested sheepishly.

His dad turned the radio up in response, but he did slow down a little. Not enough to put Granger at ease, though. The music turned to static, which made Dave curse again and smack the power button on his stereo. Twenty minutes outside of Lester the highway veered to the right, causing the rain to hit the windshield head-on. The windshield wipers worked as hard as they could to keep up, but it was like trying to mop a flooding room.

# 35

WHEN GRANGER WAS PULLED BACK to the present, he was taking gasping breaths.

"I mean it, Granger, slow down," Dave said firmly.

They hit a small bump in the road that sent them flying higher than expected.

"What's going on?" came Jake's groggy voice from the backseat.

*Jake.*

Granger had forgotten Jake was in the car. But it was too late; he couldn't stop the attack from coming.

"Do I need to drive?" Dave yelled.

"No! Never again!"

They skidded around a corner.

"Pull over, I'm gonna drive," Dave yelled.

"I trusted you!"

It was so dark, even with the lightning illuminating their path every few seconds. Granger wasn't breathing. At least, not enough.

His hand shot to the dashboard to brace himself in the passenger seat.

No.

The driver's seat. He was in the driver's seat.

Dave was driving faster and faster.

Granger was driving faster and faster. Granger took his foot off the accelerator.

"Slow down!" Granger yelled.

"Granger!" Jake yelled. "Are you okay? Granger, pull over!"

Out of the corner of his eye, Granger saw Dave looking at him from the passenger seat. Granger looked back at him.

He saw fear in his father's eyes.

Granger felt it, too. In every atom of his body, he felt it. It was going to take them all.

Granger looked over at Dave in the driver's seat, but Dave didn't look back at him.

"St-stop," a young Granger said weakly, holding on for dear life. "You're going too fast, Dad, slow down."

"St-stop," Granger said from the driver's seat, tears pouring down his face. "Stop! Why won't you stop?"

Dave looked at the high school-aged Granger, at his rapid breathing and the look in his eyes, and for the first time that night, he looked concerned.

"Hey, don't worry, son. We'll be home in no time. It's just a little rain."

Granger looked at his dad with wide eyes, his hand still on the dashboard in front of him.

"Stop," he breathed. They were going way, way, too fast. The rain was really come down now and Granger couldn't see the road at all. There was no way Dave was in control of the car.

"Slow down, please!" Granger said from the passenger seat.

"Stop the car!" Granger yelled from the driver's seat. "I need to get out. Let me out! Dad, you're gonna kill us!"

# 36

Granger leaned forward and squinted.

"Can you see anything?" he asked his dad.

He tried to keep his voice steady, but he had to yell to be heard because it was now hailing. He was listening hard for the sound of tornado sirens in the distance, but it was pointless; there was no way he'd be able to hear anything above the the sound of the hail hitting the car.

"Oh, yeah, I can see," his dad said, still not sounding appropriately concerned by the storm.

Granger didn't even see the semi parked on the shoulder of the road before they crashed into it.

Granger's airbag deployed.

The right side of his head smashed against the passenger door window, knocking him unconscious.

He didn't wake up when the ambulance arrived, or when the EMTs loaded him inside.

He didn't stir during the drive to the ER.

He didn't hear the tornado sirens go off.

He didn't wake up until two in the morning, just before a tornado ripped through the town.

# 37

GRANGER, DAVE, AND JAKE SPED down the road.

"You could've killed us!" Granger shouted, able to breathe again, for the moment.

He was momentarily oriented enough to realize he was the one driving, and it was Dave who sat gripping the door in the passenger seat.

"I know!" Dave bellowed. "I know! Pull the car over, please!"

But Granger was sobbing in the driver's seat, decreasing his already extremely limited visibility to the point he couldn't even tell if he was on the road anymore.

"I trusted you," Granger sobbed.

"Granger," said another voice.

*Jake. Jake is in the car. Jake is in danger.*

"Granger please, pull the car over," Jake pleaded.

"I will not let you hurt him like you hurt me," Granger yelled at Dave.

"Granger!" Dave sounded desperate and, deep inside himself, Granger was glad. Dave deserved to feel that desperation. That dread.

"I'm sorry!" Dave yelled. "I'm so, so sorry, Granger. Really, I am. I meant it when I said it years ago, and I mean it even more now."

When Granger looked over again, he saw that Dave, too, was crying.

"I know what I did," Dave said. "I'm so, so sorry."

"You paralyzed me! Your own son! You paralyzed me! You ruined my career! You ruined my relationship with Katie! You ruined my future!"

"I know, I know, I know," Dave sobbed over and over again.

"Granger, please," Jake said. "Slow down! It'll be okay if we just pull over. I can drive."

*Jake. We need to slow down! Jake's in trouble! How do I slow us down?*

But Granger couldn't land both feet in reality. He jumped from the driver's seat to the passenger seat in his mind. He couldn't remember what year it was, or where they were driving from. Was it a stadium? Was it a hospital? He tried to hit the brakes, but he only hit the accelerator.

*Why isn't Dave hitting the brakes?*

*Why can't I hit the brakes?*

His head was pounding.

*I just want out! Get me out! Jake's in trouble! Granger's in trouble!*

"I'm a wreck because of you!" Granger yelled to Dave. "You turned me into you! You were just so miserable you had to make someone else's life just like yours."

"I didn't want to hurt you! I promise I didn't!"

When they hydroplaned again, Granger overcorrected. They went careening off the road.

Everything was suspended. Time was suspended.

Granger could hear people's voices, but they were muffled.

*God, please help me! Can you hear me? Help me, please! Help Jake! Where's Jake? Is Jake okay?*

Granger did not get knocked unconscious when the vehicle crashed this time. When he finally came fully back to the present, he realized his tears had ceased and he was staring, wide-eyed, straight ahead into a muddy, grassy ditch.

He heard more voices. Men's voices.

"Granger! Granger, are you okay?" Dave was yelling. "Granger, answer me! Are you okay?"

Dave slapped him lightly on the face until Granger's mind and body caught up to each other. He blinked and looked around.

"Jake," Granger said. "Where's Jake? Jake! Are you okay?"

"I'm okay," said a raspy voice from the backseat.

"What happened?" Granger asked. "Wh-what… what happened?

Where are we?"

Granger became vaguely aware of Dave moving around in the passenger seat, checking Granger over for injuries, leaning into the backseat and talking to someone.

*Someone's in the backseat. Who is it again?*

Dave was dialing 911. Dave was shouting into the phone.

That was the last thing Granger heard before he slumped over the steering wheel.

# 38

"Can you describe what happened that night?"

Granger winced at the pounding in his head, and reached a hand up to the place where his stitches had been removed. He answered the prosecutor's questions as best he could, and as quickly as he could, without a single glance in Dave's direction.

The prosecutor, a tall, bald man, waited patiently for Granger to answer. Granger wanted to feel relieved that someone was finally doing something about Dave, but he didn't. It wasn't enough.

Granger occasionally peeked over at his family who were sitting behind the rail, waiting for their turn to testify. His mother sat on the edge of her seat in a charcoal-colored dress and cardigan. Everything about her had gone very charcoal-colored, recently. She had one arm around Trevor and one arm around Jakey. Trevor and Jakey sat very still on either side of her wearing matching black pants, white button-down shirts, and black ties borrowed from their grandfather's closet. It was the same thing Granger wore. They were wearing their church clothes.

Granger felt as scared as Jakey looked and as ashamed as Trevor looked, but his anger helped him maintain a neutral expression for the duration of their courthouse visit. He looked at his family whenever he felt the urge to look at Mrs. Gardner, the plaintiff. Her husband was the truck driver that Dave killed that night.

The prosecutor, Mr. Jefferson, had just finished describing what had happened prior to the wreck:

"Mr. Gardner, per his company's foul weather policy, pulled off the road onto the shoulder at approximately 10:00 that night. He radioed in to let the dispatcher know he was waiting for the worst of the storm to pass, as we heard on the recording earlier. Mr. Gardner started to set the reflective cones out around his semi, still following protocol. At roughly 10:05 pm, Mr. Kyle drove down the road going twenty-five miles per hour over the speed limit."

Mr. Jefferson looked at Granger again and asked, "could you describe what you saw just before the accident, Mr. Kyle?"

"Nothing, really," Granger said, flatly. "I couldn't see the lines on the road because of the rain and hail."

"Did you see the semi parked off to the side?"

"No."

"Aside from when you each visited the men's room, you were with your father that whole evening, correct?"

"Yes."

"In the police report, you said he was 'acting strange' after he returned from a 'long trip to the bathroom' at the baseball stadium, correct?"

"Yes."

Granger felt his face get hot, and felt Dave's eyes on him. Dave deserved what he was getting, but Granger still felt like a traitor. A snitch. He wanted justice, though, so he continued answering the questions.

"The toxicology report shows that Mr. Kyle had cocaine in his system that evening," Mr. Jefferson stated.

When Granger's mother had first heard this news, she'd burst into a violent fit of tears. She'd rocked back and forth repeating 'what did I do? What did I do?' Even now, sitting in the courtroom with wide eyes and ramrod straight posture, Granger could see she was close to breaking down.

Mr. Gardner didn't die instantly, according to the report. He was still gasping for breath and clinging to life when the EMTs got there. He died in the ambulance, minutes before Mrs. Gardner got to her husband's side.

Granger suffered several broken ribs, some deep gashes, a severe concussion, and a traumatic brain injury causing monoplegia to his left arm. But he was alive which was, according to his grandmother, "a gift from the Lord above. A true miracle." He didn't see it that way.

Grandma sat on the other side of Jakey, holding his little hand. Her chin was tilted up and she was blinking a lot. From the witness stand, Granger couldn't tell if she had tears in her eyes or not.

"Thank you, Mr. Kyle," said Mr. Jefferson, excusing Granger from the witness stand.

Dave was called up next, looking downcast. The small cuts above his eye had healed after a couple weeks. Other than going through withdrawal, he was in perfect physical health now.

*Who's really the lucky one?*

Granger wanted Dave to feel guilty. More than guilty.

He figured Dave was more worried about a prison sentence than anything else.

Granger felt guilty. People told him he shouldn't, but he could only think about the number of chances he'd had to stop Dave. In the back of his mind, Granger had suspected drugs, but he'd denied it, not willing to believe that his father was using. And on an outing with his own son, no less. Granger wondered if he could've saved Mr. Gardner's life if he'd only done something…

"I hand down the following sentence," Judge Slater finally announced. "For Mr. David Kyle, for vehicular manslaughter and driving under the influence, ten years in prison with opportunity for parole."

The officer led Dave out of the courtroom, and as he passed by, Granger turned away, his left arm hanging limp and useless by his side.

# 39

GRANGER OPENED HIS EYES A smidge, winced, and shut them again. The sun was shining through the window directly into his eyes.

He groaned and something made a rustling noise in the corner of the room. He opened his eyes again, this time shielding them from the sun.

It took a minute for him to realize he was back at the hospital. He'd awoken when the ambulance got to them, but then fallen asleep after they loaded him inside; he'd been completely fatigued. He awoke again a few minutes before they wheeled him into a room and put him under anesthesia. Things got muddy after that. Granger didn't remember being in a hospital room earlier, but maybe he had been. He looked around, trying to remember.

He heard the rustling noise again. When he looked in that direction he saw Jake half sitting in and half laying on a chair in the corner of the room. He was wearing a navy blue windbreaker jacket as a blanket, and he was just starting to stir.

"Jake?" Granger said. Jake stirred a little more and opened his eyes.

When Granger took a breath in to sit up and say more, he got a whiff of the overpowering, sterile, hospital smell. He leaned over the side of the bed just in time to retch all over the tile floor.

Jake sprung to his feet to avoid the vomit and called for the nurse.

There were a few minutes of noise and motion while his mess got cleaned up and his vitals were taken, during which time Granger fought off some major vertigo. Once it was just he and Jake again, he started to feel a little better. He opened his eyes to see the room had stopped spinning.

"How do you feel?" Jake asked, hesitantly coming over to the bed.

"I don't think I'm gonna throw up again," Granger reassured him. Jake got a little closer.

The previous night started to come back into Granger's memory.

"I made us wreck."

"Yeah," Jake said.

He looked over at Jake and quickly gave him a once over. "You were in the car, weren't you? Are you okay?"

"I'm alright." He held up his forearm. "Besides a sore neck, this was my only injury."

He had a wide, bright red abrasion that went from his wrist to his elbow. It looked like it was covered in some kind of salve.

Granger exhaled and relaxed back into his pillow.

"You have a broken right foot and a couple cuts on your face and arm," Jake informed him. "They had to do surgery on your foot."

Granger looked down at the cast.

"I'm so stupid," he muttered, closing his eyes again. "I can't believe I... well, actually I can. Trevor was right: I'm just like him."

"Trevor didn't say you were just like Dad, he said you were more like him than you think you are."

"Same thing," Granger said with his eyes still closed.

"Not exactly."

"It's close enough. The harder I try not to be like him, the more I am."

"Well, on the bright side, if there's hope for him, there's still hope for you."

Granger looked at his younger brother standing there, so full of hope and goodness.

"I'm really sorry," Granger said in a strained voice. "I let you down... just like Dave did."

Jake swallowed and walked around the bed to look out the window.

"You know," Jake said after a minute, "you make some pretty dumb decisions, and you haven't treated people the best, but I forgive you. For all of it. Sometimes I have to forgive you over and over again for the same thing, but I always do."

"I don't know how you do that, or why."

"It's a choice. I can't wait until I feel like forgiving you, I have to choose to forgive you first, and then it gets easier."

"Still seems difficult."

"It is, but it's easier than holding a grudge."

Granger looked down at the cast on his foot with disgust. He was disgusted with everything about himself, at the moment.

"You don't have to forgive me."

"Did you not hear what I said about holding a grudge?"

"I don't think I really deserve it, though."

"Does anybody? Really. We're all messed up."

"I..." Granger began, but then stopped. He looked over at Jake. Jake was watching him, waiting for him to finish his thought. Granger almost didn't continue, but the thought was on the edge of his tongue and he knew he might be sick again if he didn't purge it from his system. "I really feel like I'm trying my hardest," Granger said, staring up at the ceiling so he wouldn't have to look at Jake. "Honestly. But, it's like I just don't have what it takes to be a good, decent guy. I can't trust myself."

Jake looked down at the parking lot, looking thoughtful.

Another thought occurred to Granger, then.

"Is Dave okay?"

"Yeah," Jake said. "He's got a broken bone in his leg and a big bruise on his chest, but otherwise, he's fine."

As if he'd heard his name, Dave appeared in the doorway. He steadied himself on his crutches and looked inside. The sight made Granger feel doubly guilty.

"Can I come in?" he asked.

"Yeah," Granger said.

The man hobbled in, very uncoordinated with his crutches.

"Are you, um... did your... how... how ya doin?" Granger stammered.

"Fine, fine. It's just a little break."

Jake crossed the room and handed Dave the jacket he'd been wearing as a blanket.

"Thanks for this."

"No problem."

Dave tried to hang the jacket over one of his crutches, but started to lose his balance. Jake stepped in to assist.

Granger watched this exchange feeling out of place in the room.

Finally, the jacket was on. An awkward quiet descended over the room.

"I'm... really sorry," Granger said. "About your foot and... the accident, and... you know... all of it."

"Well, it wasn't entirely your fault," Dave said with more gravity and gentleness than Granger had ever heard from him before. "I shoulda known better."

Granger thought of that night six years ago, and a wave of fear crashed over him. "Did I hurt anyone else?"

They assured him he had not.

"But your car's totaled," Jake said.

*Nice going. Now I get to pay for a new car* and *a rental to get back to Eugene.*

"Does Mom know about the wreck?" Granger asked.

"Yeah," Jake said. "But she knows everyone's okay."

At the look on Granger's face, he added, "we didn't want to tell her, but she's still your first emergency contact, and you were asleep for a while, so..."

"The doctors told her?"

"Yeah. They also told her that 'there are too many Kyles in the emergency room right now and they don't want to see any of us in here again for at least two years.'"

"I second that," Dave said. "In fact I'm just heading out, myself. I came to say 'bye.'"

"You're leaving?" Jake asked.

"Lillian has to get back to the city and she's my ride. Plus, I have to get back in time for my shift."

"Can't you get time off for your injury?" Jake asked.

"By the time I get the paperwork finished I'll be all healed up. Trust me."

"But shouldn't you rest your foot?" Granger asked.

"Don't you worry about me, alright? I'll be fine. You guys just focus on getting yourselves all healed up, okay? Say 'bye' to your mom for me when you see her. I'll be around."

Dave hobbled back toward the door. Granger could hear that soundless, inner voice nudging him again, so he almost told Dave to wait, but he didn't know what else to say. So, he nodded and let Dave leave the room.

Jake reclaimed his seat with a yawn, but didn't tilt his head back or close his eyes again. He picked up a sports magazine sitting on the little table next to him and thumbed through it lazily. Occasionally, he'd comment on something or other in the magazine.

"What time is it?" Granger asked.

"A little after noon."

"Have you been home yet?"

"Not yet."

The poor kid had been awake for the last thirty-some hours by that time, aside from the catnaps he kept getting awoken from, and yet there he was: still at the hospital, keeping watch over his dysfunctional family.

*If Jake shares DNA with me, and we both share with Dave, then there's gotta be some hope for the two of us, right?*

"Where are the others?"

"Right now, Trevor's with Mom and Levi's with Grandma. We're rotating."

"They got time off work?"

"It's Saturday. Neither of them work on the weekend."

"You should go home and get some sleep. I'll be fine."

"They said you could be discharged within the next few hours. By the time I get home you'll be ready to leave."

"It doesn't take that long to get home. You really should get some sleep."

When Trevor came up for his turn to sit with Granger, the two were finally able to convince Jake to go home for a while. With the promise that he'd be back in just a couple of hours, he left the room.

Silence followed Jake's exit.

Trevor walked over to the chair and sat down. Granger checked the battery on his cell phone, which had been salvaged from the wreck bearing several scratches. Trevor looked over the magazines on the table next to him. Granger adjusted his leg a little for a more comfortable position. A machine next to Granger's bed beeped.

Trevor looked up. "Are you connected to that?"

"No."

"Oh."

Trevor bent down to re-tie his shoe. Granger yawned and stretched.

"You can sleep if you need to," Trevor said, also yawning.

"So can you."

"I'm fine."

Granger nodded, "same."

"How's your pain," Trevor asked.

"Not bad, at the moment."

"That's good."

Some hospital staff rolled a bed swiftly down the hall past Granger's room. The nurses and doctors spoke to each other in medical jargon as the patient in the bed moaned loudly. Though he couldn't see the patient, he could see blood on the sheets. It wasn't hard for Granger to picture himself in that bed, or Jake, or Dave. Granger felt a little woozy. He tossed his phone around in his hand to distract himself.

"I hate that you were right," he said with a hollow chuckle.

"About what?"

"About me being just like Dad. Making stupid decisions."

Trevor didn't respond right away.

"I shouldn't have said that," he finally replied.

"You were right, though."

"Yeah, I know."

Granger almost smiled. He could've sworn Trevor almost did, too.

"But we're all kinda like him," Trevor said.

Granger shrugged. Trevor was being generous. He and Jake were much more like their mother than their father.

"I don't hold it against you," Trevor said.

"You sound like Jake. The kid's already forgiven me."

"That sounds like him."

"He forgives too easily."

"Maybe."

"I wish he'd take it back," he said quietly.

More than that, he wished he could step out of his body and into another one, and this time, it wasn't because of his left arm.

*You selfish, idiotic jerk. Look how you messed things up.* You *are messed up. You've been kidding yourself. The last six years have not been 'great,' you liar. You're miserable. You're just trying to run away from your sorry self.*

He'd never loathed himself more. With every second that passed, his nausea grew.

He dragged his good hand through his hair and down his face.

*He shouldn't have forgiven me, because if he thinks I'm forgivable...*

"I'm so tired," Granger said.

"That might be from the anesthesia. You've also been up all night."

"Not that kind of tired."

Trevor seemed to understand what Granger was getting at.

"What I wouldn't give to have it all together, like you."

"I don't have it all together," he said, trying to smile. He shook his head and looked out the window.

The longer Granger looked at his brother, the more he saw. Trevor's face was set in its usual placid expression, but underneath the fluorescent lighting, Granger could see tension and strain in the muscles. At first glance, Trevor's posture looked relaxed, but he was picking repetitively, almost desperately, at a loose thread in his shirt sleeve, which was still mostly crisp and ironed even after twenty-four hours in it. Granger remembered the pills.

"Or maybe you and Jake just make it look easier than it is."

Trevor still didn't look at Granger. When he refused to talk, Granger abandoned the circuitous route.

"I wanna know about the pills."

Trevor bounced the heel of his shoe on the floor almost imperceptibly.

The brothers looked at each other, each waiting for the other to back down. Just like they used to do when they were little, right before they'd start to wrestle over some disagreement.

"Come on, Trev."

Trevor finally shook his head, "this family has enough problems already."

"You won't tell me," Granger realized.

Trevor thought about it some more. "Not yet."

They heard footsteps in the hall. Another nurse came in to check on Granger's neck and foot pain, and let him know he could be released probably within the hour.

"Thanks," Granger said. "What about Allison Benson and Julia Kyle?"

The nurse had no idea.

Luckily, five minutes later Levi came up to Granger's room. Trevor said farewell and snuck out to go check on their grandmother.

"How you feeling?" Levi asked right away.

"Not bad. I think they're getting ready to discharge me."

"Great!"

"Have you talked to Trevor?"

"About what?"

"Did you know he's taking meds for anxiety and depression?"

Levi raised his eyebrows and exhaled, "no, I didn't, but I'm glad he is."

"You knew he was depressed? And anxious?"

Levi sat in the vacated chair. "No."

"Me neither."

Levi got a text from Janessa that he had to respond to, so Granger was left alone with his thoughts for a few minutes.

*If he's on medication for it, how bad is it? What caused it? How long has he had it?*

Before long the nurse was back and Granger was getting discharged. Levi drove him back to their mom's house where Jake was passed out on the couch, sleeping soundly and drooling. A few hours later their mom was released, too, and then their grandma was taken back to *Golden Grove* in an ambulance.

And just like that, it was all over.

Granger was adamant that he be the one to take the first and longest shift sitting with their mom that evening. His brothers needed sleep, and Granger knew it was about the only helpful thing he'd be able to do over the next few days.

She was tired, dizzy, and just wanted to sleep. So, Granger was tasked with waking her up every couple hours to talk to her and make sure she was okay.

She was sound asleep, as was everyone else in the house except Granger, when some of their neighbors came home. Granger could hear their car doors opening and shutting.

"Granger?"

He looked up from his phone. The noise must have woken her up.

He sat up, "yeah? You need something?"

"My water," she said, hoarsely.

It was difficult, but he managed to lean over to deliver her water, without moving his elevated foot around too much.

"Thank you, honey. How are you feeling?"

"I'm fine, Mom. A lot better than you. Don't worry about me right now."

She gave him a tired smile. He knew it was an impossible thing to ask of her.

"What are the other boys doing?"

"Sleeping."

"Good." She took another drink of water. "Where is Dave?"

"He went back to the city with Lillian. He told us to tell you 'bye,' and that he'd be around."

"I'm glad you're all okay."

"Me too."

"When I heard about the accident..." she shook her head and her eyes got misty.

"I know. Things could've been worse. But they weren't."

"Jake told me you had another attack. That was why you wrecked."

"Yeah," he said.

"I'm surprised you let him in the car with you."

"Jake?"

"No, Dave. I would've thought--"

"Oh, yeah, I know. I should've thought of that before."

She turned her head to get a better look at him, "I know it didn't end well, but I'm proud of you for doing it."

*If only I could say the same thing.*

"Did you know," she said, "that it was your dad who called for an ambulance that night?"

"I figured it was either him or Jake."

"I'm not talking about last night," she said. "I'm talking about six years ago."

Granger frowned and wrinkled his brow. "What?"

"After he crashed into the semi, he was the only one conscious. He was the one who called the ambulance. And when the police turned up, he turned himself in on the spot."

"But… wait a minute… why… how do you know?"

"It came out during his trial."

"So, you heard it from him?"

"No, it was part of the official police report."

"But, I've never heard that before. I would've remembered that if it came out during the trial."

"Maybe you heard it and you just didn't want to believe it."

He felt the metaphorical rug get ripped right out from under him.

"I had a feeling you didn't remember," she said.

"He turned himself in?"

"He walked up to the EMTs and told them what happened, then he walked up to the cops and told them what happened."

"Everything?"

"Everything."

Granger sat back in his chair.

*He called the police? He turned himself in?*

He went through that fateful night again in his head. When he got to the part where he was knocked unconscious, he filled in the gaps with the testimonies he'd heard during the trial. For the last six years, he'd tried to block out those memories, but after last night, it was like the screws had been loosened; He didn't have to box up those memories so tightly anymore.

He could feel his mom watching him while the wheels spun in his head.

"Who did you think called the ambulance and police that night?" she asked.

"I don't know. I guess I just thought someone passing by saw everything and…"

"There was no one else around for miles."

"I… I didn't know."

"A few weeks ago, it wouldn't have changed anything for you," she observed.

"You're right."

"Does it change things for you, now?"

"It might."

# 40

WHEN GRANGER AWOKE, HIS MOTHER'S bed was empty.

He sat up with a start.

He found his crutch and tried to pull his half-asleep self upright, all the while chiding himself for falling asleep on the job. But when he got to the hall and heard his mom's voice coming from the kitchen he slowed down and, starting to wake up a little more, realized that if something had gone terribly wrong with her condition during the night, he would have heard at least something. He exhaled and, balancing against the wall for a moment, rubbed his tired eyes.

She was talking on the phone as he entered the kitchen. When she heard the noise of his crutch she turned around and immediately motioned for him to sit down at the table. When she finished her conversation she joined him at the table where she immediately rested her head in her hands.

"You okay?" he asked. "Is it another headache? Can I get you something?"

"No, no," she said without smiling. "Thank you."

The lines on her face seemed more pronounced that morning, and her hair was tousled from sleep. She was still wearing her pajamas, and the blue cotton bathrobe that hung from her shoulders was starting to look too big for her frame.

"What's wrong?"

"That was the nursing home," she said, holding up her cell phone.

"How's she doing?"

"She's sleeping. They just called to give me a readmit update."

Jake shuffled into the kitchen, his hair standing up in all directions.

"What's going on?" he asked.

"The nursing home just called to update me. She's sleeping right now."

Jake nodded and helped himself to a glass of water.

"Trev and Levi aren't awake yet?" Jake asked.

"They left town about an hour ago. They'll be back in a day or so," she said.

"Should we go up to visit her when she wakes up?" Granger asked.

"That might be difficult," their mom said. "We can still go visit her, but I have a feeling she's going to be sleeping a lot from now on."

"Why?"

"Because she doesn't want antibiotics."

"Doesn't she have some kind of infection?" Granger asked. "I thought antibiotics got rid of infections."

"Yes, but she doesn't want antibiotics."

"So… what happens then? Does she get some other treatment?"

"No, she doesn't want any treatment."

"So... will she just get better on her own?"

"No."

"But, if she doesn't take the antibiotics, she won't get better."

She nodded.

"So, then what?"

"She will probably get worse."

Granger squinted, trying to follow the logic.

"So then what happens?"

"She will probably pass soon."

Granger looked at his mom. "Pass," he repeated, flatly.

"Die," she said, quietly. "She will probably die soon."

He didn't understand.

"So, why doesn't she take the antibiotics?"

"She doesn't want them."

"You keep saying that, but she can't even make decisions

anymore, so why do they think she doesn't want them?"

Jake watched the two of them like a ping pong game.

"She filled out paperwork before her dementia got too severe. She stated very plainly that if she was ever in a situation like this, she wanted to go quickly."

"A 'situation like this?'"

"Dementia and an illness, like an infection."

Granger thought for a minute. "She doesn't want antibiotics?"

"No."

"So, she wants to just... die?"

"Yes."

A few months ago, Granger would have looked for something to throw in response to this news. But he felt the fight draining out of him rapidly.

He set his head in his palm, covering his eyes. His brain was working overtime trying understand what was happening.

*She wants to die? She's dying?*

The noise in the kitchen did not get louder, but the noise inside of his head did.

*She's dying.*

"But she doesn't understand!" he said. "She's got dementia, how could she decide anything?"

"She signed the—" Jake said.

"But that was years ago, wasn't it? What if she's changed her mind?"

Their mother did not reply. She watched Granger with a patient look.

"Can't we... I don't know... argue it, or something? Can't we convince the nursing home or... or... the hospital or some doctor or... or... someone, that her decision doesn't apply anymore?"

"But it's what she wanted," Jake said. "When she was still mentally capable. She made it clear."

Granger sighed and rubbed his forehead. "We've gotta do something. We can't just let her go."

Jake started to speak again, but he was silenced by a slight motion from their mother's hand.

"We already lost her once..." Granger whispered, feeling his eyes burn. His dinner from the night before threatened to make a reappearance.

When Granger looked up, his mother was teary-eyed but uncharacteristically resolute.

"It's better for her," she said. "It's hard for us, but better for her."

"It feels like a lose-lose, to me."

"She's not herself anymore. Even before the infection she was unhappy and unsettled. She was getting more paranoid and uncomfortable. She wasn't in a good place. She knew when she signed those papers that something like this could happen, and she didn't want to prolong the inevitable if the other option was going to Jesus."

Granger looked out the window where one of his grandmother's wind chimes hung.

"Is it going to be… like… painful for her?"

"Hopefully not. The plan is to keep her as comfortable as possible."

"How long does she have?"

"A few days, maybe."

Granger closed his eyes and rested his head in his hand again.

"I'm going to go get ready," his mom said. "We can go as soon as you want."

"Do you feel okay-enough to go?" Jake asked her.

"I'll be fine. You'll have to drive, though."

Granger's head was spinning. He avoided looking at Jake when she left the room, and luckily Jake left shortly after her. Granger sat at the table for another ten minutes, alone, trying and failing to understand it all.

Granger got out of the car and stepped onto the asphalt in the *Golden Grove* parking lot again. It took some uncomfortable maneuvering due to his cast, crutch, and unhelpful left arm, but Jake was patient and offered his assistance. Granger couldn't wait to ditch the cast and crutch; walking felt like trying to crawl using only one arm and one leg.

Granger looked at the building. A small part of him wanted to run inside. A much larger part of him wanted to run away from it. He swallowed.

The two brothers and their mother approached the building with their eyes downcast. A pre-dawn thunderstorm had come and gone, and the golden, early morning sunlight shot through the remaining clouds and reflected in the puddles. The birds were coming out of hiding and singing their songs, too.

Evangeline was stationed behind the front desk again that morning. She smiled sadly at them, and quietly asked them how they were, to which they all muttered a polite reply. When the three of them had signed in, she gave them lanyards. They were different lanyards now, they didn't say "Memory Care," anymore.

"I'm so sorry," Evangeline said.

Granger believed her.

"Thank you," their mom said, squeezing Evangeline's hand before heading down the hall.

"Thank you," Jake said with a nod.

Granger turned to follow, but he looked back at Evangeline.

"Thanks," he said.

He felt like he owed her more. Not long ago, she had been where they were now heading. But he didn't know what words to offer her. When he didn't say anything else, but still hadn't walked away, she leaned forward a little and lowered her voice.

"You and your family will get through this, Mr. Kyle. Lean on one another."

He nodded his thanks, and hobbled away.

Instead of turning right, he turned left past the sign that read "Hospice." His mother and brother walked slowly up ahead of him. For every one time his crutch hit the carpet, his hard pounded three times. His heartbeat got louder in his ears.

*Hospice.*

At the sight of that word, and knowing now what it meant, Granger felt as though he walked toward the grim reaper himself. The hall that he'd walked down before to find some respite from his family and their situation, where he'd first met Nina and Izzy, was now covered by the shadow of death.

Step.

Step.

Step.

Granger's brow, underarms, and hands, covered themselves in a cold sweat.

Death.

Death.

Death.

The word chilled him to the bone. He'd never walked this journey before, not like this, he'd only heard of others who had. He hadn't been close with any of his other grandparents, not even his dad's dad, who he lived with for so long. Grandpa Albert's death had been sudden, anyway, and had happened when Granger wasn't there.

*What will it be like?*

Fear pumped from his heart to his toes, filling every cell.

Grief pressed in stronger from all sides, taking his breath away.

Death alone was enough to chill him… but his grandmother's death…

He halted in the middle of the hall, feeling unsteady.

He looked up ahead and saw the double doors that led to the hospice unit. Death awaited him there. Death and despair and fear.

Jake and their mom walked through the double doors, so consumed by their own thoughts that they didn't notice Granger lagging behind. The doors shut behind them, and with the noise of the latch, Granger spun around and hobbled in the other direction as fast as he could. He passed the lobby and Evangeline at the front desk on his way out. He didn't stop until he was outside again, sucking in deep breaths like there wasn't enough oxygen in the air. Before he'd calmed down, Jake and their mom found him, both with looks of concern on their faces.

"I can't do it," Granger said, his voice, his good leg, and his good arm shaking.

"You might not have another chance," Jake reminded him.

Granger swallowed and tried not to throw up.

"It's okay, honey," his mom said.

He and Jake both looked at her.

"I understand," she said. "You don't have to see her."

"I thought you wanted me to see her."

"I do, but I won't push you. You know your relationship with your grandmother better than I do."

"You're not going to try to convince me to see her?"

She shook her head.

Granger felt a small weight lift off his chest.

"It's got to be your decision. On your own terms."

He sighed in relief.

Jake looked distressed by this, but he didn't say anything more as the two of them went back inside and Granger remained in the parking lot.

He sat down on a bench near the entrance of the building. When he heard footsteps again, he turned around expecting to see one of his family members coming back outside, but it was Evangeline making her way toward him.

"Mr. Kyle," said the middle-aged woman. "Do you mind if I join you for a while? I like to come outside for my breaks."

"No, go ahead," he said, starting to regain his composure.

"Thank you." She sat down lightly on the other end of the bench and smoothed out her skirt.

"You know, you remind me a little of my youngest son," she said without preamble.

It sounded like the beginning of a one-sided conversation, and his instinct was to turn off his brain while she chattered. But he restrained the impulse and did his best to give her his full attention.

"I don't see him much anymore. None of my kids live nearby."

"I'm sorry."

She tried to smile, but she wasn't fooling anybody.

"They came to visit when my mom was dying, at least. But they didn't stay long. I think it was too hard for them."

"I can understand that."

She glanced over at him. "You and your grandma had a good relationship, didn't you?"

He nodded.

"She must've had a pretty big impact on your life, given how much I've seen you in here in the last few months."

"I haven't been to visit that often," he admitted.

"More often than a lot of other people," she said. "Some of our residents see their families once a year. And some people who are dying, die alone."

He raised his eyebrows, "that's horrible."

"It is," she said, nodding. "But death scares a lot of people."

Granger remained quiet and let the sound of the birds fill the silence.

"Death is so interesting," Evangeline said after a minute. Her tone of voice, which had been very sorrowful just a moment ago, was very philosophical now. The change made Granger feel a little safer, and more curious, about wading into a conversation about death.

"How so?"

"It's not what I thought it would be."

"What did you think it would be?"

She looked ahead into the parking lot and pondered, "very violent. Horrifying. Totally devoid of light or meaning or happiness or hope. And I'm sure it is, for some people. Maybe for a lot of people. But watching my mother die, it wasn't like that."

Granger's eyes were fixed on a rock a couple feet away, but he was catching every word.

"Of course it was devastating, and I was afraid many times, but it was so... strange..."

Granger didn't realize he was holding his breath, didn't realize he hadn't blinked in a while.

"Strange how?"

Evangeline had a puzzled look on her face. "It was like I was experiencing something otherworldly. There were moments during her last days when people came to visit and pray and keep us company, and in those times, I felt some of the most joy and peace I've ever felt in my life. Sitting by my mother's deathbed! I never expected that. It was such a sacred experience, being there with her as she left this earth. And maybe all of this is unique to people of faith, but little by little, my fear had less power over me."

Evangeline's eyes had glazed over, and her voice become light as a feather again. A few months ago, Granger would have dismissed her musings and mentally rolled his eyes, but things were not the same as before.

"Death doesn't feel like I thought it would," she said. "It doesn't feel like she's buried underground in some sort of eternal, rotting, comatose state..." Granger couldn't suppress the shiver that ran down his spine, "... it's like she's simply... missing. It's as though she should still be here, and she just isn't. Like she's still out there somewhere, and we're just waiting for her to come back."

She took a slow, deep breath.

"It's awful," she added softly. "And sad. And I wish no one ever had to go through it. But I learned that believing I knew what death would be like was as silly as believing I knew what any of the future held." She shrugged. "Life and death both surprise us."

He didn't know how he felt. He was off-kilter, like he was walking with one foot on the curb and one foot on the street. But there was something new inside him now that he could identify:

Hope.

# 41

Most of the guests had gone. The few that remained were talking and laughing with his mom at the front door. The graduation party had been a success: it was a beautifully warm and breezy May afternoon, his mom had made great food, and both Trevor and Levi had come home to celebrate Granger's high school graduation.

Granger sat frowning and slumped down in a kitchen chair, fiddling with one of the graduation photos that had been displayed on the cake table.

His grandmother came into the kitchen holding a trash bag. He looked at her, and she at him, then he looked back down at the photo.

"Good party," he said, flatly.

She crossed the kitchen to collect some used paper plates from the counter.

"Yes, it was. Your mom did a great job."

"I hope she enjoyed it." He set the photo down for a second so he could take a sip from his cup.

They heard laughter from the backyard, where Trevor and Levi were playing soccer with Jakey.

His grandma tied up the trash bag, rolled up her sleeves, and grabbed a broom.

"I think she did," she said.

Granger picked at the edge of the photograph. When his grandma swept on over to his side of the table, he flipped it around and showed it to her.

"She didn't tell me she was going to use these," he said.

She looked at the photo of him, taken the summer before he started his senior year, wearing a baseball glove and a 'don't mess with me' expression on his face.

"It's a good picture. Except you're not smiling."

He gave his grandmother a look, and the look she gave in return told him she knew what he meant.

"Your baseball career is still something to be proud of," she said. "Even if it won't be the same from here on out."

"It was hard enough to miss out on my senior year season," he said. "She didn't have to rub it in my face."

"You know good and well that wasn't her intention."

"Doesn't matter if it was her intention, it's what happened."

"I'm sorry it feels like salt in the wound," she said, gentler, "but forgive and move on, or you'll only be adding more."

He took another sip and didn't say anything.

"Where's Katie?" she asked, still sweeping.

"She left," he muttered, glaring at the photo.

"So soon? I thought she was gonna stay for a while."

"She got mad at me."

"Why?"

"I don't know. We had an argument, so she left."

"You two never fight."

"I know."

She considered him.

"How far away is her college from yours?"

"About twenty minutes, driving."

"That's not too far."

"I guess."

She pulled out a chair and took a seat at the table.

"I heard your teacher asking you about your college plans. You didn't sound very excited about them."

"What teacher?"

"Shorter guy, balding, overalls."

"That's Mr. Savoy. He's not a teacher, just a maintenance guy,"

Granger said with a wave of his right hand, the one he was still holding the photo with.

"Oh. Well, anyway, you didn't seem too excited about this fall. In fact it sounded like you were kind of dreading it."

He shrugged and kept his eyes on the photo. "Hard to be excited about it now."

"So, why are you going?"

He looked up at her. She had one eyebrow raised.

"I mean, I didn't say I don't want to go."

"Do you?"

"Well, yeah."

"Why's that?"

"Because I gotta get out of here."

"Out of where?"

"Lester."

"Why?"

"Because I don't want to be stuck here forever."

"Why not?"

"I want to move on with my life. If I stay here I'm afraid I'll… I don't know… stunt my growth."

"I think it's too late to prevent that, kiddo."

He rolled his eyes at her dry joke. "Lester is just… it's dead. There's nothing for me here."

"I didn't know you felt that way."

"I guess I didn't always."

She looked through his eyes right into his soul. "You know, you don't have to worry about him coming back here. He won't be out for a long time."

He glanced at her but didn't say anything.

"Well," she said, exhaling and standing again. "I'm proud of you for looking ahead. It's good to move forward. As long as you've made peace with what's behind."

"I have."

"Because it's hard to move forward otherwise."

"I know."

"No, you don't. Not yet, at least. So take it from me."

"Yes, ma'am."

"And don't forget to come back and visit."

"I won't."

"Good. And don't throw in the towel when things get hard, 'cause they will get hard."

"Yes, ma'am."

"You've gotta trust Jesus and lean on your family, okay?"

"Okay."

"Good."

She grabbed the broom and went on her way while Granger remained at the table in the empty kitchen. It sounded like one of his brothers had just scored a goal in the backyard.

# 42

GRANGER SLEPT ALMOST TWELVE HOURS that night, but when he woke up he still felt tired.

*I'm tired when I can't sleep, I'm tired when I sleep too much. I can't win.*

He rolled over and checked his phone for the time only to see several missed texts and calls from his boss.

He set his phone down again and rolled over to go back to sleep.

Suddenly, there came a loud, strange noise from down the hall that had Granger on his feet in seconds. He lost his balance, having forgotten the cast, and fell backward onto the bed again. Finding his crutch, he hurried out of his room still in his boxer shorts, his hair looking like he'd been struck by lighting.

"What?" he called, looking around the house for the cause of the commotion. "What happened? Hello?"

He hobbled faster down the hall.

Jake was standing in the middle of the kitchen holding an envelope and a piece of paper folded in thirds. He was staring down at the paper like it had told him he'd won the lottery. Jake hurried across the room and held out the paper for Granger to read.

"I got in!" Jake said, unable to wait for Granger to actually read the letter. "I got in!"

It took Granger a few seconds to put the pieces together.

"I thought you'd decided on a college already," Granger said, fully awake now.

"I did! This school waitlisted me!"

He was still in a mild panic at the sound of Jake's yelling; Granger hadn't heard Jake that excited in so long that he'd forgotten what it sounded like. But then he understood, and with a sudden burst of pride and joy for his little brother, Granger added his own shout of celebration.

"What is it?" called their mother's worried voice from down the hall. She, too, hurried into the room.

"He got in!" Granger yelled.

"I got in!"

She grabbed the letter that Jake held in front of her and read the first line feverishly, ending with a shout of her own. She threw her arms around Jake and laughed and cried.

When she let go she did a strange little bounce. Granger watched her, trying to figure out what she was doing. Then he realized she was trying to literally jump for joy. But she couldn't. She didn't have the strength to do it. His smile faltered.

He kept watching her movements, really watching. Sure, she was recovering from a concussion, but he knew this was not a new change, it was just a change Granger hadn't given much thought to before. He couldn't deny it any longer: she was weaker.

Jake and their mom were still talking excitedly about the college when Granger heard a quiet buzzing. His mom looked down at her hand.

"Oh, here, honey" she said, handing Granger his cell phone. "When I heard you yell I went to your room to see if you were all right. Your phone was going off."

She tried to hand it to him, realized he couldn't take it from her, and so set it on the countertop.

It was his boss calling again. Granger watched the phone slide across the counter as it buzzed.

"Do you want me to answer it for you?" she asked.

"No," he said. "It's okay. I'll let it go to voicemail."

When it stopped ringing, she looked at the screen again. The icon showing the number of missed calls from work was big and red and obvious.

"Do you need to call him?" she asked.

"I will. Later. We've got to celebrate right now!"

That was all the encouragement the other two needed.

Jake rushed down the hall to text his girlfriend, Trevor, and Levi about the good news. Their mom announced she would make pancakes. Granger announced he was going to put some clothes on.

It was a trial, with only one hand and one leg to work with, but he finally finished getting dressed and went back out to the kitchen.

His mom was not at the stove. She was not at the counter. She was not at the sink or the fridge. She was sitting at the kitchen table with a whisk in one hand and her head resting in the other.

"You okay, Mom?" Granger asked, almost afraid to ask, and afraid to approach her. Her whole body looked limp and her skin suddenly looked gray-ish.

She turned her head slowly to look at him.

"Fine, honey, I just got a little tired." She did not even try to smile.

He looked around the room. She hadn't whipped up the batter, hadn't pulled out a skillet, hadn't even gotten any ingredients out yet. From the looks of it, she'd grabbed the whisk and then sat down, exhausted.

"Just give me a few minutes and I'll be okay," she mumbled.

Granger stared at her. Jake came into the room as she was trying to reassure Granger and had quickly come to the same conclusion as Granger. It was Jake who stepped up to the plate.

"I'll make the pancakes," Jake said, taking the whisk from her.

"No, it's okay—"

"No. I'm making the pancakes."

She tried to smile. "I guess I'm still recovering from this concussion."

Jake nodded.

She laid her head down on her arms on the table, and Granger and Jake commenced a brief, silent conversation about her.

The rest of the morning was much more subdued than the beginning. Jake made them all pancakes, Granger felt guilty he couldn't help, and their mom tried to pretend she had a normal amount of energy.

The college acceptance letter had been like a fast-acting energy drink to their systems. Granger hadn't realized how slowly they'd been trudging along for the last few months, half-asleep, until the letter woke him up. And then, before they'd even had a chance to store up the joy, it vanished, and the darkness felt even darker than before. Granger felt exhausted all over again.

They sent their mom off to bed, knowing that was what she would do if it was one of them who was in her place, and Jake did the dishes while Granger not-so-deftly handed them to him from his seat at the table.

Jake was quiet as he scrubbed. Granger stared off into space.

"I don't think it's just the concussion," Granger said after a few minutes.

Jake glanced over at him. "What do you mean?"

"I think this has been going on longer than a couple weeks."

Jake shook his head, "but her concussion—"

"Is part of it, yeah, but I don't think it's all of it."

Jake looked like he was about to protest, but then he shut his mouth again.

Granger wasn't sure what to say next. It felt much easier to say nothing, especially since he had a feeling that both of them were thinking the same thing, but Granger was afraid of what might happen if he didn't speak up.

"You're worried about her, too," Granger said.

"I'm thinking…" Jake sighed and paused for a moment, "maybe I should hold off on college."

To himself, Granger admitted that he'd also been wondering if Jake should hold off on college. He seemed like the most capable one of the brothers when it came to looking after their mom. But as soon as Jake said the words aloud, Granger knew it was wrong to ask that of him.

"Hold off… so you can help her out?" Granger confirmed.

"Yeah. We've got a good rhythm, with taking care of the house and both of us working. I'm just afraid that…" he didn't finish.

Granger's phone rang again. He silenced it.

"I was so ready for something like this," Jake said, pointing with his chin to the letter laying behind him on the counter. "It felt like a way to get away from all the sad stuff for awhile."

Granger looked down at the floor.

"But I think I'm being selfish," Jake said.

Granger wanted to tell Jake that it wasn't selfish, that it was normal and healthy and part of growing up and moving on, but he didn't know how true that was anymore.

Granger could read indecision and frustrating inner turmoil in Jake's movements as he scrubbed furiously at the skillet. The weight of the responsibility that the kid was assuming was becoming more than he could bear.

"Don't cancel your college plans, yet," Granger said.

Jake looked over at him, "but the school year's starting soon. They need to know."

"I know. Don't put your plans on hold, yet."

"Why? What are you gonna do?"

The look on Jake's face asked another question, but Granger wasn't ready to answer it yet.

"Just... don't put your plans on hold. You need to tell them you're coming, to reserve your spot. We still have a few weeks left of the summer. Things change. Maybe she'll start to feel better soon."

Jake looked doubtful, but he also looked hopeful. Granger remembered that, as nurturing and responsible as he was, Jake was still a teenage boy with a lot of drive, a lot of brains, and a lot of potential.

Jake needed to get away. He needed to go to college. It wouldn't be fair of the older brothers to deny him that. Granger didn't know how he was gonna make sure that happened while also not abandoning their mother, but he was going to figure it out.

This new challenge lit a fire under him, and between that and his talk with Evangeline, Granger was ready to see his grandmother.

He hobbled down the hall of *Golden Grove* in the rhythm of a funeral march. He did not let himself stop when he reached the double doors that Jake held open for him.

On the other side of the doors was an entirely different world. There were fewer people in the halls of the hospice unit, and the sound of Granger's aluminum crutch, even on the carpet, sounded harsh and irreverent in the space. The walls themselves seemed to breathe. Slowly, very slowly.

"Do you want us to go in with you?" his mother asked.

"No. Not yet," Granger said.

"We'll wait right here." And she, still looking a little gray, and Jake took up seats in the little alcove across from his grandma's room. Granger watched them walk away, seeing how his mother walked as though she was stepping from one slippery rock to another through a stream, then he turned, took a deep breath, and walked inside.

His grandma was tucked into bed beneath several blankets, looking freshly bathed and comfortable. There was only one bed in this room, a hospital bed, and two chairs in the corner by the window. A television was mounted on the wall across from his grandma, and it was turned on to a channel that played soothing music. It was a strange combination of a hospital room and a nursing home room, but whatever it was, it was not a real bedroom.

She was asleep, or whatever state it is that people fall into when they are dying. She breathed slowly, but loudly, like it was hard for her, but she had a calm expression and wasn't restless, so he supposed she was as comfortable as she could be.

His good arm and good leg were becoming fatigued, so he made his way directly over to the chairs stationed by her bed and eased down.

"Hi, Grandma," he began… and ended, because a lump the size of a meteor developed in his throat.

If he'd wondered before whether they were close to the end or not, he didn't have to wonder now. He could see. This was yet another version of his grandma, another person he didn't know and had never known. He couldn't believe how different she looked. So different, in fact, that he glanced over at the photographs displayed on a table beneath the television to make sure it was his family he saw.

There was movement in the doorway. Dave stood frozen with panic- and sorrow-filled eyes fixed on his mother. Granger had been expecting him since the night before when his mom got a text saying he was coming. Granger took a breath, ready to do the second thing that he'd come to do.

"Hey," Dave said to him without looking away from his mother.

"Hey. Come on in."

Dave looked at him. "You sure? I can come back later."

"Come on in," Granger repeated.

Dave slowly entered. His fidgety hands suggested that he felt the urgency of the situation, but he took his time walking around the room. He stopped to look at the photographs. The one closest to him was the picture of the boys on the farm with their mother, from many summers before. Next to it sat a photo of her and Grandpa Albert on their wedding day. There was also one of her, Albert, and their three children, Dave and his brother and sister. The faces of aunts, uncles, cousins, great aunts, and great uncles also stared up at them from the table.

"It's a good lookin' family," Dave said with his back to them both. "You sure are lucky, aren't you, Mom?"

He looked over his shoulder at where she continued to sleep, adding, "well, aside from the one screw-up."

For the first time, Granger realized none of his cousins, aunts, or uncles had come to visit her in the last few months. He remembered what Evangeline had said the day before.

"You're the only one of her kids who's come to visit her," Granger pointed out. "And you've come multiple times."

"I wouldn't read into that too much," Dave said, "what with Candace's health problems and Steve being in Kenya."

"It's a big deal. They should've been here."

"I have a lot more to atone for than they do," Dave said.

"Is that the only reason you've been coming?" Granger asked, knowing full well that it wasn't.

"No," Dave said, finally taking the other empty chair. "She's my mom."

Tears filled Dave's eyes and prevented him from saying anything more for a while. There was nothing performative about it. Granger believed him.

"It's good that you came," Granger said, honestly.

Dave looked at his mother while the tears rolled freely down his roughened face.

"I was such a burden for so long," he said. "I think that hurts almost as much as losing her; I can't make it up to her."

Granger looked away, feeling the corners of his mouth pulled down by some invisible force.

"I've been such a terrible son," Dave whispered, reaching out and enveloping one of his mother's hands between his own shaking ones. "And a terrible father." Dave sniffled loudly. "One of those things I can't fix now. It's too late. As for the other thing... well it might be too late for that, too."

But Dave didn't launch into a speech about wanting Granger to trust him. When he finally looked his son in the eye, he said, "don't make my mistakes, Granger. I can't have you end up like me. Can't do it to your mother."

Granger's eyes flicked to the doorway.

"I know I messed up," Dave said. "A lot. But if you give up, too, your mom won't be able to survive it. She's used to it from me, not that that makes it right, but you're her own child. She needs you to be okay. She thinks she needs you to be okay for your own sake, but she needs it for herself just as much."

Granger looked at his grandmother's shriveled hand, no longer calloused from years of hard manual labor. He thought about his mother sitting on the other side of the wall at that very moment, looking beaten down like a reed in a thunderstorm. Both women had weathered so much over the years, but his grandmother was tough. His mother had gotten so much of her strength from his grandma, and he was getting worried about how she would fare once his grandma was gone.

"But don't just do it for her," Dave implored, looking with such earnestness into his son's eyes that Granger could not help but believe his sincerity. Dave's voice was barely audible above the quiet music trickling out of the television. "Do it for yourself. Don't throw in the towel. Don't let my mistakes ruin it all for you, son."

The last word did not set Granger's teeth on edge this time. He swallowed and nodded.

The time had come. He was ready. He cleared his throat.

"I wanted to tell you," he said, looking down, "that I forgive you."

When he looked at Dave again, he could read the disbelief in his eyes. Disbelief, but not doubt. It was the look of surprise at having been given a gift both unexpected and unmerited. And for a second, Granger was afraid he had been a little hasty in wielding that sort of power. But since the moment he'd decided to do it, he'd felt yet another weight lift off his chest, one the size of an anvil. So he did not take it back, did not qualify it, did not even try to explain how he'd arrived at that conclusion. He just let the words move throughout the room, doing some supernatural something that was as tangible as it was intangible, and as real as it was impossible to understand.

Dave was too verklempt to speak. He could only grasp Granger's shoulder firmly, and nod.

The two men sat with Julia Kyle for another half hour, hardly speaking, but still sharing the sacred space and time which death often presents to those who go on living.

At the end of that half hour, Granger excused himself from the room to give Jake and his mom some time with her. He sat down in the alcove and pulled out his cell phone to look at the six missed calls and five text messages from his boss that he'd been ignoring for the last few days.

Nervous, he dialed. He didn't have to wait long before an angry voice answered.

"It's about time. Where have you been?"

"Sorry, Tony. I've been with my family. There's been more stuff going on."

"You know, kid, I'm having a hard time believing that. If that were really the case, you would have told me, and asked for time off. What's really going on?"

"It's the truth, Tony. I drove down a couple days ago because my grandma and mom both went to the emergency room. I thought I was going to drive back to Eugene that night, or the next day at the latest, so I didn't tell you."

"But you didn't come back."

"No. I, uh, got in a car accident."

"A car accident, huh?"

"Yes, sir."

"Your excuses have been stacking up recently."

"I know, sir."

"Are you back in Eugene now?"

"No, I'm still in Lester. My grandma was moved to hospice. She's got an infection, so they don't think she has long."

"Sorry to hear that," Tony said gruffly, but sincerely. "I'll make you a deal. You can stay until after the funeral. If you can get back here two days after that, I'll let you keep your job. Deal?"

"Deal. Thanks, Tony."

But when Granger hung up the phone, he didn't feel as relieved as he thought he would.

He leaned forward and rubbed his right hand roughly down his face, thinking so hard that his head started to ache.

Why was it that he was met with so much resistance lately? If it wasn't resistance from his family about how he lived his life, it was his grandma's health. If it wasn't that, it was the possibility of losing his job. If it wasn't that, it was his tumultuous relationship with his dad. If it wasn't that, it was trying to figure out how to make sure his mom was okay while still letting Jake live his own life. And if it wasn't that, it was his own dang mind and conscience, which would not. Give him. A break.

# 43

"You know, Granger," his grandma said. "Sometimes when you meet with resistance, the solution is not to keep pushing. Sometimes resistance is God's way of telling you, 'turn around, you're going the wrong way.'"

"How do you know the difference?"

"Well for one thing, pay attention to Him. He may not shout it from the rooftops, but He makes it clear enough that most of us can get the hint if we really want to."

# 44

"SHE'S GONE."

Granger was close enough to the phone to hear the news, and to hear the defeat in his dad's voice.

His mother clutched her cordless landline with both hands and let out a shaky breath.

"When?" she asked.

"Around one this morning."

Granger's and Jake's eyes wandered around the room, looking for something stable to latch onto, until they found one another. Jake looked as bereft as Granger felt. Everything around Granger seemed like it had been suddenly hollowed out.

They'd known what was coming, they'd started grieving months ago, so how was it there was any pain left to feel?

Granger felt empty and heavy at the same time. He was now living in a world where his grandmother wasn't. It wasn't good. Not at all. She needed to still be there. Like Evangeline had said, it was like his grandma had just vanished, like someone was doing some sort of sick magic trick.

The whole kitchen, where the three of them still stood while his mother talked to Dave, turned gray. He felt like he should stay to make sure his mom was alright, but he needed to get away from the sudden oppressiveness of the house.

He mumbled something to Jake about going out for a while, and headed for the front door.

The steps were difficult with the crutch and the cast, but Granger didn't notice. His body moved on its own. He looked at the ground a little ahead of him and kept going forward. His non-broken foot was barefoot, but he didn't feel the heat from the pavement. The humidity wrapped him in a suffocating hug. He walked down the sidewalk at a steady pace while the ache in his chest grew. The longer he walked, the bigger the ache. It had finally happened. She was gone.

The ache was becoming unbearable. By the time he'd circled the block and sat on the steps outside his mother's house it was the pain in his chest, not in his feet and underarm, that made him collapse.

He sobbed silently, not because he was embarrassed to be heard, but because the grief was too deep for sound to be able to come out. His whole body shook with the sobs.

But crying wasn't cathartic, at least not cathartic enough. When his breathing became more normal again, somehow the ache only deepened.

He wanted a drink.

Several.

He'd talked to Dr. Jenkins about this just a couple weeks earlier. During that session, they'd made a plan for when his grandma finally died, because they both knew Granger would want to binge drink, and Dr. Jenkins was a smart guy.

*Don't be afraid of feeling,* Granger reminded himself, hearing Dr. Jenkins' voice in his head rather than his own. *The feelings will not consume you. They will not be too much for you. They will not destroy you.*

*Don't be afraid of feeling.*

*Pain comes, and it goes.*

*Feel it, so you can move on from it.*

Granger dutifully repeated Dr. Jenkins' reminders, but the pain wasn't sheepish enough. It wasn't intimidated by Dr. Jenkins' wise words.

His chest ached more now than it did when he and Katie had broken up. It ached more than it did when Granger realized his baseball career was over. It ached even more than it did when Granger's dad had let him down six years ago. He hadn't known it was possible to top any of those experiences.

Just when he thought he couldn't take anymore, he felt another unwelcome feeling slide up next to the pain.

*You shoulda been here. You left for college and didn't come back until she was already gone. And after you'd promised her you'd visit...*

He followed this lecture with a string of unforgiving names for himself.

He cried some more.

Granger took a step across the threshold of the church, thankful to be out of the sweltering heat. His new, but not fancy, black suit had been soaking up the sunshine with all the efficiency of a solar panel, and even though one pant leg was rolled up to accommodate his cast, his foot was roasting inside.

Four days had passed since her death. Four days that, somehow, had grown harder and easier simultaneously. Harder, because with each new hour they all missed her in new ways, but easier, because as more family came into town, they realized it was better to hurt together than alone.

Janessa walked through the church doors and stopped beside Granger to give him a quick but firm side hug. He couldn't hug her back, but he appreciated the gesture more than he could say. Levi, holding baby Elizabeth, Lillian, Lillian's husband, and their Aunt Candace stood talking not far off. They waved to Granger as he walked past them into the sanctuary.

Dozens of people in formal, black attire were already making their way into the bright, glossy, white sanctuary. Granger figured the air conditioning was going to have quite the battle against the heat from the crowd and the sunshine pouring in from the windows above.

Granger looked around. He felt connected to the people coming into the church, even the strangers, in a way he'd never experienced before. He wondered if that's the kind of effect death had on most people. But at the same time, he felt like a lone lifeboat trying to stay right side up on tumultuous waves. He was grateful for every person that passed him offering their condolences, but he also wished he could disappear into the walls.

*What happens after this? How does life work after something like this? Do I just go back to Eugene and keep living life, as if she didn't die?*

Granger looked around the sanctuary again. It was filling quickly, but people still milled about, talking to one another in hushed voices. Somehow, among the sea of black outfits, Granger's eye easily picked out Nina and Izzy walking in.

Granger smiled to himself.

They didn't see him standing in the back corner of the room, but they saw his mother standing down front, and walked in her direction. Nina guided Izzy in front of her down the crowded center aisle with their clasped hands raised above the little girl's head. Granger could see Nina leaning down to say something to her daughter.

Granger, whose curiosity in the pair had not diminished, kept his attention on them. When his mother saw them she hugged them both. From the back of the sanctuary, Granger could see how thin his mother's arms had gotten. He was too far away to hear what they were saying, but whatever it was, Granger was pretty sure Nina had spoken words that would somehow both comfort and strengthen his mom. She had a knack for that. After a couple minutes, Nina and Izzy walked back down the aisle to find seats, and his mom received an elderly couple.

Granger saw his siblings, father, aunts, uncles, and cousins filter inside and head to the front of the sanctuary. He followed and sat down between Levi and Jake. On Jake's other side sat their mom, and on the other side of her, Trevor. Trevor looked calm and mostly emotionless, like usual. He also looked strangely alone, even though he, too, was surrounded by family. Granger felt a little knot tie up in his stomach. His worry for his older brother had ramped up in the last few days; Trevor had seemed to shut down even more since their grandma had died.

*What do I do about Trevor? Is there a way to help him?*

Before he could think of an answer, a man, who looked to be ten, maybe even fifteen, years older than his grandmother had been, stood up and walked slowly to the pulpit. He wasn't carrying anything; not a Bible, not any notes, nothing.

Once he made it to the pulpit, he faced the congregation and started talking before he'd even raised his eyes to look at them. He moved and spoke as one very accustomed to a life behind the pulpit.

"I was Julia's pastor for over thirty years," he began. His voice was as thin and wispy as his white hair. "Before I retired, I stood up here every Sunday, looked out over the congregation, and saw Julia and Albert Kyle in their regular spots."

Without even seeming to pause for breath, the older gentleman continued. He spoke so slowly, almost weakly, and yet something about him held captive the attention of every single person in that room.

"She asked me, about ten years ago, if I would officiate her funeral. I told her that, given her tough-as-an-ox disposition and my fragility, the odds were good that I would make it to heaven before her. But she was insistent."

It had the cadence of a joke, but the old man's expression of solemnity seemed to be etched into his face like he was made of granite.

The retired pastor went on.

"It seems she knew something I didn't, or at least had an inkling."

Granger felt a new pain join the one that had taken up the vacancy in his chest four days ago, thinking that his grandma might've known that long ago that her time was coming to an end.

"And so, here I am with you today, honoring the life of Julia Kyle, and reminding us all of the things that she believed so fervently."

He shifted his weight a little and put his hands on either side of the pulpit.

"There is no hope on this earth that doesn't come from the Lord."

Behind Granger, half a dozen people responded, "Amen."

"In John 16:33, Jesus tells us, 'I have told you these things, so that in me you may have peace. In this world you will have trouble. But take heart! I have overcome the world.' There is hope, and there is healing, and there are peace and joy in the face of death!"

Old and brittle-boned he may have been, but Granger felt the force of the words and the force of the man's conviction from the ends of the hairs on his head down to the sole of his broken foot. He understood now why his grandma had wanted this guy to speak at her service; she wasn't about to let anyone leave her funeral without feeling the power of God.

"But there is still death," he continued, sadder. "And there is grief. And there is a time for mourning."

Granger heard his mother sniffle. And he felt the sadness push on his chest again.

"And so today," said the old pastor, "we celebrate her life, mourn her death, and look forward expectantly to the day we are all reunited, standing at the throne of God and kneeling at the feet of Jesus. Because we all know that Julia is there already, alive and well."

*Alive and well.*

*Alive and well.*

His grandmother believed that, but did he?

Granger was sad to admit that, over the last six years, he hadn't exactly been living out the lessons his grandmother had worked so hard to instill in him and his siblings. Sure, her words still floated across his mind every once in a while, and his conscience was probably made up mostly of her words spoken in her voice, but he'd gotten really good at ignoring those things. He'd gotten really good at ignoring a lot.

He used to sit in those pews regularly. He'd heard more sermons unwillingly than willingly. But there, sitting in that sanctuary again, the truth of the old pastor's words started to sink in.

One time, when Granger was very young, Levi cracked a raw egg from the chicken coop over Granger's little head when he wasn't looking. It was an odd feeling as it trickled down. More than anything, Granger remembered that it felt surprisingly warm. That was how Granger felt sitting in the pew just then, except instead of a warm egg it was warm light, and instead of being on the outside of his body, it was on the inside.

Granger could go back to Eugene and let his own mind and heart continue to be his guide. It was what he'd been planning to do all along, after all. But over the last week, he'd been taking inventory and looking at his track record. Maybe it was time to put his own will on the shelf for a while.

# 45

THE SERVICE CONCLUDED AND OVER a hundred and fifty people got into their cars and followed the Kyle family to Julia and Albert's farm for the reception. Granger saw the house come into view from the backseat of Levi's car. His niece squealed from her car seat beside him, as if she knew where they were.

The facade of the two-story farmhouse looked worse for wear. On the lower half of the first floor, most of the paint was chipped away, and the plants up next to the house were overgrown and scraggly. It had never looked like that when his grandparents lived there.

"Why is the reception here?" Granger asked.

Levi was also looking at the house with a skeptical expression, "I guess it was the only place that could hold this many people. You saw how packed the sanctuary was."

"I like that it's here," Janessa said tenderly, looking out her own window. "It feels like her."

They walked through the dirt, sending up clouds of the stuff. Without the noise of the A/C or the car engine, the world got eerily quiet around them for a few seconds, and then they grew re-accustomed to the sounds of the wind in the trees and the millions of bugs singing their songs. The four of them, Jake, Trevor, and their parents were the only ones there, so far. No one talked as they walked inside, but they all looked out over the land, up at the house, down toward the creek. The farm didn't feel right anymore. It was still home, but it wasn't. In a moment of selfishness motivated by grief and nostalgia, Granger silently wished that a hundred and fifty people weren't about to descend on the farm and disturb the peace.

The porch creaked beneath their footsteps. One of the posts that connected the floor to the ceiling of the wraparound porch had been replaced by a plain wooden beam. The metal bench near the house was rusting. Granger felt heat creep up his neck as the cars started filling the property.

But when he walked inside, he was not greeted by an abandoned-looking farmhouse fallen into disrepair. In fact, it looked so much like its old self that Granger was speechless for a moment.

"Wow," he finally said. "I didn't expect it to look this good."

"You can thank your brother for that," his mom said.

He looked for Levi, but Levi was setting up the portable crib for Elizabeth in another room. Granger looked at Trevor, but Trevor was busy talking with their father near the door. Granger looked at Jake, who was hanging up his suit coat on a hook in the kitchen and pulling trays of food out of a freshly cleaned fridge.

"Jake did this?" Granger asked.

She nodded. "Between working and going to *Golden Grove*. He's been here four days every week since graduation."

Granger looked around.

*I wish he would quit setting the bar so high. Who is this kid trying to be, freaking Superman?*

People poured into the first floor of the farmhouse and Jake directed volunteers in the kitchen. The least Granger could do, he decided, was mingle and thank people for coming. So, grasping his crutch as much for emotional support as physical, he slowly maneuvered from room to room. He plastered a smile on his face and made small talk. As stilted as he felt, his gratefulness for the people who'd loved his grandmother was genuine. After fifteen minutes, the people were shoulder to shoulder in the lower level of the house, and the noise was growing.

"There he is," Granger heard a familiar voice say from behind him. He turned.

"Mr. Savoy," Granger said with an actual smile. "I almost didn't recognize you in a suit!"

"Well, I had to pull out all the stops today to honor your grandmother."

Granger nodded. "I appreciate that."

Mr. Savoy smiled at Granger with his watery eyes. "It's good to see you back here, Kyle. You seem… better… than before."

"Thank you, sir. I've had some help."

"Good. That's the only way. Are you heading out of town again soon?"

"Couple days. My boss is letting me stay until after the funeral."

"That was good of your boss to do."

"Yeah, it was." Granger felt that annoying, unidentifiable nagging inside his head again. He must have made a face, because Mr. Savoy asked:

"Everything okay?"

"Fine."

Mr. Savoy didn't say anything, just nodded like Granger had told him something in code, said farewell, and went to give his condolences to Granger's mother.

Granger was trying to understand what had just happened when he turned around and saw a woman with bright red hair going out the front door.

He froze.

*Was that who I thought it was? Or was it Jake's girlfriend, Devon? But she has darker hair, doesn't she? And Devon isn't that tall…*

He hesitated a moment, then started walking toward the front door. As he got closer, he picked up his speed a little, his heart pounding in his throat. But before he made it there, Nina and Izzy walked inside. He slowed to a stop. He looked at the door, and the clear path to it that had just formed, but didn't keep going.

When they spotted him standing nearby, he smiled.

"I saw you guys at the church," he said as they approached. "Thanks for coming."

"We were glad to come," Nina said. "She was a fantastic woman."

Even though they were all sweating, he thought Nina looked lovely in her black dress.

"Izzy," he said, tearing his eyes away from Nina. "Good to see ya. I never got to thank you for your letter."

"I put lots of baseball stickers on it," she stated, proudly.

"Yes, you did. It was very cool."

She was staring at his crutch and cast. "Did you get hurt?"

"Uh, yeah. I did. Car accident."

"The one you hurt your arm in?"

"No. Unfortunately, it was a second one."

"Are you a bad driver?"

He laughed. "Probably."

"I wish I had those," the girl said, pointing to the crutch and cast.

"She saw you at the funeral and talked about them the whole car ride here," Nina said.

"You don't have any names on it," she said.

"You're right," Granger said, looking down at his cast. "I guess I forgot."

When she looked up at his face, he could guess her question.

"Do you want to sign it?"

She lit up.

He chuckled, "I'll go find a marker."

He promptly turned around and left them. But a few steps later and Izzy was right there walking next to him.

"Does it hurt?"

"My foot? If I don't take my pain medication, then yeah. I broke it."

A peek over his shoulder told him Nina was following her daughter, like he'd expected. She gave off a chill vibe, but he could see she was observant and cautious. He didn't blame her.

"Have you ever had a cast before?" he asked Izzy.

She put her hands in the pockets of her dress as she ambled along, looking more like a middle-aged lawyer trying to win a case than an elementary-aged kid trying to comb through the memories of her short life.

"No. I had one of those other things one time, when I hurt my shoulder on the monkey bars."

"What, like a sling?"

"Did I have a sling, mom?"

"Yes."

"Yeah. A sling. But none of my friends could sign it. If I ever get a cast I'll get everyone to sign it."

"That's a good idea. Hopefully you won't have to have a cast, though."

She shrugged, "sometimes things just happen."

Granger turned laughing eyes over his shoulder to the girl's mother, who just smiled and shook her head.

They found a permanent marker in the kitchen and Izzy signed her name near the top of his cast. Then she instructed her mother to sign, as well.

"The more people who sign it, the more luck you have," she said. "When Oren broke his arm and got a cast the whole class signed it and then he got to go to Disney World in the summer."

"Hard to argue with that logic," Nina said, accepting the marker. "May I?"

"Of course," Granger said. "I would love a trip to Disney World."

Nina bent down, somehow managing to balance in her black heels, scrawled her name, and when she stood back up handed the marker to the next person Izzy had rounded up to sign the cast.

Izzy then went all around the house asking for people to come to the kitchen to help give her friend some good luck, and so one by one the faces which had so recently borne tears, appeared in front of Granger with delighted smiles at Izzy's antics.

He felt a little awkward about people getting so up close and personal, at first, but it turned out to be not such a bad thing. He and Nina leaned against the fridge while people came and went.

"Thanks for humoring her," she said.

"Are you kidding? I'd much rather do this than make small talk with people I don't know. I think this should be part of every funeral."

She laughed, but then turned serious.

"I'm sorry about your grandma."

"Thanks. Me, too."

Nina crossed her arms. "You know, your grandma and I were in the same Bible study for a few years before she started to get dementia. She prayed for you by name every week."

"Did she? I'm not surprised."

He got a little nervous, wondering what kinds of personal things his grandma had shared about him in those Bible studies.

"I used to think, 'dang, that is a fortunate guy. No matter how messed up he is right now, there's no way things won't get at least a little better for him after all that praying.'"

He looked over at her, "you think it worked?"

"I don't know you that well. I think you'd be the best judge of that."

"Well all that prayer couldn't have hurt me, I guess."

"There's no way. And she was persistent."

"Yeah, she was."

He held out his cast for another signature. When the signer was gone and Izzy ran off to find another, he added, "thanks for telling me."

"You're welcome. So, you sticking around for a while? Or are you leaving after this?"

"I…"

Granger looked across the room at his mom. Someone had pulled up a stool for her to sit on while she talked with people, and she was holding a paper plate full of untouched food in her hand.

"… don't know," he said, looking back at Nina. "Things have gotten complicated."

She looked over at his mom and nodded. "Well, whatever you decide to do, good luck." She pointed down at his cast which was now half-covered in signatures and winked. "See you around."

"See ya."

She gathered Izzy, returned the marker to Jake, and they were gone. He watched them go. Granger knew that his grandma had probably really liked those two.


The ache in his chest did not go away that day, or the day after. The pain ebbed and flowed, but it was constantly present. A lump would occasionally develop in his throat, especially while he was out at the farm. Like when he found his grandma's favorite, old apron inside a closet.

His last two days in Lester included the reading of his grandmother's will. Like they'd all expected, the house and surrounding property were all going to Dave's older brother, Steve, and the little money that was left was split between Candace and Dave. Thanks to Levi's digging into the contents of the will before she died, none of this was news to them, and they already had a plan for taking care of the farm until their Uncle Steve returned to the states from Kenya.

"What's the plan?" Dave asked.

They were standing in their grandparent's kitchen again, after making sure everything was cleaned up from the funeral reception.

"Jake and Mom will keep up with maintenance until Jake goes off to college," Levi said, "like they've been doing for the last few years. Then Trevor, Granger, and I will take turns coming to Lester to help out during the school year."

Dave looked from Levi to Trevor to Granger. Jake and their mom were in another room.

"You sure that will be enough? This is a heck of a lot of house and land to maintain."

"We can't ask Jake to put off college," Levi said in a hushed tone.

Trevor and Granger agreed.

"And none of us can move here for a year," Levi added.

"Well, add me to the list, then," Dave said. "I'll come down and help out when I can."

It helped. It wasn't a complete solution, but it helped.

"Alright, thanks," Levi said.

"And we can put the money she left me toward the house," Dave said.

"The money she left you in her will?" Trevor asked.

"It's not much, but maybe we could hire some people to come do maintenance when none of us can get down here."

"You sure?" Levi asked.

"Of course."

"None of us will think you're selfish if you keep it."

"I'm doing alright, I don't need it."

Granger was ninety percent sure that was not true, which made him want to refute it even less. It was another way that his dad was trying to show them they could trust him now.

The nudging that Granger had been feeling for days now had become a full-on gnawing feeling, and he suddenly knew what it meant and what to do about it.

The conviction hit him hard, but he was too nervous about it to voice his idea.

*What are you doing? You haven't thought this through at all! Keep your mouth shut! The feeling will pass.*

*I don't think this is one of those feelings that just passes... I think I know what I need to do. But just to be sure...*

"Hey, Trev," Granger said. "Will you help me grab something out of the car?"

"Sure," Trevor said, flatly. He kept his hands in his pockets and followed Granger outside.

"I need your advice," Granger said as soon as they were out of earshot of the others.

Trevor looked mildly surprised. "About what?"

He took a deep breath and tried to fight back the nervousness in his stomach.

"I think…"

*Are you sure about this? You're gonna throw it all away?*

*What, exactly, would I be throwing away?*

"I've been thinking I should move back. To Lester."

Trevor stopped. His eyes got wide. "Really?"

It was the biggest reaction Granger had seen from Trevor in weeks, and he was relieved to see the old Trevor again, even if it was just for a moment.

"When did you decide that?"

Granger tried to blow it off as no big deal, "oh you know, I've been kinda toying with the idea for a few weeks now. But I guess I hadn't really given it serious thought until just now."

"Are you sure you want to come back?"

"No," Granger laughed.

"Wow."

"I mean, let's be real. Dad's right. This place needs a lot more work than we can do on the occasional weekend afternoon. And… I think everyone would feel better if someone were here with mom. At least right now."

"Yeah."

"So… Do you think it's a good idea, or not?"

Trevor thought about it earnestly for a second. "I think it is a good idea."

"Okay then. I'll do it."

He still felt nervous about the upcoming change, but a load immediately lifted off of Granger's shoulders.

"So, you'll quit your job, then?"

"Guess so."

"And you'll find a job out here?"

"Yeah. I'm sure there are some restaurants that are hiring."

"Or you could apply for a teaching job, since, you know, that's what your degree is in."

"Or there's that."

Trevor stood back and considered his younger brother. "Huh."

"What?"

"This is a very cool thing you're doing."

Granger looked away and shrugged. "Whatever. I just wanna do my part."

Trevor nodded and didn't say anything more. He was withdrawn again for the rest of the day, but that evening when Granger presented his idea to the rest of the family, he gave it his full, albeit quiet, support.

"You?" Jake asked. "Come back and live here with Mom?"

"Well, I was thinking I could live on the farm."

His mom looked shocked to her core by the news.

"I think that's a great idea," Dave said, looking around at the others.

Trevor nodded.

"Would you work?"

"Yeah, I'd try to find a job, but I'd still be able to keep up the farm a lot more than if we just came down once a week."

"But... you hate Lester," Jake said. "Maybe I should—"

"I don't hate it so much anymore," Granger said, interrupting Jake before he could propose putting off college. "And I've never hated the farm."

"I'll still come down and help out when I can," Levi said.

"Yeah, me too," Dave said.

Trevor nodded.

"Great. Sounds like we have a plan: I'll move back for the next year."

Granger looked over at his mom again to see her reaction. She was smiling with tears in her eyes.

"Well, Mom? Think it's a good idea?"

She remained where she was sitting instead of coming over to him and giving him a big hug, probably because she was scared he would change his mind if she made it a big deal, but she wiped away a tear and nodded.

"Yes," she said. "I do."

# 46

"NEXT THURSDAY AT THREE O'CLOCK? Cool. Thanks so much."

Granger hung up the phone and, before he forgot, wrote himself a note so he didn't miss his first over-the-phone counseling session with Dr. Jenkins.

He left his phone on the kitchen counter and went back outside where the lawn mower was waiting for him. He wiped sweat and dirt from his forehead with his t-shirt and then hopped down the porch steps. It was a relief to have three working limbs again instead of just two.

He was tired from the last five hours of manual labor, but there was still a lot of grass to mow. He'd moved to the farm four weeks earlier but still didn't have a great system for keeping up with all the chores, yet. He was always relieved when one of his brothers or his dad showed up to help for the day. Every morning when he woke up and every night when he went to bed, he hurt all over. He was sure of one thing: by the time his uncle came to take over, Granger would either be dead from exhaustion or as ripped as a bodybuilder. He was really hoping for the latter.

He took a swig of water and took up his seat on the riding lawn mower again. At least for the mowing part, he got to sit down.

He mowed for another fifteen minutes. Every once in a while, he looked over to where his mom was working in the garden. She was clearing out the overgrown flower beds and fruit and vegetable patches. He was always afraid she'd tire herself out, but she said the sunshine and exercise were good for her. Plus, he had to admit, it was nice to have the company. It turned out that being around his mom so much again wasn't detrimental to their relationship, after all. They'd both learned a lot about each other in the last six months.

After another fifteen minutes, he had to stop to refill the gas tank.

"You wanna take turns?" his mom called from the garden.

He was about to say 'no,' but he figured driving the lawn mower might be a nice break for her after squatting and pulling weeds for the last hour.

"Sure. You wanna grab a rag to wipe off all the sweat while I get some more gas?"

She finished up what she was doing, went inside, and came back out with more water.

"Drink," she instructed.

"You, too."

Then she slid onto the lawnmower and picked up where Granger had left off.

He stretched up tall and then bent over, wincing at all the aches.

He heard the engine coming back toward him and turned around to see if something was wrong. But it wasn't the lawnmower he heard, it was a car pulling onto the property.

He didn't recognize the car. Shielding his eyes from the sun, he approached it hoping it wasn't someone collecting a payment for a missed electric bill or something. But then one of the back doors opened and a curly-haired kid hopped down into the dirt. Nina stepped out of the car next.

He relaxed and smiled.

It was the fourth time he'd seen them since moving back to Lester. The first was when they, and about a dozen other people from Good Shepherd Church, had come over to help him unload the moving truck when he moved into the farmhouse. The other two times were across the sanctuary at the church on Sunday mornings.

"We hoped you'd be home," Nina said. "I don't have your phone number so I couldn't call to check first."

"What's up?" he asked, curious and excited that they were there.

"We came to ask you a favor."

He raised his eyebrows. "What favor?"

Nina put a hand on the top of Izzy's head and looked down at her.

"You wanna ask or do you want me to?"

Izzy looked back up at him and started hopping up and down. "Will you be my coach?"

He looked from Izzy to Nina, confused. "Your 'coach?'"

"Yeah! For baseball."

Granger froze.

"Izzy's gonna play baseball through a community league this fall, but the league is still down six coaches."

He wiped more sweat off his forehead, and tried to buy himself some time to think. "Six coaches, huh?"

"Your mom nominated you," Nina said.

He chuckled and rested his hand on his hip, looking over at where his mom was mowing. She waved to Nina and Izzy. "Of course she did."

"Given your legendary talents, and recent abundance of free time," Nina said, pointing to the numerous ladders, hammers, drills, rakes, hoes, and watering cans lying around the property, "we were hoping your enduring love of the game would make this offer to coach elementary, co-ed, community baseball, for no money I might add, an irresistible proposition."

If neither her convincing speech, nor the excited look on Izzy's face as she bounced up and down, were enough to sway him, the twinkle in Nina's eye certainly was.

He squinted into the distance. "I'll have to think about it. I did get a pretty attractive counter-offer recently: Trayfield is looking for a coach for their over-50 bowling league and, well, you can see why it would be hard to pass that up."

Izzy wrinkled her brow. Nina smiled.

"What do you think, Izzy?" Granger asked.

"Be our coach!" she said, "if you're the coach we can win the World Series!"

"Wow!" he laughed. "Well in that case, I'm in!"

"Yay!" And then she turned and ran back to the car.

"Wait, you haven't told me when we start," he yelled after her.

"I'll be right back!"

He laughed again. He laughed a lot around those two.

"Are you sure you're up for it?" Nina asked.

"Sure. Might be fun," he said.

She looked over at the lawn mower. "How's your mom?"

"Doing okay. Not great. But better."

"Let me know if I can do anything to help."

"I will. Thanks."

"Granger, catch!"

Granger turned around just in time to catch the baseball with his bare, right hand. It actually kind of stung.

"Wow, good arm, Izzy. But try throwing a little lower."

He rolled it back to her in the dirt, since she didn't have a glove, either.

"Like this?"

That time, her aim was way off, and Nina had to duck to avoid getting a baseball in the face.

"We'll work on it," Granger said.

Izzy jumped up and down again.

"Do you have a glove yet?"

"I have one in the car!" She ran away again, and returned wearing an adult-sized baseball glove.

"You came prepared," Granger noted.

"She thought bringing them with her might help convince you to be her coach."

"She wasn't gonna take 'no' for an answer, was she?"

"Not at all."

Granger moved them away from the house, and Nina's face, a little bit so they could practice throwing safely. His hand was really stinging, but he didn't mention it. When his mom turned off the motor and came over to say hello, Granger heard a low rumbling in the distance. He looked at the horizon and saw some nasty-looking storm clouds looming. But he wasn't too worried; he'd handle the next storm when it came.

# Acknowledgements

I thank God that I had the ability, time, and support to be able to write this story, which I love with all my heart.

I also want to say thank you (times a million) to all the people who helped me get this story out into the world:
Roger Allen
Joy Allen
Melinda Morgan
Andrew Hilyard
Tricia Worthington
Savannah Worthington
Susan Richmond
Stephanie Koenig
Casey Wilkerson
Emily McDougall
Scott Lien

Whether you read entire drafts (Roger, Joy, Melinda, Andrew, Tricia, Savannah, Susan, and Stephanie), gave me feedback on writing a male protagonist (Roger, Andrew, and Scott), corrected my errors regarding baseball (Casey), or designed the fantastic cover art (Emily), I appreciate all the time and energy you spent in helping me fulfill a lifelong dream of mine: writing and publishing a book. I hope there will be many more books to come.